G000112897

BLOODY SUNSET

Further Titles by Christopher Nicole from Severn House

Black Majesty Series

BOOK ONE: BLACK MAJESTY
BOOK TWO: WILD HARVEST

The Dawson Family Saga

BOOK ONE: DAYS OF WINE AND ROSES?
BOOK TWO: THE TITANS
BOOK THREE: RESUMPTION
BOOK FOUR: THE LAST BATTLE

The McGann Family Saga

BOOK ONE: OLD GLORY
BOOK TWO: THE SEA AND THE SAND
BOOK THREE: IRON SHIPS, IRON MEN
BOOK FOUR: WIND OF DESTINY
BOOK FIVE: RAGING SUN, SEARING SKY
BOOK SIX: THE PASSION AND THE GLORY

BLOODY SUNRISE
CARIBEE
THE FRIDAY SPY
HEROES
QUEEN OF PARIS
SHIP WITH NO NAME
THE SUN AND THE DRAGON
THE SUN ON FIRE

BLOODY SUNSET

Christopher Nicole

This first world edition published in Great Britain 1994 by
SEVERN HOUSE PUBLISHERS LTD of
9–15 High Street, Sutton, Surrey SM1 1DF.
First published in the USA 1994 by
SEVERN HOUSE PUBLISHERS INC., of
425 Park Avenue, New York, NY 10022.

Copyright © 1994 by Christopher Nicole

All rights reserved.
The moral rights of the author have been asserted.

British Library Cataloguing in Publication Data
Nicole, Christopher
    Bloody Sunset
    I. Title
    823.914 [F]

    ISBN 0-7278-4614-0

All situations in this publication are fictitious and
any resemblance to living persons is purely coincidental.

Typeset by Hewer Text Composition Services, Edinburgh.
Printed and bound in Great Britain by
Redwood Books, Trowbridge, Wiltshire.

"In me thou see'st the twilight of each day
As after sunset fadeth in the west;
Which by and by black night doth take away,
Death's second self, that seals up all in rest."

William Shakespeare
Sonnets

CONTENTS

PART ONE *Victors*

Chapter	1	When the Earth Shook	3
Chapter	2	A Choice of Dreams	32
Chapter	3	A Glow in the East	59
Chapter	4	*Bushido*	94
Chapter	5	Rogue Sun	112
Chapter	6	Meridian	143

PART TWO *Vanquished*

Chapter	7	The Thrust	173
Chapter	8	The Decision	192
Chapter	9	The Attack	219
Chapter	10	Clouds Across the Sun	243
Chapter	11	The Working of Fate	271
Chapter	12	The Limit of Success	294
Chapter	13	The Narrow Waters	315
Chapter	14	Bloody Sunset	344
Chapter	15	Darkness	370

PART ONE

The Victors

"Ev'n victors are by victories undone."
John Dryden

CHAPTER 1

When the Earth Shook

The automobile banged and wheezed its way over the uneven road; peasants straightened in the rice paddies to either side, tilting their flat hats to stare at the unusual sight, bowing as they recognised the naval uniform of the driver. He was their superior – whatever the various decrees passed by the late Meiji Emperor in an effort to democratize Japan, it remained necessary to know one's place.

Captain Alexander Barrett nodded to those nearest the road, but for the most part he needed to concentrate. The motor car descended the slopes from the hills surrounding the old Satsuma fortress of Kumamoto towards the south-eastern coast of Kyushu. When Alexander's father had been shipwrecked off this coast in 1861 it had been known as Bungo, and had been part of the feudal domain of the Shimadzus of Satsuma. Sixty-one years later, in this spring of 1922, it was the most peaceful spot on earth, but as he neared the beach Alexander could make out the famous reef on which *HMS Juno* had stranded.

His father had been one of only three survivors from that typhoon-induced disaster. Now, at the age of eighty-three, Nicholas Barrett was the *only* survivor, after a lifetime of endeavour and battle on behalf of the *Mikado*, by whom he had so strangely been befriended, and whose cause he had adopted as his own. That cause, that determination to propel Japan not only into the modern era after two and a half centuries of isolation but also to make her a great power, he had passed on to his sons. And now the process had come to a grinding halt.

*   *   *

3

Alexander Barrett – or Barrett Alexander as he was known in Japan – was himself now forty-one years old, and had done his share of fighting for his adopted country. If the high point of his career, and indeed the careers of every officer in the Imperial Japanese Navy, had been the crushing victory over the Russians gained at Tsushima seventeen years before, they had all still dreamed of one day repeating that remarkable triumph . . . without actually having an enemy in view. Certainly it would never again be Russia, torn as that huge country was by revolution and civil war.

For Alexander Barrett, the events at Tsushima and since in Russia were the more traumatic, as he was himself half-Russian, born out of wedlock to Nicholas Barrett and the beautiful Countess Elizabeth Rashnikov. For all his six feet of height and heavy build, his fair skin, blue eyes and red-brown hair, publicly he was a Japanese, although unlike his elder half-brother he had never been made a *samurai*: the concept had been deliberately discouraged by the Meiji Emperor, who recognised that the law of *bushido* had little part to play in a Twentieth-Century Japan.

But equally had his mother never let him forget that he was a European, brought up as an English gentleman within the confines of his parents' home. In her American daughter-in-law and her Caucasian grandchildren Elizabeth Barrett had found a great deal of both comfort and happiness; she had never truly fitted into Japanese society.

Both she, and Sue-Ellen, were sufficiently supportive of their husbands to feel the weight of the disastrous news he was carrying.

The road turned parallel with the sea just before Alexander reached the beach, and was now little more than a rutted track; automobiles were not common in the country districts of Japan, and no provision was made for them – Alexander carried his spare petrol in cans strapped to the back. But now he could see the house.

Nicholas Barrett had built the house to his own design when he had retired from the Navy following the end of the war with Russia, and to please his Russian wife it was less in the Japanese style than the European, built of solid wood and with large, comfortably European-style furnished rooms, and a verandah overlooking the beach and the sea. His Japanese friends, including his very oldest and greatest friend, Admiral Togo Heihachiro, the victor of Tsushima and Japan's most famous fighting sailor, had poked fun at the idea, pointing out that all those so solid walls would come tumbling down at the first earthquake, and there was at least one earthquake every day of the year somewhere in Japan. Nicholas had contented himself with retorting that there had not been a serious earthquake in Bungo within living memory, and certainly this house had stood for fifteen years.

Now chickens squawked, dogs barked and pigs grunted as the motor car came to a halt, and Japanese servants lined up to bow before their future master. Alexander stepped down and straightened his cap, brushed dust from the high-buttoned very dark blue uniform, its black insignia almost invisible. He greeted the bowing servants, most of whom he had known all his life, and walked to the steps, where his younger children were gathered to meet him.

Elizabeth, named after her grandmother, was fourteen, red-haired, plump and vivacious; by Japanese social require-ments she should soon have to be found a husband, but Sue-Ellen was determined to defy convention and have the girl achieve a more acceptable age, to Western eyes; she also hoped, Alexander knew, that both the girls would marry a European or American, rather than a Japanese husband, although he felt this was being optimistic. Charlotte was twelve, serious and slender. Both were delighted to see their father after a six-months' separation.

"Tell us about Washington," Charlotte begged.

"Did you bring lots of presents?" Elizabeth asked.

"They're in the bags. I'll tell you all about Washington. Soon." He swept them from the ground, one in each arm, to hug them and kiss them. But his gaze had already roamed past them to the petite, fair woman who waited at the top of the steps.

Like Alexander's own mother, Sue-Ellen Cummings had elected to follow a strange and often bumpy road in marrying into the family of what many considered to be renegades. She and Alexander had met in the turmoil that had been Peking during the Boxer revolt of 1900, and fallen in love almost immediately. Forbidden to marry, or indeed, see each other they had waited four years to elope, and their wedding had been abortive for more than a year, overtaken by the Russian war. But that was a long time ago, now. Alexander embraced his wife and kissed her mouth. "Father?" he asked.

"He has waited only for your coming. Have you seen Nicky?"

Sue-Ellen had her own house in Tokyo, but had elected to live with her parents-in-law during her husband's prolonged absence with the mission to Washington; that meant she was also temporarily cut off from her son Nicholas, who at eighteen was following in the footsteps of his father and grandfather, and would soon be graduating from the Naval Academy at Eta-Jima on the Inland Sea.

"No, I came straight here. We'll see Nicky on the way home, and talk about the future."

"Is the news as bad as the newspapers say?" she asked.

"Probably worse." Alexander released her hand to take off his shoes as he entered the house, then embraced his mother.

Elizabeth Barrett was seventy-two, but remained tall and erect, even if only traces of the once glorious auburn hair could be discerned amidst the gray, and her exquisite features had become overshadowed with wrinkles. "Alex!" She held him close, then at arms' length the better to gaze at him. "You at least look well."

He kissed her. "We shall survive even the Americans." He winked at his wife.

"They're frightened of you," Sue-Ellen suggested.

Alexander squared his shoulders as he stepped through the door into the study. Vice-Admiral Nicholas Barrett sat in his easy chair, looking out through the window at the bay the sea, and the rocks. He sometimes sat like this for hours on end, no doubt reminiscing, Alexander supposed. Having spent so much of his life in Japan, the old sailor wore a *kimono*.

Alexander bowed, and then stood to attention. "I trust you are well, honourable Father."

6

Nicholas turned his head. "I watched you come," he said. "You drive that thing too fast."

"I haven't hit anything yet," Alexander reminded him, and sat down. His wife and mother had also come into the room, ·but they remained standing behind the old man.

"Well?" Nicholas asked. "Is the news bad? The newspapers say so."

"It is bad, honourable Father."

"Tell me."

"By the first clause agreed in Washington, honourable Father, the United States, France, Great Britain and Japan each guarantee each other's island possessions in the Pacific Ocean."

"Is that not satisfactory?"

"At the insistence of the United States, honourable Father, the alliance between Japan and Great Britain was thereby terminated."

Nicholas's head turned more sharply than before. The alliance with Great Britain had been the cornerstone of Japanese foreign policy for twenty years.

"The Americans claim that, with these mutual guarantees of protection, offensive-defensive alliances are unnecessary and out of place in the Pacific theatre," Alexander went on.

"Balderdash," Nicholas grumbled. "They are afraid of us and the British ganging up on them."

"I believe this is true, honourable Father. But of course they will not admit it."

"And Prince Tokugawa agreed to this?"

"He wished to disagree, honourable Father, but the British signified their willingness to do as the Americans required. The British owe the Americans a great deal of money because of the recent Great War, and they were also anxious to negotiate on other points."

"Continue."

"By the second clause, we have agreed to evacuate the Shantung Peninsular and return Kiaochow to the Chinese."

Nicholas snorted. "You will be telling me next that Tokugawa has agreed to return Port Arthur."

"No, honourable Father, we were not required to do that. However, by the third clause, all the nine powers

7

represented at the conference, that is to say, the United States, Great Britain, France and ourselves, together with Italy, Belgium, the Netherlands, Portugal and China, signed a treaty guaranteeing the integrity of China, and reiterating the principle of the Open Door."

Nicholas nodded. "That is not unreasonable. What of the fleet? This conference was really called to decide the future of naval warfare, was it not?"

"Ah, yes, the fleet, honourable Father. By the fourth clause, a naval holiday was declared. It was agreed that for ten years no new capital ships would be built by any power. For the purposes of the treaty, a capital ship was defined as any vessel over ten thousand tons and armed with any gun larger than eight-inch."

"Ha. But that surely does not affect ships already building. Our new forty thousand ton Kaga Class? And the K II's?"

Alexander cleared his throat. "I'm afraid work has already ceased on the Kagas, honourable Father. The K II's will almost certainly be cancelled."

Nicholas went very red in the face, and Elizabeth rested a reassuring hand on his shoulder.

"But there is more, honourable Father," Alexander went on. "It was also decided that there will be an upwards limit of thirty-five thousand tons for any one ship. This would in any event have put the Kagas over the top. The reason for this limit is a very simple one: the Americans have calculated that thirty-five thousand tons is the largest vessel that can pass through the Panama Canal, and they wish to be able to transfer their battleships at will between the Pacific and the Atlantic."

"And the rest of you agreed to this?" Nicholas was astonished.

"Again, we would have opposed it. But again, all the other powers owe the Americans money. In any event, argument as to the size of a battleship was entirely negated by the final agreement. Again, so the Americans claim, in the interests of peace, the navies of the world are to be limited in strict ratio one to another, at least in capital ships. This ratio is supposed to have regard to the requirements of the maritime nations. The formula agreed to

8

is five-point-two-five: five-point-two-five: three-point-five; one-point-six-seven: one-point-six-seven for the five leading naval powers. This means that the Americans and the British can each have a total battleship and battlecruiser tonnage of five hundred and twenty-five thousand, Japan can only have a total tonnage of three hundred and fifty thousand, and France and Italy are limited to one hundred and sixty-seven thousand tons each."

Slowly Nicholas sat straight. "Admiral Kato agreed to this?"

"Yes, honourable Father."

"It is a betrayal of the Empire. Great Britain at least has an overseas empire to protect. Why do the Americans require a fleet half again as large as ours?"

"They wish to be regarded, with the British, as a super-power. Sadly, honourable Father, it was the will of the majority to agree to this, and we had no option but also to agree. The fact is that alone we cannot defy the world, and even if we wished to do so, it is another disagreeable fact that we are also short of funds. In fact, Admiral Kato confided to me on the voyage home that even had we not been forced to it, he was not sure it would have been possible to lay down the K II battleships, because insufficient money has been voted by the Diet."

Elizabeth had hurried forward with a glass of brandy for her husband, and Nicholas settled back in his chair with a grunt. "We had such problems when I was first trying to create the Imperial Navy, but we got round it. If we accept this political decision on how many ships we can have . . . some will have to go."

"Yes, honourable Admiral. All our fourteen year old battleships, that is, all ships completed before 1914, will be withdrawn from service."

"Haha! You mean they will be moth-balled, to be reactivated as we need them."

"I am afraid that is not possible, honourable Father. There will be inspections to make sure that these ships are entirely demilitarised and their guns removed."

"All of those fine ships?"

Alexander could understand his father's concern; Nicholas

Barrett had himself commissioned most of them; several of them had fought at Tsushima, and indeed three were Russian battleships, captured in that battle and taken into the Japanese Navy.

"Are they just to be scrapped?" Elizabeth asked.

"Hopefully some use will be found for them, as depot ships, and the Americans suggest we use some of them as targets."

"So," Nicholas said, "we are to be left with two battleships of the Fuso Class and two of the Ise Class. What of the two Nagato Class ships: they are all but completed, are they not?"

Alexander nodded. "And they will be completed, honourable father. With their eight sixteen-inch guns, *Nagato* and *Mutsu* will be as strong as any present ship in the world."

"Still, we are reduced to six ships."

"We also have the four Kongo Class battlecruisers, honourable Father."

"All coming up to ten years old. And we cannot build another ship for ten years? Do Kato and Tokugawa understand the implications of this? How many ships are the British deleting?"

"The British are taking out seven battleships and two battlecruisers, honourable Father. That will leave them with fifteen battleships and six battlecruisers."

"Fifteen! And *Hood* is more than forty thousand tons. How do they reconcile that with the thirty-five thousand ton limit?"

"They refuse to do so, honourable Father. *Hood* is the pride of the Royal Navy; they claim she is the greatest warship in the world. The Americans conceded this point."

"But they would not concede our Kagas. They were to be bigger and more powerful than *Hood*."

"The difference, honourable Father," Alexander said patiently, "is that *Hood* is already in commission, while our Kagas are on the slip."

"Ha!" Nicholas commented again. "What of the Americans? How many ships are *they* deleting?"

"None, at this time, honourable Father, save for their old pre-dreadnoughts."

"What did you say? That will leave them also with fifteen ships."

"That is true, honourable Father. And they have four thirty-two thousand tonners, the Maryland Class, building, which will bring them up to nineteen. But the nineteen will only total a little more than the five hundred and twenty-five thousand tons they are allowed, and they have promised to delete their two oldest ships, *Florida* and *Utah*, as soon as the new ships are commissioned."

Nicholas slapped his forehead. "I cannot believe this. Only two years ago we had one of the three most powerful fleets in the world. Now we have six battleships, while our enemies have fifteen apiece, and more building."

"It's worse than that," Alexander said miserably. "The British have some seventy thousand tons in hand, and they have been given the right, despite this building 'holiday', to lay down two new battleships; they claim this right to make up for the losses they suffered in the War. These new ships have to be within the thirty-five thousand ton limit, but they are going to be armed with nine sixteen-inch guns."

"Nine! You said *Nagato* and *Mutsu* were the equivalent of any ships in the world."

"They are, at this moment, honourable Father. But when, say in five years time, the British have their new ships in commission . . ."

"We have been made into a second-rate power," Nicholas said. "By a stroke of the pen. We are disgraced. Leave me."

"Your pa is really upset," Sue-Ellen said as they drove north-west. The ferry at Shimonoseki would carry them from Kyushu to the main island of Honshu, and thence to Tokyo, still a couple of days away. The two girls were seated in the back. They had spent a week on the Bungo coast with the grandparents, but Nicholas Barrett had remained throughout morosely brooding.

"With good reason," Alexander said. "The navy he created has been virtually destroyed."

"What does Admiral Togo say?"

"I have no idea," Alexander said. "But my father is

right: Prince Tokugawa and Admiral Kato have dishonoured Japan."

"They won't be made to commit *seppuku*, will they?" Sue-Ellen's voice was anxious; like most Westerners she had never been able to come to terms with the Japanese concept of honour, especially the ceremonial suicide required of a defeated commander.

"Once upon a time they would," Alexander growled. And then smiled. "But then, once upon a time, I also would have been condemned, merely for being present as an aide. Times have changed."

"For the better, thank God," she said. "But this sudden diminution in the Navy . . . what does that mean to your career?"

"Very little, I should think." He smiled again. "My name is Barrett."

"And Nicholas Junior?"

"His name is Barrett, too."

The Naval Academy of Eta-Jima was situated on an island, a few miles away from the naval port of Kure on the Inland Sea. The Inland Sea is one of the most beautiful places on earth, and Eta-Jima personified that beauty. An enormous stretch of usually calm water, studded with tree-clad islands, some of which were mountainous, the Inland Sea was at once a seaway from the southern island to the great northern port of Osaka, an almost enclosed lake teeming with fish, and a national playground. Eta-Jima itself appeared merely as a typical island, covered in woods and little valleys, shaped roughly like a Y, dominated by Mount Furutuka in the north, and presenting no obvious military features to the casual passerby.

The Academy lay in the fork of the two arms, and could not be discerned as a naval establishment until already within the precincts, when the parade ground and the fluttering flag became visible. It was a small place; there were only forty cadets, and the prestige of having attended was great. Most of the future naval officers came from middle-class and reasonably well-to-do families, although there were always places open to sons of the previously inferior classes able to

12

qualify academically. But a cadet's background, or financial status, mattered nothing once he arrived on the island.

In the first place, he was then subjected to such a rigorous series of tests, both physical and academical, before admission that it was reckoned less than fifty per cent of the applicants ever *gained* entrance at all, and then the four-year course was so severe that it was estimated less than fifty percent of those who had gained entrance ever qualified.

Alexander himself was a graduate of the college, although he would have been one of the first to admit that had been within ten years of its foundation, and that, as he had been the son of one of the founders, his personal failure had been unthinkable. Young Nicholas had had a much tougher road to follow as standards had been raised ever higher, even if, as Alexander had reminded Sue-Ellen, his name was also Barrett. But he had not only gained entrance, he had now all but completed the course: in a few months he would be eighteen years old, and ready for graduation, to take his place in a Navy which had suddenly been cut by two thirds!

After a warm greeting from the commandant, Alexander and Sue-Ellen and the two girls met Young Nicholas in one of the private gardens. "I always feel as if I were entering a monastery when I come here," Sue-Ellen remarked, but she clung to her son, smaller than his father, but as handsome in his dark uniform; Nicholas had inherited his grandmother's titian hair and bold Russian features.

"Well, honourable Mother, we feel that too," Nicholas said. "But, when we are allowed out, then we do not feel like monks." He bowed to his father. "Is it true, what is being said of Washington, honourable Father?"

"I'm afraid it is," Alexander said. "But your career is in no doubt. Have no fear about that."

"It is the dishonour done to Japan, honourable Father, that concerns me."

"That is a matter for your elders, Nicholas," Alexander said, a trifle more sharply than he would have wished.

Nicholas bowed, and Sue-Ellen waggled her eyebrows at

her daughters; she hated this kind of man-talk. "I have had a letter from Yoshiye," the cadet said.

Barrett Yoshiye was his cousin. Although General Barrett Takamori, the Vice-Admiral's eldest son by his long dead first Japanese wife, was some fifteen years older than Alexander, Takamori had married relatively late in life, and Yoshiye, an officer in the Army, was only two years older than the cadet.

"Oh, yes." Alexander said. He did not care for his nephew.

"Yoshiye says the whole army is deeply offended by what was agreed in Washington. They say such a thing could never have happened in the days of the Meiji."

Alexander reflected that the young man, if undoubtedly speaking treason in his implied criticism of the present Son of Heaven, was equally undoubtedly right. The Meiji Emperor, who had defied the world to raise Japan to the status of a Great Power, would certainly have continued to defy the world in his determination to keep his country great. But his successor, his son Yoshihito, whose reign was known as the Taisho period, lacked the stern character of his father; there were even rumours that the Emperor was perhaps not of normally sound mind.

"That is not a matter for us to discuss, Nicholas," he said. "We serve the Emperor, wherever he leads us, as our family has always done. And remember this, no matter what the politicians may say, the Emperor has only ever led us to victory, at sea and on the land. When the time comes, should it be necessary, I have no doubt he will do so again."

"Kind of heady talk, wasn't it?" Sue-Ellen asked that night, as they lay together on their mattress on the tatami mats of the hotel at which they were staying.

"I don't want him getting mixed up in any Army absurdities," Alexander said.

The rivalry between the Army and the Navy, common in most militaristic countries, was more acute in Japan than in others, for several reasons. It stemmed from the glorious days of Meiji imperialism. In the first of the great wars, that with China in 1894–95, it was the army which had captured

14

Korea for the Empire; the Navy's business had been simply to prevent the transportation of men and material to the peninsular. While the Navy had gained the international prestige, by its victories over the Chinese fleet at the Yalu River and Wei-hai-wei, the army was chiefly remembered for the ghastly massacre it had perpetrated when it had stormed the city of Port Arthur, at the southern end of the Liaotung Peninsular – an event, Alexander recalled, in which his half-brother Takamori, Yoshiye's father, had been involved.

Even more had the Army felt hard done by following the war with Russia. Japan had mobilised a quarter of a million men, and had fought the greatest land battles ever known, before the Great War itself, always emerging victorious. Yet the war was remembered chiefly for the naval victory of Tsushima, the most decisive sea battle ever fought in terms of casualties, for the entire Russian fleet had been destroyed or captured.

But the rivalry had deeper roots than mere prestige. As with most things, it was a matter of money. Even the Meiji Emperor had never had quite sufficient funds to do everything he wished, and thus his reign had been a matter of balancing one necessity against the other. In the beginning it had been the Army which had received the most funding. But when it had been understood – Nicholas Barrett had played his part in this – that an island nation which aspired to great power status simply had to have a first-class navy, the balance of priorities had been altered – to what effect the Washington treaties indicated. No one in Great Britain or the United States had made any suggestions regarding limiting the strength of the Japanese Army; it was the tremendous power of the Imperial Navy that London and Washington had found frightening.

In seeking to alleviate a rivalry which he had discerned could be dangerous to the state, the Meiji Emperor had perhaps exacerbated it. He had decreed that, in order to split the available funds year by year in a manner acceptable to both services, there should always be, in the Imperial cabinet, are minister representing the Army and one representing the Navy. These had naturally always been senior service officers, and in such a militarily dominated society as Japan, both by inclination and by history, parliamentary politics had gradually come to be dominated by adherence to one or other of the service points of view. The Meiji himself had always been strong enough to maintain a balance, but since his death in 1912 the much weaker Taisho Emperor had been unable to control the opposing factions.

The rivalry had come to a head during the Great War, when the Prime Minister, Admiral Count Yamamoto Gombei, had resigned because of a financial scandal. Since then the parliament had been dominated by the Army faction. And now the Navy had been humiliated.

"I'm afraid there is going to be trouble ahead, anyway," he muttered, as he fell asleep.

The service rivalry did not merely rest on matters of finance or prestige. It had grown out of an intensely differing view of life, a diversity of opinion which had but increased during the brief two generations that had elapsed since Japan had once again opened its doors to the world and sought to learn the secrets of that world.

The Meiji Emperor had determined to model his armed services on the best the West had to offer. Thus it had been natural to have his sailors trained by, and in the traditions of, the Royal Navy of Great Britain. Nicholas Barrett the elder, who had begun his career in the Royal Navy, had indeed benefitted from this decision. Thus the difference between the drill, the attitudes, the *esprit de corps*, and above all, the ideals, of the Imperial and Royal Navies had been, and remained, slight. In addition to being trained in navigation and gunnery and seamanship, the cadets at Eta-Jima were above all taught to be officers and gentlemen.

For training the Army, following the defeat of France in 1870, the Emperor had turned to Germany. There could hardly have been a starker contrast between the ideals of a British Naval officer and a Prussian drill sergeant. The Army, like the Navy, had become a magnificent fighting force. The Navy had allowed the ancient Japanese traditions of ferocious inhumanity towards a conquered foe to be tempered by British traditions of fair play and generosity.

16

The Army had found much in the singleness of purpose with which their German mentors approached each task to support their age-old law of *bushido*, which could be summarised as requiring total honour in one's self and in one's dealing with one's compatriots and any equally honourable foe, and total contempt for anyone who lost his honour by surrendering.

These differences had been accentuated by the opposing experiences of the two services. The Navy gloried in its victories over the Chinese and then the Russians, but its ships had visited the many ports of the world, especially Great Britain and the United States. Its officers had studied naval history and tactics, and had been obliged to realise that there were forces in the world as powerful as theirs, if not more so. There were many Japanese officers who considered that had Togo been in command at Jutland the Germans would not have got away so lightly, but there were others who understood that they themselves might have suffered enormous casualties.

The army had no such experiences. When called upon to fight, they had done so with tremendous elan and total success. It had not seemed important that the enemies they defeated had first of all been the troops of a Chinese Empire riddled with corruption and badly led, and secondly had been Russians on the verge of revolution. Allies of the Western Powers in the recent Great War, few Japanese soldiers had been sent to the Western Front; the majority had no concept of the enormous masses of men and material which had been thrown into the conflict by both sides.

And now, in addition, the Germans, who they had been brought up to believe were the greatest soldiers in the world, had been defeated. The Japanese Army could hardly be blamed for a certain confusion as to its proper place in the world's military heirarchy, and so clung to only one tenet. Unlike all the European armies, it had never been defeated in battle.

Alexander Barrett feared the ambitions of the Army, as typified by his half-brother. Barrett Takamori was fifty-seven now, and a general. But far more than his rank he valued the fact that he was a *samurai* of the Satsuma clan. He had been adopted by the immortal Saigo-no-Takamori, whose name he bore, and who had been his father's greatest friend. They had been driven apart by the pace of Japan's progress, out of which had come the destruction of the Satsumas and their stronghold of Kagoshima, and the deaths of both Saigo and of Takamori's mother, Barrett Sumiko.

Alexander had not even been born then, and Takamori himself had only been thirteen years old. But he could remember every shriek of anguish with which the Satsuma, men and women, had died before the onslaught of the Emperor's army, in whose ranks had marched the renegade Englishman who was his father.

They had never truly been reconciled. Takamori had never been able to accept the death of his mother, for which he blamed his father, or her replacement by the Russian woman. And Nicholas had never been able to forget that Takamori was one of those who had stormed Port Arthur in 1894, slaughtering men, women and children, and even animals, in their victorious blood lust.

Alexander, essentially of a different generation, attempted to understand both points of view as he sat with his half-brother, sipping tea. The screen door stood open, and the splendid garden was redolent with the charm of a Japanese summer.

Takamori's wife, Nikijo, and Sue-Ellen, together with Takamori's two daughters, Elizabeth and Charlotte, took their tea at the bottom of the garden, in the little gazebo, so as not to disturb the men.

"There can be no doubt that we have suffered a crushing defeat," Takamori remarked.

"Absolutely," Alexander agreed.

"In real terms, it is as if we have lost a battle in which fifteen of our capital ships were sunk," Takamori said, rubbing it in.

"I'm afraid that is so, honourable Brother."

"We shall rise again," Takamori said. "The Navy will rise again. I am certain of it."

"I find your words very reassuring," Alexander said.

"Yet there are questions to be answered," Takamori said, sipping his drink. "Who do you blame for this catastrophe?"

Alexander shrugged. "It is easy to blame the Americans. They have suddenly discovered that they are the most powerful nation in the world, merely because they are the richest, and they are flexing their muscles. But I think the blame really lies with the British. I think there is a large proportion of the British, certainly in government circles, who have never felt easy with the concept of being allied to Japan."

"Little yellow men," Takamori commented.

"Exactly. I think for a long time now, these men have been seeking a way of ending the alliance, but remained afraid of weakening their position here in the Pacific. The Americans provided them with a way out of their dilemma, by this mutual guarantee of all Pacific colonial possessions. After all, in terms of territory controlled, at least, Great Britain is still the most powerful nation in the world. So they owe the Americans a great deal of money. Suppose they were to repudiate that debt? What would the Americans do? Send in the marines, as they did with Haiti? I don't think anyone has much doubt that the Royal Navy could blast the US Navy out of the water, especially if they had us to support them. No, it is the British *will* to be our friends, as opposed to being friends with their blood-relations, the Americans, who have deserted them. And us."

"There is much in what you say," Takamori acknowledged. "Have you spoken of this to our father?"

"No. I feared to do so," Alexander said frankly. "But I believe he knows the truth of the matter as well as anyone."

"And yet, much of the guilt lies here, at home. You never met the Meiji."

"I was not so fortunate," Alexander said.

"He exuded greatness, in every way. Since then . . ." Takamori glanced at his brother.

Alexander frowned. He had been brought up to an acceptance that the Son of Heaven was above criticism.

"One must face facts," Takamori said. "We in the Army are taught to face facts. There have been Sons of Heaven before who have lacked the strength to carry out their duties. Had this not been so, there would never have been a *shogunate*. The Meiji showed us that the *shogunate* was no longer necessary. But if the *Mikado* would resume his function under the gods, then he must at all times rule. The Meiji *ruled*."

"And the Taisho does not rule?" Alexander asked.

"The Taisho has never ruled," Takamori said, darkly. He pointed at his brother. "This is a private conversation."

"I understand this, honourable Brother. But I am not sure I wish to listen to it. You are planning treason."

"I am planning nothing," Takamori told him. "I am but telling you what I know. The Taisho does not possess all of his wits. This is well known."

"Yet is he the Son of Heaven."

"As I have said, there have been Sons of Heaven before who have been unable to carry out their function. Now, no one is suggesting a return to the days of the *shogunate*. What is being suggested is a regency, by which the Son of Heaven will continue to make the necessary sacrifices to the gods, but the business of ruling will be undertaken by another."

"And no doubt this other is already chosen?"

"Of course. Prince Hirohito."

Alexander's head came up.

"Prince Hirohito is the Taisho's eldest son," Takamori pointed out. "Thus, in the course of time, and by the laws of nature, he will become *Mikado* himself. He is of sound mind, and much ability."

"And he is but twenty-one years old."

Takamori smiled. "Your middle-aged conservatism is betraying you, Alexander. How old was the Meiji, when he became Emperor?"

"Seventeen," Alexander conceded, grudgingly.

"And he was the greatest emperor in Japanese history. Prince Hirohito is his grandson. And he is even more suitable to rule than his illustrious grandfather. Do you not know what the Meiji told his *samurai*, told our father, when he became Emperor? He told them that for us to be strong we had to understand our rivals, our potential enemies. He encouraged our people to travel, and learn the ways of the west. He never travelled himself: he could not spare the time. But Prince Hirohito has just completed a world cruise. He has seen for himself the forces with which we are opposed. He will make a great emperor, perhaps as great as the Meiji."

"You are yet asking me to be a party to treason, honourable Brother," Alexander pointed out.

Takamori grinned. "I am not asking you to be a party to anything, Alexander. These great affairs are not for such as you. I am but informing you of what is going to happen, so that you will not be unduly surprised. Just remember that what I have told you is confidential. Especially are you not to utter a word of it to our honourable father."

"Because he would forbid it," Alexander said.

The two young men panted as they ran, sweat staining their blue vests almost black. They were well in front of their fellows: Barrett Nicholas was the finest athlete in the academy, and Tokijo Hasueke always endeavoured to keep up with his friend. Now, as they topped the last rise before the barracks, they could relax.

"Do you believe what your honourable father said?" Tokijo said inbetween deep breaths. "That we all still have careers?"

"Of course. We are the cream of the crop."

"*You* are the cream of the crop," Tokijo pointed out. He did not have a father and a grandfather who had both been naval heroes; his father and grandfather had never served at sea at all – Tokijo was a product of the liberal regime initiated by the Meiji, intended to bring the best of his people to the fore, however humble their backgrounds. Not everyone agreed with the late Emperor's policy, and Tokijo, as the son of a farmer, had had a hard road to follow since being accepted for the academy. The friendship of *barrett* Nicholas, so big and talented and confident, was the most valuable thing he owned.

They slowed to a walk for the last half mile; even their instructors were out of sight behind them.

"What is your greatest ambition?" Tokijo asked.

Nicholas did not have to think about a reply. "To serve under my father. What is yours?"

"To serve beside you."

21

Nicholas gave him an embarrassed punch on the shoulder.

"We shall do great things together, Tokijo *san*."

"Will we ever fight in a war, do you suppose?"

Nicholas grinned. "We do not have enough ships, to fight in a war."

"I should like there to be a war," Tokijo said, somewhat wistfully. "How else may we equal the deeds of our ancestors?"

"Yes," Nicholas said thoughtfully. They were being trained as fighting seamen, and if they never fired a shot in anger their entire lives would be a waste. But the only people Japan could possibly fight at sea would have to be the English or the Americans, and he possessed the blood of both in his veins. "I am sure our honourable ancestors will forgive us," he suggested.

Barrett Takamori was proved right, and before the end of the year Prince Hirohito was made regent, because of the "illness" of the Emperor. The business was handled very discreetly, and there were no repercussions. Whether or not Nicholas Barrett understood what had really happened, Alexander was not sure, but in the new year Nicholas died.

He was given a state funeral in Tokyo, attended by all the admirals in the Navy, amongst them Togo Heihachiro, and by several generals, including of course his eldest son, who on this occasion supported the stepmother he had always hated. Also present were his grandsons, Barrett Yoshiye and Barrett Nicholas, his two daughters-in-law and his four granddaughters; the male members of the family wore uniform, the female *kimonos*.

Count Togo gave the oration: he was grey-haired and grey-bearded now, and his always sensitive features had settled into pessimistic lines, but his voice was as resonant as ever. "It was my great privilege to know Barrett *san* almost from the day he came ashore in Bungo. I was present at his first wedding, and I was present when he was inducted as a *samurai*. In later years I served with him in our great and victorious wars. He was more than just a seaman. He was a fighting sailor, but we must never forget that he also earned great fame by his fighting on land. Japan was his adopted country, by force of circumstance. I mean no disrespect to the dead when I say that he would not have had it so, that he would have preferred to pursue his career beneath the White Ensign of the Royal Navy rather than the Rising Sun of Japan. Fate decreed otherwise, and I doubt whether the Royal Navy would have provided him with as many opportunities for glory as did the Imperial Navy, opportunities which he seized with all the consuming valour of his personality. We shall not see his like again. But more than his valour, his skill, his imagination, which played so large a part in the formation of the navy of which we are so proud, he was a man, and a *samurai*, to whom dishonour was anathema. May his ancestors welcome him to their company, for he is worthy of any of them."

Afterwards, Togo spoke with Elizabeth, and Sue-Ellen and Nikijo, and Takamori and the two boys; Nicholas was accompanied by his friend and room-mate, Cadet Tokijo, and for him also the famous admiral had a word. He came to Alexander last. "It is good to know that there is still a Barrett in the Imperial Navy," he remarked.

Alexander bowed. "There will always be a Barrett in the Imperial Navy, honourable Count. My son will soon graduate from Eta-Jima."

"And what of you, at this time?"

"I am presently serving ashore here in Tokyo, honourable Count. I am hoping for a command, soon."

"Were there sufficient ships to go round," Togo said grimly. "We must look to the future. I wish you to take tea with me. Do you know Yamamoto Isoroku?"

"Indeed, honourable Count. He has just been gazetted captain."

"He has some ideas he wishes to discuss."

"With me, honourable Count?"

"With me, Barrett. But I wish to discuss them with you. Come the day after tomorrow."

Yamamoto Isoroku was slightly taller than the average Japanese, and heavy set, with broad features and a balding head – he was thirty-seven years old. Like Alexander, a

23

graduate of Eta-Jima, he was a class the junior. But both had fought at Tsushima, where indeed Yamamoto had been seriously wounded, losing two fingers of his right hand. In those days his name had been Takano, but some years later he had been adopted by the powerful Yamamoto family. Alexander knew that he was regarded as one of the up and coming officers in the Navy, and also that he had spent two years studying at Harvard University and was thus even more international in his outlook than the average Japanese naval officer. He had not known he was a friend of the famous admiral's.

Now Togo ushered the two younger men to their seats on the cushions placed on the *tatami* mats, while one of his maids served tea. The girl then left them, carefully closing the screen door as she did so, to give them privacy. "This is an entirely informal discussion," Togo said. "Captain Yamamoto, we would like to hear what you have to say."

Yamamoto had brought with him a briefcase, and this he laid on the mat beside him and opened before he began to speak. "I am sure, honourable Count, honourable Captain, we are all agreed that our navy has been put back many years by the Washington Treaty. The plain fact of the matter is that if the Treaty is left unaltered, Japan will never be in a position to challenge either Great Britain or the United States. They will say that there is no reason for us ever to *need* to challenge them. But times change. We are entitled to ask, why are the United States building a fortified naval base at Pearl Harbour in Hawaii, if they never intend to use their naval superiority in the Pacific? We are entitled to ask if Great Britain has truly ceased her colonial expansion. More than either, we are entitled to ask if our own legitimate aspirations are to be forever restrained by the will of the Anglo-Saxon powers. The answer to this last question, at the least, must certainly be no."

He drank some tea, and looked from face to face of the two older men. Alexander drank some tea as well. Togo's face remained impassive, but he could have no doubt that the young captain was suggesting setting up a scenario for a future war.

"But how may the Treaty be changed? The Anglo-Saxons

will never agree to change. Why should they? The Treaty cannot be changed, except by a denunciation on our part. And how may we denounce a treaty when we are in such an inferior position? When we denounce the Treaty, we must be as strong if not stronger than our enemies. But how is this to be done if we cannot build any new ships?" He smiled. "It is, how do you say in English, Barrett *san*, a chicken and an egg situation. There is only one solution: it lies in introducing into naval warfare an entirely new concept, which will enable us to achieve the parity, or even the superiority, we seek, without openly breaking the Treaty." From the briefcase he took a book. "I believe that the answer lies here. This book is by General Giulio Douhet, an Italian, who was head of their air force at the end of the Great War. I have had it translated into Japanese, and I have this translation with me . . ." he took from his case two bound sheaves of paper, "for you to study, honourable Admiral, and for you, Barrett *san*. Douhet was particularly impressed by the activity of the Royal Air Force in northern Italy following the Battle of Vittorio-Veneto. A not very serious Austrian defeat was turned into a rout by the bombing and machine-gunning of the British planes. Douhet considers the airplane is the future of warfare. One may take this with some reservations. But one must consider him seriously when he states that it is the future of sea warfare far more than on land.

"His theory is straightforward. A naval gun has a range of perhaps fifteen miles maximum. An airplane can fly several times that distance. It also should be more accurate, as the bomber can fly immediately above his target before releasing his bombs."

"You are looking sceptical, Barrett *san*," Togo remarked.

"Well, honourable Count, I have not read this book," Alexander said. "But I have read a great deal about the recent war. I think General Douhet may well have a point when he says that the airplane, with its bombs and its machine-guns, will be a much more effective destroyer of retreating troops than, say, light cavalry could ever be. But the scenario at sea is totally different. A retreating army has to follow certain clearly defined routes, roads or railways through valleys, or across certain specified country. It cannot

25

travel very fast. An airplane can knock out bridges ahead of it, and choose its moment for attacking the column itself. This does not apply at sea. Also, it can do a great deal of damage with bullets and what are really very small bombs. These are unlikely to have much effect on a warship, for two reasons. Our small ships, which might be damaged by such bombs, are far too fast to be at risk from an airplane, nor can their course be predicted, off shore. And our larger ships would be at no risk at all. What is the largest bomb that can be carried by an airplane? Five hundred pounds? A sixteen-inch gun delivers a shell weighing more than two thousand pounds. Yet there is no one would dare say that a single sixteen-inch shell, or even a salvo of eight such shells, will sink a modern battleship. Certainly, no modern battleship has ever been sunk by fire from another battleship. Battlecruisers, now, are a different matter because of their lack of armour, as we have seen in the recent war. Finally, there is the problem of recovery. If an airplane is going to carry a five hundred pound bomb, it needs to be a large machine. Such a machine could only land and take off from a land aerodrome. This in turn limits its field of action to a hundred miles or so offshore. No, honourable Admiral, in my opinion, the future of sea warfare lies in the hands of the submarine, by means of the torpedo."

Togo looked at Yamamoto. "Captain?"

"Barrett *san* may well be right, honourable Count. The submarine and the torpedo are certainly going to play an important part in the sea warfare of the future. But all navies have them, and the Americans and the British have more than most. I am seeking a way of obtaining an advantage, not merely of matching our enemies' strengths. I concede that an airplane can only deliver a small proportion of the weight of shell available from a battleship salvo, at this time, although I would take issue with Captain Barrett's estimate of its effectiveness. A bomb dropped from an aircraft is essentially plunging shot; a shell fired from another ship is parabolic. That is why our battleships, all battleships, carry at least twelve inches of armour on their topsides and turrets, and only three inches on their decks; this leaves the decks four times as vulnerable to a direct hit, but this can only be provided by plunging shot. I also agree that an airplane, so

26

loaded, may only fly a short distance. But we are discussing the future, are we not? And so I would ask Barrett *san* this: when his lamented but immortal father came ashore on the coast of Bungo, what was the size of the largest battleship in the world?"

"Well . . . six thousand tons," Alexander said.

"That is but sixty years ago," Yamamoto said. "Now, what was the size of the largest battleship in the world at the time with the war with China?"

"Fifteen thousand tons," Alexander conceded.

"That is, the size of battleships increased by two and a half times in a single generation. Now we are told we must not build them over thirty-five thousands tons. So they have more than doubled again in another generation, and but for this treaty limitation they could be much larger. Were not our Kagas to be well over forty thousand tons? Would you not agree that by this line of reckoning, if the biggest bomb that can be carried by an airplane is at present five hundred pounds, may it not be able to carry a twelve hundred pound bomb in thirty years time? And two and half thousand pounds in sixty years? Or that an aircraft's speed might not also be similarly improved? What was the best speed any warship could achieve sixty years ago? Ten knots. Now we are concerned when we cannot achieve thirty. Planes fly at a hundred miles an hour now. When they can fly at three hundred miles an hour, they will run rings round any battle fleet afloat. As for their range, we have already seen what men like Alcock and Brown have done. If a plane can fly the Atlantic now, their range in a few years' time will be limitless."

"Alcock and Brown were not carrying a bomb load," Alexander argued.

"Agreed. But I have surely indicated that planes will grow in size and load-carrying capacity within a very few years."

"Permit me to interrupt," Togo said. "Am I right in assuming that it is your idea that Japan should develop an air force larger than that of other countries? I had assumed this was a discussion about how we can regain parity with, or achieve superiority over, Great Britain and the United States at sea. A large air force will simply be appropriated by the Army."

"Not if our planes fly off ships, honourable Count."

"He is speaking of aircraft-carriers, honourable Count," Alexander said. "Ships like *Hosho*. She will be completed this year, will she not? The British and the Americans have already experimented with such ships, and there are even a few in commission. But they have not proved very successful."

"That is because these ships were never designed as aircraft-carriers," Yamamoto said. "They were hasty conversions made at the end of the War, or equally hasty constructions. Even *Hosho*, as you know, is only a converted oil tanker, and even with her full complement of twenty-six planes, she will hardly displace ten thousand tons. I am not thinking of such small ships. Only one British vessel, *Eagle*, is more than twenty thousand tons. I believe they plan to reconstruct one of their battlecruisers, *Furious*, as a carrier, but she too will be under thirty thousand tons. The Americans are more ambitious. They are also in the process of converting two designed battlecruiser hulls into carriers, to be called *Lexington* and *Saratoga*. These are very big ships. They will each be more than forty thousand tons, fully loaded, and carry more than sixty aircraft."

"Forty thousand tons?" Togo asked. "But they will be monsters."

Yamamoto grinned. "And they will not pass through the Panama Canal, eh, honourable Count. It will be interesting to see where the Americans station them, the Alantic or the Pacific."

"But how can they do this, without breaking their own treaty?" Alexander asked.

"It is all a matter of the small print, Barrett *san*. These ships will actually only have a drawing board displacement of thirty-three thousand tons. That is within the maximum limit. This is achieved because at Washington it was agreed, as you will remember, that in arriving at the weight of ships it was to be permitted not to include defences against air or submarine attack. Well, if you have sufficient space, the best defence against air attack is to have planes of your own, would you not say? It is when these planes, and all their ancillary equipment, are loaded that the weight goes up dramatically. But it is within the treaty. Now, Barrett *san*, is there not another English saying, that what is sauce for the goose is sauce for the gander?"

"You are suggesting that we build large aircraft-carriers?"

"I am suggesting we do a little converting of our own. We are told that we cannot continue building our Kaga class battleships, because they are too big and would put us beyond our total tonnage limit. But to be included in the total capital ship tonnage limit a vessel must carry larger than eight-inch guns. No aircraft-carrier needs guns that big. The Americans are operating on this very system. Converting the Kaga Class would give us also carriers in excess of forty-thousand tons, fully loaded. Then what of the Akagi Class battlecruisers? These were designed to equal *Hood*. Now we are told they too must be scrapped. Thus we have a total of eight large hulls awaiting scrapping. Or conversion. At one bound we could possess the most powerful naval-air fleet in the world."

Togo looked at Alexander. "Well?"

Some of Yamamoto's enthusiasm had enveloped even Alexander's conservative mind. "If it could be done, honourable Count."

Alexander was more excited by Togo's scheme than he would dare admit, even to himself. Of course, with his English blood, he had no real desire ever to go to war with the British, even if he did feel that their decision to adhere to the Americans rather than the Japanese was a sad abandonment of a long-established and entirely faithful ally. While with his American wife, he was even less anxious to fight with the United States. But if he was half-English he was also half-Russian, and he had willingly gone to war with Russia when it had become necessary.

But more than that, he was a seaman, and he did not enjoy having limits put on his navy by outside powers. It was a grim experience having to watch the famous old battleships which had gained the world's most decisive naval victory, and their younger sisters, being towed away for scrap. Only one survived. *Mikasa*, Togo's flagship at Tsushima, was to be preserved for all time as a museum piece, a reminder of the Japanese Navy's greatest hour.

But for some months he heard nothing further about Yamamoto's concept, until Admiral Kato Tomosaburo, who had headed the naval mission to Washington and accepted the infamous Treaty, and whose flag-captain Alexander had been on that occasion, became Prime Minister. Then the Navy could wait with anticipation for some forward movement, although it soon became apparent that Kato had been made Prime Minister simply to carry through the ratification of the Treaty: no other minister, and certainly no one from the Army, would so demean himself.

However, only a few weeks after ratification, Alexander was summoned to Admiral Kato's office. "I have been speaking with Count Togo, Barrett *san*. He gave me a paper prepared by Captain Yamamoto. He also informed me that you were privy to this idea."

"I am, honourable Admiral."

"It has much to recommend it," Kato said. "If we could suddenly establish a fleet of eight large aircraft-carriers, it would alter the entire balance of naval power, and do much to reverse the misfortune of the Washington Treaty. Unfortunately, the three of you, even Count Togo, omitted to take into consideration one vital objection to the concept: money. As I told you on the voyage home from Washington last year, we could not have continued with the Kagas even had there been no Treaty, without additional funding. As it is I have had to cut one hundred and seventeen million yen from the naval budget."

Alexander's shoulders sagged. "So there can be no new ships, honourable Admiral."

Kato smiled. "Yamamoto writes a very persuasive paper, Captain. I have circulated it to all the members of the cabinet, and have been pleasantly surprised by the positive reactions I have obtained. Obviously funding eight ships is out of the question. However, I have obtained agreement to proceed with two, and possibly a third to follow. The two ships we are going to convert are the battlecruisers *Akagi* and *Amagi*. In all the circumstances, I consider it only proper that these two aircraft-carriers, when completed, should be commanded by the two men who conceived their purpose. *Akagi* is on the stocks at the Kure Yard; she will

30

be commanded by Captain Yamamoto. *Amagi* is on the stocks at the Yokohama Company Yard in Yokosuka. You will command her, Barrett *san*."

"I am overwhelmed, honourable Prime Minister."

"I am sure you will prove worthy of the task, Captain Barrett. I must tell you that it is estimated it will be several years before conversion can be completed, possibly as many as four. However, I wished you to know the situation now, so that you may be entirely associated with the venture from the beginning."

Alexander bowed.

"Oh, I am so happy for you," Sue-Ellen cried. "How I wish your dad were still alive: he would have been so proud."

Alexander knew his mother would be equally proud, and wrote to her to tell her the good news.

Young Nicholas was equally delighted; he had just been posted to a destroyer. "But I would love to serve on a carrier, under you, honourable Father."

"Well, perhaps it can be arranged. But we are talking of another five years before *Amagi* can be commissioned. I would seek your own advancement, until then."

Alexander was proud himself, prouder than he would admit to his family. He was even more delighted that he was, as Kato had said, in at the beginning, rather than merely taking over a ship which had previously been commanded by someone else, and would bear the imprint of another personality. *Amagi* would be his, and his alone.

Like everyone in the Navy, he experienced a momentary pang of alarm when army pressures forced Kato to resign towards the end of August 1923. But his successor was Yamamoto Gombei, the adoptive father of Isoroku, recovered from the scandal of several years before, and the captains were immediately informed that there would be no change in the naval policy.

Nicholas continued to visit the Yokohama Yard every day, to watch the the initial stages of the conversion being carried out. He was there three days after Kato's dismissal, 1 September 1923, when the earth shook.

31

CHAPTER 2

A Choice of Dreams

Alexander had just descended from the gantry overlooking the hull. He was aware of a sense of well-being, because he adhered, whenever possible, to the Western concept of the week-end, and was now preparing to take the next thirty-six hours off and spend them with Sue-Ellen and the girls; they were, in fact, planning an overnight picnic, complete with tents, in the Hakone Mountains south-west of Yokohama. Now, as he walked towards his waiting car, he was conscious first of all of a tremendous and very odd sound, as if a giant was tearing apart several telephone books with a twist of his wrists, and then discovered himself lying on the ground, having been thrown from his feet by . . . for several seconds he could not think, and supposed he was deaf, because he could hear no sound either.

He rose to his knees, staring in consternation at his car, which had half disappeared into the earth, as if suddenly parked over a bog. He reached for his cap, which had fallen off, and was checked by another enormous sound, ending the silence with a terrifying suddenness, and followed immediately by another gigantic *yawn*. Once again he was thrown to the ground, but this time he was more ready for it, and rolled on to his back, to stare up at the gantry he had just left, and watch it collapse like a house of cards. There had been several men up there, and these fell like stones, crunching into the tumbling ironwork, and being absorbed by it. If they screamed their fear and agony, he did not hear them. He was staring at the ship – his ship; the slip on which she had been sitting had buckled, as had the ship

32

itself. His ship! But she was not the only ship, either on a slip or moored alongside, that had been wrecked in an instant: the entire naval base might just have suffered a devastating enemy attack.

Noise welled about him, screams and shrieks, wails and moans. He reached his feet, looked left and right at collapsed offices, saw bodies scattered and smoke rising. He looked up to the high headland on his left, where the American Hospital had stood in all its modern pristine glory. He gulped. The cliff was gone, and with it, the American Hospital, a tumbled mess of wreckage in the shallow water beneath. Instinctively he started towards it, towards the patients and nurses and doctors whose lives had so literally fallen apart in the middle of a sunlit morning, and was thrown down again. But this was not a tremor: this was a huge, surging blast, that rolled him over several times and left him lying against a collapsed fence, his uniform in tatters.

He blinked at the sky which had turned black with billowing oil-smoke, and realised that the huge storage tanks on the other side of the seaport must have exploded. He pushed himself up again, and heard a new sound, a sound he had heard before, often, in his years at sea. The ocean in turmoil. He turned, running to the edge of the car park to look out at Tokyo *Wan*. The huge stretch of sheltered water was, as usual, full of ships, many of them naval vessels, including some quite big warships. Most were anchored, but a few small craft were on the move. The bay was calm. But out to sea, at the mouth of the inlet, there was an immense wave, slowly curving, higher and higher, unique to his experience because there was almost no crest, as there would have been in a storm. But it was the biggest wave he had ever seen.

Among the anchored ships there was pandemonium. Even above the noises closer at hand Alexander could hear the screech of the whistles, the blare of the trumpets summoning the watches below. He saw the wisps of steam rising from the various funnels increase in volume as steam was summoned, and he listened to the rasp of the anchor chains frantically being raised. All the time the wave seemed to grow in size as it moved majestically up the bay.

He jerked himself out of his stunned state into an awareness of his position. The yard was a wreck, with great fissures running to and fro, slipways buckled, smaller vessels thrown aside to lie with their timbers stove in. The offices were collapsed, and drydocks shattered. His *Amagi* was also a wreck. But now was not the time to think about that. People were emerging from the wreckage, staring without comprehension at the bodies of their workmates and friends; several of the buildings within the yard were already ablaze, no doubt ignited by fallen electricity cables. Within seconds this entire shipyard was going to be swept away by the approaching *tsunami*.

"Run!" he shouted. "Get inland. Make for high ground." He ran *at* them, waving his arms, forcing them to realise that the two shocks had been only the beginning of the catastrophe that was Tokyo *Wan* this day. They responded to his urging and his commands, and fled for the broken gates, while behind them there came a sullen roar, as the wave rose and rose.

Fortunately the land climbed steeply on the far side of the road beyond the gates, and most of the surviving workforce had reached there before the wave hit the shore. Then the roar became an explosion. Alexander, still driving the men before him, was seized by a gigantic wet hand and thrown forward with a force that winded him. But he was also thrown against a surviving telegraph pole, and he hugged it with all his strength as water continued to surge past him and under him and over him.

The pole snapped beneath the force of the wave, immediately above where he was grasping it so desperately. As it came down in a tangle of wires, immediately to be swept away, he could only thank God that it had been a telegraph pole and not an overhead electricity cable; as the water started to retreat he could hear the sizzling sound of live electricity and salt water in contact close at hand, and heard too the screams of men being burned and electrocuted.

Then he could breathe again as he lay on the shallow hillside, soaked to the skin, nostrils and eyes burning. He had no desire to move, wanting only to remain clutching his pole with utter desperation. He lay there for perhaps

34

half-an-hour, while his hearing slowly returned to normal, and his muscles ached. The enormity of what had happened slowly sank into his stunned brain. He had to move. All around him was noise, rising in volume. It was the the roar of nature loosed, as it was the united scream of a million people in agony. He sat up, gazing first of all at the town. Yokohama was a sizeable place, and the port for Tokyo was growing every day; so fast was it expanding it was becoming difficult to discern where the port ended and the city began; the open field on which the forces of the Satsuma had defeated the Tokugawa, less than sixty years ago, was completely covered in new buildings.

Had been completely covered. The *tsunami* had swept over the low land which bordered the coast, across the highway, and struck the houses like a vast bomb. Now they had disappeared into scattered matchwood, and no doubt their inhabitants with them. He looked to his right. Yokohama had itself been flattened. The waterfront of warehouses and docks had been crumpled up as if brushed by a giant hand. Behind them the more substantial houses and the two hotels had been shattered and smashed, the smaller dwelling houses and street-side shops collapsed entirely. The wave had receded, leaving behind it a turmoil of fallen and broken wires, and fires were starting in every direction. Smoke drifted skywards into the strangely still air to join the all-obliterating shadow of the oil-pall. Those houses further back and on slightly higher ground seemed to have escaped the worst of the inundation, but there too were fires springing up. From the holocaust there rose the continuing wail of human misery. Above all was the stench of the burning oil.

Alexander looked out to sea. The bay was a seething mass of leaping waves, again strange to look upon because of the absence of whitecaps. It made him think of a bowl of water which has been violently shaken, save that these waves were not inches but feet high. The ships which only fifteen minutes previously had been riding so securely to their moorings were scattered as if they too had just fought, and lost, a battle. Several had been driven ashore, on both sides of the bay. Several more were sinking or capsized. Some had got sufficient steam up to breast the wave and remained afloat, one or two had even survived at anchor, but that the damage was immense was certain. And they were now faced with an even greater catastrophe as burning oil from the shattered tanks spread across the surface of the bay, turning it into a leaping, dancing, vision of hell. His son was out there, somewhere.

The realisation made him look up the bay towards Tokyo itself, and he caught his breath. For here too the *tsunami* had smashed into the city, even as the city itself had opened up. From his position he could see only the waterfront; that was as devastated as in Yokohama.

But behind, he could see smoke rising from the city. The rest of his family were beneath that pall.

Moored in the security of Tokyo Wan, the Imperial Japanese Navy destroyer *Sawakaze* required only an anchor watch, and on a lazy September morning that consisted of half a dozen men. A third of the crew, including the executive officer, were ashore, and Commander Nagumo was in his cabin, writing letters. That left Sub-Lieutenant Barrett Nicholas as the most senior officer on deck.

From the bridge, Nicholas could look across the immense harbour to the naval base at Yokosuka outside Yokohama; with his binoculars he could make out the huge form of the battlecruiser-cum-aircraft-carrier *Amagi* sitting up on her slip. Every time he looked at her, Nicholas felt a glow of pride. His father's ship! Soon to be his ship as well.

He had no fault to find with *Sawakaze*. She was one of the new Minekaze Class destroyers, completed only three years before. She displaced sixteen hundred tons, fully loaded, was three hundred and thirty-six feet overall length, and carried a main armament of four four-point-seven inch guns to supplement her six twenty-one inch torpedo tubes. Best of all was her speed. Powered by four Kampon boilers, she could theoretically reach thirty-nine knots. She had actually only achieved just over thirty-eight on her trials, but one of her sisters had passed forty: none of the latest British and American destroyers could even approach those speeds, so far as was known. Thus if Japan was to have only the third strongest navy in the world in terms of tonnage, it could at least claim to have the best, in terms of quality.

Yet *Sawakaze* was only a destroyer. Nicholas hoped to captain a ship like her one day. But before then he wanted to serve on the greatest ship in the world, and under his father's command.

Doing what? He recalled his conversation with Tokijo, that day at Eta-Jima, so soon before they had both been commissioned, and thus separated, although they continued to be the best of friends and corresponded regularly. Tokijo had pointed out with utter simplicity that their only real hope of advancement lay in a war, and both his father and grandfather had fought in wars. Now, almost without warning, Japan had been made too weak to fight a war with anyone.

His own flesh and blood had done that. He could not help but feel a considerable affinity for the British and the Americans. He longed to visit both countires, see for himself the differences between western and Japanese cultures, which some admired and others denigrated. Indeed, he hoped to do so: Japanese ships often made courtesy visits to foreign ports. But at the end of the day he had to accept, as every officer in the Imperial Navy was doing, that these people were their enemies, determined to maintain their own superiority in every possible way.

He wondered if his father accepted that?

"Permission to take over the watch, honourable Lieutenant." Midshipman Tono bowed.

Nicholas looked at his watch. It was five to twelve, and thus the snotty was early. But Tono was a terribly keen type; no doubt he would grow out of it. "Very good, Mr Tono," he said. "There is nothing to report."

Nicholas went to the top of the ladder, paused there to look around him. The day was absolutely still, and there was not a cloud in the sky. Beneath his feet both the generators and the boilers uttered faint rumbles, and wisps of smoke rose from the two funnels above his head: *Sawakaze* was duty ship for the squadron this week and was thus required to keep steam up even when moored, or with so many of her crew ashore.

It was going to be hot in his cabin. He thought he would instead go to the wardroom and read a book until it was time for lunch. He slid down the ladder into the bowels of the ship, went aft to the wardroom, and nodded to the steward waiting there.

"You wish tea, honourable Lieutenant?"

"Thank you." Nicholas went to the book case, and brooded at the titles. He wanted something to empty his mind of the considerations which haunted him when on watch. He reached out for a selected novel, and became aware of a noise. It was a very loud noise, but one he could not identify, because it was totally chaotic, like a huge giant belching after a satisfying meal. Then he realised he was lying on his back on the wardroom deck, with all the books from the case scattered over him and around him.

For a moment he had no idea what had happened. He had an irritating thought that some battleship had passed close by at speed and set up an enormous wake. Then he sat up, and gazed at the steward, who seemed to be pirouetting around the wardroom, while cups and saucers and the kettle of scalding tea appeared to be following him. "Lieutenant!" he was screaming. "Lieutenant!"

Nicholas reached his feet and ran into the corridor. The ship lurched again, and he was thrown against the bulkhead; he supposed he might have sprained his wrist. He ran for the companionway, and met two sailors coming down. Falling down. The entire world had gone mad.

He threw them aside and started climbing, bursting past shouting people, and reached the bridge. There he checked, gazing in horror at the sea. Only ten minutes ago, when he had gone below, there had been no breeze and scarce a ripple across the surface of Tokyo *Wan*. There was still no wind, and yet now the surface seethed as if boiling, rolling all the ships to and fro, while the worst was still to come. Even as he watched he saw a solid wall of water, a wave at least thirty feet high, rising up out of the calm and ride up the bay. He listened to sirens blaring as other ships saw the coming catastrophe, but could not turn his head. *Sawakaze* was at least facing the coming avalanche, but she had no power and but a single anchor down – no more had ever

38

been considered necessary. She was also the furthest warship out, ansd therefore first in line to be hit.

"By all the gods!" Tono gasped beside him.

One of the watching sailors moaned.

Nicholas grabbed the voice tube. "Honourable Captain!" he shouted. "*Tsunami!*" He hastily closed the tube again. "Hold something!" he shouted, and grasped the bridge rail as the tidal wave burst on the bows of the ship, completely obliterating them, forcing them down as it careered aft. Visibility disappeared in green water as the wave broke against the bridge screens, which fortunately held. But even above the immense roaring of the water Nicholas heard the *crack* of the snapping anchor-chain.

He shook his head, and stared forward as the water cascaded to port and starboard. The severed chain snaked in the air before coming down with a crash on the forward gun-turret, crushing the thin steel as if it had been cardboard. He was dimly aware of the men to either side of him scrambling back to their feet, gasping and shouting. But only the thought that his ship was adrift and out of control occupied his mind. And there was no sound from the captain, who might have been hurt in the tremendous movement of the destroyer, for all he knew. But he had no time to worry about the captain: he was the senior officer on deck, and only he could save the ship. He whipped open the speaking-tube to the engine-room. "Give me steam," he shouted. "Give me steam!"

But he knew that, although there was steam up, it would take hardly less than an hour to have sufficient power to get under way. An hour! When every second meant possible disaster.

Tono was grasping his shoulder and pointing. The tidal wave had crashed into the other ships, and several of them, too, had snapped their chains, and were drifting, colliding together, while sirens blared and bugles blew and voices shouted. Not all had survived; Nicholas saw a fishing-boat turned upside down, its crew disappeared. But he had problems of his own, for behind the wave had come a wind, hot and vicious, and strong, seeking victims from amongst the shattered fleet. It marked *Sawakaze* as its own, driving

39

her across the still turbulent sea towards the rocks on the eastern side of the bay. An hour would be too long.

"Tono," he said, "break out two more anchors. We must bring her up. You . . ." he pointed at a dazed-looking sailor. "Get down to the captain's cabin and find out what has happened." Once again he picked up the speaking tube. "Honourable Lieutenant," he said, for the engineer officer was technically his superior. "It is very necessary to have steam at the earliest possible moment. The ship is in danger."

Tono was already on the foredeck, where water still ran through the scuppers. Men were emerging from their hastily-sought shelter to assist him. Their faces were blanched with horror and fear. If they knew what had happened, they also knew that the earthquake had been on a scale none of them had ever experienced before.

But having been given the lead by their officers, they were prepared to work to save the ship. The auxiliary anchors were shackled to the spare chains with what seemed agonishing slowness, while the tumbled rocks approached ever closer; then the anchors plunged into the water, and the ship slowly came to a halt – Nicholas estimated the nearest rocks were only fifty yards astern. But the seas were already subsiding, and for the moment the ship was safe. It was time to think, to take stock, to try to understand what was happening. And what had happened elsewhere.

The noise was still tremendous. Nicholas went outside on to the bridge wing, where there was still water dripping everywhere. He felt the September sunshine incongruously hot – it was still only just after noon – and realised for the first time that he was on duty without his cap, thus contravening every Navy regulation. He gazed at the now distant Tokyo shoreline and saw that the wave, having continued up the bay with ponderous and deadly slowness, was now breaking over the docks. Even from this distance he could see the entire waterfront being submerged, small craft being tossed into the air, great warehouses being smashed down. He could not see beyond the wave, but he knew he was watching Tokyo being destroyed. Tokyo! His entire family was there.

No, he remembered. Not his *entire* family. He turned,

to stare down the bay towards Yokohama and the naval dockyard of Yokosuka. On a clear day it was possible to see not only the American hospital, but also the ships moored at the base, or building on the slipsways behind. This was an exceptionally clear day, and yet he could see nothing beyond the wall of burning water which was extending from the shore where the oil tanks had been ruptured. He heard movement behind him, and Tono pressed a pair of binoculars into his hand. He levelled them, sweeping them up and down the coast. Of course the tidal wave had swept Yokahama as well; it would have been stronger there, closer to the mouth of the bay. Even with the glasses he could make out little of what had actually happened down there. But he could see that the hospital had collapsed . . . and that the naval base was no more.

Alexander staggered down to the torn and twisted roadway. The dockyard staff were still standing around, dazed by what had happened. He knew many of them lived in Yokohama. "Go to your homes," he told them. "See what has happened to your families."

He went down to the cark park and the waterfront, trying to avoid the gigantic puddles as he did not know which of the wires lying in and out of the water were live. He looked at where he had left his car, but the car had disappeared, thrown aside by the raging sea. The docks below were shattered, and so were all the small craft which had been moored there; the wreckage burned as the glowing oil got to it. The only way he was going to reach Tokyo was on foot. He looked again at where the hospital had been, and where it had fallen. But even that wreckage was obliterated by the raging, burning sea; anyone who had survived the collapse of the building down the hundred-foot slope would have been drowned or battered to death when the *tsunami* had struck. There were already people there, clambering down the torn slopes, shouting and hallooing. One more or less was going to make little difference, and he had an overwhelming necessity to reach Sue-Ellen and the girls.

He set off along the highway, crawling in and out of the huge fissures which broke the surface in every direction.

Here at least the air was clear of smoke, although rolling black clouds were now beginning to shroud the entire area. There were fewer horrors to be seen; the odd car thrown over by the waves or half buried in the sunken earth. Some of them still had occupants, but the occupants were clearly dead. The horror that was Yokohama was behind him. The greater horror that was Tokyo lay ahead.

He got there a couple of hours later. By then he had had to ford the Tama River, for the bridge was a tangled mess of wood and steel, and there was so much water he had to make his way upstream for more than a kilometre to get across. There were people everywhere, and animals. Dogs barked, chickens squawked. Children sat by the side of the roads and screamed, either because they were hungry or terrified, or had lost contact with their parents. Men and women pulled and prodded at collapsed buildings, trying to salvage their own goods or listen for the sound of someone still alive in the debris, but Alexander was sure there was a good deal of looting going on. And more than looting, for when he rounded a street corner he saw a young woman being carried into a yard by several men. She wasn't hurt, but from her screams she was terrified at the realisation she was about to be raped.

He hesitated, knowing that he could not fight them all and driven by his anxiety for his own womenfolk. He saw to his relief a platoon of armed soldiers at the end of the street. "Here!" he shouted. "Quickly."

They ran towards him, recognising his uniform, torn and mud-stained and water-ruined as it was. The sergeant saluted. "Honourable Captain!"

"In there." Alexander pointed. "There is a woman being raped."

The sergeant barked orders and four of his men ran towards the screams. A moment later there came the reports of the rifles, and more screams, this time masculine. "We have orders to shoot looters on sight, honourable Captain," the sergeant explained. "And rape is a form of looting, is it not?"

"What about the woman?"

42

"We will escort her to a camp. But you, honourable Captain: you have relatives in the city?"

"Yes."

"Then I will give you an escort too."

"That won't be necessary," Alexander told him. "But I will ask for the loan of your pistol."

The sergeant considered for a moment, then unbuckled his entire belt and handed it over. "There are extra cartridges in the pouch, honourable Captain. Be sure you use them if you have to."

Alexander nodded, and set off into the smoke and the turmoil.

Alexander was a veteran fighting man, both at sea and on land. He had fought at Tsushima, but he had always counted his experiences in 1900. As a boy he had accompanied the allied army to the relief of the besieged legations in Peking. It had been the most unforgettably horrifying ordeal of his life. What he encountered as he made his way through the stricken city wiped Peking from his mind.

The fires were now raging out of control; whole streets were impassable because of the heat and the roaring flames, and he found it necessary to tie his handkerchief across his mouth and nose in an effort to prevent himself from inhaling smoke. He passed the Tokyo Naval Club, where he knew there had been a political meeting that morning; it was a collapsed and burning shell. He crawled in and out of gigantic fissures, which contained dead bodies and such things as tram-cars, half-buried in the earth, with human beings scattered to either side. The city electricity and gas had by now been disconnected, but all around him lay the evidence of those ghastly minutes immediately following the two shocks. Trailing wires looped in every direction, and there was an ever-present smell of gas. He stumbled upon an entire tram-car filled with people who had been electrocuted; more than twenty men and women sitting rigidly in their seats, one woman's hand still outstretched as if she had been in the act of paying her fare when the current had coursed through her body.

Even worse were the parks surrounding the Imperial

43

palace, where the firestorm had induced tremendous lethal winds which had left mounds of people dead, while in the canal surrounding the palace itself he came across more people who had sought shelter in the shallow waters, who had also been burned to death by the fearsome heat, their blackened heads protruding like fishermen's buoys. The living were even more horrific, some burned or maimed almost beyond recognition, trying to drag themselves along or screaming for help. Many were apparently unharmed, physically, yet overwhelmed by the immensity of the catastrophe, wandered to and fro, calling the names of their loved ones or just shrieking their fear. Others almost having a game, like the group of schoolgirls he saw sheltering in the entrance to a disued sewer, jumping up and down as they laughed at each other's antics.

And then there were those to whom the disaster had suggested opportunity. Alexander had encountered some of those earlier. Now he shot dead two men who were looting a partially damaged house whose owner and his wife watched without comprehension, their eyes dull. But always he was absorbed with the urgent need to reach his own home, which was situated to the north-west of the palace. He stumbled on, resolutely ignoring the chaos to every side, challenged by various armed groups, both soldiers and sailors, who were attempting to control the looting, and then allowed on his way again as they recognised his uniform. At last he reached the street where his house had been situated, and gazed at tumbled ruin. At least there had been no fire here as yet, although he knew it was coming; the entire city lay beneath a pall of red-tinged black smoke.

He stumbled into what had once been his garden, a place of peace and some beauty, with a summer-house set beside a tumbling stream which had emerged from a rockery some yards distant. Now it was split by a gigantic fissure, several feet deep, which had come back together to leave an ugly brown score across the grass, and into which the stream had been sucked, together with half of the summer-house. The main dwelling had simply collapsed into another fissure, its roof tossed one way and its

44

thin walls the other. "Sue-Ellen!" he bawled. "Elizabeth! Charlotte!"

He heard a scream in reply. "Father! Oh, Father!"

He scrambled through the wreckage to find the younger girl, sitting on the grass. Her clothes were torn, her hair wild, but not as wild as her eyes. "Father!" she gasped, as he hugged her against him.

"Are you all right?"

"I am so very thirsty!"

Alexander looked at his watch. She had sat there for some four hours. Yet her remark surprised him. "Then we'll get you some water," he said, realising he was pretty thirsty himself. "Where are your mother and sister?"

Charlotte stared at him with huge eyes. "In there," she said, as if surprised that he did not know that.

Alexander looked at the collapsed house again, then gave a shriek himself and hurled himself at the wreckage, tearing timbers apart with his bare hands. "They've been in there for *hours*," Charlotte told him.

Alexander panted as he dug into the wreckage, having to move earth now as well as broken wood and furniture. "Sue-Ellen!" he shouted. "Elizabeth!" he screamed.

The noise of his shouting brought people, including some soldiers. They used their bayonets to dig into the rubble and the earth. And after half-an-hour they uncovered a leg. Alexander sat down and stared at it. The soldiers began to scrape away at the earth to either side, slowly revealing a kimono, and an arm . . .

"With respect, honourable Captain," one of them said.

"Yes," Alexander said. "That is my daughter. Where is my wife?"

"There is another body underneath," the soldier said.

Alexander sighed. "Have you any water?" he asked. "For my other daughter?"

It was the following day before Nicholas found them. By then Alexander had carried Charlotte out of the city to one of the hastily erected camps in the north, to avoid the flames which continued to destroy what was left of Tokyo.

45

The young lieutenant had been searching half the night, and was exhausted as he knelt beside his father and sister. "Thank God, boy," Alexander said. "Your ship?"

"Survived, honourable Father. We had steam up. Captain Nagumo gave me compassionate leave as soon as we were secure. Honourable Father, how can this have happened? People are saying it is a judgement of the gods."

"I'm sure it makes them feel better to say that, Nicky. But it is simply an act of nature."

"But so many are dead. Honourable Mother, and Elizabeth . . ."

"They went into the ground, with the house," Charlotte explained. "They'll be all right down there."

Nicholas looked across her at his father, his eyes stricken.

"I will take her down to Kyushu as soon as is possible," Alexander said. "To Grandmother Elizabeth. She will know what to do."

Elizabeth held her granddaughter close. "You will live with me for awhile," she said.

On the Bungo coast the air was clean, and cool. A man felt he could take deep breaths, and that had not been practical in Tokyo. The damage had been on a scale the imagination could hardly grasp. Even three weeks after the earthquake it was not possible to be certain of the death toll, but it was estimated to be not less than one hundred and fifty thousand people, with another hundred thousand seriously injured; all the deaths had been in horrifying circumstances, some more unacceptable than others: when the Fuji cotton mill had collapsed, fifteen hundred people had been trapped inside. Most of them had survived the tremor and the falling masonry, but then would-be rescuers had been driven back by the flames, and had had to watch the entire staff burned to death.

Yet the extent of the physical damage left even those catastrophic figures far behind. Seven hundred thousand homes had been destroyed, not to mention many large buildings, including the American Hospital and the two main hotels in Yokohama, where one hundred and eighty guests had been buried alive. Seventeen libraries had been destroyed, including that in the Imperial Palace, as well as one hundred and fifty-one Shinto shrines and six hundred and thirty-three Buddhist temples. South of Yokohama, the summer resort of Sagami Wan had been utterly destroyed by the *tsunami*, while nearly all the schools and hospitals in the Tokyo area had been wrecked. The railway system had been ripped apart, literally, with every line in the vicinity of the capital buckled and broken, the stations flattened, and an entire tunnel collapsed; a train had been passing through at the time and all its passengers had been suffocated.

These horrors had been compounded by the human factor. Some fifteen hundred convicts had been released from Ichigaya Prison when the building had been threatened by fire, and these had joined the looters and rapists already loose in the city; the reaction had been natural and xenophobic. Foreigners were regarded as responsible for the anger of the gods and several hundred Korean labourers had been lynched before order could be restored. Yet order *had* been restored, within two days, just as services and, indeed, life itself, had been got back to normal as rapidly as possible. Tokyo was already beginning to rise from the ashes. But there were some for whom the agony would never end.

Elizabeth came to sit on the verandah beside her son. She supposed it had been fortunate that he had been one of those, as a serving officer, mobilised into the restoration process: for more than two weeks he had worked twenty hours in twenty-four, commanding a detachment of sailors and marines charged with maintaining the peace in an area of Yokohama. For that time, his thoughts had been chanelled, and when he had had the time to think about himself and his family, he had had to visit the camp where Charlotte was being kept.

Now that was over; he had at last been given leave. She could not imagine what thoughts must be tearing his mind apart as he gazed out at the calm September sea. "How is Nicky?" she asked.

"Nicky is fine. He is the strongest of us all, I think."

"You are all strong," Elizabeth said.

He turned his head. "What are we going to do, honourable Mother?"

47

Elizabeth squeezed his hand. "Only time will tell if the damage is permanent. I think she should stay here for the rest of this year. It will not matter if she misses one term at school."

"I wish I could have got her to you sooner."

"So do I. But it was not possible. But what of you? Your ship?"

He gave a wry grin. "Is a piece of twisted metal."

"But they will give you another?"

"That I shall have to wait and find out."

"Barrett *san*." Kato gave a brief bow in response to his subordinate's deep one. "It is good to see you looking so well. Please sit down." He sat himself, behind his desk. "When I heard what had happened to *Amagi*, I feared for you."

Alexander seated himself, his cap on his knees. "I was there, honourable Admiral. But I am afraid I went up to Tokyo as quickly as I could."

Kato nodded, understanding. "Permit me to offer you my condolences on the loss of your wife and daughter. It is a sad and tragic time for us all. But it must be reassuring for you to know that your son acted with exemplary courage and decision. Commander Nagumo has recommended him most highly. His future is assured. We must all look to the future."

"Yes, honourable Admiral." Alexander waited.

Kato tapped the file on his desk. "*Amagi* is far too badly damaged to be repaired. I have given orders for her to be broken up for scrap. We shall have to look elsewhere for a replacement. It is my intention to use *Kaga*." Alexander's head came up, and Kato smiled. "I am aware that the battleship was to be scrapped as part of the Treaty. But she is still on the stocks at the Kawasaki Yard in Kobe, and it makes no sense for us to destroy her when we can put her to such good use."

"But, honourable Admiral, her tonnage . . . she was designed as a forty thousand ton battleship!"

"Agreed. But, stripped of her heavy guns and various other items she comes out at a designed weight of twenty-seven thousand tons. This is all we need to report. When her conversion is complete, and she is fully laden – I am intending that she should carry sixty aircraft – that weight will be increased to something over thirty-three thousand tons, but that need concern no one save ourselves. We will then have two large aircraft-carriers and will be able to contemplate the future with more equanimity. Do you not agree?"

"Entirely, honourable Admiral, May I ask . . . ?"

Kato gave another of his little smiles. "You may indeed, Captain Barrett. You will have the command."

"What you should do is marry again," Takamori told his half-brother. "It is not good for a man to live alone. Servants are no substitute for a wife."

Alexander stretched out upon the cushions on the *tatami* mats in the private room of the *geisha* house. Takamori certainly seemed to need at least an *augmentation* of his wife. Takamori had married late in life, and Barrett Nikijo was nineteen years younger than her husband, which meant that she was not yet forty. She was, in fact, roughly the same age as Sue-Ellen had been, and *he* had never needed any additional diversions. But those were still thoughts he dared not think.

They had eaten well, and now were being served tea by the girls, faces painted white as they eagerly sought to please their clients. Their bodies were no less completely concealed by their flowing *kimonos*; even the tiny feet thrust into the open sandals were encased in white socks. They had already performed their more usual duties, singing and dancing for the gentlemen, while the establishment's waitresses had served the meal. But now the waitresses had been waved away, and the two *geisha* awaited the further commands of the gentlemen, for while any *geisha* would be insulted and angry to be described as a prostitute, or even to have it suggested that she might sleep with a man for money, where two such distinguished clients as General Barrett and his half-brother were concerned, they were entitled to whatever service they wished to purchase.

Takamori ran his hand over the shoulders and down the back of the girl who knelt beside him, caressing her buttocks through the silk. "Equally," he said. "Is it not good for a man to be without a woman for any length of time. For me, it is a matter of a few days. Sometimes a few hours. But you . . ."

Alexander drank some tea, and gazed at the girl kneeling beside *him*, black eyes anxiously attempting to anticipate his every whim. "I have been in mourning," he said, quietly.

"For six months. Even if your wife were royalty, you could not have paid her a more sincere compliment," Takamori said. His hand moved lower, down the girl's thighs, and then reached her ankle, to slide beneath the silk of her skirt. As his hand began to move back up her leg, while she gave a little ripple of anticipation, he uncovered her calf, which above the ankle-sock was bare, and pale, and attractively slender and well-shaped.

"Is that not a pretty sight, Alexander?" Takamori asked. "Why do you not uncover him?" he asked Alexander's girl. "*He* will be a sight you will not forget. He may be a Japanese, but he is also a barbarian. He will split you in two."

The girl gave a little giggle, and moved her lips. But she would not dare touch him until invited.

Alexander watched the other girl. She had lain down, on her side, to facilitate Takamori's exploration. Now her thigh was uncovered and then her buttocks. As her back was towards Alexander he could not see more than that, but Takamori's hand had slipped between her legs, and she was giving little moans, of undoubtedly simulated pleasure, but none the less stimulating for that.

"Do as he says," he told his girl, for now he was definitely aroused. And Takamori was undoubtedly right. A great gap had been torn in his life, but if he was going to go on living, the gap had to be filled, sexually as well as emotionally. The girl's fingers were eager as she opened his kimono and untied the cloth he wore beneath. Then she gave a little gasp. Again Alexander did not doubt it was all acting; if barbarian penises were as a general rule larger than Japanese, this *geisha* house was popular with the officers off the many foreign vessels which used Tokyo *Wan*, and he would not be the first westerner this girl would have serviced.

"Use your mouth, tonight," Takamori was saying beside

him, lying on his back. The girl shrugged her kimono off entirely, and became an entrancing sight. The diminutive naked body was at odds with the white socks and sandals, which she retained, and the magnificently coiffured hair, which remained piled on the top of her head, secured in place by ivory pins. Her expression was hidden behind her paint mask as she straddled Takamori's belly, leaning forward to obey his command, leaving her buttocks and between available to his hands.

As did the expression on his girl, Alexander reflected. She had touched him, and indeed her hand remained resting on his shaft, but she was uncertain what he might want. "I want to enter you," he said. After more than six months, nothing else would do. She released her kimono and made to straddle him as well, but he shook his head. "I wish to lie on you."

She looked at his bulk, and then down at herself. He grinned. "I won't hurt you, little girl."

When they had both climaxed, Takamori sat up. "Brandy," He said. The girls hastily dressed themselves, and hurried from the room.

"I think I should be going home," Alexander said.

"To an empty mattress? You would do better to stay here. But there are matters I wish to discuss with you."

Alexander waited. "The first concerns the subject of which we spoke earlier," Takamori said. "Would you not like to marry again?"

"I have not considered it. I could never love again."

Takamori might have been blowing a bubble. "What has love got to do with it? Men do not love. Love is a non-existant emotion dreamed up by poets and western romantics. That is the great flaw in western philosophy, Alexander: it is based on a romantic concept of life. But there is nothing romantic about life. The fish eats the raw sewage pumped from our shores, we eat the fish, we eventually become raw sewage. What is romantic about that?"

"If one adopted that point of view entirely, where would be the point in living?" Alexander asked, good-naturedly; unlike his half-brother, the more he drank the more mellow he became.

"There is certainly no point, and no benefit to anyone,

51

to fall in love," Takamori said. "Love weakens a man, and invariably ends in misery. Our business is to perform our duty, to the Emperor, to the empire, to our ancestors." He grinned. "But there is no reason why, along the way, we should not enjoy ourselves. And when the enjoyment is also a duty to the Emperor and the empire, and our ancestors, in that the result of it may result in future soldiers and sailors, future bearers of our family name and honour, why, then it is a positive crime not to indulge oneself."

Alexander sighed. "I suppose there is something in what you say."

"Why do you not let me find you a wife?" Takamori asked. "I will guarantee you four things. One, that she will be well born; two, that she will be beautiful; three, that she will be utterly subservient; four, that she will make you happier than any *geisha*." It was a singularly attractive prospect, especially when he had just been serviced by the epitome of Japanese womanhood. "I could also make sure that she is a Christian," Takamori remarked. "I am sure you would prefer that."

"Have you that wide a field to choose from?" Alexander asked.

Takamori chuckled. "I am Barrett Takamori."

"I will think about it," Alexander said.

"And so will I."

"You mentioned two matters."

"The second concerns young Nicholas," Takamori said.

"I see. You wish to find him a wife as well, is that it?"

"In the course of time, perhaps. He is very young. No, no, his problem is of more importance. I should like to sponsor him as a *samurai*."

"Eh?" Alexander sat up.

"I know you have never become a *samurai*," Takamori said. "This was the will of our father. I disagreed with him, and told him so. He was a *samurai*. Both he and I were sponsored by the immortal Saigo-no-Takamori, who was once our father's dearest friend, and whose name I bear."

"And who died in rebellion against the Emperor," Alexander said.

"He was undoubtedly mistaken," Takamri said, equably – he had been in the Satsuma fortress when it fell to the

Imperial assault, and although he had been a small boy he would have fought for his clan had he been able. "At that time we had no idea where the Emperor was going, the glories to which he would lead us. Nonetheless, Saigo died as a *samurai*, in defence of his honour and by the laws of *bushido*."

"Both of which were abolished by that very emperor we both served and revere," Alexander pointed out.

"He took away our rights. He could never take away our honour."

Alexander sat up. "Takamori, in the old days, when Japanese society was stratified into classes, *samurai*, as the only class permitted to bear arms, were of great importance. They supported the *daimyo*, the *daimyo* supported the *shogun*, and the *shogun* ruled in the name of the *mikado*. But that system was ended by the Meiji Emperor. He gave the privilege of bearing arms to the whole nation. It was not an army of *samurai* that defeated China in 1895, or Russia in 1905, or that you were so proud to command in this last war. As for *bushido*, that is medieval. It has no place in a Japan that wishes to take its place amongst the civilised nations of the world."

"Our place in the world," Takamori sneered. "What is our place in the world, honourable Brother? We earned our place in the world, by the force of our arms. And let me remind you that these peasant armies of which you speak, while they may not have consisted of *samurai*, were certainly commanded by *samurai*. There was not a general in our Army, or an Admiral in our Navy, and that includes both of the men you have most admired in your life, our father and Admiral Togo, who were not *samurai*. And we won, on each occasion, against immense odds. How do you suppose we stormed the Narrows into the Liaotung Peninsular, against Nanshan Hill, one of the strongest fortresses in the world? It was because we were animated by the spirit of *bushido*. Did not Prince Ito, who commanded the Navy against China, and Prince Oyama, who commanded our armies against both Russia and China, both commit *seppuku*, with their wives, when the Meiji Emperor died? That was the law of *bushido*, because they were his closest associates." He snorted. "Now you, and others similarly misguided, would have that spirit lost, as you

53

would have the *samurai* disappear from history. And what have been the immediate results of that puerile approach? We have never been defeated in battle, either on land or sea, yet by the stroke of a pen we have allowed ourselves to be reduced to a second-class power. A stroke of a pen, and all that our father, and ourselves, have spent our lives fighting to achieve, has been cast away. Now we are told that the Americans are intending to reduce, or end altogether, the immigration of our people to Hawaii and California. We are being reduced to the same level as China, merely a market to be exploited by the whites as they feel the need. With respect, honourable Brother."

Alexander grinned. "A man cannot help the colour of his skin. But I hope you are not seriously suggesting that a revival of the spirit of *bushido* would reverse these misfortunes?"

"Yes, that is what I am saying," Takamori said.

"You would oppose the whole civilised world?"

"As to whether it is they who are civilised, or us, remains to be established. But yes, if necessary, we will oppose the world."

"We being the *samurai*?"

"We being the Japanese Army, honourable Brother. And the Imperial Navy, of course. Will you permit Nicholas to become one of us? At this moment he is a national hero for saving his ship from the *tsunami*. He is eminently suitable"

Alexander stroked his chin. "I will have to ask him," he said.

"To become a *samurai*!" Nicholas's eyes gleamed.

"You understand that this no longer has any legal implications at all," Alexander told him. "You are joining in effect a secret society. However, I cannot deny that it may be advantageous socially, and may even help your advancement in the Navy."

"Not being a *samurai* has not hampered you, honourable Father."

"I had never supposed so," Alexander admitted. "But now I am wondering. My father was an admiral by the time he was my age. I am still only a captain, and of a ship which is still on the stocks. But you must make your own decision."

Nicholas took a turn around the room. "I should tell you," Alexander said, "that were your mother alive she would entirely oppose the idea."

"But my mother is dead, honourable Father." The young man stopped, and faced Alexander. "I would like to be a *samurai*, honourable Father."

"Then you shall be one. But Nicholas, I hope that you will always remember that honour and charity go hand in hand."

"It is the honour that counts, honourable Father."

"Your father will be turning in his grave," Elizabeth remarked.

"Nicholas is old enough to know his own mind," Alexander said. "I cannot dictate the way his life should be run." He smiled. "My father was a Victorian. But we are living in a different century."

"Yes. I'd be glad I wasn't going to see the end of it," Elizabeth said. "If it wasn't for worrying about you lot. Are you going to take Charlotte for a walk?"

Alexander nodded. The previous day he had taken his daughter into Kagoshima for a medical examination, but the doctors had been unable to offer much hope: Charlotte's brain seemed to have become frozen in time at noon on 3 September 1923, more than a year in the past now. She spoke of her mother and sister as if they were still alive. One of the doctors had recommended time and patience; the girl was still only fourteen, and was therefore not evidently retarded, at least to anyone who did not know her well. The other had recommended trying the new science of psychiatry; apparently there was a man who claimed to be a psychiatrist in Nagasaki, which was just on the other side of the island. But Alexander felt that psychiatry was less a science than a kind of mumbo-jumbo, and he wasn't sure he wanted to expose his daughter to that. He went for time.

He stood up, cleared his throat. "What would your reaction be if I said I was thinking of marrying again?"

"Alex!" Elizabeth seized his hand. "I think that's a splendid idea. Is it someone I know?"

"Ah . . . no."

"Oh. You mean she's Japanese."

55

"I imagine she's going to be. But she'll be a Christian."

"You mean you haven't even found a bride? You're just thinking about it?"

"I suspect it's gone past the thinking stage." He told her the rest of his conversation with Takamori.

Elizabeth gave a little shiver. "The whole idea is medieval."

"Takamori represents a medieval way of life."

"I have never liked him. I imagine he knows that. But you are going to accept his offer of a bride."

Alexander gazed out to sea. "Would that be so very wrong of me?"

Elizabeth sighed. "No. No, it would not be wrong of you. It might even be good for you. But Alex . . ."

He squeezed her hand. "Don't worry, Mother. My first duty will always be to Nicholas, and Charlotte, and you."

Elizabeth's smile was sad. "Don't waste your time worrying about me."

Alexander attended Nicholas's induction as a *samurai*, as a guest. Takamori himself acted as the young man's sponsor, and himself cut away the hair from the forehead, after the rest of the head had been shaved, save for the topknot. It was after the completion of the ceremony, when Nicholas was being congratulated by his fellow officers, that Takamori sought out his half-brother. "This is a great day for the family, honourable Brother. I am sure you know Fujimoto Hakesara."

Alexander bowed to the older man. "Your brother was married to our sister, and was lost at sea."

Fujimoto bowed in turn. "I was but a boy at the time. But I remember how honoured my family was to be united with yours, Barrett *san*, even if briefly. That such a unity may again be possible, fills me with pride."

Alexander glanced at his brother, and Takamori smiled. "Fujimoto *san* would invite you to dine with him, honourable Brother."

It was a small party, but an especially intimate one. Takamori and Nakijo were there with Alexander, and the number was made up to six, by Fujimoto and his wife, and their daughter.

Alexander was quite taken aback, at once by the apparent acceptance by everyone present that the matter was a fait accompli – before the meal Fujimoto Suiko showed him to her private chapel, where she and her family worshipped before an ikon of the Virgin Mary – and by the girl herself. Fujimoto Christina was no more than sixteen years old. She was as pretty as a picture, wearing a pale blue kimono, her black hair swept up in a chignon and secured with ivory pins, her face untouched by paint, her mouth quick and mobile, her black eyes darting and intelligent. Too intelligent, he thought; she had certainly been told what was expected of her, and her attentions were deliberate, if, he could not help but feel, slightly mocking. Because . . . "I am nearly three times your daughter's age," he said to Fujimoto, when the ladies had left them after the meal.

"Does that not make your heart beat faster?" Fujimoto asked.

"Of course it does. But what of hers?"

"My daughter is overjoyed at the thought of marrying so famous a warrior, Barrett *san*," Fujimoto said.

"She is younger than my son," Alexander told Takamori.

"Then will he envy you the more. Why are you so reluctant, honourable Brother?" Takamori grinned. "Are you afraid of your performance? Fujimoto Christina is a virgin. She does not even have any brothers. You will be her sole yardstick as to a man's capabilities. There is nothing for you to fear. And binding Fujimoto to us is of great importance to the cause."

Alexander frowned at him. "The cause?"

"The resurrection of Japan as a great power, honourable Brother. Is this not your dream?"

"Well, of course, but . . . Fujimoto is an industrialist."

"And do we not need industrialists? Of course he is not a *samurai*. But it was the Meiji Emperor himself who told us, many years ago, that in the making of a modern great power the industrialist is as important as the soldier. When we go to war, it will be the industrial might, and the money, of men like Fujimoto behind us."

"Did you say, go to war?" Alexander asked.

Takamori smiled. "Is that not the most sublime state to which a man can aspire?"

CHAPTER 3

A Glow in the East

Barrett Alexander and Fujimoto Christina were first of all married in the Anglican Church in Tokyo, before adjourning to the garden of the Fujimoto house for the long, elaborate Japanese wedding ceremony. But at last it was over. The ceremonial toasting, the solemn exchange of gifts between Alexander and the Fujimotos was completed. Barrett Christina, as she now was, having changed from her white wedding gown into a kimono, had now changed once again into a smart pink going away outfit, jacket and skirt, and high-heeled shoes. Then she had kissed Takamori and Nikijo, Yoshiye and Nicholas, eyeing the young men with a mixture of interest and apprehension. She was six years younger than Nicholas, but as his new mother he must now obey her in all things.

Then they had driven to the hotel where they would spend the first night of their married life. Tomorrow they would drive down to Kyushu, and the house on the coast; Elizabeth had not felt able to travel up to Tokyo for the wedding, nor had she wished to expose Charlotte either to curious gazes or to the trauma of accumulating a new mother without proper preparation.

The manager bowed low as Captain Barrett and his bride entered the lobby, and the assembled staff, and not a few guests, clapped their approbation. "My humble establishment is filled with pride, honourable Captain," the manager said. "May I show you to the elevator?"

The hotel was brand new, one of those modern, western-style buildings which had sprung up from the ashes of Tokyo.

In addition to its ordinary foundations, it was surrounded by massive blocks of concrete, set some distance away from the walls, from which huge steel chains were linked to various points on both walls and roof; it was claimed that not even another shock like that of 1923 could bring this building crashing down.

The lift rode upwards, the manager smiling at his guests; the luggage would follow separately. "Where were you in the great earthquake?" Alexander asked his bride.

"I was in Osaka, at my father's house," she replied. "But you were here, honourable Husband."

He nodded. "In Yokohama. And you?" he asked the manager.

"I was here also, honourable Captain. Now, we will live forever, eh?"

The lift stopped, and he ushered them into the bridal suite, where he showed them the appointments, which were of a high standard. By the time he had finished, their luggage had arrived. Alexander handed out tips, while Christina waited patiently by the window, looking down at the street. When he closed the door, she came towards him. "I have an extra wedding present for you, honourable Husband," she said, in English.

"Wherever did you learn it?"

She smiled. "I had an English nanny. I know all things English."

He took her in his arms. "Then do you also know how Englishmen, and women, kiss?"

"I think so. But you can correct me where I am wrong." She slid her arms round his neck, and held him against her. Sixteen years old, he thought, and she is already leading me by the nose. But her mouth tasted like nectar, laced with champagne.

She stepped away, and took off her smart pink jacket. Then she took off her white blouse, and slipped her pink skirt past her hips to the floor. Beneath she wore a camiknicker, incongruous with the pale yellow skin and the upswept hair, but the more titillating for that. Perhaps it was too long since he had been sufficiently excited, about sex. "Do I please you, honourable Husband?"

"I think you are very beautiful. Will you release your hair?"

She reached up and pulled out the ivory pins, and her hair tumbled past her shoulders, straight and black as midnight. He wished to regain the initiative, stepped up to her and himself slid the straps for the undergarment past her shoulders. "Do you wear this, always?" he asked.

She shook her head. "At home, I wear the *kimono*. Would you like me to put one on now?"

His turn to shake his head, as he slowly exposed her breasts. They were small, but yet perfectly shaped. He leaned forward to kiss a nipple, and she gave a little shudder. "Do I frighten you?" he asked.

"I am here to please you, honourable Husband."

The camiknicker slid down her thighs and gathered around her ankles. Daintily she stepped out of it. Her hips were narrow and her legs thin, but the buttocks, like her breasts, were well shaped. And between her thighs were the most delightful silky wisps of hair as black as on her head. "You please me very much," he said.

She waited, just touching her lips with the tip of her tongue. He felt acutely embarrassed. Before him was youthful and innocent perfection. Before her was ageing lust. Never had he been so aware of his slight paunch. He turned away to hang his uniform in the wardrobe, slide his drawers past his thighs. He was fully erected when he turned to face her.

"Honourable Husband," she said, and fell to her knees.

He went towards her. "I did not wish to frighten you."

"But, honourable Husband, you also please *me* very much," she said, and took him into her mouth.

"She is an absolute charmer," Elizabeth said. "And you say Takamori arranged it?"

"The whole thing."

"Well, maybe he's not as bad as I thought he was. I must apologise the next time I see him. Not that I expect to do that again."

"He never visits you?"

"My dear Alex, he loathes me. Always has done."

61

"But you are his mother!"

"He has never acknowledged that either. Don't forget that your father and I couldn't get married until my first husband died, and that wasn't until 1905. Takamori was forty and already married himself. I think he just got into the habit of thinking of me as your father's private *geisha*."

"Nevertheless," Alexander said severely. "You are his mother. I will have a word with him."

"No." She rested her hand on his arm. "Please. I really don't care if I never see him again. Tell me, how has Nicholas reacted." She smiled. "I don't see too much of him, either."

"Well, that I *can* do something about," Alexander said. "He will come down here on his next furlough. He's taken it all in his stride."

"I suppose it can happen in any society," Elizabeth said. "But I imagine suddenly accumulating a step-mother who is six years younger than yourself must take a little getting used to." This time her smile was broader. "I at least was twelve years older than Takamori. But Christina is so sweet I am sure they will get on famously. As for Charlotte . . . she's fallen hook, line and sinker."

Alexander watched the two girls – they were roughly the same age – coming up the steps from the beach, where they had been walking barefoot on the sand and paddling in the sea. "I think Christina has too. But honourable Mother, what are we going to do?" For Charlotte's brain refused to be released.

"I think," Elizabeth said. "That now you have a wife, and a rebuilt home, you should take Charlotte back. If she likes Christina this much, we may have found the key to unlocking her mind. And let's face it, I haven't been very successful. But mind you all come to visit. Regularly."

"Sushi, you old devil," Nicholas said as the door of his father's house was opened for him.

The butler bowed. His name was not really Sushi, of course, but it was the only name Nicholas had ever known him by: Sushi had worked for Barrett Alexander for years.

"You are most welcome, honourable young Master. It has been a long time."

"Well, I have been at sea, and besides, I could not interrupt my father's honeymoon. Is he at home?"

"Honourable Master is in the bath house, honourable young Master."

Nicholas raised his eyebrows; it was past nine in the morning. But perhaps Father was on holiday. He strode through the house, entirely rebuilt since the earthquake, and to his room, where he changed his uniform for a *kimono*. Then he went into the garden. This too had been rebuilt, but exactly as before; the stream meandered through the centre of the lawn, the summerhouse stood to one side, and the bathhouse to the other. He crossed the lawn and tapped on the door. This was immediately opened, a crack, by one of the maidservants, who gave a little giggle as she recognised him – all the girls were very fond of the handsome young lieutenant – and was about to shout his name, but he shook his head and laid his finger on his lips.

He squeezed her naked thigh as he stepped through, for the moment blinded by steam. The second girl quickly took the kimono from his shoulders, while the first emptied a bucket of cold water over him, following which they fell to soaping him vigorously, the water draining through the slatted floor into the gutters beneath.

From the far side of the room there came splashes. "Who is that, Yenta?" Alexander Barrett called.

Again Nicholas shook his head, and himself seized the second bucket to rinse himself, then went towards the bath itself. "Home from the sea, honourable Father," he said, and checked in consternation.

The bath was deep, set into the floor. It contained as Nicholas knew, two seats, one at each end, and the occupants, once seated, would be immersed in constantly renewed hot water up to their necks; the bubbling left their bodies all but invisible. But as he emerged through the steam, Barrett Christina stood up, and stepped on her seat to climb out of the tub

She had washed her hair, which spread like a dark stain, down her back, and on to her breasts. She glowed with the heat of the water, She was the most beautiful sight Nicholas had ever seen in his life; *geisha* girls, who composed his knowledge of intimate womanhood, very seldom stripped naked, at least for second-lieutenants, while his mother had always preserved the niceties of western civilisation, and had not even allowed the serving girls into the bath house whenever she or her daughters had been indulging.

It was for that reason it had never occurred to him that his new stepmother might be sharing her bath with Father. Now he could only goggle at her, while the sight of her, and her half-smile as she looked at him, had an inevitable reaction.

"I'm sorry," he gasped, and stepped back towards the two girls; *they* had never caused an erection. Hastily he grabbed one of the waiting towels and draped it round him.

"Nicholas?" Christina's voice was soft.

"Nicky!" Alexander boomed. "Welcome home. When did you get in?"

He was again invisible behind the steam. But Christina was not, as she came towards him; one of the girls offered her also a towel, and she shrugged it aside.

"I got in this morning, honourable Father," Nicholas said. "And came straight here. I did not mean to embarrass you."

"Embarrass me?" Alexander asked, bewildered.

Christina smiled, and gently took away his towel. "You have not embarrassed us, Nicky," she said. "I was just getting out, anyway. Take my place in the tub and tell your father all about your voyage."

On 25 December 1926 the Taisho Emperor died. As Prince Hirohito had anyway been regent since 1922, politically it appeared to have little impact, but the event was a cause for the nation to go into mourning, yet Takamori was jubilant. "Now we will see an entirely different state of affairs."

He dined with his half-brother, and the two wives had followed custom and withdrawn after the meal. "How different?" Alexander asked.

"His Majesty has long felt constrained by the presence of his father. This is as it should be. But now we have a young man on the throne, a vigorous man, and a man who believes in the principles of the Army."

"You mean the principles of *bushido*?" Alexander could not believe his ears.

"Well, as to that, who can say. But you will see a change. Now, Alexander, I wish to talk about you and your family. Tell me firstly, when will *Kaga* be completed?"

"The gods alone know, Takamori. Since Kato Tomabusuro died, there are never any funds. The fact is that our new Navy Minister, Kato Kanji, is not interested in the concept of aircraft-carriers. He is not interested in any project his namesake may have sponsored. *Kaga* will be a rusting hulk before I can take her to sea. I have never felt so frustrated in my life."

Takamori grinned. "What? With a young wife to absorb your energy? Anyway, I would say that you will soon have the funds you require. Now tell me about Nicholas."

"He serves on *Naka*. She is a seven thousand ton cruiser, armed with seven five-point-five-inch guns."

"That is a new ship, is it not?"

"She was completed just over a year ago."

"Then he must be very pleased."

"He is satisfied. But he knows, as I know, that a seven-thousand ton cruiser, armed with pop-guns and with only two-and-a-half inches of belt armour, is a nothing ship; she cannot hurt anything larger than herself, and she is absolutely vulnerable. No, he is looking forward to joining me on *Kaga*."

"I can understand that," Takamori agreed. "How old is Nicholas now?"

"He will be twenty-three this year."

"Have you given any thought to a wife for him?"

"No. And neither has he. We agreed, you and I, that these are early days."

"Oh, entirely. Just as long as he remembers that it is his duty, to the Empire and to the family, to marry and have children. Now what about Charlotte."

"You saw her before dinner."

"She did not seem so very odd to me. Not that she said much."

"Well, in one sense time is helping. The memory of that day is fading. But that is our only progress. She still thinks her mother and sister are alive. She still does not seem to wish to resume her life until they return from . . . well, wherever they are.

"And how old is *she*?"

"Seventeen. She's a year younger than Christina. Thank heavens, they're the best of friends."

"At seventeen you should be thinking of *her* marriage, certainly."

"Now, Takamori, how can I possibly suggest marriage to my daughter, to anyone? We have to face facts, she's retarded."

"She has been educated?"

"Well, yes. Up to a point. But that doesn't alter the fact that . . ."

"Her mind has been affected. But not in any relevant way, Alexander. Can she cook?"

"Of course."

"And I am sure she can sew. As for ordering a household, that comes naturally, once one is given the opportunity, even if one is thinking with the mind of a thirteen-year-old-girl. Physically, she is mature. In fact, she is quite beautiful. She reminds me of your mother, when she was a young woman. Her hair is magnificent."

"It is very good of you to say so, honourable Brother. But still . . ."

"And do you not see that marriage may be the answer to all of her problems? It will make her grow up."

"It's the word 'make' that frightens me," Alexander confessed. "And what if she becomes a mother?"

"Would that not be the very best thing for her? I shall find her a husband, who will take good and loving care of her, and let you get on with the business of living your own life."

"Don't you think you have taken sufficient interest in my domestic affairs?" Alexander asked.

Takamori grinned. "What you really meant to say was, have I not *interfered* sufficiently in your affairs. But your affairs are my affairs, honourable Brother. Am I not the head of our family?"

*   *   *

Alexander could not argue with that, especially as Christina was all for the idea. Christina remained a delight to have as a bed companion; she had quite rejuvenated him. But she believed a wife should play a much more prominent role than had been the Japanese norm in the past. She appeared to be very fond of her step-daughter, but there were times when Alexander knew that she would have preferred to have the house to herself.

Nor did Charlotte herself seem averse to the idea when Alexander tentatively broached it. "I would have a house of my own," she said enthusiastically. "Honourable Mother and Elizabeth would be able to visit, when they come home."

It was Nicholas who was strongly against. "It would be almost a crime, honourable Father," he said. "Both to Charlotte, and to the man she marries."

"Would you then condemn her to a lifetime of nothing?" Alexander asked.

"Is there no hope?"

"None that is very evident. I think your uncle is possibly correct, that if she were taken right out of her home environment, given something to do, surrounded by new people and new places, she might benefit greatly."

"But her husband will have to be so very patient and kind," Nicholas said.

Alexander studied him. Nicholas might have become a *samurai*, but he remained essentially a very gentle man. "Agreed," he said, and smiled. "Uncle Takamori also thinks you should consider your own future."

"My future is to serve the Emperor, honourable Father."

"He was talking about your domestic life. Marriage."

"I am too young to take a wife."

"My own sentiments exactly. But . . . don't you have any girl you are especially interested in?"

Nicholas hesitated. "I have not the time for girls, honourable Father."

Takamori was proved absolutely correct in his judgement of the future. In April 1927 the ministry of Wakatsuki Reijiro, only the second commoner ever to become Prime

Minister, fell, and was replaced by the right-wing *Seiyukai* Party, headed by Baron Tanaka Giichi.

In his very first speech the Baron declared his intention of pursuing a more "positive" attitude towards relations with China. China had always been of tremendous importance to Japan. It was not merely that it lay as a vast continental cloud, seeming to hover above the much smaller island empire. Every Japanese statesman was aware of this. Equally no Japanese with any knowledge of history – and that meant any educated Japanese – could ever forget that under the thirteenth-century Mongol Emperor Kublai Khan, China had made two serious attempts to conquer Japan, and had been defeated less by Japanese arms than by a famous storm, since known as the Divine Wind, or *kamikaze*.

Three hundred years later the most famous of all Japanese soldiers, Toyotomi Hideyoshi, had led an army into Korea with the avowed intention of conquering China. Hideyoshi had failed – he had had no concept of the immensity of what he was taking on – and a few years later Japan had shut itself off from the world for two hundred and fifty years, yet always aware of the menace across the water. When the island empire had been forced by Commodore Perry to open its doors and look out, it was to find China ruled by the mighty Ch'ing Dynasty, and seemingly more threatening than ever.

Yet at that very moment, the reign of the Ch'ing was in jeopardy, as the Dynasty was confronted by the internal revolt of the T'ai-P'ing as well as the external onslaught of the British and French barbarians. With the decline of the Ch'ing Empire, China had become an ambition rather than a menace. Only a generation previously, the mainland country, with its several hundred million people, had been resoundingly defeated by Japan, with a population then of less than a hundred million. Since then, the Chinese situation had staggered from bad to worse. The collapse of the Ch'ing had been followed by the disintegration of the nation. The Kuomintang, founded by Dr Sun Yat-sen, had claimed to rule, but its fiat was only effective south of the Yangste-Kiang, and the north was left in the hands of several opposing warlords. Dr Sun's regime had had a socialist flavour entirely opposed to traditional Japanese political thought, even if he had broken with the Russian Communists who had initially supported him. But Sun had died in 1924, and his government, and more important his armies, were now being directed by an entirely different personality, Marshal Chiang Kai-shek, a soldier and a practical politician as opposed to a political theorist. Over the past two years Chiang had begun the reunification of China by declaring open war on both the Communists and the northern warlords, and by a mixture of military genius and utter ruthlessness had carried his arms beyond the Yangste. The concept of a man of such stature ruling a united China was not something the Japanese could contemplate.

There was a third aspect of the situation, even more recent. With the American rejection of the idea of any further Japanese immigration to Hawaii and California had come an economic boycott of Japanese goods, produced and offered at prices considerably lower than the Americans themselves could provide. The problem was that Japan had nothing of any real importance *to* sell to the world, and especially the American, market, save for rayon, the artificial silk. The Americans had a protectorate over the Philippines, from which they took most of their rice; if the quality of the silk and *cloisonné* work they could obtain from other places was inferior to that offered by Japan, these were not really commodities by which one lived or died, while American capital and oil was essential for the Japanese economy. Ever since the war with Russia, Japan had had its own small, but viable, oil industry, in the wells of south Sakhalien Island. But with the emergence of Soviet Russia as a potential enemy, and one which refused to recognise the terms of the Treaty of Portsmouth signed between Japan and Tsarist Russia in 1905, the Japanese had sought to obtain such recognition by returning Sakhalien to the Russians – with its oil. Thus all Japanese fuel now had to be imported, and paid for.

Failing the United States, the only profitable outlet for Japanese goods lay on the East Asia mainland. Japan had fought two wars at the turn of the century to secure Korea as an economic outlet. But Korea was now virtually a Japanese colony, and the Japanese population was expanding all the time. Beyond Korea there lay Manchuria, a huge area which at present was under the domination of Marshal Chang Tso-lin, who had been military governor, with Japanese approval and support, since 1911. Manchuria was just awakening to the benefits of civilisation. It was the obvious market for Japanese goods. And Chang Tso-lin was quite agreeable to accept Japanese economic penetration, so long as he was sold Japanese arms and expertise in his fight to defend himself against Chiang Kai-shek. No one in Japan could doubt that, were the Kuomintang to win the civil war, that potential economic lifeline would be snapped.

Thus any 'positive' Japanese attitude towards China had to involve the checking of Chiang Kai-Shek's advance to the north. Within a month of Tanaka taking power, Japanese troops had moved back into the Shantung Peninsular, threatening Chiang's forces from the flank.

The Shantung Peninsular was another continuous, if more recent, bone of contention between China and Japan. While it was undoubtedly Chinese territory, it formed the southern arm of the Gulf of Chih-li, that large stretch of water restricted on the north by the Liaotung Peninsular, at the southern end of which was situated the strategically important, ice-free harbour of Port Arthur. Between them, the two headlands dominated the mouth of the Pei-ho, the river that led to Peking, no longer the capital but still the most important city in China.

It had been to secure Port Arthur as much as to achieve political and economic dominance over Korea that the Sino-Japanese War of 1894–95 had been fought, in the course of which the Japanese had not only captured the northern arm of the Liaotung, but had also, in their determination to eliminate the remnants of the Chinese fleet after the Battle of the Yalu River, landed an army in Shantung and captured most of that as well. In both events Barrett Nicholas the elder and Barrett Takamori had covered themselves with glory.

Totally victorious, Japan had been forced to relinquish her Chinese gains by a concert of the Great Powers, led by Russia, France and Germany. Out of that humiliation had come the alliance with Great Britain which had lasted down to 1922, and out of *that* had come the war with Russia in 1904–05, victory in which had given Japan final possession of the Liaotung.

Shantung, however, had been relinquished, only to be regained in the Great War of ten years later. As an ally of Great Britain, Japan had entered that contest, and had been entrusted with the reduction of the German naval base at Tsing-tao, on the southern side of the peninsular. The work had been carried out in conjunction with the Royal Navy, with speed and efficiency, and Japanese troops had remained in the peninsular. Towards the close of the War, indeed, the then Japanese Government had sought to impose itself upon the various warring factions in China, and had made demands which, if accepted, would have virtually left China a Japanese protectorate. The Chinese, for all their immense population and area militarily helpless, had procrastinated, and Japanese ambitions had been overtaken by the end of the War, and the subsequent humiliations.

Among the provisions of the Treaty of Washington had been Japanese withdrawal from Shantung. Now Tanaka boldly ordered Japanese troops to be returned to the peninsular, with the avowed object of protecting Japanese citizens and businesses, but the real intention of preventing Chiang Kai-shek's advance, with the possibility of a reunification of the Dragon Empire.

"Will there be war?" Elizabeth asked, when Alexander and Christina visited her in the spring of 1928.

"I do not think so," Alexander said. "Tanaka will obviously go as far as he can. But the Chinese are adopting a policy of passive resistance, boycott of Japanese goods, that sort of thing. More importantly, the country does not want war. There have been demonstrations against the government in Tokyo. I think he's just gone too far too fast."

Indeed the matter was soon patched up, and an agreement was reached by which China would pay an indemnity – no one seemed quite sure for what reason; it was, actually, a ransom – and Japanese troops again would be withdrawn by the summer of 1929. The whole thing had been rather a fiasco, but then it took a nasty twist. Chang Tso-lin's private train was blown up by a huge bomb that summer, with the marshal and most of his family on board. The Japanese government immediately denied any involvement in the affair, but it was widely known that it and Chang had had a difference of opinion as to future tactics, with Chang insisting upon a more independent line for himself, and there was worldwide condemnation at what was seen as a Japanese murder plot. Worse, Chang's surviving son, Chang Hsueh-liang, while retaining his father's Japanese links, began negotiations with the Nanking Government of Chiang Kai-shek. Japan had received a severe setback to go with its loss of international standing. Takamori was furious. He did not deny that the whole episode had been instigated by the army; what angered him was the inept way it had been handled. Having lost the support of the Army minister – he had never had the support of the Navy – Tanaka's government fell in the summer of 1929, being replaced by the Liberal *Minseito* Party, with Hamaguchi Yuko as Prime Minister. But from Alexander's point of view, while, in common with most officers in the Navy, he had not approved of Tanaka's aggressive foreign policy, the right-wing ministry had achieved for him his greatest ambition: in March 1928 *Kaga* was finally completed.

Seven hundred and fifteen feet long, she displaced thirty-three thousand tons fully loaded, and her four-shaft geared turbines could push her along at twenty-seven knots. She had ten eight-inch guns as well as several huge batteries of anti-aircraft equipment, eleven-inch belt armour, and carried sixty aircraft, while her crew totalled over thirteen hundred men. "Now, Barrett *san*," Yamamoto said when he came to inspect the new ship. "Between us we have the ability to take on any navy in the world."

For if the two big American carriers had also recently been completed, and were slightly larger, they were in no way more powerful, and indeed, were less thickly armoured and had fewer guns. While Britain, still laboriously converting ships originally designed for other duties, had nothing the least comparable.

"But Britain has those two big new battleships, *Nelson*

and *Rodney*," Alexander pointed out. "They are the most powerful ships in the world."

Yamamoto grinned. "Oh, indeed they are. I understand they will displace forty-one thousand tons deep-loaded, which makes a nonsense of their designed thirty-three thousand, eh? They have fourteen-inch belt armour, and nine sixteen-inch guns. They could blow our two ships out of the water with no effort at all. But . . ." he raised his finger. "They have to be within range, eh? Ten miles or so. If we are more than fifty miles away from them, they cannot touch us. But, Barrett *san*, our planes can touch *them*!"

"Do you really think our planes will get through their anti-aircraft defence, remembering that the big ships will always be surrounded by their destroyers and cruisers?"

"I believe they will," Yamamoto said. "I believe, as I have told you, that this is the entire future of sea warfare. Fortunately, it seems that few others realise this. But we must not be complacent. Have you ever heard of an American named Billy Mitchell?"

"Of course. He was commander of their air force in the War."

"Then you will know of his trial and conviction for insubordination. For daring to suggest that the United States Navy is not taking sufficient precautions against air attack. He has now resigned. So, the American armed forces are as short-sighted as armed services so often are. But we must assume that the Mitchell affair has made one or two of their top brass think; they may be short-sighted, but it would be a mistake to assume that they are also fools, eh?"

"Like the British, they have faith in their battleships," Alexander suggested.

"Perhaps. It will be our business to disabuse them. I have to tell you, Barrett *san*, that I will no longer be commanding *Akagi*."

"What?" Alexander was astounded.

"I am being seconded to a new department," Yamamoto explained. "It is all very hush-hush, but I can tell you that my brief is to investigate to the limit my premise that naval success in the next war will rest with the superior air strike force rather than battleships."

"You speak as if the next war is just around the corner," Alexander chided. "Are not the British and the Americans working upon a plan which predicates that there will be no major war for at least ten years."

Yamamoto inclined his head. "Then, of course, there will be no war for that period. But still, ten years is not such a long time."

He left Alexander wondering just what he had been told. Of course there could be no war, if the other side refused to fight. But that did not mean the aggressor could not be aggressive. He found that extremely disturbing, but his concern on that front were very rapidly replaced by others.

That autumn he left with *Kaga* for her shakedown cruise. "Our first separation," Christina said.

"Well, it was your choice to marry a sailor."

"I would not mind if you were not so obviously anxious to be away," she complained.

He kissed her. "I am anxious to be away; she is one of the finest ships in the world. But once I am away, then I shall be anxious to get back, to you."

"Three months," she pouted.

Kaga was a dream ship, even if it took Alexander some time to acclimatise himself to commanding a ship at sea from beneath the top deck; like *Akagi* her landing platform was flush-decked. But as he watched his planes taking off, roaring above his head as they soared out to sea, he felt a glow of tremendous confidence. And anticipation?

The mood was felt by his crew. "All we need is someone to fight, honourable Captain," said his executive officer, Commander Asabe.

"Yes," Alexander agreed, while realising that, as Japan could not contemplate taking on the might of the United States or the British Empire, the only possible enemy was China. And that could hardly be considered a fair fight.

He was delighted when, in the spring of 1929, Nicholas was finally seconded to the ship, even if he had to make it perfectly plain to the young man that he could treat him only as any other officer. But it was a pleasure to have

74

his own son serving under him. He recalled what a thrill it had been to serve under his own father in 1900, during the march on Peking to relieve the Legations under siege from the Boxers. And there could be no doubt that Nicholas was a most efficient officer; what was disturbing was the way he was revealed as a loner, who kept much to himself, seldom took part in any of the high-spirited horseplay so enjoyed by the Japanese, and appeared totally disinterested in women. He did have one close friend, his old room-mate at Eta-Jima, Tokijo Hasueke, with whom he regularly corresponded. But this in itself was disturbing. If there was no condemnation of homosexuals in Japan as there was in the West, Alexander retained too much of his ancestral ethical viewpoint to be happy about his son perhaps being one.

By the early summer of 1929 he felt he had both ship and crew licked into shape, and was therefore the more surprised when he was summoned to the Admiralty to be informed that he was not going to continue to command his aircraft-carrier.

"There is to be another Naval Conference, Barrett *san*," said Admiral Ishishada. "It begins in January next year, in London. This time they wish to speak about limiting the size and number of ships smaller than battleships and battlecruisers. Our mission is being headed by ex-Prime Minister Wakatsuki Reijiro, but as it is to be mainly a naval conference the Navy Minister, Admiral Takarabe is also going. He wishes to have Captain Yamamoto and yourself as his aides."

"I am flattered, honourable Admiral." And delighted, Alexander realised. To be visiting England for the first time, and with Yamamoto . . .

"Your task, and that of Captain Yamamoto, will be to assist Takarabe in representing our interests. You were at Washington. You know these people." Ishishada gave a brief smile. "You are one of them."

"I understand, honourable Admiral," Alexander said.

"However," Ishishada went on. "There are two instructions I must give you in the strictest confidence, Barrett *san*. One is that undoubtedly the West will be informed about our two new carriers. They may seek some more information about them, in order to establish that we have exceeded our allotted tonnage in capital ships."

"I understand, honourable Admiral."

"The second is that you should attempt to discover their own plans, not only in ship sizes, but in strategic placing of ships, as well. We are moving into a period of crisis, Barrett *san*. I cannot tell you more than this, but I can tell you that we, the Navy, must be prepared for any eventuality over the next few years. Go and prosper."

"I don't like the sound of that at all," Alexander told Takamori, when he called to say goodbye. "I really thought the China business was settled."

"How can the China business ever be settled?" Takamori asked. "We are having trouble with this fellow Chang Hsueh-liang. After accepting a great deal of support from us, in money as well as materiel, he is now asking for more, and threatening that if we do not give him what he wants he will surrender Peking to Chiang Kai-shek. Honestly, these people are nothing more than brigands."

"I don't see that there is a lot we can do about it," Alexander said. "Save tell him to go to the devil and cut off all aid."

"If he called our bluff, then Chiang would re-unite all China," Takamori pointed out. "Would you believe that Chang is a Christian? It ruins one's faith in religion."

"So you intend to do something about it," Alexander remarked.

"Something, certainly. As Ishishada said, we must be ready for all eventualities. Do not surrender too much in London." He grinned. "And who knows, by the time you return, I may have found a husband for Charlotte."

Nicholas was heartbroken. "To lose your ship, honourable Father," he complained. "*Our* ship."

"It is still your ship, Nicholas," Alexander reminded him.

"I wished only to serve under you."

"I imagine you will find it much easier to serve under someone else. Now, Nicholas, I wish you to do something for me. When you return from your next cruise, you will be given leave. I wish you to go down to Bungo and visit your grandmother. She is getting very old and frail, and she complains that she does not see enough of you. I know this will be an imposition, but I would like you to do it, especially as I shall be away for several months."

"I understand, honourable Father."

"You may take honourable Stepmother and Charlotte with you."

Nicholas's head jerked.

"You come so seldom to the house," Alexander said. "Honourable Stepmother is beginning to feel that you do not like her."

Nicholas opened his mouth, and then closed it again.

"I understand that perhaps you feel resentful because she has taken your mother's place," Alexander went on. "But you cannot live in the past, Nicky, any more than I could. This visit will give you a chance to get to know her better, and enable to realise what a nice person she is, and how much she cares for you, as she does for Charlotte." He smiled. "I give you permission to drive my car."

Nicholas's face, which had become rather gloomy, obviously, Alexander supposed, at the thought of being stuck with the two women, lit up again. "The Panhard? Honourable Father, I am delighted."

"Just don't smash it up," Alexander warned.

Only a couple of weeks before Alexander was due to sail for London with the Naval delegation, news arrived of the stock market crash in New York.

"What will it mean?" Christina asked, nestling against him.

"That the Americans have been spending more than their incomes," he said. "I doubt it will affect us."

"I am sure it will mean something," she grumbled. "From the prominence it is all being given in the newspapers. And now you are going away again."

"Well, if I hadn't been sent to London, we'd have been separated a week ago, when *Kaga* sailed on her first cruise." Under her new captain, he thought bitterly.

"I know, I suppose I am still not used to being a sailor's

77

wife. Except for those three months last year, you have always been here."

"You'll have to blame the state of the country's finances for that. Now listen, when Nicholas returns, it'll be in about three months time, he's going to take Charlotte and you down to see my mother." The room was dark and he could not see her face, but as there was no immediate reply, he said, "You do not object to that?"

"Does Nicholas object? He seems to avoid me as much as possible."

"I know this. I have spoken with him on the subject. I would like you and him to be friends."

"So would I. I should like to visit honourable Mother," she said. "But . . . will you not be back in three months?"

"I doubt it. Not judging by the length of time taken by the Washington Conference."

"And you will be missing Christmas as well," she grumbled.

"You wanted to be a sailor's wife," he chided her, not for the first time.

The Japanese delegation sailed on the small, three thousand ton, light cruiser *Yubari*, it being no part of their plan to display any naval might when they were trying to improve their position relative to Britain and the United States. They reached Southampton at the end of the second week in January, seven days before the Conference was due to open. Alexander was delighted to have the opportunity to explore, and show Yamamoto, some of the places his father had told him about. His other ambition was to be able to visit Russia, and especially Moscow and St Petersburg, but that appeared a remote possibility as the hand of the new Communist leader, Stalin, closed like a vice on that unhappy country.

London seemed equally pleased to see him, as his father was a well-remembered renegade whose life was now being offered as a supreme example of that romanticism which seemed to have disappeared with the Great War, and, as the creeping weight of the depression spread across the world, equally seemed unlikely ever to return. All the

78

naval delegates were thoroughly well-entertained, to dinners and dancing, and the tall, red-haired, distinguished-looking captain was eagerly sought after, whether as a dining partner or on the dance floor. Or even for bed, he quickly gathered. But he had not come away to be unfaithful to Christina.

"If international affairs could be left to charm and the ladies," Yamamoto remarked, "we would be certain of a triumph here, Barrett *san*."

But then the conference began, and Alexander quickly realised that Takarabe's team was in a much stronger position than Kato Tomasaburo's had been at Washington, eight years before. The principal effect of the stock market crash had been that American investors were hastily withdrawing their funds from Europe in the hopes of plugging the gaps. This was leaving every Eueropean government short of funds, and the Americans were equally so. Whereas Japan was virtually unaffected by the financial debacle, excluded as she was from so many of the world markets.

The result was that Takarabe was able to resist the pressure of the western powers far more successfully than Kato had in 1921. Thus the suggestion of the British Government that all capital ships be reduced to twenty-five thousand tons or less was successfully resisted, although as a compromise, the building holiday for big ships was extended until the end of 1936, when a new conference was envisaged. It was also agreed that capital ship quotas would be reduced, to fifteen each for Britain and the United States, and nine for Japan, but this actually improved the relative ratios as regards Japan.

Cruisers were next tackled, with the British volunteering to reduce their previous standard requirement for the protection of the Empire from seventy to fifty ships, and also to take second place to the United States in terms of tonnage. Thus it was settled that the USA would have one hundred and eighty thousand tons, Britain one hundred and forty-six thousand, eight hundred, and Japan one hundred and eight thousand, for ships armed wih six-inch guns or better – up to eight-inch. Ships with smaller than six-inch guns were also allotted in proportion, as were destroyers, in which Japan was allowed one hundred and five thousand tons as opposed to a hundred and fifty thousand each for the United States and Britain.

"This keeps us firmly in our place," Alexander grumbled to Yamamoto. But his friend smiled. He had a plan, and he gained the day, in that while all future destroyers were to be of fifteen hundred tons or less, the twenty ships of the Fubuki Class which Japan already had in the water or building were allowed to remain, and these displaced two thousand tons, deep loaded. "One of our ships," he told Alexander, "is worth two of theirs."

The Japanese did even better with regard to submarines. They were prepared to go along with the desire to regulate submarine warfare, both by limiting the tonnage and the size of guns to be carried by submarines; the Imperial Navy had never been truly interested in undersea craft – here the old *samurai* spirit was for the good. While the Japanese were great believers in sneak attacks carried out even before a declaration of war, as against the Russians in 1904, they still felt that a man should face his opponent fair and square when it actually came to fighting; the attack on Port Arthur had been carried out by torpedo-boats. As a result, there were only fourteen submarines in the Imperial Navy, and even their proper role had never been identified. In the main they were regarded as weapons to be used against enemy warships, and indeed there were building at that very moment four new vessels with a surface range of twenty-four thousand miles, which it was hoped would enable them to strike at any enemy in his home waters. But as regards tonnage, just on two thousand, and guns, a couple of five-point-five-inch, they were within the parameters the British and Americans wished to establish. Now they were given parity with the United States and Britain, at fifty-two thousand seven hundred tons each.

Then the western powers wished to talk about the limitation of aircraft-carriers; undoubtedly they were concerned about the emergence of *Kaga* and *Akagi*. Alexander and Yamamoto were able to assure their British and American counterparts that the Imperial Navy envisaged only one additional carrier – she had already been laid down, but would displace, fully-loaded, well under fifteen thousand tons, and carry only forty-odd aircraft.

There followed the usual discussion and promises concerning the scrapping of certain ships. It was at this stage, when the conference was virtually over, that Wakatsuki, the civilian leader of the Japanese delegation – again a carefully planned manoeuvre to remove any ideas of militarism from Western minds – sprang a surprise. "While of course the Imperial Navy wishes in every way to co-operate with all other navies in reducing armaments to a level consistent only with national safety," he said smoothly, "I am sure that all the governments in the world realise that a situation *could* arise where any given nation might find itself faced with a problem which might require additional forces, again, simply in order to protect its sovereignty. We in Japan, for example, are very conscious of the nearness of Soviet Russia, a vast country which is growing stronger by the day. Has not Monsieur Stalin just embarked upon a five-year plan intended to make the Soviet Union the equal of any industrial power in the world? The history of the past hundred years reveals all too clearly that industrial strength is invariably followed by an increase in military strength." He smiled. "And we are forced to remember that the Russians and ourselves were not always friends."

That provoked another discussion, but the western powers could not argue the truth of what Wakatsuki had said; they too had their eye on the Soviets, an emerging power which the Americans had not yet recognised as a government.

"Tell us what you want," they suggested.

"I want nothing, honourable sirs, at this moment. I am merely seeking what we might call an 'escalator clause' in our treaty, permitting any signatory to exceed the specified tonnages should a critical situation arise with regard to its security. With due notice to the other signatories, of course."

He got what he wanted, and at this time it was agreed that the treaty, with its restrictions on both numbers and size of ships would be reviewed at the end of six years rather than ten, as before.

"Now we can go home and get down to designing some real warships, Barrett *san*," Yamamoto said jubilantly.

"Will we not have to provide a reason for this?"

"In due course. It will take a year or so to get the designs

81

ready, and then at least another three years before any new ships will be in the water. Then we may be asked to explain our actions, but in five years time, we will almost certainly have discovered a reason. Besides, the treaty expires in six years time. We must look to the future, Barrett."

"Nicholas!" Christina greeted her stepson with a chaste kiss on the cheek. "We are all ready."

He had telephoned her two days before to tell her that he was about to commence his furlough, and asking her to be ready for the drive down to Bungo. Now she stood back to admire him, for he wore uniform, while she was in a kimono.

"And Charlotte, honourable Mother?"

"I am here." Charlotte bustled out, red hair floating in the breeze. "Do you think Mother and Elizabeth will have got to Grandmama's yet?"

"I do not think they will be visiting this time," Christina said with total composure.

"You are very good with her," Nicholas remarked, when they had a moment alone.

"She is my daughter," Christina reminded him.

It took them three days to drive down to Bungo, as the only car ferry was at Shimonoseki. They stopped at hotels in Osaka and Hiroshima, Christina and Charlotte sharing a room. Nicholas was very careful not to encroach on their privacy in any way, and as was his practice, never entered the bathhouse until he was sure they were finished.

Christina made no comment on this, but she did remark, on the last evening in Shimonoseki, as they sat on the hotel balcony and looked out at the Sea of Japan, "I feel that I am getting to know you for the first time, Nicholas."

"And I you, honourable Mother."

"And you are soon to be twenty-six years old. We must set about finding you a wife."

"Time enough for that, honourable Mother. I have my way to make in the Navy, first."

"Ah," she said.

82

Grandmother Elizabeth was indeed old and frail, much more so than Nicholas remembered from his last visit, two years before. She was now eighty, but more than her age, he thought, was her sense of being cut off. She was Russian, and there had been no communication with her homeland for fifty years; she did not even know if her brothers and sisters were alive or dead – as she had belonged to an aristocratic family, it was extremely unlikely they had survived the Communist revolution.

These tragic reflections had not been allowed to become overwhelming as long as the admiral had been alive, but since his death they had had a profoundly depressing effect on her personality. Then there was the problem of Charlotte, who was now twenty, with her mind still locked seven years in the past. Yet Elizabeth's mind seemed as active as ever, as she answered Charlotte's questions about the well-being of her mother and sister without the least hesitation, engaged Christina in conversation about domestic matters, sought the latest news concerning Alexander, and queried Nicholas about both his social and professional life.

They spent several very happy days there, Nicholas sitting on the verandah with his grandmother while Christina and Charlotte went swimming in the bay – as was the Japanese habit, the women did not wear swimming costumes. But after ten days, the end of Nicholas's furlough was within sight. "I must be returning to Tokyo," he told them.

"Oh, what a shame," Elizabeth said. "But, Christina, surely you and Charlotte can stay awhile longer?"

"Charlotte certainly can," Christina agreed. "But I should be getting back as well: Alexander will be home in a couple of weeks, and I must have the house ready for him. I will send for Charlotte in due course."

They left the next morning, the car bouncing across the uneven road as Nicholas headed back to Shimonoseki. "How do you think your father will react to honourable Grandmother's death?" Christina asked.

"I think he will be very upset," Nicholas said.

"Because it will soon happen," Christina remarked.

"I know."

They drove in silence for a while, then Christina observed, "It is a pity you will never be the head of the family."

"Do you think so? I find it a great relief."

"You should not. Do you get on with your cousin?"

"Who, Yoshiye? I hardly ever see him."

"You understand that one day *he* will be the head of the family?"

"Do you know, I've never thought about it."

"It is logical. General Barrett is sixty-six years old. Your father is fifty-one. Then it will be Barrett Yoshiye."

Nicholas grinned. "Both honourable uncle and honourable father are very fit men. You look too far ahead, honourable Mother." He pulled into the forecourt of the hotel.

They ate together in the dining room; it was still only March and there were only half-a-dozen other guests in the hotel.

"What is your greatest ambition?" Christina asked.

"Mine? To command the Imperial Navy."

Christina conveyed a grain of rice to her mouth with her foodsticks. "You know that can never happen. Because you are not truly Japanese. It will never happen to your father, just as it never happened to your grandfather."

He knew she was right. But he had not expected to hear a Japanese, even his stepmother, say it. "What are you suggesting, honourable Mother?" he asked. "That I should resign, and emigrate. Back to England, perhaps? Honourable Father would never forgive me."

"I was not suggesting that, Nicholas," she said. "I was suggesting that you should aim at a more attainable target."

"Well, then, to command my own ship."

"Even that honour was denied your grandfather."

"But not my father, honourable Mother."

"That remains to be seen." She smiled. "I do not wish to think gloomy thoughts. I wish you to be happy, Nicholas, as I am happy. Why do you not marry?"

"Why is the subject repeatedly being raised, honourable Mother? There is much time."

"Perhaps," she said, and rose. "What time do you wish to leave in the morning?"

"As soon as we have bathed, honourable Mother."

"Ah, so," she agreed.

After Christina had gone to bed, Nicholas remained for some time staring out at the setting sun. Up until now, this trip had been a very public matter, first with Charlotte always present, and then with Grandmama. Now suddenly it had become a private matter, with just the two of them, and another whole day left before they could regain Tokyo, even if he drove non-stop – and he certainly intended to do that.

If only he could tell what went on behind those glowing dark eyes, that serenely beautiful expression. His stepmother could hardly have been unaware of the effect the sight of her naked body had had on him that terrible day he had walked in on her and his father in the bathhouse, even if Father, in his combined state of confident euphoria and sexual innocence had apparently not noticed anything at all. Father had not even noticed anything odd in the fact that his son should have attempted to distance himself from his new stepmother, beyond the obvious conclusion that he resented someone, anyone, attempting to take his mother's place. Was Christina that blind to the truth, that her stepson had fallen totally in love with her at that sight of her naked body? He could not accept that, where a woman as intelligent, as sexually alert, as she was concerned.

If that were true, then she had been almost insane to have agreed to this trip. But then, so had he. They had both been obeying the wishes of her husband and his father, who sought only a happy and contented family. Knowing the risks, he had obeyed his father, because he had not been able to believe she might even consider any breakage of the rules of the marriage bed, and thus all he had to do was preserve his usual perfect propriety until they returned home. But suddenly he was unsure just what Christina might wish, or desire, or even intend. The thought was terrifying . . . and yet, irresistible, from a woman who was in any event six years younger than himself, and remained the only woman with whom he had ever been in love.

Christina! Why was she his stepmother? That raised all manner of thought. He well understood that there had almost certainly been nothing sinister in her marriage to

85

his father; spring/autumn marriages were the norm in Japan, rather than the exception. And in any event there could be no possible reason other than parental command for her to have married Barrett Alexander, who had no political power, and, as she had just pointed out, no real prospects of naval power either, and who was by no means wealthy. While even had Nicholas not totally admired his Uncle Takamori, and knew that the marriage had been arranged by his uncle, there was no possibility of there being anything sinister in that, either: Barrett Takamori did not need any hold over his half-brother – he was already head of the family, and so far as Nicholas was aware, his father had never opposed his uncle in any way.

Of his father's happiness with his young bride over the past four years there could be no doubt. Again, it was obvious that Barrett Alexander would find more to enjoy in Christina than she in him. But that was the lot of many Japanese brides. They were not expected to love their husbands; indeed, there was no word for romantic love in the Japanese language. All she needed to do was honour and respect him, satisfy his sexual requirements, and bear him children. Christina had, obviously, failed only in the last one, and the fault need not be hers. But that did not mean she was contented with her lot. So just where did that leave him?

It was not a question he dared answer.

Next morning he waited in the hotel lobby for his step-mother to appear. She kept him waiting for some time, before the bellboy brought down her cases and loaded them, Nor did she address him, as they got into the car together, and he drove off, taking the coast road north along the shore of the Inland Sea for Osaka. "This is so beautiful," Christina remarked. "Have you ever swum in the sea?"

"Yes," he replied.

"In the Inland Sea?"

"Yes."

"I never have. I would like to." She waited, and as he made no reply, but continued driving at the same speed, asked, "Is it not possible?"

"Of course it is possible, honourable Mother."

"Then let us find a convenient stretch of beach."

"Have you not bathed already this morning?"

"Yes. But you did not. I find this unbecoming. Why is it you never bathe in my presence? Is it because you are deformed? I did not notice that when . . . we first saw each other."

He continued to drive, preferring not to answer her immediate question. He really did not wish to offend her, and it would be catastrophic if he suggested what was in his mind and it was not actually what she had intended. "Then I apologise, honourable Mother. I must have been tired after my drive of yesterday."

"And now you are intending to drive all day today as well. You will be even more tired by this evening. And where is the hurry? You are not due to report for duty for another four days. I think today we should linger, take it more slowly, enjoy the countryside. It is a beautiful day. The Inland Sea has never looked more beautiful. Look, is that not Eta-Jima?"

They had just skirted the port of Kure, and the island was clearly visible. "My Alma Mater," he commented.

"It is behind you now. Look, there is a little beach. Stop the automobile."

Nicholas hesitated, then pulled off of the road and drove down the grassy incline to a spot just above the sand, where he braked. Christina stepped down. "This is heavenly." She kicked off her sandals, stood on one leg to pull down her socks.

"You will find the water very cold, honourable Mother," Nicholas commented.

"It will tingle my blood," Christina said. "And yours."

"I will stay with the automobile, honourable Mother, and make sure you are not interrupted."

"Nonsense. There is no one for miles. I have never bathed in the sea before. I am afraid. I wish you to come in with me."

As she spoke she stepped out of the *kimono*, and dropped her underclothes on top of it. Nicholas found himself staring at her, partly because she so obviously wished him to, remaining facing him while he got out of the car, but equally because at twenty-one she was so much more beautiful than he remembered her at seventeen.

"What you wish is criminal, and dishonourable," he said, his voice thick with desire.

"What I wish is between you and me, Nicholas. No one else. Therefore it can affect neither the law nor your honour. And besides, do you not wish it too? Do you not realise I have known this, for three years? It has been a matter of achieving the right moment."

"And my father?"

"He will never know of it."

"Do you believe that one only sins if one is found out? You are speaking of my *father*."

"He is hardly able to do me justice. What would you have me do, take a lover? Is it not best to keep these things in the family?" Now at last she turned away from him, and waded into the water. It lapped around her knees and then her thighs, came up to her waist, and she turned on her back, to float, her toes just visible. Her hair was still piled on top of her head. "I am waiting for you."

Nicholas undressed and ran down the beach, Christina smiling as she saw how aroused he was. Then he was in the water, which was distinctly cold. He ducked his head and swam vigorously, some distance out to sea. When he was out of his depths he stopped, and trod water, turning back to look at her, watch her doing a slow breast stroke as she followed him. "I did not know you could swim," he said.

"I learned as a girl," She came up to him, panting a little. "But I have not swum recently. You are right; it is cold. Let us go in."

He swam beside her, slowing his stroke to match hers, until it was shallow enough to drop his feet and stand up. "I am exhausted," she said, and put her arms round his neck.

He brought her against him, and she dropped her legs in turn, although as she could not stand she kept her arms round his neck. Or perhaps she would have done so anyway, he thought, as she kissed him on the mouth. Now he could feel her hard nipples pressing into his chest, while she wrapped her legs round his thighs, and she could certainly feel *him*, caught between their crotches. She pulled her head back, mouth drooping in a half-smile. "I want to have a child by you."

"This is madness," he protested. "Criminal madness."

"The crime is already committed," she said. "In both of our minds. Carry me ashore."

He swept her legs up, and carried her through the shallows. While he did so she kissed him again and again, and by the time they reached the beach he was as hard as a rock. "Lay me on my *kimono*," she commanded.

He obeyed, kneeling beside her, watching her shiver with the chill, her hair just starting to come down. "Now mount me like a barbarian," she said. "Push him in as far as he will go."

He hesitated, and she spread her legs. There was no way he could stop himself now. "Use your fingers first," she told him. "Make me ready."

Again he obeyed, and she sighed her pleasure. Then he was in her, and her legs were again wrapped round him as he thrust to and fro, timing the surges of his thighs to hers. When he lay still, she ran her fingers through his hair, kissed him again and again. He rolled on his back, stared at the brilliant blue of the sky. "I am dishonoured."

Christina rose on her elbow. "And will now commit *seppuku*? Are you that stupid?"

He turned his head to look at her. "It is the law of *bushido*."

"That is old-fashioned nonsense. Anyway, it applies to defeat in battle."

"It applies to *honour*! I have just dishonoured my own father."

"Who will never know of it. While, if you were to do something as stupid as to cut open your belly, it would kill him. Would that not be a greater crime than anything you have just committed? I absolutely forbid you, as your mother, to even think of such a thing."

She got up, and picked up the *kimono*, clucking her tongue as she discovered how wet and sandy it was. She rolled it into a ball, climbed up to the car, opened one of her suitcases, and took out a clean *kimono*, as well as a towel, with which she proceeded to dry herself. Nicholas watched her, mentally inhaling the beauty of her, trying to reconcile what he had done with what could be his if he just accepted what she offered. He stood up as well. "Then now I am your slave, is that it?"

Christina laughed, and threw him the towel. "Were you not my slave already, as you are my son? *Now* let us hurry; we have three more days before you must rejoin your ship. I would like to spend them at home, with you."

Barrett Takamori read through the text of the London Treaty; he had come out to meet his half-brother on board *Yubari*; he had known Admiral Takanabe for years. "But this is brilliant," he said. "You have obtained everything we wished. My most sincere congratulations."

"Are we now enabled to proceed with our plans, honourable General?" Takanabe asked.

"I should think so, honourable Admiral."

"What plans are these, honourable Brother?" Alexander inquired.

"The improved prosperity of Japan," Takamori told him.

Alexander frowned, aware that there was something going on of which he knew nothing.

But he was more interested in getting home, to Christina. And she was as lovely and welcoming as ever, as he took her in his arms. "Honourable Husband, it has been so long."

He kissed her. "Well, now I have a month's furlough."

"Then we had best go down to Bungo," she said.

"But surely you have only just returned from there?"

"Indeed. But I am distressed about your mother, Alexander. I do not think she has long to live."

He hugged her. "Sometimes I think you regard her as your own mother."

"Well, I do, as she is the mother of our family. But you know that Nicholas and Charlotte and I went down last month?"

He nodded. "How are they both?"

"Oh, very well. They look forward to seeing you again. Unfortunately, Nicholas is at sea. He hopes you will be resuming command of *Kaga*."

"So do I. But that is something I will have to find out when my leave is up. You were telling me about honourable Mother."

"Simply that we were all shocked at how old she is looking. I have been very worried that you would not get back in time. I did not know if I should stay down there, but in the end I left Charlotte, and came up to meet you. Did I do the right thing?"

"You did as you thought best," Alexander acknowledged. "But I would not like Charlotte to be the only member of the family there when honourable mother dies. We must get down there immediately."

She hugged him in turn. "I am so glad you have returned."

They left the next morning, and were in Bungo three days later. But they were too late; Elizabeth Barrett had died in her sleep only hours before they arrived.

Barrett Takamori and his wife, as well as Yoshiye, came down to Bungo for the funeral; Barrett Nicholas was unfortunately away on his ship and could not be present, but there was a considerable local turn-out, for the one-time Russian countess with the flowing red hair and the ready smile had been a popular figure.

"She's not coming back, is she?" Charlotte asked her father. She had coped with the situation of being the only family member actually present at the death with amazing self-possesion, and he had been terrified for her mind.

But now he seized his opportunity. "I'm afraid she isn't."

"Just like Mummy and Elizabeth. They aren't coming back either, are they, honourable Father?"

"No, they aren't," Alexander said.

Christina took the young woman in her arms and looked at her husband.

"It is strange, how things work out," Takamori said after dinner. "Will she remember anything of the past eight years, do you think?"

"I think she does, and will," Alexander said.

"Then, will she understand that she has not been altogether sane, during that time?"

"I doubt that. Few people recognise any mental lack in themselves. But now I do feel we can think of marriage."

"Indeed we must. I have the very man, Lieutenant Mori Toshiye. He is a brilliant officer and a dedicated one. He will go far."

"Have I met him?"

"I do not think so. But I will arrange it as soon as possible."

"Then he has never met Charlotte, either."

"This is true. But it is not something with which you need concern yourself. He is content that his marriage should be arranged between his father and I. We are old friends."

"Meaning he is a *samurai*."

"And you object to your daughter marrying a *samurai*? Your son is one."

Alexander knew he had no reasonable objections to make; it was simply that he was certain Sue-Ellen, were she alive, would not approve of such a marriage. Indeed, Sue-Ellen would not have approved of her daughter marrying a Japanese at all. But that was absurd, really. Charlotte, for all her Caucasian looks, was as Japanese as the next woman; she had never lived anywhere else, and she had no heady Western notions of feminine equality.

"How old is Mori?"

"He is twenty-four."

So there could be no reasonable objections on that score, either.

"Well, then, I would say the sooner I, and Charlotte, meet this young fellow the better."

"Absolutely. He is presently serving with his regiment in Manchuria. But he is due for leave later this year. Then I will bring him to meet you, and we will organise the wedding."

Alexander decided to leave acquainting Charlotte with the plan until after the young couple had actually met; he certainly wasn't going to force his daughter to marry anyone to whom she had taken an instant dislike. Besides, he had more important things on his mind: he had only been back two months when to his great delight Christina announced that she was pregnant. He was the happiest man in the world until that November when Prime Minister Hamaguchi was murdered by a right-wing fanatic, together with several of his ministers.

CHAPTER 4

Isolation

The nation was shocked, and Hamaguchi was replaced by Wakutsuki, a man in whom all sides could have confidence, for his second term as premier. In the midst of the upheaval, Christina gave birth to a baby boy, who they named Alexander. "He looks just like you," she cooed at her husband.

Charlotte was delighted to have a baby step-brother, but Nicholas, who had hardly visited Tokyo all year, busy as he was with naval duties, sent only a curt card of congratulation.

"I fear he still does not approve of me," Christina said sadly.

"And I had hoped that trip to Bungo would have brought you closer together," Alexander said. "I will have another word with him."

"No," Christina said. "I do not wish to force him to endure my company. He will come home, when he is ready."

Not even Wakutsuki could stem the tide of events, and in July 1931 a Japanese officer was murdered in China, apparently by Nationalist troops. All leave was immediately stopped, although the news was not generally released until 17 August. Takamori himself told Alexander, calling one morning very early, and surprising both his half-brother and Christina in bed. For once Christina, who was still feeding Baby Alexander, was embarrassed, and hastily wrapped herself in a dressing gown. But she was too interested to leave. "What does it mean?" she asked.

"That the time has come to settle with those insolent dogs once and for all," Takamori said angrily.

Alexander got up. "Surely we cannot be contemplating going to war because of a single murder?"

"Ha! Did not all Europe go to war because of a single murder, in 1914?"

"Yes, but really, all Europe was just waiting for a *casus belli*. And the victim was an archduke."

Takamori gave a savage smile. "Have we not been waiting for a *casus belli*? And is Nakamura so inferior to an archduke? They were both men, and representatives of their country's power."

"The League of Nations will not stand for it," Alexander warned.

This time Takamori's smile was genuine. "What do you suppose they will do, honourable Brother?"

A month later Japanese troops, alleging that Chinese forces were threatening the Japanese-controlled railroad from Port Arthur to Mukden, seized the city of Mukden itself during what were officially described as 'manoeuvres.' The Chinese were forced to withdraw, and the Japanese continued their advance. By the end of the year all Manchuria was under Japanese control. The Army action, which had not been sanctioned by the Wakatsuki ministry, brought a political crisis in its wake; the liberals fell from power, and the *Seiyukai* again took office, officially headed by Inukai Ki as prime minister, but the real power in the cabinet was the war minister, General Araki Sadao.

"Will there now be war?" Christina asked, cradling the babe against her breast.

"I very much fear so."

"Will the Navy be involved?"

"If there is war, the Navy will have to be involved. I must see Yamamoto." He watched the concern in her face, and kissed her forehead. "There is nothing to be afraid of: China does not have a navy."

But he went to see Takamori first; he knew that his half-brother was a close friend of Araki's. "We cannot possibly be intending to hang on to Manchuria," he said.

"Why not? It has long been our aim to obtain an area of growth on the continent."

"The world will not stand for it," Alexander said. "It is naked aggression. You may well ask what they can do, but in so blatant a case they may well do a great deal. Economic sanctions, to begin with."

"We do not believe such sanctions would have much effect," Takamori argued. "They would have to be applied universally, and we do not believe this will happen. You describe our takeover of Manchuria as an act of naked aggression. Suppose I was to tell you that we have acted at the request of the Manchurians, who have been a pawn on the Chinese political board for too long?"

"I would be bound to reply that you must think I am a fool, honourable Brother."

Takamori smiled. "I believe you are a highly intelligent and honourable man, Alexander. But also a man who is interested in the preservation of peace. Which is why you will find it difficult to reject the evidence I shall provide. Have you ever heard of Pu Yi?"

"Well, of course I have," Alexander said. "He was the last emperor of Manchu China."

"Who was forced to abdicate when Yuan Shih-k'ai seized power in 1911. Well, we have found this gentleman."

"Eh?"

"He has lived in retirement since 1911. Earning his living as a clerk, would you believe it? But he has not forgotten who he is, what he once was. Now he has signified his willingness to resume his role, as Emperor of Manchuria."

"Good God!"

"And he has the support of a large number of his people, enough, anyway, amongst the upper classes, to present an irrefutable case to the world. So, the new kingdom of Manchuria – I imagine we will change its name to something less Chinese – will arise in central Asia as a client state of Japan. There is nothing anyone can do about that."

Alexander immediately applied for a sea command, but was turned down. "You are to work with Rear-Admiral

Yamamoto," Ishishada told him. "It is a matter both of design and strategic preparation."

However disappointing it was to be, like his father, kept ashore, this was actually an intensely attractive and interesting prospect. Yamamoto was clearly delighted to have his old friend as his assistant, even if he felt somewhat embarrassed that while his own career was streaking ahead, Alexander's was at a standstill. "I would not be surprised, Barrett *san*," he said after the two men had greeted each other, "if you have not given some thought to resignation."

"Because you have a thick stripe and I have not?"

"It is very unfair; we played equal parts in London, but I am rewarded and you are not."

"It was what I knew was going to happen from a very early stage in my career."

"It is still unfair. However, I am very happy to have you working with me. We have much to do."

"In which direction?"

Yamamoto grinned. "Our brief is to prepare for the next war."

"I hope you're not serious?"

"Oh, I am, Barrett *san*. I have never been more serious. However, like you, I am sure, I do not wish another war if it can be avoided. Thus by preparing for it, most thoroughly, one would hope to convince one's possible enemies that it is not worth fighting. And this is strictly a Navy affair. The Army is running things at the moment. But they are blind. They have always been blind. Their horizons are limited by Soviet Russia and China. They see nothing else. The ocean to them, is the ocean. There are no enemies out there, they think. But if, as is quite possible, things take a turn for the worse, they will discover that we have enemies enough across the sea, and then they will have to turn to us, to keep themselves alive. It is an interesting prospect."

Not for the first time, Yamamoto was correct in his prognostications. Manchuria was declared independent on 18 February 1932, as the State of Manchukuo, with the ex-emperor Pu-Yi as president, but by then the situation had sharply deteriorated. A month earlier, the United

States Secretary of State Henry Stimson had announced that his country would recognise no territorial gains achieved through armed force. This amounted to a denunciation of the Japanese action, and encouraged the Chinese to intensify their boycott of Japanese goods, to the extent that trade with China fell to one sixth of its normal value.

There was an immediate response by the Army, which landed seventy thousand troops at Shanghai, covered by the Navy, and drove the Chinese 19th Route Army out of the vicinity of the city. This was an act of war which could not be disguised by diplomatic manoeuvre or language, and provoked the mostly lively debate, not only in the League of Nations, but in the Japanese Parliament as well. The result was that the League of Nations began a detailed investigation into the whole matter of Sino-Japanese relations, while Premier Inukai became more and more at odds with his cabinet, still dominated by General Araki.

Kaga, with her war planes required to support the Army, was involved in the Shanghai landings, and when she returned to Tokyo *Wan*, Alexander made a point of going on board to congratulate her officers, and especially Barrett Nicholas. "Are you really proud of us, honourable Father?" Nicholas asked.

"No, I suppose there is not a great deal to be proud of," Alexander conceded. "Was there any opposition?"

"In the air, virtually none. A couple of old biplanes which we disposed of very rapidly."

Alexander nodded. "It is a distasteful business. But it is the policy of our masters, and as we serve them, we must obey them in the best possible spirit. Now, you will be given leave. I hope you are coming home."

"There is so much to be done . . ."

"I can see that you are a dedicated officer," Alexander acknowledged. "But there is an old English saying that all work and no play makes Jack a dull boy. Besides, your stepmother is worried about you. She worried very much about your involvement in the Shanghai business, anyway." He grinned. "I could not convince her that, as you say, the Chinese have no navy. Now she feels that you dislike her."

Nicholas made no reply, merely bowed. "Besides," Alexander went on. "Mori Toshiye will be home at last. We are to have a betrothal party."

"Would you believe it?" Takamori demanded. "The League of Nations is actually sending a commission, to decide for itself what is going on? Headed by some English lord. With respect, honourable Brother, but suppose we announced we were sending a commission to some British colony, to see how it was being run? The arrogance of these Westerners beggars belief."

"I would suggest it would not be quite the same thing," Alexander ventured.

"Well, you would. Now come . . ." he gazed across the crowded room. "Tell me what you think of Mori?"

"He seems to be a very decent fellow," Alexander said.

"There is a glowing testimony," Takamori said, sarcastically. "Well, Charlotte is pleased with him. That is very obvious."

Charlotte glowed. But then so did Christina, Alexander thought proudly; he loved to see her standing next to Nicholas, the one so small and dainty, the other so tall and strong. When he died, as by the nature of things he would do long before either of those, it was good to think that they would be able to continue the name, and bring up little Alexander in the best traditions.

"I see so little of you," Christina complained, when she managed to get Nicholas in a corner.

"I would have thought you had seen more than enough," he muttered, in a feeble attempt at humour.

"I can never see enough of you. And you do not pay proper respect to our son."

"Are you mad? Anyway, how do you know it is our son?"

"Do you really suppose it is your father's?"

He bit his lip, and smiled across the room at his sister. "Charlotte at least is happy."

"There is no reason why we should not be happy," Christina pointed out.

"The two greatest sinners on earth."

"Sin is a point of view. The important thing is never to be found out."

"Barrett *san*," said Mori Takashida. "I am the happiest man on earth. I hope you feel the same."

"I am delighted, Mori *san*. I can think of no better husband for my daughter than your son."

"I am flattered. Now, we must choose a date for the wedding. In these troubled times, I would say, as soon as possible."

"Absolutely," Alexander agreed.

"Then, shall we say, 30 May?"

Just over a month away. "That will be ideal," Alexander agreed.

But on 15 May, Prime Minister Inukai, like Hamaguchi before him, was assassinated by military reactionaries who felt he had been too eager to reach an agreement with China.

The country was again plunged into a state of shock, and the Army was for the moment totally discredited. Several senior officers committed *seppuku*, and Alexander feared for his half-brother. Much as he would have condemned Takamori for any involvement in the murder, he would not have wished the head of the family to have to commit suicide. But Takamori stoutly denied any involvement, and as there was no proof against him, his word was accepted. Takamori was now sixty-seven years old, and one of the most senior officers in the army; he was nearly as respected a figure as his old compatriot, Admiral Togo.

Alexander privately suspected that young Yoshiye *was* implicated, but he also entirely denied it, and here again there was no proof. Young Mori also appeared innocent of any involvement. In all the circumstances, however, it was decided to postpone the wedding for six months.

This apart – and Charlotte took the disappointment very well – from Alexander's point of view the event turned out better than he could dared have hoped. With the Army in disgrace, the new Prime Minister was Admiral Saito Makoto, a disciple of Kato Tomosaburo.

*   *   *

This promised stability, as well as increased support for the Navy. Obeying Yamamoto's instructions, Alexander got down to investigating and studying every aspect of Japan's position, supposing there was ever to be a war with one or more of the Western Powers, or with the Soviet Union. The more he studied the situation, the less he liked it. He realised with increasing certainty that such a war, if it ever happened, had to involve the Imperial Navy on an even greater scale than the Army. But the Navy did not have either the ships or the men, as virtually every resource of the country for the preceding ten years had been poured into the Army. Yamamoto studied his figures with a grim face. "Obviously things must be changed," he agreed. "Prepare a detailed report, Barrett *san*, and we will go and see the Prime Minister together. We can at least be sure of a sympathetic hearing."

Alexander had only just completed a final report when, towards the end of 1932, Lord Lytton was ready to present *his* report to the League of Nations. A copy had of course been sent to the Japanese Government before it was made public. Premier Saito immediately summoned a meeting, not only of his cabinet, but also of his naval and military chiefs. To Alexander's surprise, he was also required to attend. He seated himself discreetly at the back of the room, while the Prime Minister addressed the assembly. "This report," Saito said, "entirely condemns our action in Manchuria. To summarise, it says, firstly, that our reaction to the incidents in the summer of 1931 were unjustified, and secondly, that it can find no evidence that the people of Manchuria actually wished their country to be made a protectorate of Japan. Well, this is nothing less than we expected, gentlemen.

"However, the report does not end with these condemnatory remarks. It then goes on to make recommendations, the important one of which is that Manchukuo should be made an autonomous state, but under Chinese sovereignty." There was an angry rustle round the room, and some hissing.

Saito waited for the noise to subside, before continuing. "It recommends that this new state, which is to be renamed Manchuria, should have an international police force, and that its government be assisted by international advisers."

More rustles and hisses. "Finally," Saito said, "presumably as a sop, it recognises that Japan has considerable economic interests in Manchuria. However, all Japanese forces must be withdrawn from the area." He raised his head to look at his officers.

"This report means that we are being told to give up our entire conquest, honourable Prime Minister," declared Barrett Takamori.

"That is what it appears to mean, yes."

"That is intolerable."

"It is unacceptable," Saito said carefully. "At least in the present circumstances. However, our response must be carefully decided."

"Bah," Takamori declared. "What can they do? They are all bankrupt."

"But so are we," Saito pointed out with brutal frankness. "Our only advantage is that we know what we are going to do, and they do not."

"And that they are slow to act, honourable Prime Minister," Yamamoto said quietly. "Certainly in concert."

"This is very true, Admiral Yamamoto. These two assets we must put to the most use. Our first weapon must be absolute legality. We have claimed, and we will continue to claim, that we were invited by the Manchurians to take over their country. We can produce evidence to support this. No doubt the League will present evidence to support Lord Lytton. We must argue the point. I am informed that the debate will not take place until early next year, so we have that much time. Now, if, as seems likely, we are outvoted and condemned on the floor of the League, and commanded to withdraw our forces from Manchukuo, our ambassador to the League will be instructed to refuse to accept that resolution, and should it not be withdrawn, to announce our intention of abandoning the League."

This time the hisses were of approval. Saito held up his hand. "By the rules of the League, there must be two years' notice of withdrawal. This we will give."

His officers stared at him in consternation. Saito smiled.

"Legality, gentlemen. That is the secret of the game. As long as we protest our innocence of any wrong-doing, as long as we take no precipitate steps, as long as we do everything by the letter of the law, the Western Powers will continue their inability to act, in unison. There will always be one of them to say, soon there will be a change of government in Japan, and the new government will accept the League resolution." He smiled. "They may be right. In the meantime, we will have secured two years, two years in which we will continue to occupy Manchukuo, to seek to extend and strengthen our domination of China."

"And at the end of two years, honourable Prime Minister?" someone asked.

"If the resolution remains in force, we will leave the League."

"Will they not then act against us?"

"That remains to be seen," Saito said. "There is one big flaw in this League of Nations: while its rules provide for action against any member state which refuses to accept its resolutions, there is no provision for any action against a nation which is *not* a member. Of course, if every member of the League of Nations were to agree to act together against such an outsider nation, the consequences could be disastrous. But I do not think this will happen, and we must never forget that the United States, potentially the strongest of any possible enemies of Japan, is not a member of the League."

"She is acting with them in this condemnation of our actions," Takamori grumbled. "This fellow Stimson is a menace."

"She is acting with them in condemning us, as you say, General Barrett. But there is absolutely no possibility of her undertaking any military action in concert with the Europeans. I have this on the best authority of our ambassador in Washington. No, no, it is my opinion that if we do everything 'by the book', as the Europeans say, they will find it very difficult to close ranks against us. In the meantime, we will have Manchuria, and we will be preparing ourselves for whatever may lie ahead . . . and who can say what the world situation will be in two years' time? This depression shows no sign of lifting, that is certain. Thank you, gentlemen. Admiral Yamamoto, you will remain."

Yamamoto motioned Alexander also to remain, as the other officers and cabinet ministers filed from the room, muttering amongst themselves. "Come forward, gentlemen," Saito invited, when the room was emptied.

"I have asked Captain Barrett to remain with me, honourable Prime Minister," Yamamoto said. "He is the officer who has prepared the report I have submitted. It occurs to me that you may have some questions to ask him."

Saito nodded. "Sit down, gentlemen. We are all naval officers, so I know there will be a complete unanimity of purpose between us, and also a complete honesty. This is a very gloomy report, Captain Barrett. Is it your true opinion that the Americans are the decisive element here? You heard what I told the assembly just now: our ambassador in Washington is certain they will never act in concert with the Europeans."

"I am sure he is right, honourable Prime Minister, as regards military force, at least in the present circumstances. But they do not have to."

Saito frowned. "You think America would go to war with us, unilaterally, over Manchuria? That is against all of their principles. And all of my information."

"They do not have to go to war, honourable Prime Minister. None of the Western Powers needs to go to war. They have only to cut off our oil supplies, and also our rubber. Then we would not have the means to continue our campaign on the continent. Or even to maintain ourselves there in any force."

Saito frowned. "We get our oil from the Dutch East Indies, and our rubber from British Malaya."

Alexander nodded. "These may well be prepared to co-operate with the Americans."

"All of these nations are in considerable financial difficulty," Saito argued. "Would they really be willing to abandon their trade with us at such a time?"

"I believe it is possible, honourable Prime Minister. The

104

Western nations operate on points of principle. These are dear to the hearts of their politicians because they are dear to the hearts of their electorates. Besides, they will suppose that the mere threat to cut off our supplies of essential commodities will bring us to heel."

"And where do the Americans fit into this?"

"Most of our overseas investments are in the United States, honourable Prime Minister. If the Americans were to freeze those assets, it would be very difficult for us to pay for our necessities."

"And you think they may do this? Is not the present Administration about to lose office?"

"That is what the experts say, honourable Prime Minister."

"Well, then at least we will be rid of the detestable Stimson, our arch enemy."

"That may be, honourable Prime Minister. But I do not think our troubles may necessarily be over. If this man Roosevelt wins the election, he is coming to office on a promise of sweeping away all the errors of the Hoover Administration, and launching America on to the road to recovery. The measures he is advocating are severe. He may well find it expedient to present to his people the image of Japan as a menace to be combated. This, honourable Prime Minister, is a time-honoured way to gain, and keep, the support of the masses; did not Genghis Khan advise his sons always to maintain peace at home, but that the way to do this was always to maintain troubled borders?"

"Ha!" Saito gave a brief laugh. "You are comparing Franklin Roosevelt with Genghis Khan? An effete aristocrat with a warrior from the steppes?"

"With respect, honourable Prime Minister, did not Toyotomi Hideyoshi, the greatest warrior ever produced by Japan, consider his rival, Tokugawa Iyeyasu, an effete aristocrat? And did not the Tokugawa conquer?"

Saito stared at him for several seconds. "Very good, Captain Barrett," he said at last. "You have suggested that our enemies may be able to do us much harm. But do you also consider that they will entertain the use of military force against us?"

105

"No, honourable Prime Minister. At least, not at the present time. That would be against all of their principles. Especially as they will believe we can be forced to withdraw from Manchuria without the use of such force."

"So, what is your solution?"

Alexander glanced at Yamamoto, who cleared his throat. "You have bought us two years of time, honourable Prime Minister. Our first priority must be to stockpile as much of those essential commodities such as fuel and rubber, tin and steel, as is possible."

Saito nodded. "That we will do. But it is not possible to accumulate sufficient reserves for more than a few years."

"Less, if it comes to a war," Alexander put in.

"Having stockpiled what we can," Yamamoto went on. "And presuming that there are no advantageous changes in world opinion or world politics, then, honourable Prime Minister, we will be faced with either having to fight to hold what we have, or withdraw from Manchuria."

"Such a withdrawal would mean the fall of this government, and perhaps even civil war," Saito said. "It would be a disgrace few of us in power could survive. The nation would not stand for it."

"I understand this, honourable Prime Minister."

"Therefore our only alternative would be to fight. Can we defend our position, successfully?"

"We could fight a defensive war, honourable Prime Minister, only for a limited time. Much would depend upon the resolution of our enemies, and I doubt they have that much resolution, where they themselves are in no danger. But as our sources of supply would be cut, we would eventually be defeated, simply because we would lack the resources to continue waging war. Our only hope of ultimate victory would be to wage an *aggressive* war."

"Against whom?"

Yamamoto glanced at Alexander, and cleared his throat. "To maintain our position, honourable Prime Minister, it will be necessary to ensure our supplies of those raw materials which are essential to our military survival. I am speaking of oil and rubber and tin. The nearest worthwhile source of these raw materials is South-East Asia."

Saito also glanced at Alexander. "You are speaking of the Dutch East Indies and Malaysia."

"That is correct, honourable Prime Minister."

"Then you are speaking of war, with Great Britain and the Netherlands."

"Regrettably, honourable Prime Minister. Although one suspects that there would be little chance of the Netherlands going to war, even to protect their richest possessions. Their record for the last hundred years has been one of wishing to remain at peace, regardless of the provocation."

"But this would not apply to Great Britain."

"No, honourable Prime Minister."

Saito stroked his chin. "Could we win such a war, Admiral Yamamoto?" He continued to look at Alexander.

"At this moment, no, honourable Prime Minister," Yamamoto said. "Simply because this would, necessarily, be a war of navies, and thanks to the Washington and London treaties, we are in a position of considerable inferiority to the Royal Navy."

"And as long as we adhere to those treaties, we can never achieve parity," Saito mused.

"I would suggest that the treaties are part of our membership of the League of Nations, honourable Prime Minister," Yamamoto said. "In any event, the treaties expire at the end of 1936, and, if you proceed with your programme, we should leave the League at some time during 1935. These dates are conveniently close."

"And then challenge the world," Saito said soberly.

"At least, have our preparations to do so well in hand."

"And what of China? The Army commanders, and they include your brother, Barrett *san*, are convinced that our destiny lies on the mainland."

Yamamoto nodded to permit Alexander to take up the case himself. "I believe they are mistaken, honourable Prime Minister," Alexander said. "For four reasons."

"Speak."

"Firstly, to commence an all-out war with China will distract our very slender resources, exposing us to aggression by the Western Powers. Secondly, China has nothing to offer us, save markets for our goods. These markets are there,

107

whether we fight her or not. Indeed, it is probable that they will be more readily available if we remain on the best possible terms with Chiang Kai-shek. Is it not so that the only result of our aggression on the mainland is a complete boycott of our goods by the Chinese? Then thirdly, China can give us none of the things we desperately need if we are ever to defy the Western Powers: I am speaking of oil and rubber."

"You mentioned four reasons, Barrett."

"The fourth is the most vital of all: I do not believe we can conquer China."

Saito raised his eyebrows. "Does your brother share this opinion?"

"Indeed not, honourable Prime Minister. But he is considering only the military aspect of the situation. Of course we can defeat the Chinese armies, whether they be led by Chiang Kai-shek or any of the warlords. But we simply do not have the resources to conquer the entire country. The Chinese will not give up. They will continue to resist, so that we will find ourselves engaged in an unceasing war, in which all of our resources will be consumed. It would make sense if we could obtain the raw materials we need from those parts of China we could seize and control. But as we cannot, we would only be shortening the length of time we could hold out if the Western Powers sought to implement their resolutions."

Saito stroked his chin.

"Would you like this opinion in writing, honourable Prime Minister?" Yamamoto asked. "I will of course associate myself with Captain Barrett."

Saito considered for a few minutes longer, then he shook his head. "I think such a report, coming from two senior officers in the Navy, would merely exacerbate the differences that already exist between the Navy and the Army. It will be my business to maintain the situation for the time being. But I have no doubt that we have a crisis in prospect, in only a few years time. I would like you, gentlemen, to consider the future – I am speaking of the next ten years – from every conceivable angle, but from the viewpoint that should it come to war with any Western power, or, incidentally, the United States, because there is always the possibility of a change of heart there, it will be the Navy that will have to be the dominant service, both in securing our essential supplies, in protecting the homeland, and in defeating our enemies. I am sure, when the time comes, that even the Army will appreciate this."

"To carry out the role you have designated, the Navy will have to expand, honourable Prime Minister."

Saito nodded. "I understand this. So here is another brief. When you have prepared your scenario of possible political and economic developments over the ten years, I then wish you to draw up an estimate of the navy you would require to carry out such courses of action as you may recommend. You should work on the assumption that you will not be restricted as to size of gun or of tonnage, either regarding individual ships or regarding the combined tonnage of the fleet, either because the building holiday will be ended, or because we will have left the League. Do you understand me, gentlemen?"

Yamamoto rose, and bowed, as did Alexander. Outside the office, the Admiral seized Alexander's hand. "We have just been given the most important assignment in Japanese history."

"To draw up a blueprint for disaster."

Yamamoto grinned. "It will be an exciting disaster, at any rate."

The work was certainly immensely interesting, even if the situation seemed to grow daily more acute. The Army tightened its grip on Manchukuo, and even expanded into Jehol, bringing more cries of protest from China and the West. The Lytton Report was duly presented to the League and Japanese action condemned, whereupon Japan gave formal notice of its intention to leave the League in two years' time. "What will it mean?" Christina asked.

"Hopefully, not a lot," Alexander told her. "At least in the short term. Let us think about the wedding."

Having been postponed for several months, it was at last possible. It was an elaborate affair, as Captain Mori was not a Christian, and therefore the couple had to be married twice, once by a priest and once in a Shinto ceremony. Alexander had not seen as much of Mori as he would have liked since the betrothal. He had been assured by Takamori that his prospective son-in-law had been fully briefed regarding his wife's psychological problems, and that he was prepared to accept them, and, if necessary, cope with them. Now, the seemingly endless toasting ceremonies of a Japanese wedding drawing to a close, Mori bowed to his father-in-law. "This is the greatest moment of my life, honourable Captain," he said, his eyes bright with the amount of *sake* he had consumed.

"And one of the saddest of mine, Mori *san*. I am but relieved that my daughter is going to the care of a man such as yourself."

"Her care shall be my constant concern, honourable Captain," Mori said.

They bowed to each other. Charlotte had already left, to toast her new parents, because by Japanese custom and indeed law, she was no longer a Barrett in any way, but a Mori.

By now most of the guests had left as well, and Alexander, thrusting his hands into his pockets, could saunter out on to the lawn behind his house. It had been the centre of activity following the ceremony, and was now a litter of paper and discarded crockery and cutlery, being assiduously collected by the various servants. Alexander greeted them by name as he sauntered through their midst towards the gazebo at the foot of the garden. It nestled amidst the dwarf trees which clustered there, beside the goldfish pond. He was tired, and he had had a good deal to drink. He knew that he should be happy. But this was difficult.

Obviously it had to be better for Charlotte to be married, and hopefully to have children, and live as normal and fulfilling a life as possible. But could she do those things with Mori Toshiye, who, however charming kind and patient on the surface, was yet a *samurai*, and who would therefore be, at heart, an upholder of all the old noble, but harsh and stern, values of Japan? Even more disturbing was the certainty that Sue-Ellen would never have permitted this marriage. Sue-Ellen would, if necessary, have taken her daughters back to the United States to find them husbands,

110

rather than permit them to marry Japanese. So Sue-Ellen, even if she had rebelled against her own parents, could have been classified as an old-fashioned racist. It was nonetheless what she would have done, and therefore she would most heartily have to dispprove of what he had permitted.

Now, he supposed, she would disapprove even more, when Nicholas sought a Japanese wife. This was as certain as anything in life. He paused in surprise, because there was the young man, emerging from the gazebo, buttoning his tunic.

And emerging behind him, but checking at the sight of her husband, was Christina.

CHAPTER 5

Bushido

Nicholas stood still at the sight of his father, and seemed insensibly to come to attention. Christina stepped past him. "Why, honourable Husband," she said. "You surprised us."

Alexander, unsure of what reply to make, took refuge in the obvious. "You were not with me to bid our guests goodnight."

"I am a wretched creature," Christina agreed, "I wonder you do not beat me, honourable Husband. Go to bed, Nicholas. We will continue our discussion another time."

Nicholas looked as if he would have said something, then glanced at his stepmother, and bowed before hurrying for the house.

"Discussion?" Alexander inquired, and found himself walking behind his wife as she also set off for the house.

"Your son is unhappy, with the direction our country takes," Christina said, over her shoulder. "Are we at peace with the world, or at war with the world? Are we the lackeys of the Western democracies, or are we the rising tide of nationalist Asia?"

Alexander was totally surprised. "He has never spoken to me on this subject."

"I know this," Christina led him into the house, where again servants were busy cleaning up the mess. "Nicholas is not sufficiently close to you. Not close as perhaps Yoshiye is to Takamori. Will you say goodnight to Baby? I came in before, and he was disturbed by the noise."

"That was to be expected," Alexander pointed out. But once again he was following her. As he had followed her all of his married life? "But you . . . where did you get such opinions?"

"Ssssh," she commanded, opening the nursery door. The nanny, asleep in the corner, hastily sprang up, realised who had come in, and knelt, head bowed.

"He is asleep, honourable Mistress," the girl whispered.

Christina nodded, bent over the cot for a moment, then stood aside to let Alexander look at the babe. Then she stepped outside again, and waited for him to close the screen. "You do not think a woman should have political opinions," she remarked.

Alexander had momentarily lost the thread of their conversation. "I am presuming that a wife, concerned as she is with the domestic management of her husband's affairs, must necessarily hold such opinions at second hand."

Christina slid back the screen to their bedchamber, where several maidservants were hastily placing vases of flowers and arranging the mattress; this had been part of the reception room only an hour ago. "You are right," she said. "I am too interested in matters that do not concern me. You should beat me."

He wished she wouldn't keep saying that. Although he knew that many Japanese husbands did beat their wives, quite regularly, he had never beaten *her*. The trouble was that he had often felt like doing so – and she knew it. "I still feel he should have discussed the matter with me, rather than you," he grumbled.

"I agree with you, were you not so unapproachable. You do not understand, but to Nicholas, you are not merely a father. Far more are you a senior officer in the Navy. You are too much his superior for him to confide in you." She clapped her hands, and the girls hastily bowed and filed from the room. "Do you never feel the urge to mount one of those girls?" she asked.

"To . . . my God, the things you think of, Chrissy."

Christina undressed. "I do not have great ships to command, great plans to make. So I think of natural things, of men and women, and their relations to one another. You have been married to me now for seven years. You know every nook and cranny of my body, do you not?"

"But not of your mind," he remarked, half to himself.

"Well, a person's mind is his last refuge of privacy. Or hers." Naked, she undressed him in turn. "So, as a man, you would not be normal did your desires not occasionally embrace other bodies. I know there is always the *geisha* house. But is it not true that with a *geisha* a man is almost a suppliant? Even if you have paid her well, she gives you what she wishes to give, and withholds what she wishes to withhold. There is no mastery, and does not a man seek mastery over every woman with whom he couples, or indeed, has any kind of relationship? But with a servant, now, you would be total master. And those girls are young, and willing, and eager."

He frowned at her. "You mean you would *like* me to take one of them?"

"I wish only to see you happy, honourable Husband."

"And you do not think you make me happy?"

"I hope I have made you as happy as one woman may. Now I would make you happier yet."

He took her in his arms. "I am perfectly happy with you, Chrissy. Even if I do know your every nook and cranny. It is your nooks and crannies that I like best."

She kissed him. "You mean you aren't going to beat me?" she whispered.

It was next morning before Alexander realised he had never asked her why she and Nicholas had found it necessary to hide themselves away in the gazebo to have their little chat. But by then he had decided not to probe. He was actually delighted that she and the boy should have become friends at last, and besides, much of what she had said made sense: he *had* never been truly close to his son, and now they were likely to drift even further apart. He was well aware that to many of the younger officers, more particularly in the Army, the country seemed to be stagnating, just keeping its head above the financial flood, maintaining itself in Manchukuo to be sure, but making no further inroads into China.

114

They blamed the government. Indeed, their hostility to Saito forced his resignation in the summer of 1934, but to their chagrin he was replaced by another Navy minister, Admiral Okada Keisuke. Although Okada was forced to accept a "hawk", Hirota Koki, as his foreign minister, few people doubted that Saito remained the real power behind the scene. Despite this, as with a dozen years before, Alexander could not help but wonder if the change at the top would mean a change of policy, but Yamamoto was immediately assured, in secret, that there would be no change, and that he was to proceed with his project.

From Alexander's point of view, the most exciting aspect of their task was that of designing a new battleship which would be able to dominate all other navies. But this was only a part of the overall strategy.

Yamamoto called in his chief draughtsmen to tell them what he had in mind. "This is a hypothetical design," he assured them. "We are looking to the future. Now, there have been in all history only seven radical changes in the design and construction of first-rate ships. The first was when oars gave way entirely to sail, at least on the oceans. The second was the introduction of ship-smashing cannon as against man-killing missiles. The third was the coming of steam power which made a fleet independent of the winds, but at the same time limited its range of action by the necessity periodically to refuel. The fourth was the introduction of iron and then steel as defensive armour. The fifth was the invention of the armour-piercing, explosive shell. The sixth was the invention of the turbine which enabled much greater speeds than had ever been supposed possible to be achieved. And the seventh was the concept of the all big gun ship, the dreadnought. I believe that we may be on the verge of an eighth revolutionary advance, the development of aircraft, and therefore aircraft-carriers, as the principal strike weapon of a modern fleet.

"Let us therefore consider aircraft-carriers first. We have two major fleet carriers, *Akagi* and *Kaga*. Both of these, however, are inferior in size and aircraft-carrying capabilities to the American Lexingtons. In the first instance, therefore,

I wish designs prepared to enlarge these two ships. I am thinking in terms of increasing the overall length by about fifty feet; this is mainly to obtain additional space on the flight deck. I also wish the hangar space increased, so that instead of sixty planes each ship will carry ninety."

"With respect, honourable Admiral," said one of the officers. "Such changes will involve an increase in weight of perhaps nine thousand tons, full load. Will that not put these ships considerably over the limits established by the Naval Treaties?"

Yamamoto smiled. "Prepare the design, Captain Usugi. Actual work will not commence for a year or so, by which time the Naval Treaties will be on the point of expiry, and Japan will have left the League of Nations. However, I am informed that no matter what we do, we will be unable to increase the speed of the ships to thirty knots, much less anything more than that, and the American Lexingtons can exceed this. Thus we will bear in mind this all-important factor as we talk about new construction. There is also the matter of time: we do not have very much of it. We need to improvise, as well as build. Firstly, there is the submarine support vessel *Taigei*. She has been launched, and completion is scheduled for next year. I intend to take her over and reconstruct her upper works as a carrier. She is only fifteen thousand tons, and will be unable to carry more than thirty planes. But she will be a useful auxiliary on the lines of *Ryujo*. As regards absolutely new construction, it is important that we make the right decisions, and this means understanding what our plans will be if it comes to war.

"As it will be a naval war for the most part, it will be a war of great movement. Movement, to be effective, requires speed, and this is what I consider we must plan for. It is impossible to construct an aircraft-carrier capable of carrying the kind of armour that would be needed either to stand up to a sixteen-inch shell, or, let us be honest about this, two or three five hundred pound bombs, and which would also be capable of moving at any speed. The only true defence available to a carrier is speed and punch. Our carriers must never be allowed within range of an enemy battleship, and, having delivered their own assault with their aircraft, they

116

must be able to escape a counter-strike, by their speed. Should a counter-strike become inevitable, then they must be defended by their own aircraft, to keep the enemy planes away.

"So, what I am looking for is a design for two new ships, fleet carriers, but with a speed well in excess of thirty knots. *Kaga* and *Akagi* have a maximum of twenty-eight knots, and as I have said, this is not good enough. The new ships must be as big as possible, bearing in mind the speed requirement. They must also carry as many aircraft as possible, again bearing in mind the speed requirement. That is the overriding factor."

He paused while the designers made their notes. "Now we come to battleships," he went on. "There is nothing new we can do with a battleship, save make it bigger and stronger, in order to withstand air attack. Stronger means the biggest main armament and the thickest protective armour practical. Thus here again I intend to make some conversions. I wish the four Kongo Class battlecruisers entirely rebuilt. They are powerful vessels with their fourteen-inch guns, but we all know how vulnerable battlecruisers are to plunging shot. I wish their armour brought up to battleship strength, I wish their anti-aircraft batteries doubled, and I wish their engines replaced to increase their present speed of twenty-five knots to thirty. I know these are old ships, but if we can turn them into a squadron of fast battleships they will do much to redress the balance until our new construction comes along. Don't tell me: what we are doing is contrary to the regulations of the Treaty of Washington." He smiled. "By the time anyone *knows* what we are doing, the Treaty of Washington will be a dead letter. Now, as to new construction, I wish the maximum in everything. Guns?"

"The heaviest guns presently available are eighteen-inch, honourable Admiral. They could be mounted in four turrets of two."

"Why not three of three?" Yamamoto asked. "That would give us an extra gun. I also wish the maximum armour. Here I am thinking of sixteen-inch belt, nine-inch deck, and as high as two feet on the turrets."

The designers exchanged glances. "With respect, honourable Admiral, the weight will be excessive."

"Thus this battleship will need a length to accomodate such weight."

"Something around eight hundred feet," Alexander remarked; he had also been scribbling sums. "*Nelson* is well under seven hundred."

"We are speaking of a displacement of close to seventy thousand tons," Kato said.

"A monster!" someone else remarked.

"The greatest battleship ever conceived," Yamamoto said. His eyes gleamed as he smiled at them. "Design her for me, gentlemen."

"The cost will be considerable, honourable Admiral."

"Design her," Yamamoto said again. "Let me worry about the cost."

"Now let us speak of the political situation," Yamamoto said, when he and Alexander were alone. "It has changed somewhat since you undertook your examination of our prospects."

It had indeed, changed so considerably that Alexander had found it necessary to revise his estimates again and again. "At the moment," he said. "It is most favourable to us. Roosevelt is fully occupied with his domestic problems; it appears that not all of his reform programme is going to be accepted by the Supreme Court, and this will obviously cause a constitutional crisis. Besides, his mandate is to make America rich again, not to become involved in international crises. The European democracies are fully committed to keeping an eye on Germany since this man Hitler has come to power."

"Unfortunately," Yamamoto said, "the moment is *not* favourable to us, with regards to strength. Barrett *san*, it is necessary for me to ask you two questions. The first is commonplace: do you consider that the Hitler regime in Germany can last?"

"There can be no doubt that Herr Hitler intends to set up a dictatorship in Germany," Alexander said. "In fact he has already done so. Therefore everything will now depend upon the attitude of the German Army."

"Surely the German Army is a nothing, since the Treaty of Versailles? Is not all power in the country controlled by the Brownshirts, who are controlled by Hitler?"

"The Wehrmacht is still perhaps the most potent force in German political life, honourable Admiral. Certainly the officer Corps. I agree that there are reputed to be several hundred thousand Brownshirts, and only about a hundred thousand regulars. However, there can be no doubt that the Army could eliminate the Brownshirts, if it determined to do so. This is because it would have the support of the German people. It would mean civil war, of course, and I should think this is something Herr Hitler is most anxious to avoid. He has come to office at least partly on a promise of restoring the Army to its former power and glory. Much will therefore depend on how quickly and how well he manages to keep that promise."

"Will the democracies allow this?"

"That too is of vital importance. It appears that Mussolini, at the least, is determined to stop him becoming too powerful. But whether anyone, even Mussolini, will ever take the irrevocable step of using force to halt him, with the financial catastrophe that would imply to the already fragile Western economies, remains to be seen."

"Do you consider that it would be worth our while to pursue a relationship with Germany, after we leave the League? On the basis that we might both be opposing the Western democracies?"

"I doubt it," Alexander said. "No matter what happens, it must be a considerable time before Germany has any influence on world affairs. More importantly, from our point of view, she has no fleet, nor any prospect of building one under the rules of the Treaty of Versailles, so she can be of no possible use to us. Was that your second question, honourable Admiral?"

"No," Yamamoto said. "My second question is this: you are actively preparing a scenario for a possible war with Great Britain. But you are half British yourself. What are your personal feelings in this matter?" He saw Alexander's hesitation. "What I am saying is that if you have any reservations, I can have you relieved of this onerous duty,

119

and given a sea command. Perhaps you would prefer this, anyway."

Alexander considered a few seconds longer. Of course he would like a sea command. But at the same time he did not wish to consider any other man creating *this* scenario. "I am a Japanese officer, honourable Admiral. At Eta-Jima I swore an oath to the Emperor. But, as you well know, I am deeply desirous to avoid a conflict with the British."

"Yet it is inevitable. If we ever determine to move south, against the Dutch East Indies and Malaysia, there will be war."

"Agreed. But with every day it becomes more impractical. At this moment, even with an inferior navy, it is almost possible that we could wage a very short war, that is to seize Dutch oil and British rubber, with every possibility of success. But military action, and military success, against the British and Dutch, will turn us into an international pariah, which is what we nearly are as it is. While once this moment passes . . . you know the British are fortifying Singapore? They are turning it into a massive naval base, which could sustain the entire Royal Navy, if it became necessary."

"But this can never happen, because of the Royal Navy's other commitments."

"As there is no other nautical enemy in sight, honourable Admiral, this would actually be perfectly practical. There are only three worthwhile navies in the world other than the British and ourselves. The United States we have agreed will never become involved in a war, the French and the Italian are staunch supporters of the League of Nations, which, in naval matters at least, is led by Great Britain. At this moment, were we to go to war tomorrow, Britain would be in an inferior position, as her nautical lifeline to Malaysia would be several times longer than ours. Once Singapore is completed, the situation is entirely reversed. They can maintain a fleet on the spot, and our lifeline back to Japan suddenly becomes comparatively very long indeed. There is more. Were we to go to war with Great Britain it is extremely likely that France would come in on the British side, if not militarily, at least with moral support. This could easily include granting the British the

120

use of air bases in French Indo-China. With those they would dominate the South China Sea, while we would be operating from carriers in that sea, forced to return in rotation to refuel, and vulnerable to enemy air attack, no matter how fast our ships are."

"Then our position is more serious than I thought. You are saying that it is possible for us to be squeezed out of existence? Returned to the level of a third-rate power?"

"I am saying that there are some very difficult decisions to be made, honourable Admiral. Unless, and this could always happen, there were to be a dramatic re-alignment of forces in Europe."

Yamamoto nodded. "It is our business to make those decisions, Barrett *san*. Or at least recommend them to our superiors. But now I have some splendid news for you. Lieutenant Barrett Nicholas is to be gazetted Lieutenant-Commander. And we have a ship for him: *Hatsuharu*."

"I am so very pleased for you, Nicky," Alexander said, shaking Nicholas's hand. "You are on your way to a distinguished career."

"Is it possible to have a distinguished career without seeing action, honourable Father?"

Alexander suppressed a sigh. The boy was so uprightly anxious to make his way, and be worthy of his name. But the slight air of defiance with which he always faced his father would not go away. "I would say it is very possible, and more worthwhile, Nicholas. Now come and be congratulated by the family."

They were all assembled, Nicholas saw with concern. He came to his father's house as rarely as possible. He saw the family as little as possible too. His apparent coldness, his inability to make close friends amongst his brother officers – he had even drifted apart from Tokijo, although they still corresponded from time to time – had obviously been noted by his superiors. On the other hand, he had no visible vices, and displayed an utter devotion to his duty and his career. He spent all his leisure time at his books and was always willing to give up that leisure time to carry out any naval requirement. They had been pleased enough to give him this

121

early promotion. He was just thirty, and he was to have a command. What man could ask for anything more? Save that he had no doubt that his rapid climb up the ladder had also been in part due to his name and his antecendents, and that he did not want. And to the influence of his stepmother?

Christina smiled at him, and held him close for a chaste kiss on the cheek. "We are all so very proud," she told him.

Then she stepped back, and their eyes held for a moment. Knowing her now for what she was, he had to wonder how often she had betrayed his father with another man: at least she had not again become pregnant.

The amazing thing about his stepmother, Nicholas thought, was that she revealed no remorse, no suggestion of conscience, no indication that she even considered they had done anything wrong. Whereas he had hovered on the brink of suicide for four years. And remained alive! There were several arguments for what he had done, or perhaps, not done. For him to die, by *seppuku*, would have raised more questions than it could have answered, because, as she had so brutally pointed out, it would have answered none. No *samurai* committed *seppuku* without a most compelling reason, and he, son of a famous house and with an unlimited career in front of him, had less reason to end his life than anyone else in Japan -- on the surface. The deed would have plunged his father, and his sister, into a deeper pit than he had dug for himself, and had the truth then come out, he might even had condemned the child, his son. Far better to sit it out, and hope to atone for his sin, and die gloriously, in some battle. If there could ever be a battle? Or was he just a coward?

In either event, commonsense as well as honour dictated that he not compound the crime, however often temptation was thrust in his way, as at his sister's wedding, when Christina had virtually dragged him into the gazebo and attempted to all but rape him! "I am fortunate, honourable Mother," he said,

Christina gave a little moue, then another flashing smile. "You know everyone here, I think."

Nicholas bowed to his uncle. "I greet a future admiral of the Imperial Japanese Navy," Takamori said.

Nicholas shook hands with Yoshiye, wearing the uniform of a major in the Army. "We are the future of Japan," Yoshiye assured him.

Nicholas kissed Barrett Nikijo and her two daughters, and then Yoshiye's wife. "Your success is our success," Nikijo told him.

Mori Toshiye, also a major now, bowed and shook hands. "My congratulations, honourable Brother."

Charlotte was last. Taller than her husband, she seemed more Russian than English, with her titian hair looking ready to tumble out of its restraining chignon as she hugged her brother. "I am so happy for you," she said.

Here was real pleasure. Nicholas had come into very little contact with Mori Toshiye, but there could be no questioning the happiness that he had brought Charlotte. When Nicholas remembered back only a few years, to the young woman on the brink of madness, and compared her with this confident, smiling wife, he felt he was looking at a different person.

Last of all was Yamamoto Isoroku. Nicholas paused in consternation. Wrapped up in his family, he had not taken proper notice of the naval officer standing at the back of the room. Now he clicked his heels as he bowed. "Honourable Admiral. This is a great honour."

"On the contrary, Commander Barrett," Yamamoto said. "It is I who am honoured by being invited to such a family gathering. As your cousin has so aptly put it, I am looking at the future of Japan."

"Will it be as fruitful a future as was our past, honourable Admiral?" Nicholas asked boldly.

"One would hope so, Commander," Yamamoto said.

Hatsuharu was the name ship of her class, the very latest to be completed; there were to be six in all, but three of them were not yet delivered, although launched. The ships had been designed very strictly in conformity with the requirements of the London Naval Treaty, being one thousand four hundred and ninety tons standard displacement, although this was increased to eighteen hundred when they were fully loaded. Just under three hundred and sixty feet overall length, they had been estimated to make thirty-six knots. Armed with five five-inch dual-purpose guns, *Hatsuharu* had originally been designed so that while four of the guns were twinned in two turrets, one aft and the other on the raised fordeck, the fifth gun was above the foredeck pair, in order to superfire. This however had impaired stability, and only a few months earlier a much smaller destroyer, *Tomozuru*, had capsized because of the additional weight of the superfiring forward gun. *Hatsuharu* was undergoing a rebuild, with the superfiring gun being moved aft, where it was nearer to the waterline. In addition to her dual-purpose guns, she was armed with two thirteen-millimetre anti-aircraft guns, nine twenty-four-inch torpedo tubes, and fourteen depth-charges.

"You understand, Commander Barrett, that the rebuilding will mean a substantial increase in tonnage," the superintendent at the Sasebo Yard in Kyushu explained. "She will now displace seventeen hundred standard, and two thousand deep-loaded."

"But will this not exceed the Treaty limits?" Nicholas asked.

The superintendent shrugged. "I have been told not to concern myself with this. What *is* of importance is that the increased tonnage will involve a reduction in speed, to thirty-three knots."

"But that is three knots slower than the latest British and Americans," Nicholas protested.

"If our reports are correct, it will be *four* knots slower than the new American design, the Porters," the superintendent said. "But it is not possible to improve the speed without installing new engines, and that is not practical at this time. I have been instructed to prepare the ship for sea in the shortest possible time."

"Which will be when?"

"Another six months, honourable Commander."

"I am sadly disappointed," Nicholas told Yoshiye, who came to Sasebo for a visit.

Yoshiye stood on the bridge and looked over the foredeck; being in dry dock, there was a far greater awareness of height than had the ship been at sea. "Over the loss of three knots?"

he asked. "I think you have a splendid ship. I wonder if I should not have been a naval officer."

"Why aren't you?"

Yoshiye grinned. "There are two compelling reasons. The first is that my honourable father would never have forgiven me, and the second is that I get seasick."

"Almost everyone gets seasick at some time or other," Nicholas told him. "You would soon get over it were you to spend any time at sea. But honourable uncle, no, I do not suppose you would get over his disfavour." Barrett Takamori was about the only man in the world he was actually afraid of.

"Honourable father stands for everything that is great about Japan," Yoshiye asserted.

"I won't argue with that," Nicholas agreed.

"Thus it is our business to live up to his ideals, at all times."

"Do we not do that?"

"Honourable father is sorely distressed at the state of the country," Yoshiye said.

"I thought we were doing rather well," Nicholas said. "You must admit that since the Navy has been holding the premiership the country has known more political stability than at any time in the past twenty years. Nothing has been done about the Lytton Report, because the democracies are entirely bound up with their financial problems. We still have Manchukuo, and as long as we have there, and the rest of China, as a market, we shall not starve, even if we may not actually be prospering at this minute. By the end of the year we shall be out of the League, and next year the Naval Treaties expire. *My* honourable father has told me that then there will be a considerable expansion of the Navy. And as the rest of the world pulls out of the Depression, and we are, shall I say, forgiven for our misdeeds and thus faced with lower tariff walls, why, I see nothing but prosperity ahead of us."

"You are incredibly naive, honourable Cousin," Yoshiye remarked. "But then, you always were."

Nicholas waited to be enlightened, as to his naivety; he did not take offence because Yoshiye, like his father, was always this intense.

"Do you really suppose that the rest of the world, by which I understand you to mean the western block of powers, will ever treat with Japan as an equal, unless we force them to do so? Have they ever done so?"

Nicholas considered.

"They have accepted our expansion into Manchukuo simply because we warned them we would brook on inter-ference from them," Yoshiye continued. "They have taken what revenge they could by raising their tariffs against our goods, but that is the revenge of a child. Yet what do we see now? A government which persistently says it wishes peaceful coexistence with the West, which has declared its wish to work for lower trade barriers, in effect, to crawl on its belly to Washington and London, not realising that our enemies will merely step on our head. But that head will be Japan. You speak of political stability? All colonial peoples have political stability, where the colonising power is strong enough and ruthless enough to enforce it. And ever since the end of the Great War the Western Powers have been working to reduce Japan to the equivalent of a colony. And now we have this government of ours summoning a general election, inviting the people to confirm them in their ridiculous path. And the people, besotted as they are with all the ideals of peace and its supposed benefits, will probably give them their mandate."

"I sincerely hope they will. And I do not think your facts are absolutely correct," Nicholas ventured.

"It is a fact that throughout history," Yoshiye went on, ignoring the protest as he warmed to his theme, "the only prosperous and successful and, I may say, happy nations have been those who have been stronger than their neighbours, and have demonstrated their strength, by means of war. Victorious war!"

"Oh, come now . . ."

"Why do you not listen? Was not the fifth century B.C. the greatest in the history of Greek art and literature and sculpture, a time when they made their greatest contribution to the thought and progress of mankind? And it was a century of unending warfare, against Persia and even against each other."

"Yes, but . . ."

"And when did Shakespeare and Marlowe and Spencer and Milton flourish? When England was fighting for its life against Spain, or during the great civil war."

"Well, I suppose there is some argument in that direction," Nicholas agreed, unable to think of a counter at such short notice.

"We in the Army have long recognised these facts," Yoshiye said. "We have always conceived it to be our duty to remind the nation of these facts as well, to raise it to a full understanding of its duty, not only to itself, but to posterity. And what do we now see all around us? A people sunk into slothful anxiety only for peace and a preservation of the status quo, encouraged in that direction by the white-livered government which is now in power."

"The government represents the people," Nicholas suggested. "That is its prime duty in life."

"Bah! When have the people mattered? When have the people truly known what they wanted? It is us, the *samurai*, the leaders, who matter."

Nicholas glanced left and right to make sure none of the shipyard workers were within earshot. "I think you should reflect very carefully about what you are saying, before you continue, honourable Cousin."

"Or you will have me arrested for treason?"

"Of course not. But you may say something you regret."

"How can I? You are my cousin. May not one cousin speak freely to another? But I will ask you to swear to me that you will never repeat a word of what I am now about to tell you."

"Perhaps it would be a better idea for you *not* to tell me at all," Nicholas suggested.

Yoshiye was not to be deflected. "Swear, by every ancestor of ours who ever wore a sword, and most of all by the bones of our grandfather."

Nicholas opened his mouth to protest, and then closed it again. He was suddenly curious to know what Yoshiye, and presumably his Army friends, had in mind: he could not possibly hope to stop, or even check, their proposed action without knowing what it was. "I will swear," he said.

127

"On one condition, that you are not speaking of revolution. If you are, I *will* have you arrested, cousin or not."

Yoshiye considered him for several seconds. "No," he said at last. "We do not intend revolution. Because, as you are aware, we would not succeed. There are too many people in the country supportive of the government of Okada and Saito. It is our purpose merely to awaken the Japanese people's hearts to the glories of the past, the glory that should be their future, the shame that is their present."

"We?" Nicholas asked.

"There is a group dedicated to this task. Not large, but large enough, with every man carefully selected and utterly determined."

"A group of which you are a member?"

"Yes."

"And just what does this group intend to do?"

"On a given day, should the present government be reelected, we intend to seize the various government offices, including the parliament house and the cabinet office."

"And you do not describe that as revolution?"

"It is not. It would be a revolution if we were meaning to take control of the country afterwards. But we do not mean to do so. It would be a revolution if we intended any bloodshed. But we do not intend to shed any blood, except our own. We have taken an oath to this effect. We merely mean to protest, in the most public possible manner, against the sloth and downright dishonour which is pervading our current government."

"I think you are quite mad," Nicholas said. "Have you given any thought to the consequences of this action?"

"Indeed we have. What do you suppose will happen after we have seized these buildings, and the fact becomes generally known?"

"His Majesty will instruct the military governor of Tokyo, who happens to be your own father, to call out his troops and place you under arrest. Or are you anticipating that your father will refuse to act? Is he in the plot? Then you are forcing him to commit *seppuku*."

"My father is not in the plot, because it is not a plot. It is

128

a planned protest. I have no doubt at all that he will carry out whatever orders he receives."

"Then . . ." Nicholas took off his cap and scratched his head. "I do not understand. You will have to surrender."

"Exactly. And then?"

"My God! You will be charged with at least mutiny. Probably treason. Either way you will be condemned to death. Do you realise that?" He frowned. "Or do you mean to use your trials as some kind of political springboard?"

"There will be no trials," Yoshiye declared. "We intend to anticipate our sentences."

"You . . . ?"

"In public. Before all of Tokyo."

"You *are* mad."

"We are *samurai*."

Nicholas realised that his cousin was in deadly earnest. There was no society in the world which would accept such a course of action – except the Japanese. There was no society in the world which would react to such a course of action except in terms of revulsion and horror – save the Japanese. But Yoshiye . . . "You intend to participate in this?"

"I have been elected leader."

"What of your father? You will destroy him."

"My father, like myself, is a *samurai*. He will understand, and honour me for what I have done."

"You also have a mother."

"So have all of my fellows."

"And you think I shall not attempt to stop this craziness?"

"Of course you will not attempt to stop me, honourable Cousin. You have given me your sacred word. To break your word would be to break every law of *bushido*. You would disgrace yourself, and you would disgrace the name you bear and every member of your family. You would drive *your* father to *seppuku*. Can you contemplate that?"

Once again he was in earnest, and he was right. It was necessary to be sure that every man, woman and child in Japan would condemn what Yoshiye was proposing to do. But it was also necessary to understand that they would accept the atonement he was proposing – and even more was it necessary to understand that they would abhor the man, and especially the blood relative, who would attempt to dissuade him from what he considered an honourable course. Nicholas sighed. "Then why have you come to me at all and told me all this? You do not seriously suppose I will join you?"

"Of course I do not expect you to join us. But there is something I wish you to do for me." Nicholas waited. "The Admiralty is one of the buildings we intend to take over," Yoshiye said. "In fact, it is the most important of our objectives, and for that reason I intend to lead the assault on that myself. Now, I understand that honourable Uncle Alexander is presently working there."

"Yes, he is."

"Now, you must understand, Nicholas, that while we have set our hearts and our minds resolutely against bloodshed, there is no man can say what will happen on the day, should anyone we encounter react rashly. You must also understand that we are hoping not to have to undertake this action at all. It is entirely dependent upon the outcome of the elections. If, as we hope, the electorate show a swing to the right and turn out Saito and his crew, then there will be no necessity for action at all. However, if, as we fear, the people are sucked in by these liberal promises of peaceful prosperity, it will be necessary to act promptly."

"And you fear my father may react 'rashly', as you put it? He will certainly resist you. And I must warn you, Yoshiye, that oath or no oath, if any harm befalls my father, I will kill you."

Yoshiye studied him for several seconds. It was not the sort of declaration he had ever expected to hear his essentially passive cousin make, but he recognised that Nicholas meant what he said. "It is this possibility I am determined to avoid," he said. "Thus, on receipt of a message from me, you must act yourself, immediately. The message will contain but a number, nothing more. The number will be the day on which our action will take place, in that month. On receipt of such a message I wish you to keep honourable uncle away from the Admiralty on that day."

"That is madness. Suppose I am away on my ship?"

"You will have advance warning of the month. And your ship is not going to be ready for sea trials for another six months. That will be well after the election. We intend to act, if we have to, before then. Have I your word?"

"That I will not betray your crazy plan?"

"And that you will keep your father away from the Admiralty on the appointed day."

Nicholas tried to think coherently. He was, in effect, being asked to accept, and not to betray, a *coup d'etat*, even if the *coup* was intended to win men's minds rather than their bodies. Because he knew that if Yoshiye was telling the truth, and he could not doubt the word of his own cousin, the conspiracy did intend only a formal group suicide to remind the nation of the laws, and the obligations, of *bushido*. It was an absurd concept, viewed with any Western or Christian ideas of either logic or ethics, but it was entirely Japanese. Thus, he was being asked to acquiesce in his own cousin's suicide, because it would be an even greater crime against *bushido* to attempt to dissuade him. So, was *he* now accepting *bushido* as a way of life? But he had accepted that when he had become a *samurai*.

"Will you swear to me that you and your friends contemplate no assassinations, and no subversion of the legally elected government?"

"I have already done so."

"I wish you to do so again."

"Then I do. I swear, as did you, by the bones of our honourable grandfather. Will that satisfy you?"

Nicholas sighed. "It seems it must. I think you are wrong. Utterly wrong. I think you will bring great misfortune and misery to your family. And I also think you will bring great misery to Japan."

"But you will do as I ask?"

"It is that, or hand you over to the *Kempei-tai*." The secret police.

"And you will never do that, my honourable Cousin." Yoshiye smiled, and put his arm round Nicholas's shoulders. "When you command this beautiful ship into battle, remember that it was my friends and I who got you there."

*　　*　　*

131

What have I done, Nicholas wondered, when he was alone. I have agreed to the ritual suicide of my cousin. Because I cannot stop him without losing my honour. Never had he felt so alone. Up till now, indeed, he had welcomed his loneliness, deliberately cultivated it, because a close friend would necessarily have been too close to his secrets. Now he needed such a friend.

He was tempted to approach Takijo. But Takijo was no longer the intimate of their Eta-Jima days. Thus in the end he opted to let events take their course, relying on the possibility that Yoshiye and his friends would have more sensible reflections, or that the Navy party would lose the election – much as he wanted them to win.

He concentrated on preparing himself and his ship for sea. He saw nothing more of Yoshiye, and kept himself too busy to visit his father, even for Christmas. He could feel that the whole conversation had been nothing more than a nightmare. January passed, a cold January, with snow thick on the streets of Tokyo. The entire country became caught up in the vigorous, and at times violent electioneering, to the extent that what was happening in the rest of the world, the brutal elimination of the Brownshirt leadership in Germany on the occasion known as the Night of the Long Knives, or the amazing agreement reached between Britain and Germany by which Germany was to be allowed to re-build her fleet, providing only that it did not exceed one third of the British tonnage, and even the reportage of clashes between Italian and Abyssinian troops, seemed quite irrelevent.

In January, *Hatsuharu* was at last pronounced ready for sea. The crew reported, and Nicholas greeted his executive officer, Lieutenant Hamasada. Then the ship was ordered to proceed to Yokosuka, preparatory to beginning her shakedown cruise. Nicholas was concerned that he might be required to take his ship to sea immediately, but to his relief his orders indicated that he should not leave until after the election.

It was only two days after his arrival in Yokosuka that he received an invitation to a reception at the British Embassy.

*　　*　　*

132

Such invitations extended to Japanese naval officers by foreign embassies were not uncommon, although they were seldom offered to those under the rank of captain. Nicholas telephoned his father to ask whether he should accept. "There is no reason why you should not," Alexander said. "However, be circumspect about what you say. You've been invited because of your background, obviously."

"I understand, honourable Father," Nicholas said. "You think they may regard me as a soft touch for giving away information. But I have very little to give them, anyway."

"They may well be interested in *Hatsuharu*, since her refit," Alexander warned.

Nicholas felt rather like a sacrificial lamb as he entered the brilliantly lit embassy. But a lamb who knew what he was about, he reminded himself. There was a reception line, at which he was greeted by the Ambassador and his wife, with surprising warmth – they both spoke of his father and grandfather with some affection – and then handed over to the naval attache, Commander Richards, to be introduced to those of the other guests he did not already know.

Actually, most he had met on various other social occasions, and there were several other Japanese officers present, all senior to himself. There were also quite a few women, Japanese wives of the other officers, or guests from other embassies, and some members of the embassy staff itself. Standing somewhat apart from the others at the end of the room was a tall, willowy young woman, with soft yellow hair lying straight on her shoulders. "Linda Wells, may I present Commander Nicholas Barrett," Richards said. "Linda is a recent arrival in Tokyo," he explained. "She is our new decoding clerk. Play your cards right, Barrett, and she may let you into a secret." He grinned at them both, and left them.

Nicholas found himself attracted. Linda Wells had what could be described as a plain face; she had no very prominent features apart from a small nose and flat mouth, dominated by deep green eyes. But he couldn't doubt that she had a splendid figure beneath the red cocktail dress, and her smile was sufficiently enigmatic to be most interesting.

133

"I like you too, Commander," she remarked. "And I have the advantage."

He raised his eyebrow. "I know all about you," she pointed out.

"I'm flattered."

She gave a little shrug. "Goes with the job. People one should know, or know about, in Japan."

"And the famous renegade comes top of the list, is that it?"

"I don't know about renegade, any more. But obviously someone of English descent serving with the Imperial Japanese navy is of considerable interest."

"And not only to you, Miss Wells. I am half-American as well, at a first generation level, but I also have a good deal of Russian blood. Or did you know all of that?"

"Your background is fairly well covered, yes."

"Then you owe me one, Miss Wells."

"I'm sure it would bore you, Commander."

"I think I should be the judge of that. Dinner?"

Linda Wells' eyebrows arched in turn. "I had heard Japanese were the most polite of men, when they are not actually killing you."

"Is it impolite to ask a woman out to dinner? I think you now owe me two."

"You're a glutton for punishment, Commander. Don't you think it's at least forward to ask me out to dinner within ten minutes of our first meeting?"

"Ah, but you have just confessed that you have, in effect, known me for a very long time. Just about from childhood. I am merely trying to catch up."

She regarded him for several seconds, then smiled. "Then I shall be pleased to accept your invitation, Commander."

Nicholas found her the most fascinating woman he had ever met. This was at least partly because, in her Western-style clothes and demeanour, and her refusal to accept an inferior status, she was entirely different to any Japanese woman he had ever met, and most especially Christina. On their first date they caused some embarrassment by both instinctively attempting to enter the room first through a somewhat

134

narrow doorway. But he and the waiters were the ones embarrassed, not Linda.

They dated four times before he kissed her, and then he got the impression that she had been waiting for some time. "It is not something that happens very often, in Japan," he attempted to explain, as they sat in his car looking out at the waters of Tokyo *Wan*.

"Kissing?"

"No. Dating."

"I've read about it. You look the field over, say, I'll have that one, and if your dad can agree with her dad, the poor girl has had it."

"You'd be surprised," Nicholas said seriously. "How many Japanese marriages turn out very well. Most Japanese women would be appalled if they were to be given the freedom of you Westerners." Or violently abuse it, he thought, thinking of his stepmother.

"I suspect it's rather like someone who has never been taught to read refusing to learn, because she'd then be expected to turn the pages," Linda suggested.

"But you know how to turn the pages," he said, and kissed her again. "Linda . . ."

She shook her head. "No, Please don't ask."

"Not ever?"

"Not until we know each other a whole lot better."

He grinned. "I'll work on it. I'll take you out to a special dinner after the election."

She raised her eyebrows. "Are you involved in politics?"

"I'm an officer in the Navy. Of course I'm involved in politics. We are going to celebrate a naval victory."

In Japan it was necessary either to belong to the right, which was basically the Army, or the Liberals, the Minseito, which supported the Navy point of view. On the night of 20 February it became clear that the Minseito had gained an overwhelming victory. Nicholas had to go up to Tokyo to vote, as he was registered in that district, and was amused by the enthusiasm of the victorious crowds. He was cheered because he was wearing naval uniform. He was tempted to visit his uncle, to see if Yoshiye was there, but felt this might smack of crowing, nor did he wish to become involved in a political argument with his uncle. On the other hand, while the scenario Yoshiye had feared had come to pass, the vote in support of the Liberal regime had been so massive he felt that even Yoshiye would have to accept that he was hopelessly out of step with current Japanese thought.

He preferred to think of the coming date with Linda. Did he know what he was doing? But there was no doubt that Father would be happy about it, even if Christina would probably spit blood. But Christina's opinion didn't matter, and her weight would be removed from his shoulders. Now there would be a relief. Next morning he returned to the yard; *Hatsuharu* was nearly ready for sea. He found both the shipwrights and the cadre of officers and petty officers who had already reported for duty in a jubilant mood, which he felt increasingly able to join as the week slipped by and he heard nothing from his cousin. Clearly the hotheads had realised they would be flogging a dead horse in their hopes of persuading the people to revert to a policy of aggression.

His only disappointment was that Linda could not keep their date; she had gone down with influenza. "Give me a week," she asked.

"A week it shall be," he promised.

It was six days after the election when the yard superintendent told him, "One more month, Commander, and you may take your ship to sea."

"Now that is good news," Nicholas said.

"Now I must tell you that there has been a telephone message for you."

"Who from?"

"The caller did not state his name, honourable Commander. He said you would know it, on receipt of the message."

"And the message?"

"It is simply a number: twenty-six. Why, that is odd, honourable Commander: it is today's date."

For a moment Nicholas was unable to think, as a thousand

and one reflections galloped through his brain. Yoshiye had promised him more notice than this. And for it to happen now, when the government had just received the most conclusive vote of confidence in Japanese political history, was sheer desperation. But the more dangerous for that.

They had been speaking on the quarterdeck. Nicholas ran up the ladders to the bridge, where there was still a telephone link to the land, and had the operator connect him with his father's Tokyo house. "Hello? Hello? Who is that?"

"It is Christina, Nicholas. Why are you shouting like a madman?"

"I wish to speak with my father, honourable Mother."

"He is not here. He has gone to his office. He always goes early. Is there something wrong?"

"Something! Listen, honourable Mother, will you telephone him at the office and ask him to return home. *Tell* him to."

"Nicholas! Are you drunk?"

"I'm in deadly earnest, honourable Mother. Please do as I say. Listen, tell him Little Alexander has been taken ill. Tell him he must hurry. But get him out of his office."

"Nicholas . . ."

"Please," he shouted. "His life may be in danger. Please do as I ask." He hung up, buttoned his jacket. "I must go into Tokyo," he told Hamasada.

Ratings stood to attention as their commanding officer ran across the gangplank to the dock, his steward hurrying behind him, carrying his cap and sword. Nicholas threw them into the back of the car and gunned the engine. If he knew that Christina had a much better chance than himself of making Alexander return home, he still wanted to be there just in case she failed . . . whatever the consequences. He swung on to the main road, went through a red light, and immediately heard the howl of a siren behind him. Well, that was to the good: the more policemen he accumulated on his way to the Admiralty the better, just in case. In case of what? He simply didn't know what he expected to find. He glanced at his watch, while his left hand pressed the horn: it was twenty minutes to eleven. With luck he wouldn't find anything – save an angry father.

The car slid round corners, scattering pedestrians with its blaring horn, and once cannoned off a lamp post to leave a deep gash in its rear mudguard. But now Nicholas could see the Admiralty building. He braked in the drive, and showed his pass to the marine guardsman. "Have there been any visitors to the Admiralty yet this morning?" he asked.

"Why, yes, honourable Captain," the marine replied. "A group of Army officers, led by Major Barrett, arrived only ten minutes ago for a conference."

"Shit!" Nicholas growled, his fingers curling round the wheel. The conspirators were already inside the building. Doing what? According to Yoshiye, they would already be preparing themselves for *seppuku*. To go crashing in now might be to bring about the one thing he wanted to avoid, some kind of reaction on the part of the Admiralty staff. But just to sit here . . .

A motorcycle drew up beside him. "With respect, honourable Captain," said the policeman. "But you have violated every traffic regulation in Tokyo."

"Not enough," Nicholas snapped. He would have to go into the building, come what may. But he had to be prepared for any eventuality. "Have you got a weapon, constable?"

"Of course, honourable Captain," the policeman said, frowning as he reached for his book of tickets.

"Good. I will need you to come with me. You . . ." he turned to the guardsman. "What weapons do you have?"

"Weapons, honourable Captain?" The man looked astonished. Nicholas knew that even his rifle would be unloaded. But he could see past him into the guardroom, where a sergeant was sitting at the desk, and hanging from the hook behind him was a holster and cartridge belt. "Sergeant!" he shouted.

"Honourable Captain!" The sergeant got up and saluted.

"Are there bullets in that gun?"

"Why, yes, honourable Captain. It is fully loaded."

"Give it to me. Together with the belt."

"Sir?"

"That is an order, Sergeant."

The sergeant hesitated, glanced at the private, then took down the belt and handed it to Nicholas.

138

"I have written out these tickets, honourable Captain," the policeman was saying. "If you will kindly . . ."

"Yes, give them to me." Nicholas crammed them into his pocket, unclipped the holster, took out a nine-shot Luger automatic pistol and checked the magazine. "Now, Sergeant, I want you to turn out the entire guard, and make sure that they are armed and their weapons are loaded. Then I wish you to enter the Admiralty and arrest every officer wearing an army uniform. Understood?"

"Yes, honourable Commander," the sergeant said, although he looked totally mystified – and even more unhappy.

"Then get to it. You . . ." he turned to the policeman. "Come with me."

"Me, honourable Commander? I cannot enter the Admiralty compound without a pass."

"I have given you an order, Constable," Nicholas told him.

The policeman looked as if he would have protested further, when suddenly there came a flurry of shots from inside the building itself. "God Almighty!" Nicholas shouted, and gunned his engine. Behind him he heard the wail of the siren. Maybe that would distract them from whatever they were doing.

He braked at the front entrance, ran up the stairs, and bumped into the marine doorman. "Honourable Commander," the man panted. "There have been shots . . ."

Nicholas pushed him aside, ran into the hallway beyond the swinging glass doors, and looked left and right. On this floor there were only clerks, but all the doors to the various filing rooms were opening, and people were looking out, asking anxious questions. There was another burst of firing from upstairs. Nicholas took the steps three at a time. Arriving on the first landing, he was faced by a man wearing the uniform of an army lieutenant, and carrying a revolver. "Stop there," the lieutenant said. "And return downstairs. No one is allowed past this point."

"Drop your weapon, and raise your hands," Nicholas snapped. "I am placing you under arrest." The lieutenant raised his revolver instead, and Nicholas shot him. Blood spurted from the khaki tunic, and a look of utter surprise

139

crossed the young man's face as he slumped to the floor, while Nicholas stared at him for a moment – he had never shot anyone before in his life, but the reaction had been instantaneous.

Now there was pandemonium from all around him. Someone stepped out of an office and fired at him, but missed, because he was already on the next flight of stairs; he was interested only in his father's office. This flight had a right-angle bend, and he checked there, listening to the bark of the policeman's gun from behind him, and to more wailing of sirens in the distance. The next landing appeared deserted, but as he ran up to it another army officer appeared. This time Nicholas did not even challenge him. He fired immediately, three times, and the man came tumbling down. Nicholas jumped over him, gained the corridor, sent a shot winging in the direction of a door which opened towards him, and then himself pulled open the door to Alexander Barrett's office. He leapt in, gazed in horror at his father, lying on his side on the floor, still half-sitting in his overturned swivel chair; from his shoulders a trail of blood drifted towards the wall. "Christ," Nicholas said. "Oh, Christ!"

He felt something hard jab into his back. "Drop your weapon," a voice commanded.

Nicholas hesitated, then obeyed. The gun barrel jerked against him, and he moved away. He turned, to see a man he did not know, but that he was responsible for the murder of his father could not be doubted. "Commander Barrett," the man said contemptuously, and raised his revolver, but hesitated in turn as the door burst open and Yoshiye ran into the room.

"I was told you were here," he snapped at his cousin. "Why on earth . . ." he looked past Nicholas at the body of Alexander Barrett. "You shot him?" he gasped, turning to the captain. "You shot my uncle? In the name of the gods . . ."

"In the name of the Army," the officer said.

"But . . ." Yoshiye looked at his uncle again, his face betraying utter horror. Then he looked at Nicholas. "You were to keep him away."

"And you swore to me that there would be no killing," Nicholas retorted.

"I . . . there was not to be. I have tried to stop it." Yoshiye turned to the officer. "You have dishonoured me. You have dishonoured us all!"

"And you are a fool, *honourable* Major," the officer sneered. "Did you not realise that it was our purpose to rid Japan of this whole liberal blight that lies across our country like the winter snow? You were always a fool. Now I will complete the job."

The gun exploded before Nicholas knew what was happening. He was aware of a temendous jolt in his chest and of turning right round, before finding himself on his hands and knees beside his father. Amazingly, he heard no sound for several seconds. He tasted blood, and seemed to be on some kind of a roller-coaster, from which he now fell, hitting the floor with a crash. The fall seemed to restore his hearing. Dimly he heard other shots, and the heavy thud as of a body hitting the floor. Then Yoshiye was kneeling beside him. "Nicholas," he was saying. "Oh, Nicholas . . . listen, I will get help."

Nicholas could only gasp for breath, and stare in horror as the figure of his father moved.

"Uncle?" Yoshiye whispered. "Uncle? You are alive?"

"You are dishonoured," Alexander Barrett said, blood dribbling from his lips as he spoke. "In the name of your illustrious ancestor, I curse you from here to eternity, Barrett Yoshiye. You are *dishonoured*, and with you, the Army." Then his head drooped as he died.

"I swear," Yoshiye said. "I swear . . . I am indeed a fool."

The office door swung open, and Nicholas heard the gasp as the new arrival took in the charnel-house that the office had become. But he had even more important things on his mind. "The building is surrounded, honourable Major," the man said. "And we have accomplished our purpose. We must go to the balcony and commit *seppuku*. Will you not lead us?"

Yoshiye gazed at him, then looked down at his cousin. "Help will soon be here," he promised. "I will fetch it for you

141

myself." Slowly and carefully he lowered Nicholas's head to the floor, and stood up.

"We must hurry," the man said.

"I am not coming with you," Yoshiye said. "I am going downstairs, to surrender, and fetch a doctor."

"Surender?" The man's tone was incredulous. "But you will be dishonoured, honourable Major. You will be stripped of your rank. You will be cashiered. You will be condemned to death. And you will die in shame."

"Yes," Barrett Yoshiye said. "As you have forced me to live in shame, honourable Captain. Can I die differently?" He walked through the door.

CHAPTER 6

Meridian

Pain. Nothing but pain. Pain whenever Nicholas breathed, pain whenever he moved. And pain whenever he thought. And weakness. Of the mind as much as of the body. Nothing was distinct any more. He had no idea where he was, only with difficulty making out faces through a thick haze. Christina, weeping. Charlotte, weeping. Mori, looking suitably grave. Little Alexander, peering at him. But not his father. Never his father again.

Gradually his surroundings began to swing into focus, and the pain subsided. Only the weakness remained. But now he could see, as well. "Oh, my darling," Christina said. "Oh, my darling!"

Christina! But there was an insuperable problem, at least until he was strong enough to face it.

Two doctors came in; they conferred, and then nurses unbandaged his chest. He tried to look down, but they were careful not to let him. "You were very fortunate," one of the doctors told him. "The bullet only nicked a lung, and then exited to the right, through the shoulder." He smiled. "The shoulder is the most serious, now."

Nicholas wished he hadn't said that, because now he was aware of where most of the pain was coming from. "Will I lose the arm?" he asked. He was right-handed.

"No, no. But it will take time. A very long time. As will the lung. You must be patient. I repeat, you were very fortunate. It seems that your cousin shot Captain Tarawa at the same moment as the captain shot you, and this threw the captain's aim off."

"My cousin," Nicholas said. "Tell me of my cousin."

The doctor's face clouded. "It is not my place, honourable Commander, to speak of your cousin." He left the room.

"Tell me what happened," Nicolas begged Christina, when they were left alone.

"You must rest," she said. "Excitement is the worst possible thing for you."

"And do you not think I will be excited, and stay excited, until I know what has happened?"

She sighed. "It was just terrible," she said. "There were several groups, and they took over nearly all of the government buildings. But Nicholas . . . they had planned wholesale assassinations from the start. They even killed Viscount Saito."

"Saito? What of the Prime Minister?"

"Oh, they knew Okada was a nonentity. It was Saito who mattered. And Takahashi, the Finance Minister, and . . . oh, the list is endless."

"And Father."

"And your father, yes."

"Was he not also your husband, honourable Stepmother?"

Her eyes were clouded. "He died honourably."

"And you have no regrets."

Christina raised her head. "No wife can regret the honourable death of her husband. It is the future to which we must look. Our future."

"*Our* future," he said bitterly. "The most dishonourable future in Japan."

"You will feel differently when you feel better," Christina said, complacently.

It was even possible she was right; he was too exhausted to confront her. And there was so much to consider. "If Saito is dead," he said. "What has happened to the government?"

"In that respect, the conspirators achieved their aims," she said. "Okada has resigned, the country has been placed under martial law, and the Army have taken over. The new Prime Minister is Hirota. He is retaining charge of the Foreign Office."

144

Hirota Koki, Nicholas thought: the ultimate tool of the generals. "And what of the conspirators?" he asked.

"Most of them committed *seppuku* on the spot," Christina said. "On the balconies of the various buildings, in front of all the crowds, exhorting the people to remember them and to be ready to do the same, for the honour of Japan. They are being spoken of as heroes. Martyrs."

Which was what they had intended. "What of Yoshiye?"

Christina's lip curled. "He refused *seppuku*. You know that. They tried twice. When he didn't do it on the day, and allowed himself to be arrested by the police, he was given his swords and left in a cell by himself. But when they returned the next morning, he still had not done it. So they handed him over to the *Kempei-tai* for interrogation."

"The *Kempei-tai*? My God! What happened to him?"

"I do not know. Save that he is to be placed on trial, together with the other survivors; some of them were too badly wounded to commit *seppuku*. He has brought disgrace upon the entire family. He deserves to be beheaded. He probably will be beheaded."

Nicholas sighed. She was so vehement in her hatred of a young man who had been her friend. "How has Uncle Takamori taken it?"

"How did you expect him to take it. He and his wife have killed themselves."

Nicholas's head turned, sharply, and a surge of pain shot through his chest. But what else could he have expected?

The nurse came in. "The honourable Commander must rest now, honourable Lady."

Christina got up, stood above the bed, looking down at her stepson. "I will come again tomorrow."

"Thank you," Nicholas said.

Christina made as if to leave, then checked. "There is someone asking to see you, a young woman," she said, her voice again loaded with contempt. "A young *Englishwoman*. A secretary at the Embassy. Her name is Linda Wells. Do you know of such a person?"

"Yes," Nicholas said. "We have met."

"And now she wishes to visit you in hospital? I have told the staff here that it is quite impossible."

145

"I would like to see her."

"Why?"

"Because I wish it, honourable Stepmother."

Christina returned to the bedside. "You know this woman?"

"I have said, we have met."

"Ha!" Christina commented. "You mean she is your mistress."

"I would like to see her," Nicholas said again.

"I will not permit it."

"If you do not permit it," Nicholas said, as evenly as he could. "I swear by the bones of my father and my grandfather that I shall never enter your house again, honourable Stepmother."

Linda came the next morning. She looked highly nervous, which would have been understandable in any event, given the etiquette of a Japanese naval hospital. "Nicky," she said, sitting beside the bed. "Are you really going to be all right?"

"So I'm told." He let his hand lie on the covers, and she held it, lightly but possessively.

"That stepmother of yours is a bit of a dragon," she said. "I haven't spoken with her, but it seems she didn't want me to come."

"She's pretty upset."

"Of course. I understand that. What a terrible tragedy. It was in all the papers, worldwide, apparently. I don't think what happened was properly understood in the West. You know, the whole idea is foreign to our way of thinking. They're calling it a *coup d'etat* that failed. But it was never meant to be a *coup d'etat*, was it?"

"No," he agreed.

"It's all so . . ." she gave a little shiver. "Primitive? Or am I being intolerably smug?"

"You're not being smug. But maybe primitive is the wrong word. It has to do with ideals that have become submerged in the west beneath the worship of the great god Mammon."

"You admire those men?"

Nicholas considered. "Yes, I think I do. I do not agree with what they did. If their actions turn Japan towards aggression, I will disagree with them even more. But I think anyone who has the courage to die for his ideals must be admired."

"Where does that leave your cousin? You heard about his father and mother?"

Nicholas nodded. "I think my cousin is probably the most courageous of the lot. He believed there was to be no bloodshed. When there was, when he realised that my father had been killed, he felt that for him to commit *seppuku* would have *been* the act of a coward."

"You know," Linda said. "I have studied Japan and the Japanese for eight years now, and I still do not understand your ethos. I suppose I never will."

"Then do not try. Will you come to see me again?"

"Would you like me to?"

"Very much."

She gave a quick smile. "What about Stepmama?"

"You leave Stepmama to me," he said. In every possible way, he reflected, as she kissed him goodbye.

Three days later, Vice-Admiral Yamamoto was announced. "Well, Nicholas *san*," he remarked as he entered the room. "What does it feel like to be a hero?"

"Am I a hero, honourable Admiral? What did I accomplish? Am I not as guilty as anyone?"

Yamamoto frowned. "Listen to me carefully. Your stepmother came to me with some story about how you attempted to make her get your father to leave his office, minutes before the mutiny. I told her that she must be mistaken, and not to mention that to a soul." He held up his finger as Nicholas would have spoken. "I think I understand. Barrett Yoshiye was your cousin. You could not betray him, even if you had some idea of what he and his colleagues were intending. But you could not let your father die, and you determined, however late, that the mutiny could not be allowed to proceed. I have no doubt that you had no idea of the scale on which this insurrection was planned. So you nearly got yourself killed attempting to protect your father. That is all that need be said about the matter. That you happened to be arriving at the Admiralty on the morning of 26 February, and

147

heard shots coming from the building, and leapt into quite remarkable action, is at once a coincidence and an event greatly redounding to your credit. Remember that."

"We will never make that story stick, honourable Admiral. I had already summoned the guard before the first shots were fired. I am surprised that I also have not been arrested."

Yamamoto smiled. "There was some talk about that, to be sure. But I would brook no argument from the *Kempei-tai*. You have come through the whole affair with exemplary honour, in the eyes of the nation. You are a hero, while your cousin is disgraced. These things are well understood. Now it is your duty to get well again as quickly as possible. The Navy has need of you. I have need of you."

"I would like to see my cousin, honourable Admiral," Nicholas said.

Yamamoto's smile changed into a frown. "Why? He betrayed you. He is responsible for the death of your father. You should hate him."

"He did not intend my father to die, honourable Admiral. And he saved my life. And he is my cousin, my last remaining blood relative, save for my sister. I would like to see him."

"Then you will have to get well even quicker. He will never be allowed to come here. But if you can leave the hospital before he is executed . . ."

"Which will be when, honourable Admiral?"

"Oh, not for some time. He has not even been tried yet, much less convicted. There is time. I will see what I can arrange." He stood up. "But remember, his is the disgrace, for all eternity. He broke the laws of *bushido*, in every way. He is the one who has lost his honour."

It was May before Nicholas was allowed to leave the hospital, and then only into Christina's care. Charlotte came with her stepmother to escort him home. By then much of the furore over the attempted *coup* had died down, but the new regime was still firmly in control of the country, and obviously intended to remain that way: the trials of those officers unable or unwilling to commit *seppuku* were just beginning. Nicholas had wished to give evidence, but his doctors ruled against it. Both Christina and Charlotte agreed with them.

148

"You were shot through the chest," Christina reminded him. "You still cannot breathe properly, and the slightest exertion leaves you exhausted. Do you have any idea how lucky you are to be *alive*? Half-an-hour in court could start the haemorrhaging again."

She was the most solicitous of nurses, and never once raised the matter of their relationship, past, present or future, for which he was grateful. Not that he doubted for a moment that she had plans for that future; she too was waiting for him to regain his strength, and she brought little Alexander to play at his feet every day. But he also was content to wait, even if ideas had been forming in his mind over the weeks in his bed: Linda had been to see him several times.

He made a deposition, which he was promised would be read to the judges. "It can, of course, have no effect on the verdict," Yamamoto told him on one of his weekly visits. He was a regular caller, and so solicitous that Nicholas could not help but wonder if he was contemplating adopting the son of his great friend. This would be in keeping with Japanese practice, as Yamamoto had himself been adopted. It was a heady thought; to be adopted by the most brilliant of Japanese naval officers would ensure his own future, and it would also remove him from the looming confrontation with his stepmother.

But it would also mean that he would have to live his life to an impossibly high standard, which might rule out Linda altogether. Now the Admiral added, "Your cousin has confessed to treason. But I have arranged for you to be able to see him."

Nicholas went to the prison on 30 June. Christina accompanied him to drive the car, as he was still very weak and his right arm remained useless. But she waited in an antechamber while he was taken into a private room, where Yoshiye was brought to him. Yoshiye bowed as he came through the door, flanked by guards. "Honourable Cousin! It deeply grieves me to see you still so weak. I would not have had it so. But I am told you will make a full recovery."

"Yes," Nicholas said, studying him. Yoshiye had been interrogated by the *Kempei-tai*, whose methods were only

149

ever discussed in whispers: no one knew for sure what happened in those cells, only that the depths of inhumanity were reached as a norm. So, had Yoshiye's head been bound in a slowly tightening steel wire? There was no evidence of it. Then had his testicles been squeezed between the jaws of a pair of pliers? He moved freely enough, but then, he had had time to recover. "Why did you lie to me?" Nicholas asked.

"I never lied to you."

"You told me I would receive forewarning of your *coup*," Nicholas said. "Your message reached my ship half-an-hour before you entered the Admiralty."

Yoshiye nodded. "I have been told this. I gave the message to my secretary the day before, to telephone you. He did not do so until he felt sure it would be too late for you to intervene. He betrayed me."

"You also told me there was no bloodshed intended. How can a cousin lie to a cousin?" Nicholas asked again. "A *samurai* lie to a *samurai*?"

Yoshiye sat down before the table. "I did not lie to you, Nicholas. What I told you was what I understood was going to happen. What I had organised. What I commanded. It was to be a protest, nothing more. I did not realise that there were others planning more, behind my back." He shrugged. "Yet in many ways it *was* nothing more than a protest. None of my people attempted to seize power. I did not lie about that."

"But they committed wholesale murder."

"Of men who were not fit to live," Yoshiye insisted.

"My father?"

"I would have saved his life, had I known what was intended," Yoshiye said.

"But you think he also deserved to die."

"Since you press me, yes, I think he deserved to die. He has consistently opposed every plan for increasing the greatness of Japan, and supported every plan to perpetuate our inferiority to the Western Powers."

"You are a fool," Nicholas said. "Whatever his personal feelings, my father of all men in Japan would have done his duty, to the Emperor, regardless of what was involved. Even if it involved war with all the world. Do you suppose you can replace him?"

150

Yoshiye sighed. "It is not my province. It has all been a great catastrophe, and now my mother and father are also dead." He stood up. "You have paid me much honour in coming to see me, honourable Cousin. To everyone else in Japan I am a traitor and a coward. There is no man in all the history of our nation as dishonoured as I."

"You saved my life," Nicholas said, also rising.

"That was read out in court," Yoshiye said. "And I am grateful for your act of gratitude."

"When are you to die?"

"Next week."

"You are told so far in advance?"

"Perhaps they think it is an additional punishment. But it is good to know, so far in advance, do you not think? I am not a coward, you know, Nicholas, no matter what they say of me."

"I never supposed you were." Nicholas went round the table.

"It is not permitted to touch the prisoner," one of the guards said.

"Then arrest me," Nicholas told him, and embraced his cousin. "Would you like me to be present?"

"No, thank you," Yoshiye said.

Nicholas sighed. "To know the future," he said. "Oh, to know the future."

Yoshiye smiled. "I think we are fortunate not to have to bear that cross as well, Nicholas. Tell me one thing: do you forgive me for what happened? For the death of your father?"

"I forgive you for the death of my father, because I know you did not intend it."

"Then there is nothing more to be said."

"Yes, there is," Nicholas said. "Do you believe in your course, the course of the Army? Do you believe it is the right course for Japan?"

"Naturally," Yoshiye said.

"And do you know that you have probably achieved your objective? That there is now a military government in Japan?"

151

"Yes."

"Then can you understand that I am against their principles? That I believe they will lead to the destruction of the country?"

"I understand that you are against our principles, Nicholas. Only time will tell which of us is right. And I . . ." he smiled again. "I will not be there to share in either the triumph or the defeat. But I would like to be sure that *you* understand that I have only ever had the glory of Japan, and of our name, at heart."

"I understand that," Nicholas said.

"Then I will say, the gods bless you, and keep you, in the great times that lie ahead." Another quick smile. "They will be tumultuous. My only regret is that I shall not be able to stand at your side when the bullets begin to fly." He bowed, and turned, and left the room.

"And they call him a coward," Nicholas said bitterly, sitting in the garden watching Little Alexander play, while Christina poured tea.

"He killed my husband and your father," Christina said. "He deserves to die."

"Will you answer me one question, honestly, honourable Stepmother?"

"Certainly."

"Do you regret my father's death?"

Christina made a moue. "In view of the great discrepancy in our ages, I have long known it was something with which I would have to come to terms, one day."

"You never loved him."

"That kind of love is a Western ideal. I respected him, and I gave him the use of my body. That is all I was required to do."

"How can you say you respected him?"

She studied him for several seconds. "I am a woman with an appetite for sex," she said at last.

"Which you satisfy with whoever is available."

"I think you mean to quarrel with me, Nicholas. But I do not wish to quarrel with you. You are my son. I must ask you to behave like my son."

152

"That I will do, honourable Stepmother. But nothing more."

"Have I asked for anything more? There are some messages for you. One is from that Englishwoman, inviting you to a party at the Embassy. I have refused on your behalf."

"You have done what?"

"You are not well enough to attend a party. Nor are you strong enough to have sex. Do not bother to look surprised; do you not suppose I know this woman is your mistress?"

Nicholas bit his lip. "The other message," Christina went on, "is from Vice-Admiral Yamamoto. He wishes to see you, in his office, tomorrow. I have said that you will be there."

"But I am not strong enough to go to a party, or to have sex."

Christina smiled.

"Come in, Commander Barrett, come in." Yamamoto Isoroku rose from behind his desk, and gave a suitably short bow in response to Nicholas's deep one. "It is good to see you in uniform again, although I had not expected it so soon. You cannot be ready for duty again, already?"

"I believe I am, honourable Admiral. My doctors are talking of months, yet. Months!"

Yamamoto gestured him to a chair. "Can you use your arm?"

"Not yet, fully. But surely it is no longer part of a naval officer's duty to lead boarding parties, sword in hand?"

"And your lung?"

Nicholas shrugged. "My chest aches, and sometimes I have difficulty breathing. But . . ."

"You are also far too pale and thin. The doctors have spoken with me also, or rather, I have spoken with them. As you say, they recommend at least six months more of convalescence. Then you will be fit again, at least for light duties. That is the Barrett Nicholas I wish."

"Six months, honourable Admiral?"

"It is not so long a time. Do you know what I recommend for you? That you take that so beautiful mistress of yours for a long holiday. Go down to Kyushu, and soak up the sun, and eat lots of rice, and drink lots of *sake*, and return to

153

me, next year, with some weight on those shoulders, ready for work."

Nicholas gulped; did all the world know about Linda? She certainly did not realise that. And as for whether she would be willing to make a public display of their relationship by going away with him . . . they did not even *have* a relationship as yet.

"There is something else that I strongly recommend, Commander Barrett."

"Honourable Admiral?"

"That you marry the girl."

"Marry her?"

"Is that not what you wish to do?"

"Well, of course, honourable Admiral. But . . ."

"There have been those, senior in your family, who might have objected? But Nicholas, there is no longer anyone who can gainsay you. Are you not the head of your family, now?"

"Good heavens," Nicholas remarked. It had not occurred to him before. But, for all her attempt at dominance, it was he, and not Christina, who was indeed the head of the family. Or soon would be, as soon as Yoshiye died.

Yamamoto seemed able to read his thoughts. "It is truly said that out of evil cometh good. Not always a commensurate amount of good, to be sure. But we are thumbing our noses at the gods, and at the fates they control, if we do not attempt to extricate at least *some* good out of every misfortune that overtakes us. I recommend that you follow that line of thought. There is no need – indeed, I doubt that it would be appropriate at this time – for you to have a great wedding. But both you and Miss Wells are Christian, are you not? You can therefore hold a small private ceremony to satisfy the dictates of your religion, and it can still be registered as a legal marriage."

"Why, honourable Admiral, I am quite overwhelmed by your interest. I do not know what to say, except thank you. I shall most assuredly follow your advice. Always supposing the lady will say yes."

"She will, of course, have to give her up job at the British Embassy, and indeed, become a Japanese citizen." Nicholas

154

waited, and Yamamoto smiled. "It is not considered correct for a naval officer who will soon be in your position, to be very close friends with a member of the staff of a foreign embassy, regardless of their sex."

"I understand, honourable Admiral. But . . . my position?"

"Do you think the young lady will agree?"

"I . . . if she accepts my invitation to Kyush, honourable Admiral, I think she will agree."

"Then that is settled. After which, it will be necessary for you to return to your career. There is much to be done."

"It is my career that I wish to discuss, honourable Admiral," Nicholas said. "That is, if I still have a career. Is not my family disgraced?"

"Your family is honoured, Commander Barrett, because you belong to it. Only your cousin is disgraced. You should always remember this. I wish to hear no more talk of disgrace. You have a great future in front of you, one that I have mapped out with care. You are no doubt aware that your father and I were working together?"

"I knew this, honourable Admiral. My father was proud to be your associate."

"He was, of course, very senior to you. However, I discern in you the same qualities that he possessed, and I would make use of them, if I can. You understand that in view of your wound, and the lengthy convalescence that is involved, the command of *Hatsuharu* has had to be given elsewhere."

"I understand this, honourable Admiral."

"And this saddens you. Do not let it. There will be other commands. I give you my word on this. However, until you are fully recovered, and an appropriate ship is available, I would like you to work with me, here at the Admiralty. Do not look so despondent. You will be my flag-commander. At the moment, it is a desk job. But soon enough our activities will be broadened. And you will be gaining seniority all the time, for that command I have promised you. Nor should you make the mistake of assuming that a desk job, in this age, need not be even more interesting than commanding a ship at sea. Your father and I were working on many projects. I will show you one of them. You understand, Barrett *san*,

155

that not a word of what I am about to say to you, much less what I am about to show you, must ever leave this room. I am particularly referring to your wife." He raised his finger as Nicholas would have protested. "Whenever she becomes your wife. Far less, before she becomes your wife. You see, I am placing a great trust in you, because of the immense affection and respect I felt for your father. You will not fail me in this."

Nicholas understood. "I will not fail you, honourable Admiral."

"I did not suppose you would." Yamamoto got up, went to a filing cabinet in the corner, and from one of the drawers took a roll of stiff paper, which he proceeded to spread on his desk, holding the edges down with various paperweights and inkwells. When the plan was fully extended, he looked up. "What do you think of her?"

Nicholas stood beside him, and looked at a sketch of quite the most beautiful warship he had ever seen, with magnificent flared bows, a fighting top as high as an apartment building, and three obviously massive gun turrets. There were no scales shown, so it was impossible to estimate her actual size – but he was certainly looking at a very large battleship indeed. "This is only an artist's impression, of course," Yamamoto explained. "The plans are still on the drawing board, being worked over, and she is still being costed – I have not yet had even the design presented to the Diet. But they know what I have in mind, and they will undoubtedly be prepared to fund it. Or rather, them. I would like to have a squadron of these ships."

"She is certainly a lovely looking vessel," Nicholas ventured.

"She will be the greatest fighting ship in the world." Yamamoto sat down again. "She will displace seventy thousand tons, deep loaded."

"Seventy . . ." Nicholas sat down again himself, without meaning to. "But that is double the Treaty limit."

"The Treaty is expired, Barrett *san*. And we no longer belong to the League of Nations. Thus we are no longer going to be bound by any restrictions whatsoever. Let the British and the Americans rack their brains about how to

156

fit sixteen-inch guns and adequate armour into thirty-five thousand tons. Let the Americans worry about whether or not they can afford to widen and deepen the Panama Canal. We are going to *do*, and when it is done, we shall possess a fleet which no one will dare oppose. Do you see those guns? They will be eighteen-inch. Eighteen-inch! Do you realise that each gun will hurl a shell of more than three thousand pounds in weight? As they can all fire to either side, that means a broadside of twenty-seven thousand pounds. More than two tons of armour-piercing exploding shells!"

Nicholas scratched his head. He had never supposed he would hear the normally impassive Yamamoto sound so enthusiastic. But the idea of any vessel being hit by two tons of flying high explosive, or indeed, even being near-missed by such a colossal discharge, was mind-boggling. "She will have twelve modern boilers, Nicholas, developing one hundred and fifty thousand shaft horsepower. That will give twenty-seven knots. These ships will not only be approximately double the size of *Nelson* and *Rodney*, and far more powerful, they will be four knots faster. And yet they will be the best-protected ships in the world as well. Those turrets will have twenty-five inches of steel around them; the bridge will have nineteen inches; the hull will have sixteen and the deck, the *deck*, Nicholas, will have nine inches of steel. Aerial bombs will merely bounce off that. They are a dream. They have been one of my dreams, ever since I was in the design office myself, when such things could only *be* dreamed of. But now I am going to make my dreams come true. I am going to command this ship, Nicholas, as Commander-in-Chief of the Imperial Navy. I have been promised this, by our new masters. And you will stand at my side. I hope that prospect pleases you."

It was an overwhelming thought. The design of the new battleship still lay on the desk, but in Nicholas's imagination he was already standing on its bridge. She would be virtually unsinkable. No other ship, or even combination of ships, would be able to fight her. And if there *were* ever to be a squadron of such ships . . . But Yamamoto's last words had taken him by surprise. He needed to select his reply with care. "But with the government in the hands of the

Army, honourable Admiral, will the necessary funds be voted?"

"I have said they will. As I have also said, out of evil can come good."

"You mean you privately approve of what was done? Of the murder of my father?" Nicholas was aghast.

"Nothing can excuse the murder of your father. Or of Viscount Saito, or any of the other men who died. But as regards the principle of the matter, it cannot be denied that the nation certainly needed to be reminded of who and what we are," Yamamoto said evenly. "I do not hold with assassination. It has always seemed to me to be the ultimate in cowardice, to surprise a man with the intent of taking his life. But those officers at least had the courage then to take their own lives. Most of them."

"And are now considered martyrs," Nicholas said bitterly. Yet he had expressed the same opinion to Linda.

"Every nation needs a few martyrs, now and then," Yamamoto reminded him. "Your father is no less a martyr."

"And so now the Army is in control of our destiny," Nicholas said. "Utterly and completely. Do you not regard this as a grave development, honourable Admiral?"

"That remains to be seen. They are proceeding with suitable caution at the moment. And at least, with the Army in command, I am going to be allowed to create the kind of Navy Japan needs. This kind of navy." He tapped the plan. "The most powerful in the world. That can be no bad thing."

"And are we going to fight the rest of the world, honourable Admiral? When we have created this navy?"

Yamamoto sighed. "You are too eager to adopt an apocalyptic view of the situation, Nicholas. So was your father. I cannot help but believe it is a result of this Christianity you espouse. Having the greatest fleet in the world does not mean we wish to destroy every other fleet: it means every other fleet in the world will have to think twice about fighting *us*. That is the important factor. As for being isolated against the rest of the world, that is changing, most rapidly. This too, is confidential, but if it will reassure you, we are about to sign a treaty of friendship and alliance with Germany."

Nicholas frowned. "With Germany? With respect, honourable Admiral, can Germany possibly be of any assistance to us?"

"You have not kept up with recent political events, Nicholas. You still think of Germany as a defeated nation. Well, perhaps she is. But under her new government, under the leadership of Adolf Hitler, she is determined to regain her former Great Power status, and she is doing it. She is now rearming at great pace, and she is building a new navy, as well. No one is objecting. The British have even given this new navy their blessing. And they are seeking to borrow our expertise, in battleships and aircraft-carriers." He smiled. "We shall not, of course, let them into *this* secret." Once again he tapped the drawing.

"But you see, Nicholas, it is as I have always felt, that we have but needed to be patient, for the circumstances of which we have always dreamed to fall into our lap. There are cracks appearing to that monument of hypocrisy, the apparent unity of the Western powers, which has been so dismissive of our ambitions. Our necessities, indeed. Italy has become engaged in a wild African adventure, and is herself now an outcast from the League of Nations. Spain is on the verge of civil war. And Germany foresees that the real enemy of the future is international Communism. Well, so do we. That is the official reason for our coming pact with Hitler. However, in the short term, the Army still considers China to be our prime enemy and therefore our prime target. Your father was, amongst other things, my political adviser, and did not agree with this. I believe he was right. The Army is driven by basic economics: we need markets for our goods and only China can provide such markets at this time. We in the Navy are driven by basic logistics, which indicate that Japan can never be a great power in this modern world without adequate supplies of oil and rubber, tin and aluminium. A war which does not have the obtaining of these basic necessities as its objective is a nonsense; it will merely consume such stocks of essential material as we possess. However, this is a matter which will be debated, and we must hope that our point of view will prevail. The importance of our new relationship with Germany is that we are no longer isolated, and that no one at this moment is in a position to point a censorious finger at us, except the Americans, of course, and they have been doing that for years – without much effect.

"Believe me, Nicholas, I am as much against mad adventures as your father was. But I wish to see Japan as strong and respected as she should be. I will do everything in my power to accomplish that, and I expect my officers to share my point of view. I know that you do. Now go and take that holiday. And marry that girl. And come back to me, ready for work."

Nicholas used a telephone in the Admiralty to call the British Embassy. He felt almost intoxicated. Yamamoto had that effect on men, he knew, but there was more. It was almost as if he had been reborn, suddenly made conscious of his powers. The life that lay ahead was his to grasp, and there was nothing he need fear. Least of all his stepmother.

He knew it should be wrong of him to feel so happy with the father he had so grievously betrayed recently dead, and while his cousin lay awaiting execution. But Yamamoto had put that in perspective as well. The past was the past. He could do nothing to help Yoshiye now. But he could do a great deal for himself. "Nicky?" Linda sounded surprised; he had had to give his name to the telephone clerk.

"I'd like to see you."

Almost he could see her frowning. "Your stepmother said you were't well enough to come to the party."

"I think she meant it would be inappropriate in the present circumstances."

"Oh. Yes. Of course, I understand. But you . . ."

"There is something I wish to discuss with you. Can we meet for lunch?"

She looked more attractive than ever in her white linen frock and smart hat, her neatly dressed hair. "You look very pleased with yourself," she remarked.

160

"I *am* very pleased with myself. Vice-Admiral Yamamoto has invited me to be his Flag-Commander."

"But that's brilliant," she cried. "You mean you're ready for duty again?"

"Not quite. I'll join Yamamoto when I return from my convalescent leave. I'm to go down to the Bungo coast. We have a house there."

"Oh," she said.

He brushed his *sake* cup against hers. "I . . . ah . . . wondered if you'd care to join me."

"At your family home?"

"Well, it isn't really, any longer. I mean, the servants are still there, running the place – it's a bit of a farm, you see – but . . . there won't be anyone else."

She raised her eyebrows. "Not even Stepmama?"

"Least of all Stepmama." He could feel the heat in his cheeks, and she could see it.

"That's quite a proposition," she remarked.

"There are so many things I wish to talk to you about," he confessed. "So many things I wish to ask you."

She considered him for several seconds. "There are some things that are better not asked, Nicky."

He grinned at her. "Then I'll just ask one: will you come?"

She toyed with her fork. "When?"

"Well, I was going down next week."

"For how long?"

"I have been given six weeks leave of absence."

"Obviously I can't take six weeks. I could take a week."

"Beggars can't be choosers."

"When? I mean, do you wish me at the beginning, or the end?"

"What a decision. I think I'd rather have you to look forward to, than look back upon."

Her eyes were sad. "Then, I shall be there in five weeks. You'll have to tell me how."

"I'll do better than that," he promised.

"Assistant to Admiral Yamamoto!" Christina was enthusiastic. "But that is splendid news. When is your posting?"

161

"When I return from Bungo."

"Of course. You must be fully fit. I will pack immediately."

"If you will excuse me, honourable Stepmother," Nicholas said. "I wish to go alone." Christina frowned at him. "I will get well more quickly, by myself," he said. "Besides, I wish to think. I have a great deal to think about."

She pointed. "You mean you are taking that English-woman with you."

"No, I am not taking Miss Wells with me, honourable Mother."

"Do you suppose you can lie to me?" Her eyes were blazing with jealous anger.

"I suppose I can do anything I wish, within the confines of my own house," Nicholas said, quietly.

"*Your* house?"

"Admiral Yamamoto has made me aware of many things, honourable Mother. He has reminded me that, sadly, when Yoshiye dies next week, I will be the very last Barrett, saving Alexander, of course, and that I will also be the head of the family."

"And you will then put me out on the street, is that it?"

"You are being hysterical, honourable Mother. Of course I will not put you out on the street. I would just beg you to understand the situation. I wish to be alone for a while. I wish to think. And I wish to regain my health, as rapidly as possible."

"And then you will return to me." Her voice was eager.

"Why, yes, honourable Stepmother. Then I will return to Tokyo," he said carefully.

Although he would very much have liked Linda to be with him from the beginning, Nicholas was in many ways happy to be on his own. He *was* anxious to regain his full strength, and he *did* need to think. With startling suddenness his life had taken on an entirely new dimension, and an entirely unexpected one, as well. Obviously, being the head of a family was far less important in 1936 than it had been even a generation earlier, and especially a family which

162

had virtually destroyed itself. Yet it was a position of great responsibility, and would become more so as Little Alexander grew up, and if he were to marry and have other children.

Christina remained the biggest problem, because of the terrible secret they shared. It was not something she was likely to shout to the world, except in *extremus*, but he knew he could not afford to quarrel with her. At the same time, as Yamamoto, ignorant as he was of the true facts, had pointed out, he couldn't let her dominate his life either. His business was to make sure she never got around to that. By confessing to Linda? Before, or after, they were married?

He did indeed have a great deal to think about. But part of the process was also just to think about himself, understand himself. It was not something he had ever done before; introspection had not been encouraged at Eta-Jima, and even less in the Imperial Navy. There was also the consideration that Japan was looking ahead to a confrontation with the Western powers. Should that disturb him? Both his father and his grandfather had earned distinction in war; but those wars had been skirmishes compared with prophesies of what might happen in the next war – if there ever was one. And war with Britain or America . . . however Japanese he might be by birth and upbringing he was half-British and half-American. And he was going to marry an Englishwoman.

The concept did not seem to worry Yamamoto. So why should it worry him?

Bungo was the pleasantest place on earth. Father had kept the farm going even after Grandmama's death, and Nicholas did not intend to change that arrangement. The servants of course knew of Barrett Alexander's death, and were suitably consoling, but they also made their new master very welcome. Equally, once they discovered that he wished to be left alone, they did not intrude. Nicholas spent long hours walking the beach, slowly and painfully at first, breath quickly coming in huge gasps, but gaining in strength all the time. After a fortnight he felt strong enough to enter the sea, and a week later he was jogging.

163

The scar on his chest remained ugly and slow to fade, but it was reassuring to feel the strength flowing back into his muscles. And all the while he was counting the days, until he drove the Panhard across to Shimonoseki to meet the train from Tokyo.

Linda looked nervous, and her kiss was tentative, as she glanced left and right at the other people on the platform. "I've never done this sort of thing before," she confessed.

He grinned at her. "I should hope not. But if you keep your gloves on, people will think we're married."

She gave him a quick glance as he settled her in the car, while a porter tucked her bags into the back.

"Is it a long drive?" she asked.

"We won't get there until tonight."

Soon she was lost in the beauty of the Kyushu scenery, as they skirted Mount Aso, driving across the huge outer crater. They lunched in Kumamoto before proceeding down to Fujibaka and Shibushi-*wan*. "You must hate having to live in Tokyo with this place always beckoning," Linda said.

"In the past it's always been associated with my parents and grandparents," he said. "I'm only just coming to terms with the fact that it's actually mine."

"Your stepmother isn't here, is she?" she asked, suddenly anxious.

"There's no one here, save the staff."

"*They'll* know we're not married."

He squeezed her hand. "They are absolutely faithful to their master, who now happens to be me."

She exclaimed in delight again when she saw the water and the house. "It's so un-Japanese!"

"Grandpa built it to his own design." He introduced her to Sushi, who had moved down here soon after Alexander's marriage, and the other servants. It was just on dusk, and the lanterns were lit. "No electricity down here," he explained. "So we tend to live a dawn to dusk existence."

"I think that sounds just marvellous," she said.

Supper was waiting for them, and they lingered over their

sake and green tea, listening to the mutter of the rollers on the beach.

"Can there be a more heavenly spot on earth?" she asked.

"I'm so pleased you like it. And guess what? There's even a four-poster bed. That was Grandma's idea. She never did get on with sleeping on the floor."

"I wish I'd met your grandparents. I've heard so much about them. Do you miss them very much?" She frowned at his expression. "I'm sorry, that was tactless, in all the circumstances."

"Don't be sorry. Yes, I miss them. Although I think I was always rather afraid of them. But it was long ago. So was Mother. One day Father will be long ago as well. Now, I'm head of the family. That's taking a bit of getting used to."

"What exactly does being head of the family mean?"

He smiled. "Just that everyone has to do what I tell them to."

"What an awesome power. Does that include your step-mother?"

"Of course. She isn't too happy with the idea, but she'll get used to it. It also means that I don't have to ask anyone for permission to get married, and that I can choose my own bride."

She drank her tea. "Now, that is an awesome responsibility."

He was tempted to ask her there and then, but decided against it. They had a whole week, and she was falling in love with his home, with what would be *her* home, if she said yes. There was no need to rush his fences.

"Care for a swim?" he asked.

"Oh! Do you know, I quite forgot to bring a costume with me. You didn't say anything about swimming."

"Here in Bungo, we don't wear costumes."

"But . . . the servants . . ."

"Have all gone to bed. Anyway, they don't wear costumes either." She didn't realise how important it was. Whatever they had shared in the past, this was what he had first shared with Christina, and this was how Christina had to be exorcised from his mind and his heart.

165

"Oh," she said again. "Well, I suppose, when in Rome . . ."

He held her hand as they went down the steps and across the lawn to the beach. Then he released her and undressed, facing her. After a few seconds she began undressing as well.

Even when she was naked, a silver of pale flesh in the darkness, he resisted the temptation to take her in his arms, held her hand again instead, and led her down the sand into the water. She gave a little shiver as the water lapped at her ankles. "We need to get right in," he told her.

"My hair!"

"I'll wash it for you," he promised.

She gave a little laugh, and let him draw her forward on to her belly, then turned on her back and foot-stroked herself into deeper water. He swam beside her, then turned and held her round the waist. Her feet dropped, and she went beneath the surface, emerging with spluttering laughter while he took her in his arms. "I'm out of my depths," she gasped.

"I'm still standing," he assured her and kissed her. In the same instant her legs wrapped themselves round her body, and he was inside her, without the least resistance: he realised she had wanted it as badly as he. For several seconds they both surged back and forth, until his heat overcame the chill of the water.

"Oh," she said, hugging herself against him. "Oh. I never knew that was possible."

He released her, and she floated away from him. He held her ankles, and gently drew her back to him, she opened her legs again to imprison him, brought him against her so that her wet body hair tickled his stomach. "I want to marry you," he said. "Please say yes."

She kissed him, several times. "Please ask me again," she said. "In a day or two."

He could not object to that, because he knew that he had jumped the gun. Meanwhile she was there to be enjoyed. It was not simply a matter of sex. That, certainly: in the solitude of Bungo they could share everything, and did, from their bath to their bed. But there was also their relationship,

166

which reached a mental intimacy they had never attempted before. Linda didn't really wish to talk about herself or her job, but she wanted to know all about his background, about his father and his famous grandfather, about their part in Japanese history, just as she wanted to know about Charlotte and Christina. This was as it should be, he told himself, as she would understand that by Japanese ethics she would be, in effect, marrying them as well, or at least Christina – Charlotte was a Mori now.

He was tempted to tell her the truth about Christina, but his instincts warned him against it, until she had definitely said yes. That was cowardly of him he knew, and dishonest, but he was so afraid of losing her.

"These have been the six most beautiful days of my life," she told him, as they walked the beach on the afternoon before they were due to return to Tokyo. "I want you never to forget that, Nicky."

He checked in dismay. "That almost sounds as if you are saying goodbye?"

She licked her lips. "I'm afraid I am. I've been transferred."

"Transferred? To where?"

"Hong Kong."

"When?"

"I leave in a fortnight."

"I meant, when did you know about it?"

"Six months ago."

"Six months . . ." while he had been fighting for his life in hospital. "Don't you think you should have told me?"

"I didn't think it was any of your business, then."

He sat on the sand. "I love you," he said.

She knelt beside him. "And I love you. I think."

"But you only agreed to come down here because you were leaving Japan anyway."

"I suppose so."

He turned his head to look at her. "I asked you to marry me."

"And I am most terribly flattered, Nicky. But . . ."

"You're not the marrying kind," he said bitterly.

"I don't think I could ever possibly be a Japanese wife."

"For Heaven's sake, I'd treat you as a European."

"Of course you would, Nicky. You're the complete gentleman. But whatever the colour of your skin or your hair, or whatever church you worship in, you are Japanese."

"Meaning you've been warned off me because of the possibility there may one day be a confrontation between Japan and Britain."

"No, I didn't mean that, and I sincerely hope there will never be such a confrontation. Meaning that you're a *samurai*. Supposing that you felt it necessary, would you not commit *seppuku*?"

"It is not unknown for British naval officers to take their own lives, you know."

"Of course it isn't. But it is an event entirely out of the ordinary when it happens. It is not part of the code of the Royal Navy that you *must* commit suicide in certain circumstances."

"I think that is a rather flimsy reason for not marrying someone you love. If you love him."

"It's just an example, Nicky. I told you that however long I lived in Japan I could never come to terms with your system of ethics, with *bushido*. Those young men, your own cousin, you feel they did the right thing. I just can't accept that. I never would be able to."

He had no reply to make to that, because she was speaking the absolute truth.

"Please understand, Nicky. Marriage between us would be a disaster, because I would be, consciously or subconsciously, opposing you in everything. While the thought of a child of mine being brought up in your ethical code, well, it's just not acceptable." She waited, and as he still did not reply, said, "Would you like me to leave tonight?"

He looked up at her. "Of course not, Linda. But I'll have the servants make you up a separate bed."

"Only if that's what you want," she said.

"You mean you still want to sleep with me?"

"Very much so. I love you, Nicky. I just can't marry you."

* * *

168

"Ha!" was Christina's greeting. "You lied to me. Do you not suppose I know that woman has been with you down in Bungo?"

"I did not lie to you, honourable Stepmother," Nicholas said. "You asked me if I was taking her with me, and I said no. I did not take her with me."

"Words," Christina grumbled, and then began to weep. "How could you treat me so, Nicky?"

How indeed, Nicholas thought. No doubt Linda was right, and a marriage between them would have been a disaster. But that did not make him feel any the less bitter, or indeed, humiliated. It was as if she had rejected him because he simply did not match up to her ideals, when everyone knew that the Japanese ideals were the highest in the world. Well, he thought, bugger her. Perhaps he should have done that, if he was to be considered a savage. As for the future . . ." he took Christina into his arms. "Linda Wells is leaving Japan," he said. "I will never see her again. I have been away, honourable Stepmother. But now I have returned."

PART TWO

Vanquished

"O goodly usage of those antique times,
In which the sword was servant unto right;
When not for malice and contentious crimes,
But all for praise, and proof of manly might,
The martial brood accustomed to fight;
Then honour was the meed of victory,
And yet the vanquished had no despite."

Edmund Spenser
The Faerie Queene.

CHAPTER 7

The Thrust

Admiral Yamamoto Isoroku smiled at his senior captains, assembled in the wardroom of the battleship *Nagato*, and gazing at him in rapt attention; their eager tension filled the air.

"Last night, gentlemen, 7 July 1937," Yamamoto said, "Army elements clashed with Chinese forces on the Marco Polo Bridge at Lukouchaio north of Peking. As a result of this incident, on orders from the Government, our forces are now advancing on both Peking and Tientsin. It is expected that these two cities will be in our hands by the end of the month. For political reasons, there will be no declaration of war: for international consumption what is happening will be described as a series of 'incidents'. However, I do not wish you to be under any misapprehension: as of this moment we are at war with China, and this is a war we are determined to carry through to a successful conclusion." He grinned at them. "We are no longer subject to any restrictions or even criticism by the League of Nations.

"Now, I understand that this is what you, all of us, have waited for all of our lives. We are fighting seamen, who have only ever wished to be given the right to fight. Some of us, indeed, may have from time to time doubted that right would ever be ours again. But how may a man endure an entire lifetime, and never see action? That would be against the very laws of Nature.

"Alas, my comrades, I can promise you little glory in this enterprise. Yet this is not to say your duties will be anything less than arduous, and at times even repugnant;

they must still be carried out with ruthless determination. China, mighty China, more than five hundred millions of people, now united and determined under Marshal Chiang Kai-shek, has thrown down the gauntlet to little Japan. Make no mistake, they consider this a war of revenge, for 1895. They would wipe out the memory of the catastrophe of the Manchu, the memory of our past successes. And do not make the mistake, either, of assuming they will be easily defeated; their very numbers make the task difficult. Yet defeated they must be, and crushed. They have chosen to throw down the gauntlet to us; we must seize this heaven-sent opportunity to settle with them once and for all.

"Our leaders are aware that it would be quite impossible for us to seek to conquer such a vast country. Nor do we have any ambitions to try. Our aims are, first, to fight the Chinese armed services wherever they can be encountered, and utterly destroy them. Secondly, to seize, and keep control of, all the great seaports, and indeed, the entire Pacific coastline; by doing this, we control all the great rivers, and thus we control all China – nothing will be able to enter or leave the country without our permission. Once that is accomplished, all else falls into place. The third objective we have is to install in the rest of China a government which will support our aims, and not pursue ambitions of its own. But that is a political matter, and does not concern us in the Navy. Our responsibility is the second aim, the sealing up of the Pacific seaboard.

"To do this, we must first of all defeat the Chinese fleet. Well, there hardly is a Chinese fleet worth mentioning. They have eight light cruisers; the largest is the *Hai Chi*, at just over four thousand tons. She is armed with two eight-inch and ten four-point-seven-inch guns, and has a designed speed of twenty-four knots. But she was launched in 1898, and in fact four of the eight date back to the last century; two of the others, the *Ying Swei* and the *Chao Ho*, were launched in 1911. Only two, the *Ning Hai* and the *Ping Hai*, are modern vessels. Both were launched after 1930, but they are only two and a half thousand tons each, and are armed with popguns. There are also three destroyers and some gunboats and torpedo boats. So you will see that

174

a fleet action is hardly likely. However, every Chinese vessel must be destroyed wherever it can be found. This includes civilian vessels, as our aim is to end all Chinese trade with the outside world. There must be no hesitation in this. And such destruction must be carried out in a totally ruthless manner. Our principal aim is to break the Chinese will to resist, make them rue the day their leaders chose to oppose us, and therefore make them repudiate those leaders. Thus no Japanese ship will ever stop to pick up Chinese survivors. I wish this clearly understood. Every Chinese man, woman and child, every Chinese dog, is as of this moment our enemy and must be destroyed. Those who put to sea must perish, and those who remain behind must be made afraid to put to sea." He paused, to look from face to face. "At the same time, I must impress upon you that no shots must be fired at foreign vessels, whatever the provocation. I am thinking here principally of those flying the Union Jack or the Stars and Stripes. It is not our intention to offer the Western Powers the slightest reason for intervention to save China from her just desserts. Remember this.

"Our secondary task is to assist the Army in securing the seaports and the river mouths. The rivers we will simply blockade. Support to the Army will be given by bombardment as and when necessary. However, you will be pleased to learn that the reduction of the greatest port in China, Shanghai, has been allotted to the Navy alone. The battle fleet, led by *Mutsu* and *Nagato*, will sail immediately for the mouth of the Yangste, both to close the river and to launch our assault before the Chinese are properly mobilised. Now here again, gentlemen, I must impress upon you that you must carry out your duties with the utmost determination. You will blast Shanghai as directed, regardless of whether fire is returned or not, regardless of whether you may be inflicting civilian casualties or not, until ordered to cease fire as the city has surrendered or is about to fall to assault. Is this understood? I repeat, civilian casualties must be accepted as a necessary concomitant of war, and the Chinese government should have taken the possibility of such casualties into account before provoking us. Of course it goes without saying that no gun will be aimed at the International Concession. Thank you, gentlemen, that will be all. The honour of Japan is in your keeping. Your *safe* keeping."

The officers bowed, and filed from the wardroom. Nicholas remained sitting at his desk in the corner, where, as Yamamoto's secretary, he had been recording what was said. "Well, Nicholas *san*," the Admiral remarked, when they were alone, "the hour of reckoning has arrived."

"You have no doubts, honourable Admiral?"

"Which doubts were you thinking of?"

"That we can do the job?" Nicholas temporised.

"That is in the main the Army's business," Yamamoto said. "I know we can do *our* job, Nicholas, simply because, as I said just now, there is no real opposition. Shanghai is hardly a fortress. But I see no reason why the Army should not also accomplish its set purpose. It needs only not to make the mistake of attempting physically to conquer China, and become bogged down in some endless guerilla warfare in the interior. But I am sure our military masters have sufficient sense to understand that."

"Well, then, honourable Admiral, no doubts that the Western Powers may intervene?"

"None at all. At least, overtly. They are in a mess. The depression lingers on, and now they have fallen out amongst themselves, with both Italy and Germany and now Franco's forces regarded as renegades – they have too much to worry about at home. Besides, the last two attempts to create an international consensus to enforce League decisions have proved humiliating failures for Britain and France. I have no doubt they will criticise us, and perhaps even condemn us for waging war with all our might, as if they would not do the same in similar circumstances. That sort of criticism we can treat with contempt. They will also undoubtedly sell arms and munitions to Chiang Kaishek, but they are also selling such items to us, and once we have sealed the Chinese coastline Chiang will be cut off. That will probably upset them more than anything. Making money is all they really care about."

"My father told me that you were against a war with mainland China, honourable Admiral."

Yamamoto shot him a glance, then sat at his desk. "Your father was right. I have always felt that our main business lay elsewhere. But one should be prepared to modify one's position as events themselves are modified. Four years ago, when the Lytton Report was presented, and world opinion seemed so hostile to us, I felt that to dissipate our resources in a war with China would be a mistake, especially the sort of war the Army then wished to wage, a war of conquest rather than control. But now the situation is entirely different. Germany is an ally. Italy wishes to be an ally. Britain and France, as I have said, are humiliated and weaker than ever. The Americans are concerned only with America. And the Army has at last modified its ideas to control, which is important, rather than mere occupation, which is a waste of time. It is now entirely possible that we may be able to achieve our objectives before any Western Power is in a position to interfere, and once we *have* achieved our objectives, they will accept it, as they always do accept *faits accompli*. One only has to look at the way they have accepted the Italian occupation of Ethiopia. Then it may be possible to consider our situation in an entirely different light. Think of it, Nicholas. In four years time the first of our new battleships will be in commission, with the rest soon to follow. We will also have our new aircraft carriers. We will have the most powerful battle fleet in the world. And we will have all the economic resources of China at our disposal. Then it will really be possible to dominate East Asia, and more. Now, did not your great poet Shakespeare say that there is a tide in the affairs of men, which needs to be grasped, and which if missed, may never return?"

"Well, then, honourable Admiral, if I may ask a last question?"

"Of course, Nicholas."

"Have you no doubts concerning the *morality* of what we do?"

Yamamoto regarded him for several seconds, as if considering the point, but Nicholas knew that he was only considering his reply. "No, Nicholas," he said. "Because a man can afford no morals when the existence of his people is at stake. China is, and always has been, and always will

177

be, our enemy. You know this as well as I. During the next few months we are going to be given the opportunity to eliminate her as a threat to our future prosperity, perhaps for a century, if not forever. The crime would be not to take that opportunity. More, possession of the entire Pacific seaboard of Asia will enable us to develop that industrial strength which is so essential, and so elusive. The Japanese people can only benefit from this war. Now you tell me, do *you* have doubts?"

Yes, Nicholas thought. I have doubts. We are about to commit murder, murder on an unimaginable scale, but perhaps even more terrible, murder of a country, simply because we wish to be greater than we are. That is to cast all morality out of the window. But had he not cast all morality out of the window, long ago? There had been excuses, once. He had even fought against it, once. But Linda had seen through the facade, and realised what lay beneath. Since then there had been no more fighting against the role fate had given him to play. So he said, "I always have doubts, honourable Admiral. But none that will interfere with my duty. If you will tell me what that is."

"Why, to continue working with me," Yamamoto said. "I know: you would like a command. And I have promised that you shall have one. But now is not the time. I have told you, there will be no honour to be found in this war. There will be no fleet actions. It will simply be a matter of destruction of enemy lives and property. From a naval point of view, we are using a sledgehammer to crush a nut. But I am sure we will find enough to interest us."

"War!" Christina's eyes gleamed. "You will not be in danger?"

"None at all. It will be less dangerous than manoeuvres."

"Will you kill many Chinese, honourable Cousin?" Alexander asked. He was a big boy now, six years old, a curious combination of auburn hair and Japanese features. And he still did not know the truth of his parentage. But he could never know the truth of his parentage

Nicholas ruffled his hair. "Many Chinese," he promised.

*   *   *

178

Charlotte and Mori came for supper.

"I embark next week," Mori said. "For Tientsin."

"I sail tomorrow, for Shanghai," Nicholas said.

"We will toast our victory together, in Nanking," Mori promised.

Charlotte was afraid. "Suppose he gets killed, Nicky? Suppose *you* get killed?"

"I am actually in more danger of being knocked down by a tram here in Tokyo," Nicholas assured her. "It is the Army that will be doing the fighting. But Mori . . . he will survive." He kissed her. "Only the good die young."

"What are you brooding on?" Christina asked, when they were alone.

He shrugged. "I was wondering if Yoshiye knows what is going on. He died to create this situation. He must be very pleased."

She gave a little shiver. "I do not like that kind of talk. Nicky, I think you should get married."

Nicholas turned his head, sharply. He had never expected such a suggestion from *her*, of all people.

"Well . . ." she had the grace to flush. "You are thirty-three years old. There is the family name to be considered. I know you have Alexander. But would you not like to have children you can legitimately call your own?"

He studied her. "I think you need to be honest with me, honourable Mother."

"Well . . ." she twisted her fingers together. "I know how guilty you feel, about us. Well, you have told me this, often enough. I do not think a man should go off to war, feeling guilty. If you went off to war, knowing that when you came back, you would be properly married, it would be much better for you. For us. I know Yamamoto would be pleased."

"And what would happen to you, honourable Step-mother?"

"Me? Well, perhaps I also could marry. Again. If you would give me your permission."

"Ah." Nicholas understood at last. "You are asking my permission to marry again?"

179

"If it will make things easier for you."

"The name of the man?"

She gulped.

"Oh, come now, honourable Stepmother, I am really not as much of a fool as you imagine. I am quite sure you have not only chosen your next husband, but sampled him."

Christina sniffed. "His name is Takeda Konoye."

"He is a major in the *Kempei-tai*!"

"He is in intelligence, yes."

"The *Kempei-tai* have a very bad reputation, honourable Mother."

"If you mean they deal harshly with those who seek to harm Japan, then you are entirely right. Major Takeda is well thought of. He is a *protégé* of General Tojo."

"I don't consider that a recommendation either," Nicholas remarked. Tojo Hideki's nickname of The Razor fairly summed up the man, in his opinion; he had just been transferred from command of the secret police to that of the Third Army, engaged in China. No doubt, Nicholas supposed, this was to terrify the Chinese.

"You intend to refuse me permission, honourable Son?" Christina asked.

"By no means, honourable Mother. You have my permission." And heaven help you, my dear Takeda, he thought.

"Ha! You would like to get rid of me."

"I think you are right, and that it would be best for us to seek different directions. Tell me about the boy?"

"That decision is yours."

"I see." Which confirmed his suspicion that she was already Takeda's mistress. "Then he will stay here with me, and be brought up as my son."

"I had assumed you would say that, as he *is* your son."

"And I assume you have not told Takeda this?"

"Well, of course I have not."

"Because if you do, he will certainly kill you. And should he fail to do so, then I will."

Christina sniffed. "I know you hate me, Nicholas. But the boy will need a mother. Thus I will . . ."

"No, honourable Mother. I will choose my own bride."

"When?"

"Whenever I can obtain leave. It will not be for a month or two yet. I am sure you can wait that long."

Christina sniffed again.

Nicholas discussed the situation with Yamamoto, as *Nagato* and her fleet sailed south. He told the admiral the absolute truth, omitting only the background. That Barrett Christina, only twenty-seven years old and still very beautiful, and now a widow for more than a year, should wish to marry again was entirely reasonable. That she might wish to leave her only son in the care of his half-brother, as was supposed, to continue the family name, or that Nicholas might insist she do so, was equally reasonable, to a Japanese. "You should adopt the boy," Yamamoto recommended. "That would be best."

"Then I shall do so, honourable Admiral. But yet he should have a mother."

"And since the departure of your English beauty your bed is lonely," Yamamoto smiled.

"That too," Nicholas agreed. "Unfortunately . . ." he hesitated.

Yamamoto gave a shout of laughter. "You have lived such an inverted social life you do not know where to turn. I may as well tell you, Nicholas, there are those in the service who have from time to time wondered if you were interested in women at all. In Japanese woman."

"Linda Wells was an aberration, honourable Admiral."

"I wouldn't have said that. She was a very handsome woman. But now you need a bride. But for what happened last year, your Uncle Takamori would have arranged the matter."

Nicholas nodded. "It was a hobby of his, arranging marriages."

"But now he is dead, so you must turn to me. I will see to it. Indeed, I know the very girl."

"Honourable Admiral?" Nicholas was astonished.

"Hitachi Aya. I am sure you have met her, or at least know of her. Her father is very wealthy."

"I know this, honourable Admiral, and I have met his daughter. But . . ."

181

"He is also looking for a husband for Aya. I know this, because he has told me."

"Yes, but honourable Admiral, she is very young."

"Fifteen next birthday."

"And I will be thirty-four next birthday."

"So?"

Nicholas swallowed. He could not possibly tell Yamamoto that he did not wish to repeat his father's experience without explaining what that experience, however inadvertent, was. Then he remembered that *his* son was only six years old. "Besides," Yamamoto said with a smile. "If the Chinese prove recalcitrant, Aya may well be sixteen by the time she comes to your bed."

The Chinese did indeed prove recalcitrant, expecially around Shanghai. In the north the Japanese Army, already in position and with full knowledge of the various Chinese dispositions, advanced steadily – Peking fell 28 July – until halted as much by logistical factors as by increasing Chinese resistance. The marines put ashore at Shanghai found themselves beleaguered by vastly numerically superior Chinese forces. Angrily Yamamoto ordered the battleships to open fire, and the sixteen-inch guns of *Nagato* and *Mutsu* began belching steel and smoke, supported by the aircraft from *Akagi* and *Kaga*, but even so he had to call for military support. An army was landed, and it was not until after three months of bitter fighting that Shanghai surrendered on 8 November.

But the concept of a quick, merciless campaign was negated. And by then world opinion had been shocked by the nature of the Japanese strategy and tactics. Before the city even fell Nicholas found himself sitting on Yamamoto's left facing the consuls of Britain and France in the wardroom of *Nagato*. Situated as they were in the International Concession only a few miles outside the Chinese city, the diplomats had watched the holocaust of destruction in total consternation. "I am sorry, gentlemen," Yamamoto said. "But this is war. You have fought wars yourselves, in your past history."

"But this indiscriminate shelling of civilians," the French minister protested.

"The Chinese have but to surrender," Yamamoto pointed out.

On the quarterdeck to take tea, Nicholas was tackled by the British Naval attache. "Can you really support such action?" asked Commander Dutton. "It is against all the tenets of civilised behaviour, not to mention the rules of war."

"I am obeying the orders of my government, as I am sure you would obey the orders of yours, Commander," Nicholas pointed out.

"Japan stands condemned before the world," Dutton insisted.

"I suspect that is rather a sweeping statement, Commander. *All* the world? You mean Great Britain, France and America. That is a rather small proportion of the world, I would say. I would also say it is rather hypocritical, coming from the representative of a nation which less than fifty years ago used machine-guns, repeating rifles and expanding bullets to defeat various tribesmen armed with spears and matchlocks, in order to create an empire."

Dutton's eyebrows arched. "Do you mean to insult me, Commander?"

"I am stating an historical fact, Commander," Nicholas said.

"One day, sir, there will be a reckoning," Dutton warned. "One day quite soon."

"When that day comes, Commander, Japan will be ready to answer at any bar in the world," Nicholas said.

But for all his bravado, he could not help but be concerned. After Shanghai had surrendered, he went ashore to look at the city, and inhaled the stench of decaying flesh. He looked at the still unburied corpses, of women and children as well as men and animals, lying sprawled in the ungainly ballet of death on the streets and in the wreckage of their houses. Many of the women, dead or still alive, had been raped. Nor could he escape before seeing a group of men, accused of resisting after the surrender, being marched out to summary execution by firing squad. While already the Japanese forces were pushing on up the Yangste, their target now Nanking, the Chinese capital, and tales were returning of more ruthless bombardments and massacres.

Nicholas knew that all the so-called civilised powers had waged war like this within virtually living memory, but in two generations the world had chosen to forget that. Nor, in his opinion, did the behaviour of other troops in other times excuse this bestiality. While there was now no hope of even a ship-to-ship action. The small Chinese Navy had attempted to take refuge up the rivers, and by the middle of October every single surface craft of any size had been scuttled or sunk by aerial bombardment. The two relatively new ships, *Ning Hai* and *Ping Hai*, were to be salvaged and incorporated in the Japanese fleet as the *Ioshima* and *Yashoshima*; the remainder were rusting hulks.

Yamamoto could see that his *protégé* was disturbed, and called him into the Admiral's day cabin. "I suspect that being cooped up on board a ship which is doing nothing more than lie at anchor firing its guns at a target which cannot reply is depressing you, Nicholas," he said. "I think you would do well with some active service."

"Honourable Admiral?" Nicholas felt his heart sink even as he knew the Admiral was right. But he had no desire to be sent up the river.

"I am going to second you to *Shiratsuyu* as commanding officer. Her captain has been taken ill and sent back to Japan. She has just rejoined the fleet from a sweep to the south. You will carry out another sweep, pending the arrival of her new commander. Does that please you, Nicholas?"

"I am overwhelmed, honourable Admiral."

Yamamoto pointed. "Remember your orders. Seek and destroy, anything Chinese."

Nicholas bowed.

He was indeed delighted. *Shiratsuyu*, the first of a new class of ten ships, only launched the previous year, was a larger, improved version of the Hatsuharu Class. Three hundred and fifty-two feet overall, she displaced just under two thousand tons and would make thirty-four knots. Like *Hatsuharu*, her principal armament was five five-inch guns, two in a single turret forward and three aft, but in the newer ship the design had been kept simple, and the fifth gun, mounted in a separate turret, was immediately forward of the after turret, thus making it a broadside weapon. Her complement was one hundred and eighty officers and men. His first independent command! Nicholas felt as if he would burst with pride and delight as Lieutenant Yashiwara, his executive officer, at his side, he gave the order which had the destroyer steaming away from the fleet and to the south.

Yashiwara was concerned about the weather, which was threatening as they passed through the Taiwan Strait, but although the seas were lumpy, they reached their allotted patrolling area, south-east of the British island colony of Hong Kong, without difficulty. Hong Kong, Nicholas thought, lying in his bunk and enjoying the movement of the ship. He wondered what Linda, supposing she was still there, would say were he to pay Victoria a courtesy call? His voice tube whistled, and he picked it up. "The wind is rising, honourable Captain," Yashiwara said.

"I will come up." Nicholas replaced the tube, put on his cap, and went up to the bridge. It was blowing about forty knots, he estimated; the seas were big, and were starting to topple over in foaming white and blue crests, and the swell was already high enough to half-lose the destroyer in each trough; yet with the sun peeping through the clouds it was a scene of wild beauty. And *Shiratsuyu* rode the sea as buoyantly as a duck, sliding down, skimming up, her bows cutting the waves, her engines never losing their even beat. The bridge hummed with the subdued sounds of the various navigating and radio equipment, always reassuring.

Everything about the ship was reassuring, Nicholas thought; she was the most beautiful thing he had ever handled, more of a pleasure to be on than even *Nagato*, with her much more stable platform. He had no doubt he could drive *Shiratsuyu* through a typhoon, if he had to. But he did not think this was going to be anything more than a storm: the distinctive cyclonic pattern of a typhoon was missing. However, the motion was growing increasingly severe, and they were merely on patrol, some seventy miles off the Chinese coast, not actually going anywhere. "Reduce speed,

Mr Yashiwara," he said. "Twelve knots will be sufficient until the wind drops."

"Aye-aye, honourable Captain." Yashiwara gave the necessary order to the engine room, and the movement became perceptibly easier.

Nicholas sat in his chair, bolted to the deck but mounted so that he could see down through the bridge screens and over the bows, and gazed at the seas. He was happy. He was always happy to be at sea, regardless of what the weather might be doing, and in the prevailing political conditions it was only possible to be happy *when* at sea. The world was becoming an increasingly grim place; no one could doubt that Europe was heading towards war, as Germany continued to expand, regardless of promises given to the Western democracies, and as Great Britain and France became increasingly aware that Herr Hitler was not to be trusted. Yamamoto kept assuring him that even if there was a European conflagration, Japan would not be involved; the pact with Germany did not require physical support in the field or at sea, only moral. Yet there could be no doubt that it was events in Europe that had encouraged Hirota and his friends to begin this operation against China: they felt safe from intervention. And there were Yamamoto's words that once China was a satellite, it might be possible to review the entire situation in East Asia. That had to mean a confrontation with the British.

That dilemma had never confronted either his father or his grandfather. If they had known themselves to be renegades, they had also known who were their enemies, countries such as China or Russia, against both of whom Grandfather had fought as an officer in the Royal Navy; he had merely changed flags, not adverseries. His Father had spent a major part of his active life with Japan allied to Britain, sworn to stand shoulder to shoulder in time of crisis. Nicholas supposed it was ironic that he, who after three generations could hardly any longer be considered a renegade, might be the first member of the family to be required to fight against a people he still had to identify with. He wondered if he would be able to do it?

"With respect, honourable Captain." His midshipman

stood to attention at his shoulder, a sheet of paper in his hand. "A radio message."

Nicholas frowned at the words: *Imperial Japanese Ship Shiratsuyu from His Majesty's Ship Flamenco. Assistance required. Position twenty-one degrees two minutes North Latitude, one hundred and eighteen degrees twelve minutes East Longitude. Civilian vessel in danger of sinking.*

Nicholas handed Yashiwara the paper, then looked at the chart, where *Shiratsuyu*'s position was plotted every hour. "He is not ten miles away," he remarked. "How the devil did the Britisher know we are in his vicinity?"

"He will have been listening to our radio traffic, honourable Captain." Since the Chinese fleet had entirely disappeared, the Japanese had ceased to bother with either radio silence or coded messages when on patrol.

"Hm," Nicholas commented. "What is *Flamenco*?"

Yashiwara had already opened his reference book. "She is a river gunboat, honourable Captain. Two hundred and sixty tons and armed with two three-inch guns. She can make fourteen knots. Presumably she is her way to Hong Kong, for refitting."

"Does she not know this is a war zone?" Nicholas grumbled. But of course, as war had not been declared, there could be no official war zones. "Well, if there really is a civilian vessel in difficulties . . . make the necessary course alteration, Mr. Yashiwara, and increase speed to twenty-four knots." Which was as fast as he wanted to go in such big seas. He turned to the midshipman. "Make to *Flamenco*." The boy poised his pencil above his pad. "Message received and understood," Nicholas said. "Will be at your position in thirty minutes." The boy bowed, and hurried to the radio room.

Yashiwara stood beside his captain. "You do not suppose it could be some kind of trap, honourable Commander?"

"Set by a British gunboat?"

"Who can tell if it is truly a British gunboat?"

"I do not think it is a trap, Lieutenant. Great Britain and Japan are at peace, and there is no Chinese vessel afloat capable of fighting us."

"I was considering a torpedo boat preparing a strike, honourable Captain."

Nicholas glanced at him. It was certainly a possibility, one which had not occurred to him. But in this weather . . . "Double your look-outs," he said, and reached for his own binoculars.

Now *Shiratsuyu* was crashing through the waves as her speed increased, but now, too, she was running downwind, and the motion was easier, save when she overtook a wave in front of her and buried her slender bows in the back of the swell, sending hundreds of tons of green water cascading along the deck, and white spray splattering over the windows of the bridge. It would, Nicholas reflected, be quite impossible for anyone to launch a torpedo in these conditions with any hope of hitting his target; he did not think he would be capable of hitting anything with his guns, as the ship rose and fell some twenty feet every few seconds. As for being is this sea in a river gunboat, with her shallow draft and low freeboard . . . "There!" said Lieutenant Yashiwara.

Nicholas levelled his glasses and made out the shape of the British ship, bravely trying to keep herself between the worst of the seas and a very large junk, several times her size, which was wallowing in the troughs, having been dismasted earlier in the storm. Some of the waves were breaking right over the British vessel, but the white ensign still fluttered bravely in the breeze.

"Message from *Flamenco*, honourable Commander," said the midshipman. Nicholas read: *Thank God for your presence. Ship Sun Lily dismasted and making water. We are unable to take off so many people. Can you put down oil, approach to leeward, and take off as many as possible?*

An oil slick would stop the waves from breaking, as long as it held together, which could be perhaps for half an hour, long enough to remove the people on board the junk. It obviously had to be in grave danger of sinking, as the British ship felt unable to leave her position as breakwater. As her captain had indicated, it was all the little gunboat could do to maintain station without being herself overwhelmed. Nicholas levelled his binoculars again, looking beyond the warship at the merchantman. She flew no flag, all her rigging having gone overboard. But she was crowded with people, waving and shouting in panic.

188

"We will have to lower our boats, Lieutenant," Nicholas said. "But first, we will do as the Britisher suggests, and put down oil."

"With respect, honourable Commander," Yashiwara said, "that is a Chinese vessel."

Nicholas lowered his glasses, and gazed at his second-in-command. "Our orders, honourable Commander," Yashiwara said, "are to destroy every Chinese vessel we encounter, and all who sail in such ships."

Nicholas looked at the junk and the British gunboat again. But Yashiwara was right: the junk was most certainly Chinese. And they were allowed no room for discretion in their orders. Not to destroy the junk, and all on board, would be a dereliction of duty. But the thought of disobeying the eternal law of the sea, and steaming away from a vessel in distress . . . Yashiwara smiled. "A single shell would finish the job, honourable Commander."

"The junk is sinking anyway, Lieutenant."

Indeed, the junk was getting lower in the water with every minute, and the panic on her deck was visibly increasing. "It is our business to make sure of it, honourable Commander."

Still Nicholas hesitated. What he was being asked to do was mass murder. But it was what Yamamoto had instructed his captains to do, and had reminded him of that duty just before he had undertaken this voyage. Without Yamamoto he was nothing: any other naval officer whose cousin had disgraced himself would have been left without a future. If he let the Admiral down . . . on the other hand, he had also been explictly ordered not to clash with the Royal Navy in any way. Was that a way out? "If we open fire," he said. "The Britisher will think we are firing at her."

"Then we must send the Britisher away, honourable Commander," Yashiwara suggested. "Tell them we will be responsible for the junk.

Nicholas nodded. "Make to *Flamenco*," he told the waiting midshipman. "Are you escorting *Sun Lily*?" Oh, how he hoped and prayed the answer could be yes. If the junk could be under the protection of the Royal Navy . . .

"Reduce speed, Mr Yashiwara," he commanded. "We are close enough."

The midshipman was back. Nicholas scanned the paper. *Negative. We sighted and answered distress rocket. May I suggest speed is imperative? Sun Lily is sinking.* "Reply," Nicholas said. "You have done your duty. I congratulate you. You may now leave *Sun Lily* in our care."

Speed had been reduced to ten knots, and the destroyer was riding the waves easily enough. The British gunboat was just over a mile distant, keeping station to windward of the junk. The midshipman returned. *We will remain to assist. You cannot save entire crew and passengers on your own.* Nicholas looked at Yashiwara.

"He must go, honourable Commander."

"If we keep talking the junk will probably sink anyway. Make to *Flamenco*, assistance not required."

Yashiwara was staring through his glasses. "It could take some time, honourable Commander. They are pumping with all their strength. They even have small children pumping."

Nicholas also stared at the Chinese ship. They were so close now that with his glasses he could even make out individual faces, individual expressions; the crew were busy passing up towing hawsers to the bow, as the Japanese ship approached, anticipating that they might be taken in tow. The midshipman presented a new message: *Regret decision but will withdraw. Good luck. Flamenco.*

Yashiwara swung his binoculars and watched the gunboat begin to steam round the junk and head north-west for Hong Kong. "I suggest we sink the enemy now, honourable Commander," he said. "It would be quickest and best. A single shot into her waterline should suffice."

Yet again Nicholas gazed at the junk. The expressions of the people on deck were changing from hope and relief to amazement and despair as the destroyer continued slowly around the sinking vessel's stern, leaving her exposed to the seas, having made no effort to close her or put down oil. The Chinese captain was on deck, using a megaphone – he obviously had no radio – shouting into the wind, but his words had no hope of carrying across the storm. Waves were now breaking right over the junk's deck; even as Nicholas watched, a gaggle of people were swept away, screaming and holding on to each other. "Message from *Flamenco*, honourable Commander," said the midshipman.

Nicholas took the paper, read, *In the name of humanity, make haste.* He crumpled it into a ball. "There is no reply."

"The Britisher is returning, honourable Commander," Yashiwara remarked.

Nicholas watched the gunboat turn again and come back towards them. "Make to *Flamenco*," he told the midshipman. "You must leave. This is an order. You are in a war zone."

"I was wrong," Yashiwara said. "About the need for a shell. The pumps seem to have jammed."

The *Sun Lily* was now almost submerged, a hulk swept by every huge wave; more and more people were being washed away. Some, despairing, were actually jumping into the seething waters to drown the more quickly. Others knelt and prayed, staring at the Japanese warship. "*Flamenco* is preparing her boats, honourable Commander."

Nicholas nodded. He felt sick and ashamed. "That is a contravention of your orders, honourable Commander," Yashiwara said.

"My orders are to destroy all Chinese ships, Lieutenant," Nicholas said. "As you have remarked, the weather is doing that for us. As for the crew, I cannot stop the British picking them up, if he can, without firing on him. And I have been specifically ordered not to do that." How calm and resolute was his voice, in contrast to the seething misery in his gut.

"Well," Yashiwara commented. "She is gone anyway."

For indeed the *Sun Lily* had slipped beneath the waves, leaving only human and animal flotsam desperately trying to keep afloat as the gunboat nosed her way up to them, putting down her two boats whatever the danger, to pick up as many people as they could. "Alter course due north, and resume cruising speed, Mr Yashiwara," Nicholas said.

As he turned away from the bridge windows to go below, the midshipman came out of the radio room. The boy's face was flushed. Nicholas took the paper. *May God have mercy on your soul. If you have a soul. Flamenco.*

191

CHAPTER 8

The Decision

"Message from flagship, honourable Commander," Lieutenant Yashiwara said.

Nicholas jerked his head, as if awakening from a deep sleep. Perhaps he had been sleeping, for a very long time, enduring the most persistent of nightmares. The sea was calm; the storm might never have been. How marvellous it would be if the *Sun Lily* had never been, either. Now . . . he took the sheet of paper. *Proceed Hong Kong to take on board Yosunobe Asawa and family. Then return to Tokyo. Yamamoto.*

Nicholas raised his head; obviously Yashiwara would have already read the message. The lieutenant grinned. "We will need thick skins, honourable Commander."

"Alter course two points to port, if you will, sir," the pilot said. This was as many consecutive words as he had uttered since coming on board; there could be no doubt that *Flamenco* had reached port, and told her tale. And there she was, Nicholas realised, lying alongside, and in a berth immediately behind the one to which *Shiratsuyu* was being directed. He glanced at the pilot, who was glancing at him.

"The port is very crowded right now, sir," the pilot said.

The Japanese destroyer berthed with none of the usual whistle-blowing from the other ships in Victoria Harbour. The dockside indeed was both quiet and virtually empty of spectators. Nicholas looked up the hillside, past the teeming high-rise buildings of Victoria to the various houses scattered amidst the greenery beyond the city. Then he looked across the harbour to the mainland of Kowloon. The British had held Hong Kong now for very nearly a hundred years, and their mark was everywhere. But it was that coastline, Kowloon apart, that the Japanese intended to occupy; plans were already being laid for the capture of Canton, seventy miles up the Pearl River, which debouched into the sea a few miles south of the colony.

The gangway was opened, and a moment later Commander Toshida, the naval attache, was on board. "I must apologise for the welcome, honourable Commander," he said, giving Nicholas a quick bow. "Or perhaps I should say, the lack of it."

"I didn't expect to be popular here, honourable Commander."

"You were doing your duty," Toshida said severely. "These people cannot understand such things; the only important matters in Hong Kong are cricket and horse-racing. Mr Yosunobe and his family will be joining you this evening, and you will sail at dawn."

"Who is this Yosunobe, anyway?" Nicholas inquired.

"He is a businessman who has been attempting to set up an office here in Hong Kong," Toshida explained. "Unfortunately, he has fallen out with the Colonial Government, and has been asked to leave."

"And there was no merchant vessel available to give him passage?"

"Our Government wished him to leave on a ship of the Imperial Navy."

Nicholas scratched his nose. "You mean he is actually a government agent."

"I do not know about this, honourable Commander. I do know he is a personal friend of General Tojo."

"Then you mean he has been in Hong Kong as a spy."

"Again, I do not know this, honourable Commander. And it would be best for neither of us to inquire too deeply into the matter. As I say, he will be on board this evening, with his wife and daughter. But you will meet them before that. I am afraid, in all the circumstances, that it would be very unwise for you to give any of your men shore leave. The British have

193

very sensibly placed armed guards on this dock, so your ship will not be molested in any way, but of course they cannot offer any protection to Japanese sailors on the town. Feelings are running strongly. The *Sun Lily* was a regular visitor to Victoria, and her crew had many friends here."

"I understand this," Nicholas agreed.

"However, the Consul wishes to throw a small party this evening, for you and your executive officer, honourable Commander, and also as a farewell to Mr Yosunobe. I trust this is in order?"

Nicholas considered. It went against his instincts to attend a party when his crew were to be allowed no liberty. "The Consul would be very upset if you did not attend, honourable Captain," Toshida pointed out. "It is essential that we do not give the impression that we are in any way ashamed or guilty about the loss of the Chinese junk."

"You mean this is to be a big party."

"No, no. But in Hong Kong, every party is soon reported. And the guest list. I will send a car for you at seven, honourable Commander."

"Commander Barrett! Yours is a famous and welcome name!" Kayama Setsuko gave a quick bow. "My wife."

Nicholas bowed in turn to the Consul's wife. "My Executive Officer, Lieutenant Yashiwara." Yashiwara's bow was deeper.

"Now let me see," Kayama Yoko said, gesturing Nicholas to precede her into the reception room of the consulate. "Commander Toshida you already know. Honourable Commander, allow me to introduce you to Yosunobe Asawa." Nicholas and the 'businessman' bowed to each other. Yosunobe was a handsome man, with paler skin and more aquiline features than the average Japanese. This was not so uncommon in Japan, and although there were many theories put forward to explain the phenomenon, Nicholas went for a bloodline back to the Ainu, the Caucasian people who had inhabited the Japanese islands in the dawn of history before being overrrun.

Yosunobe's wife Aiwa was more orthodoxly Japanese, but her daughter Sumiko had her father's features, and was a

194

remarkably attractive young woman, dressed Western-style in a clinging sheath with a slit-skirt – in contrast to her mother's kimono – and high heeled shoes. She was wearing Western-style makeup, as well, which enhanced her beauty, and her hair was loose on her shoulders like a black shawl, rather than in a traditional chignon like her parent. "Sumiko was the name of my grandfather's first wife," Nicholas remarked.

"I am flattered," the girl said.

Nicholas wondered how old she was, but he was being drawn away to meet the rest of the guests, several of whom were members of the English community or Hong King residents. These were formally stiff. But at the end of the room there waited Linda Wells.

Nicholas was taken entirely by surprise. Linda was as lovely as ever, and her face wore a somewhat defiant expression. "I think you already know Miss Wells," Kayama Yoko suggested.

"Yes," Nicholas said.

"Then I will leave you to renew your acquaintance." His hostess slipped away.

"Quite a surprise," Nicholas remarked. "May I ask what decided you to come?"

"I was invited," she pointed out. "Besides, I wished to see for myself if you have become the monster you are considered."

"I obeyed orders."

"That has been the soldier's, and the sailor's, argument for centuries," she agreed. "I am not sure it is any longer valid."

"Neither am I."

She raised her eyebrows and he smiled. "Even a sailor is from time to time allowed to question an order."

"But not to disobey it."

"No," he said. "Orders cannot be disobeyed."

"I gather your stay in Hong Kong is going to be brief," she remarked, changing the subject.

"Unfortunately."

"Well, it has been nice meeting you again."

"I wouldn't like it to be as brief as all that. Dinner?"

"Ah . . . no, Commander."

"Afraid I might ask you to marry me again? As a matter of fact, I probably shall."

"But you won't, because I haven't accepted your invitation."

"I think I have a right to know why."

She made a moue. "I think, orders or no orders, your behaviour was despicable."

He studied her. "Then marry me, and reform me. I love you."

"There's not enough time for that," she said, and smiled at the man behind him.

"I am glad to be away from that place," Yosunobe Sumiko confided, as she stood on the bridge of *Shiratsuyu* and watched the islands fall away behind her. The sun was just rising out of the Pacific and it promised to be a glorious morning, but Nicholas had not expected any of his passengers to be on deck so early. "And actually to stand on the deck of a Japanese warship, oh, this is heaven!"

He wondered how she was going to get on back in Japan, for she was wearing trousers and a loose shirt, a most unJapanese-like ensemble, even if it had recently become very popular with English and American women. "Are you glad to be going home?" he asked.

"I think one must always be glad to be going home, honourable Commander."

"How long have you been away?"

"Six years. Honourable Father was in Singapore before he went to Hong Kong."

Six years, he thought; she would have been nine or ten when she left Japan. Saito would still have been alive, and so would Yoshiye and my father. And Uncle Takamori. And all of that time her father had been a spy! He wondered if she knew that, and if she cared? But she was utterly attractive, and she had allowed herself to become westernised. He wished to know what she thought of it all. "When you left Japan, we were at peace," he remarked.

196

She gave a quick smile. "Are we not at peace now, honourable Commander? No war has been declared."

She was no ill-informed Japanese flower, that was certain. But then, he did not wish her to be. "I would like to ask you a question," he said.

"Please do."

"I have been roundly condemned in Hong Kong for my action in leaving the Chinese junk to sink."

"It was in the newspaper," she agreed.

"How do you feel about that?"

"I think it was wrong." She turned her head to look at him. "But I understand why you had to do it."

Yamamoto Isoroku stood on the gantry, looking down on the dry dock and the monstrous hull which sat there, waiting to be launched. "What do you think of her?" he asked.

The hot July sun glinted from the freshly painted steel, flickered from the hard hats of the myriad construction workers down there. It flickered too from the guns and bayonets of the guards who constantly patrolled, not only the gantry but the dockyard floor itself. No ship could ever have been constructed in greater secrecy. But she was more than the answer to a dream, the battleship of the future, which would revolutionise naval warfare as much as the British *Dreadnought* had done in 1906: in this summer of 1940 she had become a necessity.

For not even Yosunobe Sumiko could now argue that the world was not at war, at least in Europe and on the high seas. Japan remained at peace, officially, but her armies were still heavily engaged in China, and more importantly, had fought pitched battles with Russian forces along the borderline of the Amur River, although these huge and bloody conflicts had not been widely reported, on either side. And if Great Britain was wholly committed to Europe, and was clearly teetering on the brink of defeat, the Americans were daily growing more bellicose in their condemnation of Japanese actions: they had been stirred to anger by the 'accidental' sinking of one of their gunboats up the Yangste-Kiang in 1938.

But not even the Americans had anything to match this

197

monster. "She is incredible," Nicholas said. "What is to be her name?"

"*Yamato*. Is that not fitting?"

"Indeed, honourable Admiral."

Yamato was an alternative name for the Empress Himiko, the first known ruler of Japan, in the first century, B.C. The word also encapsulated the very spirit of militant Japan.

"And she is only the first of several. The keel of her sister, *Mushashi*, is already laid. But you will serve on this ship, with me. She will be the flagship of the new Imperial Navy. I am therefore seconding you now, to oversee the preparations for her launching. You will work with Commander Tomowara, who will be her executive officer. Part of your job will be to keep the shipyard up to scratch. I want this ship in full commission by the end of next year, at the latest."

"We are at war, honourable Admiral," Nicholas reminded him. "Regardless of what the politicians may say. Should I not continue to serve?"

"You will be performing a far greater service by having *Yamato* ready for sea by December 1941 than you ever could by sailing up and down the Chinese coast," Yamamoto told him. "Anyway, you have had four tours of patrol duty, and what is there to do out there?" He gazed in Nicholas's eyes. "Save sink unarmed junks. Or rather, watch them sink."

"Yes," Nicholas said.

"You are aware that Lieutenant Fushiwara filed a report on your actions, regarding the junk *Sun Lily* and the British gunboat *Flamenco*, year before last?" Yamamoto asked.

"I was not aware of it, honourable Admiral. I was in fact surprised that he had not appeared to do so."

"I suppressed it," Yamamoto said. "I think your attitude was entirely correct."

"Thank you, honourable Admiral." But Nicholas could not stop himself adding, "I was endeavouring to obey your orders."

"You and I, Nicholas, are fighting seamen. We must always find commerce-destroying repugnant. It is the tragedy of my life that I have never had the opportunity of leading a fleet into battle. However, that day will surely come, and sooner than you think."

"Honourable Admiral?" Nicholas was mystified.

"Consider recent events, Nicholas." Yamamoto led him down the ladders from the gantry to the waiting automobile, got into the back seat, and gestured Nicholas to sit beside him. "When, last September, the democracies finally summoned the courage to go to war, no one knew what was going to happen. I can tell you that our political masters were very worried. Had Germany collapsed as it was forecast she would, our position might have become serious, as we would have been exposed to a hostile world, and one which, moreover, was mobilised and had tasted blood. But what do we see now? France has surrendered to Germany, after a campaign so brief it makes one wonder if this new Germany is really something to be afraid of, or if it is merely that the French army is rotten to the core. However, whatever the reason, it is a momentous event. It means not only that Great Britain now fights alone, and will thus have to concentrate all her forces upon Europe, but more important from our point of view, all the various French overseas possessions have now been at least neutralised. Tell me, have you read those papers I gave you? The various scenarios and possibilities investigated by your honourable father?"

"I have, honourable Admiral." Suddenly Nicholas's heart began to pound.

"Can you recall his conclusions?"

"Yes," Nicholas said. "That any positive movement of the fleet to the south would expose it to attack by shore-based bombers from Malaya and French Indo-China."

"But now French Indo-China is to be regarded as at worst a neutral," Yamamoto pointed out. "While, if *we* had the use of those air bases instead of the British . . . I can tell you that we have already opened negotiations with the Vichy Government for the use of bases there. Continue. What next?"

"My father was of the opinion that any violent expansion to the south would bring us into conflict with the Royal Navy," Nicholas said, feeling exactly as he had done when watching the Chinese women and children drown.

"But the Royal Navy is fully committed to the North Atlantic and the Mediterranean. Are you not aware that both *Bismarck* and *Tirpitz* are virtually complete? The Royal Navy will soon have its hands full. Go on. What else did your father say?"

"That any movement of our armies to the south would expose us to invasion by Russia in the north," Nicholas said desperately.

"Yes. But I can tell you in confidence that Foreign Minister Matsuoko is on his way to Moscow now to finalise an arrangement with Molotov. But there was a fourth hazard mentioned by your father."

"The most important one, in my opinion, honourable Admiral: intervention by the United States. There is a battle fleet of at least six battleships and three aircraft-carriers in Hawaii."

"Agreed. When your father made that objection, there seemed little chance of the United States interfering with our plans, due to their own internal preoccupations. Now, I think the situation may have changed. I think the most significant thing that has happened this last year, even more significant than the French surrender, is Roosevelt's announcement that he intends to run for a third term. This is entirely against American history. He is attempting to justify his decision by saying it is necessary because of the world situation. This can only mean that he intends to take a more prominent part in world affairs. He is already assisting Britain against Germany by all the means in his power short of actually declaring war, which he cannot do without the consent of Congress. But should we go south, he may well order that Hawaiian fleet to sea, and it could prove a considerable problem. I mean, consider the situation if we were engaged against say, the British and Dutch, and an American warship, whether instructed to do so or inadvertently, strayed into the battle zone? We could well find ourselves at war with the United States without meaning to."

"Yes," Nicholas said, most vehemently.

Yamamoto smiled. "If we ever have to go to war with America, it should be done deliberately, do you not agree?"

"Absolutely, honourable Admiral."

"Therefore I would like you to use all of your father's papers and assessments, bearing in mind the alterations in

200

fleet strength since he made those assessments, and prepare for me a scenario for defeating America."

"Me, honourable Admiral?"

"I think you have your father's brain. What is more important, I know you have his detachment. I want a cool, unemotional approach to this problem. This is very important to the future of Japan."

"Honourable Admiral, I do not believe Japan can defeat the United States in a war. It might be possible to defeat their navy in one big battle, but . . ."

Yamamoto tapped him on the knee as the car drove into the Admiralty grounds. "Tell me how to win that one big battle, Nicholas: that is all I wish. Now, let us speak of less bloodthirsty subjects: your marriage. Your stepmother has remarried, and you need a mother for your young brother. I have spoken with Hitachi Kano."

"With respect, honourable Admiral . . ." Nicholas flushed.

Yamamoto raised his eyebrows. "You have changed your mind about the girl?"

"I have found the woman I would have as my wife, honourable Admiral. For myself," he added, somewhat defiantly.

"Tell me of her."

"Yosunobe Sumiko."

"Ah so," Yamamoto said thoughtfully. "You know, of course, that Yosunobe Asawa is an agent of the *Kempeitai*?"

"I am sure his daughter is not, honourable Admiral."

"And she is very beautiful." Yamamoto grinned. "Then marry her, and be happy, and prepare my war plan. But . . ." he wagged his finger. "Do not tell your wife of it."

"My lord!" Yosunobe Sumiko knelt before Nicholas in the privacy of their bedroom. Outside the noise of clearing up the debris of the wedding continued, for they had been married in a Shinto ceremony, which had been attended not only by Yamamoto, but by General Tojo himself. But in the bedroom it was quiet.

Sumiko raised her head when he did not immediately

201

reply. "Is that not the proper form of address, honourable Husband?"

Nicholas did not suppose he would ever be sure when she was mocking him. The very deference with which she acted the part of a Japanese wife was a mockery, when taken with the flashing black eyes, the curiously arrogant twist of her lips. "It is the proper form of address, yes," he said.

He stood above her, more than twice her size. Mock him she might do, but yet she was now his wife, to be possessed. It was a salutary thought, which had crossed his mind more than once during the past few weeks, during this evening, in fact, that in her and through her he sought to avenge his father, and the wrong done him by Japanese womanhood in the person of Christina, so proud on the arm of her new husband throughout the ceremony. And yet . . . Sumiko could never know the depths of his emotions, the depravity of his past, but she had become his bride, and he was certain she was no typical Japanese. "Do you love me, Sumiko?"

"I am your wife, honourable Husband."

He untied the obi, slid the kimono from her shoulders. She was seventeen years old, somewhat more than the average Japanese bride; it was almost as if she had waited these two years for him. Or perhaps he was the first man of her acquaintance bold enough to marry into the *Kempei-tai*. She was not very tall, but she had a much fuller figure than the average, too. He cupped her breasts, and stroked the nipples with an elongated forefinger, awaiting a response, but she did no more than stare at him. "Then tell me why you married me."

"It was my father's wish."

"Do you always do as your father wishes?"

She unfastened his obi in turn. "Of course. But it was my wish as well." She looked down his body, slowly and appraisingly, without any suggestion of either coquetry or embarrassment. Then she raised her head to look at his face.

"You know I will hurt you," he said.

"Then hurt me," she said. "Hurt me, hurt me, hurt me!"

He took her in his arms, and kissed her mouth, savagely. So savagely that he tasted blood. But when he released her she was smiling. "Fuck me like a European," she said. "Lay me on my back and ram me."

He obeyed her, and she arched her body to receive him. She was far stronger than she looked, and was not overwhelmed by either his weight or his passion. When she lay back beneath him he felt her legs wrap themselves around his body to draw him ever more into her, and where he had expected at least a grunt of pain there was only her wide-smiling mouth and even a hint of laughter. He rolled off her, more sated than ever before in his life. "Where have you been, all of my life?" he asked.

She raised herself on her elbow. "Waiting for you."

He gazed at her face, so beautiful and so innocent. And yet, not innocent at all. "Where did you learn words like fuck and ram?"

She made a moue. "I have read many books."

"What books?"

"Books I found in Singapore and Hong Kong. Books by a man called Henry Miller, and others. But Miller I liked best."

"How on earth did you get hold of books by Henry Miller?"

"Honourable father brought them home, for himself and honourable mother to read. He said it was necessary for them to understand the depravity of the Western mind."

"And he gave them to you as well?"

Sumiko lay down again, pillowed on her hair, legs flung wide. "No. I read them when he and honourable Mother were out."

It was his turn to raise himself on his elbow. "And do you think the Western mind is depraved?"

"I do not see how sex can be depraved. Without sex, without the enjoyment of sex, none of us would be here. Thus the gods, who meant us to be here, must also mean us to enjoy sex. But from what I have read, in the newspapers and in other books, I think the West thinks of *itself* as depraved. Certainly it thinks of Mr Miller as depraved. I think that is an absurdity."

"I am of the West, in blood."

She smiled at him. "But you are not afraid of sex."

203

"No," he said. "Not with you, anyway. We are going to be very happy together, Sumiko."

Her smile faded. "Honourable Father says there is going to be a war."

"There already is a war."

"Pouf." Her lip curled, contemptuously. "I am not speaking of China. Honourable father says there is going to be a war with the West. I would not like this. You would not like it either, honourable Husband, as you are of their blood."

"And why would you not like it?"

"Because I like the West. I like Singapore and Hong Kong. I like the clothes and the people and the way of life."

"Even if they might think you depraved?"

"They do not know me," she said wisely. "But more than any of that, a war would mean you would have to go away, and perhaps be killed. I do not wish you to go away, honourable Husband. And if you were to be killed . . ." her fingers closed on his wrist. "I would kill myself."

He put his finger on her lips. "Do not talk like that. You will have your children to care for."

"How can I have children to care for if you are away at a war?"

He kissed her. "We are attending to that matter now, and will continue to do so for the next fortnight."

But she returned to the subject when he was again spent. "Do not let there be a war, honourable Husband."

"I'm afraid it is not in my province, my dearest girl, either to start a war, or prevent one happening."

"You are a friend of Yamamoto. Everyone knows this. Thus you are at the very centre of power."

He kissed her again. "But only a very small cog in the machine."

Yet the cog with the mightiest task of all. And as he sat at his desk and gazed at the papers he had prepared, he was horrified at the conclusions to which he had been drawn. But he had been commanded to draw them. It would be war, on the biggest and most bloody scale the world had ever seen; the German *blitzkrieg* which had proved so successful in Europe would be a tea party compared with this war.

He had no desire to go to war, with anyone, much less America and Britain. He did not even like this war with China. All he wished to do was go home to his beautiful and so eager bride every evening, and forget all the other women who had so tormented his life. The thought of leaving her, even for a short while, much less forever, was like a knife turning in his stomach. Yet he had to agree with Yamamoto that if there was going to *be* a war it had to be won, or at least, the Japanese aims had to be achieved – and it was better that its conduct be left principally in the hands of the Navy, rather than the Army.

He gathered his papers and went to Yamamoto's office. The door was opened for him, and he checked in surprise, for not only the Admiral was present; with him were Prince Konoye Fumimara, the Prime Minister, and, biggest surprise of all, Tojo Hideki, who Nicholas had supposed was commanding an army in north China.

"Come in, Commander," Yamamoto said. "Gentlemen, may I present Commander Barrett, my Director of Operations? I think you have already met Commander Barrett, General Tojo."

Nicholas bowed deeply to the three men. "I met you at your wedding, Commander," Tojo said, eyes glinting behind his steel-framed spectacles. "Yosunobe Asawa is proud to be your father-in-law."

"I am very fortunate, honourable General."

"Sit down, Commander," Yamamoto said. "I would like you to give these gentlemen the conclusions you have reached about the possible next stages of our programme."

Nicholas looked at his chief in consternation. "Exactly as you have put it to me, Commander," Yamamoto said, quietly.

Nicholas licked his lips as he looked at the faces in front of him; Konoye and Tojo were interested, certainly, but also somewhat sceptical that a mere naval commander should be telling them what needed to be done. He cleared his throat. "The aim of Japan is to regain great power status and to obtain the necessary markets for its goods, and room for expansion for its people. These aims are resisted by the Western democracies, and especially the Anglo-Saxon nations."

205

The men waited. "Occupying the seaboard of China is a first step in this direction, as has been the rebuilding of the fleet. By the end of 1941 Japan will have a battle fleet second to none in the world. Especially will it be equipped with battleships unmatched in the world. However, the basic problem, of expansion and the obtaining of essential raw materials, has not yet been solved. We have stockpiled sufficient oil for four years, but at a peacetime rate of consumption; it would be wholly inadequate in time of all-out war. The same goes for rubber and tin. There is a serious shortage of steel. This last will be difficult to overcome, but oil, rubber and tin lie in abundance to the south of us.

"At the present time, the situation with the Western democracies is very favourable. France has been crushed, Great Britain is beleaguered and is expected soon to seek to make peace with Germany. At the moment, she has neither men nor ships available for the Far Eastern theatre. However, should peace be concluded with Germany, we do not know what the situation will then be. Germany is our ally, but Hitler has shown a distressing trend not to inform us of his proposed actions. In the past he has made a condition of peace the surrender of the Royal Navy. This would suit us admirably. But it is possible that he may change his mind and seek compensation elsewhere, thus an end to the European War could release the entire Royal Navy for action in the Pacific.

"Politically, therefore, the situation is perhaps as favourable as it is ever going to be, for a strike against Malaya and the Dutch East Indies. However, our new battleships and aircraft-carriers are not yet in commission. The decision must be taken as to whether to strike now, with inferior forces, or wait eighteen months, when we would be able to defeat the Royal Navy in battle, regardless of the number of ships they have available." He paused, and again looked from face to face.

"If you are certain you will be able to defeat the Royal Navy in eighteen months time, then we should wait," Konoye remarked, looking at Yamamoto.

Yamamoto nodded to Nicholas. "There is, however,

another factor to be considered," Nicholas went on. "The attitude of the United States. The Roosevelt Administration is becoming more and more hostile to our advance in China. They are leading the world in accusing us of atrocities in places like Nanking. Although they have accepted an indemnity for the sinking of their gunboat *Panay*, there can be no doubt that the incident still causes deep resentment. I know it is against American policy and history for them to go to war where their immediate national interests are not threatened, but we must take them into consideration. There are now nine American battleships and three aircraft-carriers based on Pearl Harbour in Hawaii, and more ships could of course be transferred through the Panama Canal if required. This is a formidable force. We could not guarantee victory against such a force. If it were to be supported by the Royal Navy, we would be unable to fight a battle in favourable circumstances."

His listeners exchanged glances. "It follows therefore," Nicholas went on, "that the United States must be neutral-ised, in one way or another. Either she must be so placated diplomatically that there will be no chance of her interfering, or she must be eliminated from our calculations as a possible antagonist. The first option can never be anything more than a temporary arrangement, as it will depend entirely upon which administration is in power in Washington; this is liable to change every four years. The second involves a great risk, but we believe it can be satisfactorily accomplished."

"How?" Tojo demanded.

"If the American Pacific fleet could be eliminated, both before it could unite with the Royal Navy and before it was itself ready for war."

"You mean, a surprise attack, as we launched on the Russians in Port Arthur in 1904," Konoye said. "Before a declaration of war."

Nicholas looked at Yamamoto. "This would make us even more an outlaw amongst nations," Yamamoto said. "But such a surprise attack could be delivered within a very short space of time *following* the declaration of war, providing the Americans know nothing of our intention to *go* to war until the declaration is made."

"That will be a very finely defined business, Admiral," Konoye said.

"The entire business will have to be very finely defined, honourable Prime Minister," Yamamoto pointed out.

"You are talking of an attack on Pearl Harbour," Tojo said. "How can you get within range of it without being discovered?"

"That is the Navy's concern," Yamamoto said.

"Very well. And having got within range, you believe that you can eliminate the entire American Pacific Fleet? I do not recall that the Navy was entirely successful in Port Arthur."

"This attack will be far more decisive, because it will be delivered in greater strength, and by planes rather than torpedo boats. I am not guaranteeing to destroy the entire American fleet. I am guaranteeing so to reduce it that we can then force the remnants to a fleet encounter in favourable circumstances."

"And you believe such a defeat will force the Americans to sue for peace?" Konoye asked, looking at Yamamoto.

"No, honourable Prime Minister. We must be very clear about this. The Americans will not sue for peace because their fleet is destroyed. They will, in fact, wish to fight the harder. And in the long run they will prove the stronger, both because there are more of them and because they have the greater natural resources. It must be our business to use the time we will have before they can mobilise their full strength to create an impregnable fortress within which we can live and prosper in our own way." The Admiral got up from his desk and went to the huge wall chart of the Pacific. "Our first step must be to obtain bases in French Indo-China." He looked at Konoye.

"These are virtually conceded," the Prime Minister said.

"Then, once those bases are operational, we will be in a position to attack Malaya and the Dutch East Indies in great strength. This attack must be carried out at the same time as the attack on Pearl Harbour, and this means that we must also attack and occupy the Philippines, before the Americans can fortify those islands and increase their strength there." It was Yamamoto's turn to look from face to face. "I know this sounds like an immense undertaking, but it is necessary, and once these initial objectives have been achieved, it will be necessary to attack again, in another wave." He picked up a wand from his desk and began tapping the chart. "Our aim must be to create three concentric rings of fortified positions. The outer ring will be this natural arc of islands. You see, it stretches from the Aleutian Islands in the extreme north, past Midway Island to Christmas Island, thence round to Fiji and New Caledonia, and thence back to New Guinea and along to the Dutch East Indies, thence up to Siam. It should incorporate Siam as well up to the southern borders of China, which we will then also occupy."

His listeners stared at the map in consternation, and Yamamoto grinned at them. "In terms of square mileage, it will be the greatest empire the world has ever seen."

"Your line is within a few hundred miles of the Hawaiian Islands," Tojo commented. "Would it not be simpler to occupy them as well?"

"We must be careful not to overplay our hand," Yamamoto explained. "You will see that these islands which do fall inside the perimeter, and I am not just talking about Midway and Christmas, Fiji and New Caledonia, but those which lie immediately behind them, such as the Marshalls, the Gilberts and the Solomons, are all sparsely populated and will be easy to dominate and fortify. They are all also beyond the range of the most advanced American bombers. Hawaii is not. It is also heavily populated and very pro-American. Besides, once the fleet is eliminated, Hawaii is of no importance; it can be neutralised as we choose by bombing raids from Midway." He tapped the map.

"Your proposed perimeter abuts both Australia in the south, and India in the west," Tojo remarked. "But these are not to be attacked?"

"Australia is a waste of time, just a desert. Once our perimeter is complete it will be entirely cut off from the rest of the Anglo-Saxon world. It can become a satellite. But to invade it would be a waste of men and resources. All that is necessary is to occupy Port Moresby on the south coast of New Guinea; from there our air force will dominate the Australian mainland. India is obviously beyond our scope.

We simply do not have the resources to conquer so vast and heavily populated a territory. However, as I am sure you know, honourable General, there is considerable unrest with British rule in India. I should imagine this unrest can be encouraged, and will grow, when the British have been thrown out of Malaya and south-east Asia in general."

Tojo nodded. "The man Bose."

"Absolutely. He has been in both Moscow and Berlin touting for help. They can give him none. We can. The point I am making, gentlemen, is that once we have established our perimeter, to be supported by our fleet, we will have created a position against which the Americans will hurl themselves in vain, and which they will have to accept as a *fait accompli*."

"And if they do not?"

"Then, honourable Prime Minister, our fate is in the lap of the gods."

"What have we to fear, if we have Indonesian oil and Malayan rubber and tin?" Tojo demanded.

"With respect, honourable General, I feel it is necessary for you to consider some statistics. We have now been at war for three years. Do you know how many machine tools are being operated in Japan? Sixty-seven thousand, two hundred and sixty."

"That is very impressive," Tojo said.

"Yes, but do you know how many machine tools are at this moment in use in the United States? A country which is still at peace? Nine hundred and forty-two thousand."

There was a stunned silence, and Yamamoto delivered some more hammer blows.

"In Germany, working at full capacity, there are just under one point two million tools in use. Now I imagine we might be able to double our capacity, by devoting all our steel and energy to that purpose. The Americans can double theirs almost at will, and without disorganising their economy. Then let us consider shipping. Forget the fleets, for the time being. The American merchant navy has a total tonnage of over eleven million. Ours is five-and-a-half million. The Americans produce twenty-nine billion tons of pig iron a year; we do not produce two billion. The Americans produce forty-two billion tons of steel a year. Again, we do not produce two! Most important of all, the Americans produce more than one and a quarter billion barrels of oil a year. We produce none. The Dutch East Indies, if we can seize it, produces fifty million. Now I will grant you that the Americans also consume oil at an enormous rate. The current figure is one billion, one hundred and sixty-seven million barrels a year. But that still leaves them with an oil surplus in the nature of a hundred million barrels, which can be increased by increasing their production, while their consumption can easily be cut by rationing. Here in Japan we are currently consuming thirty-four million barrels a year, and we have almost no room for cutting that figure as we are already on rationing anyway. Thus even with the Dutch output we would have a surplus of only sixteen million barrels. And I need hardly remind you gentlemen that while all America's production is home grown, ours will all have to be transported by tanker back to Japan, even if we manage to establish bases in south-east Asia, as I fully intend to do."

"What you are saying is that we dare not go to war with such a monster," Konoye remarked.

"What I am saying is that we dare not fight a war of attrition with such a monster, honourable Prime Minister. We must force them to make peace very rapidly."

"How rapidly?"

Yamamoto grinned. "Given the scenario outlined by Commander Barrett, which pre-supposes a continuation of the war in Europe and our ability to destroy the American Pacific Fleet at the outset of war, I can run wild for a year. After that . . ." he shrugged.

Konoye glanced at Tojo, then looked away again. "A year," he muttered.

"Our course is very plain," Tojo said. "Admiral Yamamoto is correct when he says that our armies are becoming bogged down in China. If we are to continue to expand it must be in other directions. This means that war with the Anglo-Saxons, or at least the British, is inevitable. Let us therefore prepare for that. But it can only be a successful war, again as Admiral Yamamoto has outlined . . ." he glanced at Nicholas in grudging admission of his part in drawing up the scenario,

211

"if the Soviet Union and the United States are eliminated as immediate enemies. We must therefore first of all try to eliminate them diplomatically, while preparing to eliminate them militarily, if we have to. While doing this, we will bring our fleet to its maximum efficiency and preparedness. As we will prepare our Army for whatever lies ahead. I believe that we can achieve the perimeter Admiral Yamamoto envisages, and I believe we can hold it, long enough at any event to make the Americans agree to a peace. They are not fighters, the Americans. They like money too much, and a comfortable life. I do not see them as a serious problem. The Russians now, are different. We must tell Foreign Minister Matsuoko to put forward his very best efforts to overcome Marshal Stalin's suspicions and make him an ally. After all, he is virtually allied to Hitler. Why should he not be allied to us?"

Yamamoto and Nicholas both looked at Konoye. Tojo had been speaking as if he were running the government, rather than the Prime Minister.

But Konoye did not seem offended. "Yes," he said. "That is what we must do. Is there anything else?"

"There are two vital questions which the Navy must address," Tojo said. "The destruction of the American fleet and the capture of Singapore. Until Singapore falls, Malaya will not fall, and that means the Dutch East Indies will not fall. Once Singapore falls, south-east Asia is ours, and we dominate the Indian Ocean. I assume you have given this some thought, honourable Admiral?"

Yamamoto bowed.

"He is right, of course," Yamamoto told Nicholas when they were alone. "Singapore is the key to south-east Asia."

"It is very strongly defended, honourable Admiral," Nicholas pointed out. "These plans have been prepared by Yosunobe Asawa, during his stay there, and I believe they are accurate."

"I am sure they are, as he is your honourable father-in-law," Yamamoto agreed, studying the several sheets of stiff paper.

"The only weakness is the absence of any capital ships,"

Nicholas went on. "However, this would obviously be remedied once war between Britain and Japan became likely. Great Britain is well on the way to completing her new battleship programme. There will be five of these new ships. They will be over forty thousand tons, deep-loaded, and will be armed with ten fourteen-inch guns. All have already been launched, and the first, *King George V*, is expected to be in commission before the end of this year. By the middle of next year the British may well be able to spare a squadron for the Pacific."

"That will entirely depend upon what use the Germans make of *Bismarck* and *Tirpitz*," Yamamoto argued. "They displace over fifty thousand tons and have eight fifteen-inch guns. That makes them more powerful than any Royal Navy ship, including the five coming off the stocks. Then there are the two battlecruisers, *Scharnhorst* and *Gneisenau*. They displace nearly forty thousand tons, and have nine eleven-inch. That is a formidable squadron. I do not believe the Royal Navy will be able to spare any ships from the North Atlantic until such a fleet has been eliminated, and all Hitler has to do is keep that fleet in being. He doesn't have to risk a battle until he is absolutely ready. And that will not be until the first of his aircraft-carriers is completed, at the least."

"He has an aircraft-carrier?" Nicholas was surprised.

"He is building two twenty-eight thousand tonners, and the first, *Graf Zeppelin*, is already in the water, although she is several months from completion. No, I do not think we have to concern ourselves with the Royal Navy in the Far East. Singapore may be a powerful base, but no base is worth much when it has nothing based on it. Our main problems are Russia and America. You have worked out the strategical plan, Nicholas. Now I wish you to work on a tactical one, for the destruction of the American fleet. Let me have your dispositions as soon as possible."

"Yes, honourable Admiral. And Russia?"

Yamamoto shrugged. "For that we must wait on Ambassador Matsuoko."

"Can you tell me what is on your mind, honourable Husband?" Sumiko asked.

213

"I am afraid it is naval matters," Nicholas said. He sat in the gazebo, and watched Alexander and some of his friends at play on the lawn, kicking a football about. Alexander was ten now, and a big, strong boy: he was going to be a true Barrett. If he was ever going to be given the chance to be a Barrett at all.

It was incredible that he should be sitting here, in the warm May sunshine, watching his son at play, enjoying the loving company of his beautiful wife, when tomorrow he would return to his office and continue planning the greatest war history would ever have known. And against his own blood! But they were his enemies, because his grandfather had adopted the Japanese as his people. Yet how he prayed that there could be some spectacular collapse of the Nazi regime, which would leave Britain as powerful as it had ever been in the past. The tragedy was that there would still be a war; the Japanese military machine had simply gone too far already. If that were the case, then the war had to be won, or everything he held dear would be lost. If it could be won.

Sumiko kissed his cheek. "Perhaps it will not be as bad as you think," she murmured.

Only a week later Nicholas was summoned to Yamamoto's office, to find his chief standing, staring out of the window. When he turned, his face was grim.

"These Germans know nothing about warfare," he said. "They have lost *Bismarck*!"

"Honourable Admiral?" Nicholas was astounded.

"Instead of waiting for *Tirpitz* and *Graf Zeppelin* to be commissioned, as any sane commanders would have done, or even trying to link her up with *Scharnhorst* and *Gneisenau* to make a battle squadron, the fools sent her out by herself, with only the cruiser *Emden* as escort; they did not even provide her with a destroyer screen. So she has been hunted down and sunk. The tragedy is, that she has shown what could have been done: with a single salvo she sank *Hood*."

"Then that is surely a triumph, honourable Admiral? *Hood* . . ."

"Was the Royal Navy's most famous ship. She was also one of the oldest, Nicholas. What is more, it has always been known that battlecruisers are vulnerable; I would have undertaken to destroy *Hood* by aerial attack within an hour. So, the Germans have sacrificed their newest and greatest warship for the Royal Navy's oldest and most vulnerable. What is more, they have now forever lost their chance of putting a battle squadron into the Atlantic. They have not only ruined themselves, given the British a great propaganda victory – two of their new battleships, *King George V* and *Prince of Wales*, took part in the battle, although I understand *Bismarck* was finally sunk by torpedoes – but they have completely upset our plans. It now appears entirely likely that the British will be able to spare a battle squadron for the Pacific."

Nicholas said nothing; it was what he had always suspected might happen. But it was also what he had always most wanted to happen. "So we will have to think again," Yamamoto said. "You must work on the assumption that when war comes, Singapore will be the base for a British squadron. Assume that it will contain at least three battleships and one aircraft-carrier."

"Yes, honourable Admiral. However, I am bound to say that in those circumstances it will be very difficult to envisage a favourable sea battle off Malaya. The enemy will not only have Singapore to fall back upon, but will be able to use land-based aircraft to offset any advantage we may hope to gain by possessing bases in French Indo-China."

Yamamoto stroked his chin. "War, they say, Nicholas, is a choice of difficulties. Let me see those plans Yosunobe prepared."

Nicholas spread theme before him, and Yamamoto pondered. "It is certainly a mighty fortress," he remarked at last. "Designed and equipped to repel any seaborne attack. But have you noticed something, Nicholas? There is not a gun, not an emplacement, not a single weapon, pointing north across the Strait of Johore to the mainland."

Nicholas frowned as he stood at his superior's shoulder. "That is because there can be no seaborne assault from the north, honourable Admiral. The Straits of Johore are in places hardly more than a hundred yards wide."

"Absolutely. But do we not have an army?"

215

Nicholas stared at him, open-mouthed. "We intend to seize Malaya in any event," Yamamoto pointed out. "The original concept was by seaborne landings *after* the fall of Singapore. But, Nicholas, suppose we reverse the process, make our seaborne landings at the north end of the peninsular, and capture Malaya *first*. What then, do you suppose?"

The immensity, but also the simplicity, of the plan, took Nicholas's breath away. Yet . . . "It will mean defeating the British forces on the ground, honourable Admiral, while their fleet is in being."

"Will we not have to defeat their army anyway, even if Singapore fell first? You do not expect the British to surrender, do you? It is more than a hundred and fifty years since a British army surrendered to anybody, and Cornwallis only had eight thousand men. Percival has *eighty* thousand. Nor can their battleships do much to help them ashore, save by bombardment. That is something our people will just have to put up with."

"But, honourable Admiral, even if defeated, they will have Singapore to retreat upon. Once they cross the causeway, if they blow it up, as they will, they will be on an island."

"Created by a strait which as you have pointed out is in places only a hundred yards wide. That is surely not an insuperable obstacle. Nor will the enemy be able to move those massive guns to face north. Consider it, Nicholas. Singapore, already one of the most crowded places on earth, jammed with eighty thousand troops, only two water reservoirs, and an already active Japanese fifth column . . . it will be a massacre."

"Yes, honourable Admiral," Nicholas said grimly.

"So, prepare plans for an invasion of Malaya from the north. I understand that it will be necessary to liaise with the Army, but we will not do so until our own plans are ready."

"Yes, honourable Admiral. May I ask a question, sir?"

"Certainly."

"We obviously would intend to knock out all the British possessions in the Far East?"

"All which fall within our designated perimeter, of course. But I have established that we will not be attempting to occupy Australia and New Zealand."

216

"I understand this, honourable Admiral. But it would include places like Hong Kong?"

"Of course."

"It truly grieves me to see you so down-hearted, honourable Husband," Sumiko said as they lay together on their mattress. She was the more upset because he had been impotent. "I am sure if you were to share your burden with me, I would be able to relieve you of at least part of it."

He hugged her. "And I wish I could, share my burden."

"We are going to war," she said.

He looked down on the crown of her glossy head. "Who has told you that?"

"Honourable stepfather-in-law."

"Takeda? Well, he should know. He is in the secret police. Do you see him often?"

"Honourable mother-in-law comes to call, often. Well, she wishes to see Alexander. She tells me what her husband says."

Nicholas hadn't realised there was any intimacy between his wife and his stepmother. Nor did he much like the idea of it. "What else does she tell you?" he asked.

"What else is there to tell? Except about you."

"Eh?"

"Honourable stepmother-in-law is very fond of you, honourable Husband. I think she loves you as much as Alexander."

"No doubt I remind her of my father," Nicholas said, and stared at the ceiling.

Yes, he thought, we are going to war, and a huge number of innocent people are going to be killed. A huge number of innocent people were already being killed. But it was the one's in the future that concerned him. Presumably Sumiko and Charlotte were safe enough; Japan was simply too far away from any hostile country, apart from China, ever to be bombed, and China was now virtually a Japanese province, save for the interior, many hundreds of miles away. But what of Linda Wells, enjoying the good life in Hong Kong, and not realising the immense threat that lay over her? There was nothing he could do about it, save pray that Russia

217

might prove so intransigent that even the Army would not dare turn its back on the bear.

Only a month after the sinking of the *Bismarck*, Yamamoto called him into his office. "Everything comes to he who waits, Nicholas," the Admiral said with a broad grin. "This morning the Germans invaded Russia."

CHAPTER 9

The Attack

Nicholas could not believe his ears. "But that is madness."

Yamamoto shrugged. "I agree that no one has ever successfully invaded Russia since Genghis Khan, and then Russia didn't exist. But that is not our concern. Hitler presumably thinks the war in Europe is won. The important thing is that Russia need no longer be considered as a threat; whether or not they can cope with Hitler they certainly cannot afford to fight us as well. In fact, I can tell you in confidence that the Russian ambassador has already called upon the Foreign Office to ascertain our intentions."

"And what *are* our intentions, honourable Admiral?"

"Why, to remain strictly neutral. The Russians would like to move the troops they have maintained along our border for the past ten years and use them against the Germans. We have assured them that they may do this, as we have no intention of ever crossing the Amur. We have bigger fish to fry."

"That will not please the Germans."

"Oh, we are assuring Hitler of our moral support, but are explaining that with our commitments in China we are quite unprepared for any additional war. They understand this. Anyway, as they embarked on this adventure without informing us, they really cannot expect us to go charging in. No, no, Nicholas. Everything is falling into place. There remains only America."

Nicholas felt he was perhaps the only sane man in a world that was going mad. He carried out his duties, and prepared the plans that Yamamoto wanted. Just how serious, and how imminent was the situation, he realised when he was sent down to Kyushu, ostensibly on holiday, but in reality to locate an area where the topography approximated Diamond Head in Hawaii; this was for the Navy pilots to train in identification and approach.

He duly found the required cliff, close to the seaport of Nagasaki. Sumiko accompanied him on his 'vacation', thrilled on this her first visit to the old family home on Subashi *Wan*. Even Nicholas managed to relax for a few days – although the place brought back so many memories of Linda – but when he returned to Tokyo it was to sit down with Yamamoto and General Yamashita, who it appeared had been already designated commander-in-chief of the Army of Malaya, to follow through the plan for capturing Singapore from the north. With them was Yosunobe Asawa, to give them the benefit of his on-the-spot observations.

"You will understand that this is some of the thickest jungle in the world," Nicholas's father-in-law explained. "Are any of your men trained in jungle warfare, honourable General?"

"No," Yamashita said. "That is something that must be attended to. Where can I find a suitable jungle?" He was not joking.

"We have already demanded, and been granted, the use of bases in French Indo-China," Yamamoto said. "Some of these will be air bases, but others can be used for jungle training."

"That is some of the thickest jungle in the world."

"It is the jungle in which you will have to fight, or something very similar," Yamamoto told him.

"My men will not like it," Yamashita said.

"It is a matter of not being afraid, of the noises and the leeches and the snakes," Yosunobe said seriously. "These things are a nuisance, but a soldier should always remember that he stands far more chance of being killed by an enemy bullet than of dying from snakebite."

"I will make that point to my people." Yamashita said, and peered at the map. "What is more important is the lack of roads, or railways, in Malaya." He looked at Yamamoto.

"Are your people going to be able to land us further down the coast?"

"Not if there is a British battle squadron sitting in Singapore," Yamamoto said. "That is the whole reason for making it a land campaign. There *are* roads." He prodded the map. "Here, and here, and here."

"Half a dozen roads which could possibly support tanks or heavy artillery, and which, as the enemy will be aware of this, can easily be blocked." Yamashita scratched his chin. "I am told I can have no more than eighty thousand men," he said. "That is the same size as Percival's garrison. And those are men who are used to the terrain."

"With respect, honourable General," Yosunobe said. "I do not think that is correct. Most of them are raw troops, and traditionally, Anglo-Saxons are afraid of the jungle."

"You do not think my men are going to be afraid of the jungle?"

"Aren't there Indians in Percival's force, honourable Father-in-law?" Nicholas asked. "These men will certainly be used to jungle warfare." If the general could become sufficiently discouraged . . .

"They also are raw troops," Yosunobe assured him.

"Speed is the essence of any campaign," Yamashita grumbled. "Yet you are asking me to move my army three hundred and fifty miles, from the Siamese border to Singapore, in the face of equal numbers and with half a dozen roads and no railways."

"Are you saying it cannot be done, honourable General?" Yamamoto asked.

"I am saying it will take a long time."

"And we do not have a long time. It is essential that Singapore falls just as rapidly as possible. All our plans hinge on this." Yamamoto looked at Nicholas.

Nicholas sighed. But he could not let Yamamoto down. "With respect, honourable General, we will possess certain advantages. The element of surprise, certainly. The fifth column in Singapore itself. The fact that the defenders will be composed of disparate elements, British, Australian, Indian . . . if the attack could be carried out with sufficient boldness and imagination . . ."

Yamashita snorted. "The boldest and most imaginative general in the world still needs to be able to move his men from A to B, quickly and efficiently."

"The secret of this campaign will be to flow like the tide," Yamamoto said. "Go to the beach, honourable General, and observe. The incoming tide seeks its way by gullies and inlets. When it meets a rock, it does not waste its time battering against it; it flows round it, and within minutes the rock is surrounded."

"Men are not as mobile as water," Yamashita objected.

"They can be." Yamamoto snapped his fingers. "Bicycles."

Yamashita stared at him. "There *are* roads in Malaya," Yamamoto said. "Many more than appear on the map. Most of them are tracks, and few of them, as you say, honourable General, could be used by a military column. How do the natives get about, Yosunobe?"

"Of course, honourable Admiral. They use bicycles."

"There is your mobility, honourable General. Train your men in jungle warfare. But also train an advance guard to carry bicycles, infiltrate round the enemy strongpoints, and use their bicycles to spread terror in the rear. Then, when the strongpoint defenders are looking over their shoulders, send your tanks down the main roads."

"An army, advancing on bicycles?"

"Did not the French, and the Germans, use bicycles at the start of the Great War, honourable General?" Nicholas asked.

"That was twenty-seven years ago, Commander. And as you say, it was at the start of that war, not the finish. They had progressed beyond bicycles by then." Yamashita stroked his chin. "But it might work, if only for the surprise element."

"It will work," Yamamoto insisted. "Once the enemy have had one experience of being infiltrated and attacked in the rear, they will be always looking over their shoulders. That is a victory in itself."

"And terror," Yosunobe added. "Have your men act with great brutality to any captured soldiers, and to any Europeans. Tell them to loot and kill without mercy. That will cause great distress."

"With respect, honourable Father-in-law," Nicholas protested.

"Commander Barrett is right, Yosunobe," Yamamoto said. "That is no way to wage war."

"It is the way we waged war in China, honourable Admiral," Yosunobe said. "With great success."

"And great international condemnation," Nicholas remarked.

"Do we care for international opinion, when we are fighting for survival?" Yosunobe demanded.

"The campaign will be fought at the discretion of the general," Yamamoto said, and looked at Yamashita.

"My men will fight according to the laws of *bushido*," Yamashita said.

"It is not proper, for a son-in-law to correct his father-in-law," Yosunobe Asawa remarked, when he and Nicholas left the Admiral's office.

"Then I apologise, honourable Father-in-law," Nicholas said. "But I believe you were wrong to advocate mistreatment of prisoners and civilians. Are we not attempting to regain our place amongst the great nations of the world? To do that means we must also endeavour to make that world a better place to live in."

"A better place to live in," Yosunobe sneered. "Christian claptrap! In the first place wars are won by breaking the enemy's will to fight. This is best done by terrifying him. In the second place, I am speaking of the Anglo-Saxons. You may have their blood, Nicholas, but you have never had to live amongst them, as I have done, to be treated as an inferior, to be refused entrance to the Raffles Hotel in Singapore or the Jockey Club in Hong Kong. They have never endeavoured to make the world a better place for anyone to live in, save themselves. If I had my way, I would not take a single Anglo-Saxon prisoner, man, woman, or child."

"Spoken like an employee of the *Kempei-tai*," Nicholas remarked.

Yosunobe glared at him, then walked away.

*　　*　　*

Sumiko bent her head over her screen, on which she was painting, with considerable skill, a pastoral scene dominated by a huge red torii, the gateway to a shinto shrine. Nicholas had come home early, and Alexander was still at school. "It is sad, when a husband quarrels with his father-in-law," she remarked, quietly. "You did not tell me of this, honourable Husband."

"Our difference was over a highly confidential matter, Sumiko. You mean *he* has told you of it?"

"Only that you disagreed before senior officers. This was humiliating for him."

"It was a point of principle." He sat beside her, and would have kissed her mouth, but she turned her face away, and he kissed her cheek instead. "Surely it is unbecoming for a wife to take *anyone*'s part against her husband?" he chided, playfully.

"I am sad," she said.

"Then I am sorry. But your father was advocating a point of view, which could become a plank of government policy, with which I could not possibly agree. Had I done so, I would have been betraying my own principles."

"Men are allowed to have principles," Sumiko remarked. "Women must make do with feelings. Thus I am sad. When I should be happy."

"I would always wish you to be happy, my dearest wife."

"I should be happy, now," Sumiko said, "because I am to bear your child."

His eyes were wide. "Are you sure?"

"I am as sure as it is possible to be." At last she smiled. "It would seem that we both enjoyed our holiday in Bungo." Now she allowed him to kiss her lips.

Nicholas realised he was in the deepest of cleft sticks. He had actually been toying with the idea of resigning his commission, while knowing all the while that it was impossible. Western ideals did not obtain in Japan; the only acceptable protest against one's superiors was *seppuku*, and he had already rejected that. Perhaps Christina had made a coward of him. More realistically, she had made him understand his position. As well as being unique, it was in many ways an

224

untenable one, and becoming increasingly so. He had been brought up as a Christian, and to have a considerable respect for the Anglo-Saxon people from whom he was descended. Christianity apart – and the modern Japanese were utterly tolerant of other people's beliefs – he had not found his ethics out of step at Eta-Jima; every naval cadet was taught to respect the ideals and traditions of the Royal Navy from which their own navy had taken so much, and in any event he had been protected by the aura of his father and even more his grandfather.

He felt that the average Navy officer had not changed that much, although perhaps he was in the process of changing – Lieutenant Yashiwara was an example of that. But as long as their commanders were men of the stamp of Yamamoto they had nothing to fear, ethically. Save that Yamamoto was himself now being gripped by the paranoia that seemed to have the entire country by the throat. If only the English and American admirals and politicians who had attended the Washington Conference had been able, or sufficiently interested, to understand the people with whom they had been dealing. The Americans, like Henry Ford, might dismiss history as "bunk", yet they remained proud enough of their own, as evidenced by the huge volume of books and films dealing with the civil war and the conquest of the West; the only other universally popular subject for Western literature and art was the legend of the Christ. But they had been quite unable to grasp that to the Japanese, whose religion consisted of actually worshipping the past, history was the very breath of life. And if the Japanese were proud of their antique heroes such as Yoritomo and Hideyoshi and Iyeyasu, how much prouder were they of the achievements of their fathers and grandfathers, who by an excess of zeal and courage and determination not equalled by any people in the world, had in a single generation, leapt from being a small and backward people, ripe for exploitation if not indeed colonisation, into the very forefront of nations, able to stand with the best. That was indeed a unique achievement.

But at Washington in 1922 the Americans had dismissed them with a wave of the hand, and told them to return to the place they really belonged, in the ranks of the second-class powers. And the British, who should certainly have known better, had spinelessly fallen into line behind their American creditors. No one had ever troubled to find out what the Japanese felt about it. Nicholas had no idea what successive British and American ambassadors, or naval and military attachés, had reported to Washington and London. But as far as he was concerned these gentlemen mostly fell into the stuffed-shirt variety anyway. The League of Nations had sent Lord Lytton and his team to Manchuria to find out what the people there felt about the Japanese takeover, but no team had been sent to Japan to find out what the people *there* thought about the situation.

While throughout all of those years the Japanese had boiled in resentment. There were still those who thought that the Tokyo earthquake was a divine punishment for the supinity of their leaders in accepting the diktat from Washington. Equally were there those like his father, and himself, who had felt, or at least, hoped, that what was happening was a temporary upheaval, which eventually could be guided back into the realm of peaceful co-existence with the rest of the world. The response to Yoshiye's mad adventure had given the lie to that. The Japanese people felt rejected by the rest of the world, well, then, they would fight the rest of the world. That they had allied themselves to a German regime which seemed to have similarly suicidal tendencies was their misfortune.

And *he* had been required to create the scenario for the coming conflict. Easy to say, as had his father recorded in Alexander Barrett's private notes, that if it had not been him it would have been someone else. Father had worked on the principle that with him dictating the strategy, war might possibly be avoided, or its effects could at least be mitigated. Yamashita and Yosunobe had given the lie to that. Nicholas remembered the horrors he had read about and seen photographs of in Nanking, had seen for himself on a smaller scale in Shanghai. Could he really envisage such scenes on the streets of Hong Kong? Could he possibly imagine Linda lying on her back, her hands bound behind her, her skirt thrown about her head, her underclothes ripped apart, her violated body skewered on a bayonet?

226

The concept made his blood run cold. But it was extremely likely to happen.

So what was he going to do. To attempt to warn her would be to commit treason; she was intelligent enough to read between the lines of any reason he might give for her leaving Hong Kong, and she worked for the government. Supposing she would even pay any heed to any warning he might give. Back to *seppuku*? That would be an act of betrayal to Alexander and his unborn child, not to mention Sumiko. Sumiko! Yosunobe's daughter. He wondered what she thought of it all.

How he wished he could get together with Takijo, and discuss the whole situation. But Takijo was at sea, in command of a destroyer. He would have no idea that there *was* a situation, as yet.

Sumiko herself gave him his cue. "Sometimes," she remarked a few nights later, as they ate their evening meal, "I wonder if you will ever smile again."

"I would hope to," he said. "But it is difficult as things are at the moment. You do understand that there is a grave risk of war with Great Britain and the United States?" He was not revealing any secret that was not being daily discussed in the newspapers.

"I understand this, honourable Husband. But you must be the only officer in the Imperial Navy, not to mention the Army, who does not look forward to this. Is it because you are really one of them?"

"My blood plays a part in it, yes. But I am more concerned with the effects of war. I saw some of it, in China."

"Surely that can never happen here?"

"Indeed not. But it can happen in other places." He glanced at her. "What is your opinion about this?"

She looked surprised. Like most Japanese women, she was unused to having her opinion asked on any subject which was not strictly domestic. "I mean, you have lived in Singapore and Hong Kong. You must have had friends there."

"Some friends, at school," she said carefully.

"Are they still there?"

"I suppose so."

227

"Does it distress you to think of them being blown up by our bombs? Or raped and murdered by our soldiers?"

She frowned. "Are we going to attack Singapore and Hong Kong?"

He had nearly said too much. "If there is a war, with Britain and America, the nearest British possessions are very likely to be involved." She did not reply, so he went on. "Your honourable father is of the opinion that, should there be a war, it should be waged with all the ferocity we can manage. That we should use terror towards prisoners and civilians to rob them of the will to fight."

Sumiko raised her head. "Is this what you quarrelled about?"

He nodded. "Do you think he is right?"

She shuddered. "War is terrible. If it must be fought, it will be terrible."

"Then you do agree with him."

"Perhaps it will not happen," she said. "But if it does, then we must pray that it will be over, quickly. And that you will not be harmed." Only victory, and personal survival, was important. But was that not perhaps the only way to look at it?

Mori and Charlotte came to dinner. "I am so envious of you," Charlotte said. "How I want a son. Honourable husband wishes a son, too. But now . . . it will never happen."

Sumiko giggled. "Who can tell? You must keep trying. That at least is pleasurable, is it not?" The two women had not a care in the world, except pregnancy, or lack of it. Perhaps they honestly believe it will never happen, Nicholas thought. Yet the evidence that it *was* going to happen was all around them.

"To keep trying, I need honourable Husband," Charlotte pointed out. "And now he is being sent away."

"Where is he going?" Sumiko asked.

Charlotte shrugged. "He will not tell me."

Mori sat with Nicholas to drink his tea. "It is confidential," he said. "But I suppose you will know of it soon enough; I am being sent to French Indo-China. My entire regiment is going. We are to be trained in jungle fighting."

228

"Ah," Nicholas said. "Are you looking forward to it?"

"To the jungle? I am terrified of it. And why? Can you tell me why we are being trained to fight in the jungle? There is no proper jungle in China. Do you think we are going to take over Indo-China?"

"It is possible," Nicholas agreed. He hated deceiving his brother-in-law. "On the other hand, presumably you are going there with the consent of the French Government."

"Well, yes, that is true." Mori gave a little shudder. "You know, Nicholas, the jungle is something one only reads about, in adventure stories. When I think of snakes, and leeches, and crocodiles . . ."

Nicholas fell back on first principles. "Do you know how many people, in the whole world, died of snakebite or were eaten by crocodiles, during the last year?"

"I have no idea. Do you?"

"No. But I imagine it could be several hundred, world-wide."

"There, you see."

"But now let me ask you this: do you know how many people were killed by bullets or bombs, during the last year?"

Mori frowned at him. "I would estimate, when you think of Russia and China, not to mention Europe," Nicholas said, "that you could be talking about several hundred *thousand*."

"Do you think that is reassuring? If we have to fight someone in the jungle, I will have to contend with snakes and crocodiles as *well* as bullets."

The logic was inescapable. Nicholas could only say, "At least you know that you should worry about bullets more than reptiles."

"Ha! It is all very well for you. You will be on a ship, far away from these things."

"Ships get sunk, sometimes," Nicholas remarked, mildly.

"Not Japanese ships," Mori grumbled. "Nicholas! If I do not return, I have made it plain to my family that I wish Charlotte to come back under your roof. I hope you will not object to this?"

"Of course I will not. But will your family agree? Charlotte is a Mori."

"They have already agreed. They do not really understand Charlotte. Her . . . well, you know her problem. She will be better off with you, than with them." He gave an anxious glance at his brother-in-law. "She does not know of this, of course."

"Of course. Nor should she. She will be welcome here, but . . . you will be coming back, Mori." He grinned. "There is a saying in English that only the good die young."

Yet the news that Yamashita was beginning to train his men meant that the die was cast. Certainly it was seen so by the West. On 26 July, only three days after the news of the agreement with Vichy France was released, Britain and the United States froze all Japanese assets in their territories, and two days later, the Dutch banned all oil exports from the Netherlands East Indies; these had previously gone mainly to Japan. While despite Japanese protests, the British had already re-opened the Burma Road – closed earlier at the demand of the Japanese Government – by which Chiang Kai-shek obtained most of his supplies.

But despite these counter measures, as the year advanced, the situation seemed to become ever more favourable for Japanese ambitions. The German armies were biting deep into the Russian heartland, and there seemed no doubt at all that Moscow would fall before the end of the year, despite the onset of winter. The British were attempting to help their strange new allies, whose political system they had opposed for so long, with the result that they had little equipment to spare elsewhere, and in North Africa their army was being routed by the German Afrika Corps.

At sea they were engaged in a life-and-death struggle in the Atlantic with the U-boats. But capital ships were of little use here, and they were too vulnerable. As Yamamoto had feared, the loss of *Bismarck* and Hitler's decision to use *Tirpitz* and his battlecruisers in an attempt to block the northern lifeline to Russia rather than risk them in a fleet encounter – there was no longer any word of a completion date for *Graf Zeppelin* – left the Royal Navy with capacity to spare. "Look at this." Yamamoto handed Nicholas a signal from the *Kempei-tai*, received from one of its agents in England. Both he and his flag-commander had recently returned from a rigorous four-day exercise in the North Pacific, in which most of the Japanese fleet had been involved. "*Prince of Wales* and *Repulse* left England over a week ago, for an unknown destination. But the crews were issued with tropical kit. I should not think they are going for a holiday in the West Indies, eh? This is just what I feared would happen. Those ships are bound for Singapore."

"But surely they would not send two capital ships east without air cover, honourable Admiral?"

"Well, obviously they will have air-cover once they reach Singapore," Yamamoto said. "But I agree that would limit their field of action. However, what of that other report we received some time ago, that the aircraft-carrier *Indomitable* is working up in the Caribbean. Now, for what purpose, do you suppose? Tell me about her."

"*Indomitable* is a new ship, honourable Admiral; she was completed less than a year ago. She is an improvement on the Illustrious Class. That is, while she displaces approximately the same as the Illustrious ships, nearly thirty thousand tons, her design has been altered to permit her to carry forty-five aircraft instead of thirty-three. Also she is capable of thirty-plus knots. Obviously she is not a match for our new Shokakus, but she is capable of providing air cover for two battleships."

"So that is a neat little squadron, eh? One thirty-thousand ton aircraft-carrier, one forty-thousand ton, ten fourteen-inch gun battleship, and one thirty-seven thousand ton, six fifteen-inch gun battlecruiser."

"Will this alter our plans, honourable Admiral?" Nicholas asked, somewhat hopefully.

"No. Because our plans have already been altered, eh? Let them sit in Singapore and fire their big guns out over the jungle. We have other fish to fry, at least in the beginning. I have just been informed that the completion of *Yamato* is going to be delayed by some weeks, and *Mushashi* is unlikely to be completed before the middle of next year. Thus I am going to need every ship I have."

"To fight the Americans?"

231

"To carry out our initial attack and eliminate their Pacific Fleet, yes."

"Is it that imminent, honourable Admiral? I had thought the Americans were being more co-operative. And Kurusu Saburo's peace mission to Washington . . ."

"In some ways the Americans are trying to defuse the situation, Nicholas. That cannot alter the fact that they are irrevocably opposed to our policies and our ambitions, and thus have to be considered as our enemies. In addition, by controlling so many of our overseas assets and supply lines, they are in a position to apply enormous economic pressure as and when they choose, and this they are already doing. To break free from those shackles, to regain our freedom of action, means fighting them. The die is cast. Kurusu's mission is to keep them talking until we are ready to strike."

"But with respect, honourable Admiral, the odds are enormous, especially if we are forced to fight before *Yamato* is commissioned. We have ten battleships. *Mutsu*, the newest, is twenty years old. The Americans have got nine battleships in the Pacific. Admittedly these too are old ships, but there are still nine to our ten. Those odds are not sufficiently favourable. And their two new ships, the North Carolinas, are already in commission. Nearly forty-five thousand tons, nine sixteen-inch guns. These can be quickly transferred to the Pacific. There are also the three carriers."

"Nicholas, Nicholas," Yamamoto said. "After all I have taught you, you are still thinking in the past. Those nine battleships are sitting ducks, as would ours be were they subjected to a concentrated air attack. It is the aircraft-carriers that matter. As you say, the Americans have three based on Pearl Harbour. But *Yorktown* and *Enterprise* are mere twenty-five thousand tonners, and their big ship, *Lexington*, is nearly fifteen years old. I am sending six against them. Granted that *Akagi* and *Kaga* are also veterans, and *Hiryu* and *Soryu* are both only twenty thousand tons. But as you say, the Americans have nothing to compare with *Shokaku* and *Zuikaku*. Thirty-two thousand tons, Nicholas. Thirty-four knots. Seventy-two aircraft each. Between them, and allowing for fighter cover to be retained for the fleet, those six ships will be able to launch three hundred and fifty

232

aircraft against Pearl Harbour. I meant what I told Konoye and Tojo. The Americans will in the end be able to outbuild us. But if we can destroy the Pacific Fleet we can still win a tactical war against them."

Nicholas was silent for some minutes. Then he said, "Will you command the fleet, honourable Admiral?"

Yamamoto shook his head. "No. Obviously, if it is to be a surprise attack, the fleet will be completely out of radio contact for several days. I must be here, especially if there is a British battle squadron in Singapore. No, Nagumo will command. He is an experienced seaman. He will have the battleships *Hiei* and *Kirishima*, both better than thirty thousand tons with eight fourteen-inch each, amd a suitable escort of light vessels. Our main battleships must remain on this side of the ocean."

"With respect, honourable Admiral, Vice-Admiral Nagumo has never commanded aircraft -carriers."

"That is not relevant, Nicholas. All he has to do is escort them. He is to hit Pearl Harbour, and withdraw again, with all speed. There will be no fleet action. The Americans will be too surprised. And . . ." he gave one of his grim smiles, "hopefully, they won't have enough ships left."

"Then, honourable Admiral . . ." Nicholas drew a deep breath. "I would like to request a sea posting."

Yamamoto frowned. "A command?"

"I do not care whether it is a command or an executive position, honourable Admiral."

"But you wish to fight? And perhaps die, because you do not agree with our policy?"

Nicholas flushed in confusion, because that was the exact truth. Yamamoto smiled. "That is very commendable, Nicholas. And you will fight, believe me. But you will not die. You will fight at my side, as I have long promised. But for the time being, you will remain here, also with me, directing affairs rather than participating in them. I need you. And the fact is, Nicholas, I do not think it would be a good idea for you to go to sea at this moment. I was able to suppress Yashiwara's report on the *Sun Lily* incident, as far as any official comment or action was concerned. I was not able to prevent Yashiwara from speaking of it, to his fellow officers."

"You mean my loyalty is in doubt."

"If your loyalty was in doubt, Nicholas, you would not be in my office now. What is in doubt is your ability to be as ruthless in war as will be required. And please understand that this has nothing to do with your Anglo-Saxon background. Your ill-judged humanity was revealed towards Chinese, not Britishers. I am sorry to have to speak so frankly, but you have forced me to it. As I have said, I need you more than any of our ships. Now let me see again the calculations you have made for the main fleet."

Nicholas extended the chart. "The fleet must be assembled a fortnight before D1," he said. "I do not know how you intend to do this, honourable Admiral. Will you hold another fleet exercise?"

"No. It would be too soon after the last one. What that exercise proved is that the fleet *can* be assembled in four days. This time it will be done in total secrecy."

"Very good, honourable Admiral. Then ten days must be allowed for the crossing of the Pacific to the position from which the strike aircraft can attack Pearl Harbour and be recovered."

"Ten days?"

"I think this will be necessary, honourable Admiral. If we intend to use the northern route, and I feel this is essential. It greatly lessens the risk of the fleet being seen by any American vessel or submarine."

"Ten days *increases* the chances of the fleet being spotted by an enemy observer, surely."

"This has always been a risk, honourable Admiral. But I do not think it is a considerable one, firstly, by using the northern route, and secondly because of the probable American reaction even if the fleet *is* sighted. I understand these people; they are my own. Even if, say, an American submarine, were to sight the fleet, it is extremely unlikely it would regard it as an attacking force."

"An American submarine commander, seeing a Japanese battle fleet steaming east, is not going to assume it is on its way to attack something?" Yamamoto was incredulous.

"I will tell you how it will go, honourable Admiral. The submarine commander will say, this is odd. Can it be

234

an attack? No, it cannot be, no war has been declared. Then he may well report the fleet movement to Pearl Harbour. At Pearl Harbour, several hours later, they will say, this is very odd. Can it be an attack? No, it cannot be. No war has been declared. They will then relay it to San Diego. By now at least a day will have passed. San Diego will say, this is very odd. Can it be an attack? No, it cannot be, no war has been declared. But we had better inform Washington. Washington will say, this is very odd? Can it be an attack? No, it cannot be, we are at peace. Now, honourable Admiral, it is just possible that someone in Washington may say, perhaps we should tell Pearl Harbour to increase its vigilance. They will discuss it, and then a signal will be sent. By now we are probably three days after the fleet has been sighted. And even so, it is extremely likely that the commander at Pearl Harbour will be more irritated than alerted by such a signal, and will just regard it as Washington having the jitters. Not for the first time."

"I never knew you had a sense of humour, Nicholas. Well, I hope you are right. I have not told you this, but when I presented your plan to the cabinet it was rejected as being too complicated and risky." Yamamoto grinned. "I told them that if they did not accept it I would resign as commander-in-chief. That made them change their point of view. If we were now to fail . . . but can you have any doubt that we shall beat people who are that unable to separate reality from self-deception?"

"Wars have a habit of separating the dead wood from the live, honourable Admiral, especially if the dead wood is all killed or captured at the start."

Yamamoto nodded. "That is true. It has happened here in Japan as well. Tomorrow Prince Konoye will resign."

Nicholas gulped. "Who will replace him, honourable Admiral?"

"General Tojo."

"Then it is irrevocable," Nicholas muttered.

"It was always irrevocable," Yamamoto said. "We have merely endeavoured to make it happen at the best possible time for us. Obviously the best possible time for the Navy would be when we have *Yamato* and *Mushashi* in commission. However, their delay may well take us past our best time from other points of view. And in any event, *Yamato* will only be a few days late."

Nicholas frowned. "We are going to war by the end of this year?"

"Yes. The date has been chosen: 8 December. That will be 7 December in the United States, and in Pearl Harbour. It is calculated that Moscow will have fallen by then, or be about to fall, and this moment will have the greatest impact upon our enemies. Equally, we must act before the British squadron can link up with the Americans, as may well be its intention. So, you will prepare the plans, and have them ready to circulate to our commanders. By your own reckoning, the fleet must be ready to sail on 26 November. So we have just under three weeks. I do not have to remind you that this is absolutely top secret."

"I understand, honourable Admiral. And the British squadron?"

"My information is that it may well reach at least Colombo by the end of this month. However, as I have said, no offensive action will be taken against those ships, unless they actively attempt to interfere with our plans. Vice-Admiral Ozawa is commanding the Southern Invasion Fleet. They will leave Canton 5 December. His orders are merely to put the troops ashore and protect them. Once the Americans have been dealt with, then we can think about the British. Understood?"

"Understood, honourable Admiral." Nicholas bowed, and went to the door, and there checked. "Honourable Admiral, is it because this decision has been taken that Prince Konoye resigned?"

"Very probably so," Yamamoto agreed. "I was not present at the cabinet meeting."

Nicholas stood on the waterfront, and watched the sun prepare to dive into the mountains to the west. As Yamamoto had said, the die was cast, and before the end of the year Japan would be at war, not merely with China, but with Britain and America as well.

Now was not a time for wishing that things could be different. For him the die had been cast many years before he had been born. His grandfather had become a renegade because he had happened to be in Kagoshima, a shipwrecked sailor, when the Satsuma capital had been attacked by a British squadron. Nicholas Barrett the elder had been forced to command the Satsuma guns, and thus, when the city had fallen, he had been branded a traitor by the British. From that moment forth he had known no home but Japan, no loyalty save to the *Mikado*. He had always known that such a loyalty might one day again require him to fire upon his erstwhile comrades; he had counted himself fortunate that it had never happened. But Nicholas did not doubt that his father had also considered that possibility, perhaps the more seriously since 1922.

Well, then, what would Father's attitude be now, were he still alive? Nicholas could have no doubt about that. Father would say that if the war had to be fought it had best be fought quickly and successfully, and ruthlessly, in order to end the suffering and the casualties on both sides. But would Father accept that this war *had* to be fought? And what would be his attitude to men like Yosunobe, and his belief in the validity of terror?

"I shall be going away for a few days," Nicholas told Sumiko and Alexander at dinner.

"Is there to be another fleet exercise, honourable Father?" Alexander asked.

"Ah . . . yes," Nicholas said. "And this one will take longer than before."

But he had hesitated for a moment before replying, and when the boy had gone to bed Sumiko sat beside him. Sumiko was still not showing, as she was only four months pregnant. "Is it to happen, so soon?" she asked.

"You know I cannot answer that."

She sighed. "I had hoped you would be here, for the birth of our child."

"Of course I will be, Su. I am only going away for perhaps a fortnight."

"But will you return?"

He grinned at her. "I should think so. I am not leaving Japan."

He thought she understood; certainly she seemed reassured. He packed his bag and went to the Admiralty, where a room had been arranged as sleeping quarters. Yamamoto had also taken up residence in the building. By now all the orders had been sent, merely instructing each ship to be in a certain position on 25 November. None of the captains knew more than this, and although they might be able to guess they were intended to make a pre-emptive strike they would not know where or when.

Even Nagumo Chuichi had not been fully informed as to the plan. But he was summoned to the Admiralty with his flag-captain on 23 November, and Yamamoto gave him his orders, Nicholas standing at his shoulder. Nagumo was a strong-faced man, like Yamamoto, nearly bald. He studied the orders and the chart, frowning. "This is madness," he commented.

"In what way, honourable Admiral?" Yamamoto inquired, softly.

"It has got to be madness to attempt to carry out a surprise attack across four thousand miles of sea. It has never been attempted before."

"Thus it will come as the greater surprise to the enemy."

"If we are located," Nagumo said, "or shall I say, *when* we are located, we will be sitting ducks. You expect me to pit two old battleships against nine? I must have more support."

"Chuichi," Yamamoto said winningly. "You have six aircraft-carriers. Four hundred and seventy-two planes. You need fear no battle squadron in the world."

"The Americans also have aircraft-carriers," Nagumo grumbled.

"Three. And you will have the advantage of surprise."

Nagumo brooded at the chart. "And if the battleships are not in Pearl Harbour, but at sea?"

"The harbour is being watched by our submarines," Yamamoto said patiently. "So you will be informed of any American fleet movements. The submarines will also assist in your attack, of course, with their midget vessels."

"It is still possible that some of their battleships may be able to fight their way out of the harbour and attack my fleet, while all my aircraft are airborne," Nagumo said.

Yamamoto raised his eyes to heaven. "Are you really suggesting, Chuichi, that an American battleship can raise steam, cast off, put to sea, locate your whereabouts several hundred miles away, and attack you before you can recover and re-arm your aircraft? What are these Americans? Supermen? I have given you a perfectly straightforward task. It is threefold. You will attack and destroy as many of the enemy battleships as is possible. You will attack and destroy as many of his aircraft-carriers as possible, hopefully, all of them. And you will attack and destroy his fuel installations. Do not suppose this last is any less important than attacking his ships. The American fuel stockpile is all they have available in Hawaii to fight the war with, thus if it is destroyed, their radius of action will be substantially reduced until it can be replaced. That probably makes it the most important of your three duties. Vice-Admiral Nagumo, you have your orders. All you have to do is carry them out."

Nagumo's already stiff features closed even further. He stood to attention, gave a quick bow, glanced at Nicholas, and left the office, followed by his aide. "Phew!" Yamamoto commented.

Nicholas said nothing, and Yamamoto glanced at him. "I know what you are thinking, Nicholas. But . . ." There was a knock on the door. "Come," Yamamoto said.

A rating entered the office, gave Nicholas a note, bowed, and left. "Well?" Yamamoto sat down.

"It is from the *Kempei-tai*. Their agent in Colombo reports that *Prince of Wales* and *Repulse* arrived . . ." he checked the date of the despatch. "Four days ago. They could well be in Singapore by now."

"Does their agent not list *Indomitable*?"

"No, honourable Admiral. He does not."

Yamamoto frowned. "Then she must still be on her way. No naval commander would be so presumptious as to risk two capital ships without air cover in potentially hostile waters."

"As you have said before, honourable Admiral, they will have cover once they reach Singapore."

"But will be restricted to short-range land-based fighters. I still think *Indomitable* must be on her way. However, if she is late, that is to our advantage," He drummed his fingers on the desk. "Nicholas, you recently requested a sea posting. I am going to give you one."

"Honourable Admiral?" Nicholas could not believe his ears.

"It will be non-executive, I am afraid, but it will only be for a limited period. I am going to send you to *Hiei* to sail with Nagumo. You will be my liaison officer with the North Pacific Fleet."

"My orders, honourable Admiral?"

"Your orders are to make sure that Vice-Admiral Nagumo understands *his* orders. Is that understood?"

"Yes, honourable Admiral. And if he does not?"

"I am sending you, Nicholas, because you understand my thoughts. I am not asking you to commit mutiny, or to be insubordinate. However, I will give you a letter informing the Vice-Admiral that you are my representative with the fleet. I understand that this is not an easy task. You must do your best. What you must remember, and make sure Nagumo remembers, is that all our hopes rest on this strike being decisive. The American Pacific Fleet must be crippled for a period of several months, so that we can occupy and fortify our perimeter. This is a matter of life and death for our country, Nicholas."

"I understand this, honourable Admiral."

"Then go. And may the gods go with you."

Vice-Admiral Nagumo read Yamamoto's letter, then looked up at the Commander standing before his desk. He did not look terribly pleased. "Welcome aboard, Commander Barrett," he said. "It is a pity Admiral Yamamoto did not inform me that you were joining when we met in Tokyo. Now I shall have to find you accomodation. Commander Hirishawa will see to it. As for this letter, all we can do is our best. I hope you agree with that?"

"Of course, honourable Admiral."

Nagumo nodded to indicate that the interview was at an end.

*   *   *

The fleet weighed anchor at dawn the next morning, steering north-east. Only a few fishermen saw them go, on their way to a date with destiny, Nicholas thought.

If he was entirely opposed to the concept of this war, on the grounds of morality, necessity and blood relationship with the enemy. As he was forced to fight it, he had to remind himself that there was no reason it could not be won. If, in September 1903, the year before he had been born, anyone had suggested that Japan could dare take on the might of Tsarist Russia with any hope of success – anyone outside Japan, at any rate – he would have been laughed to scorn. But the colossus had been found to have feet of sufficient clay to enable the Meiji to win the limited victory he sought.

Now again Japan was seeking a limited victory. The question was, did the United States have feet of clay?

The days drifted by as the fleet steamed on a parabolic course, north and then east, intending to approach the Hawaiian Islands from the north-west, where they would be least expected. The November/December weather was cool and gray, with limited visibility. This was all to the good, and they saw no other ships, no suggestion of any American planes or submarines. Even Nagumo was moved to say, "It is going very well, so far."

Meanwhile the pilots studied maps and photographs of the Hawaiian Islands and especially Oahu and Pearl Harbour, from every possible angle and point of view, so that they would know exactly what to expect.

Although the fleet was maintaining the most rigorous radio silence, not even using low power amongst themselves but sticking to flags during the day and lights at night, they could of course listen to the various signals being sent to them. On the morning of 5 December, when they were still some thousand miles from Hawaii, they received the coded message that Admiral Ozawa's fleet had left Canton for the south. Up to that moment it had still been possible for the mission to be aborted. Now it was too late, barring a miracle. Mori would be mobilised and ready to go, Nicholas thought; he wondered if his men, and their commanding officer, had overcome their fear of the jungle. Equally, in Hong Hong, Linda would be peacefully asleep, unaware of the catastrophe hanging over her head. He wondered if she was sleeping alone.

The following morning came the message they had all been waiting for. The submarines on watch off Pearl Harbour, signalled condition Green, which meant that the American fleet was in port. There was only one important message left to be received, and that was the most important of them all. It came that night. *Proceed to destination.*

Nagumo invited his senior officers to join him in his day cabin for a drink. "Gentlemen, the declaration of war is at this moment being decoded in Washington. Tomorrow morning we commence the operation. I will wish you good fortune." He raised his glass. "*Tora, tora, tora!*"

CHAPTER 10

Clouds Across the Sun

As with every other officer in the fleet, save the engineers, Nicholas was on the bridge to watch the aircraft take off. It was well before dawn, and the planes themselves were merely ghostly images in front of their exhaust flames, but there were lights on the various flightdecks as the attack was launched. All three hundred and fifty-odd planes were airborne in forty-five minutes, and when they were gone, the morning was suddenly hushed save for the hum of the engines, and even these were operating at low speed; the fleet's business was to maintain station until the attack aircraft had been recovered. "Well, gentlemen," said Vice-Admiral Nagumo. "All we can do is wait." He went into his day cabin.

"This is the hardest part," remarked Captain Asabe. Fifteen years ago he had been Barrett Alexander's Executive Officer on board *Kaga*, and he was one of the few officers in the fleet who had a soft spot for his old chief's son.

Nicholas continued to gaze to the east, and the huge glow which was emerging out of the darkness. Those aircraft would be flying into that rising sun, the emblem of Japan, the emblem they carried on their wings and painted on their fusilages. They could hardly fail to be inspired. Gradually the sun rose into a cloudless and cool December day. Now binoculars were sweeping the sky, although it was too soon for the aircraft to have returned. Nagumo emerged on deck, having bathed and shaved. "Use low power to signal the fleet," he commanded; the need for radio silence continued. "The greatest vigilance is now required; there may well be a counter-strike."

Nicholas went to the radio room, where the operators could make little sense out of the faint jangle of sounds coming out of the ether; they were too far away to pick up any ground signals, and the pilots were shouting in a meaningless melange of words. He returned to the bridge, and heard the cries of "There!" "There!" Little specks appeared out of the eastern sky, and then whole clusters.

"Signal *Kaga*," Nagumo said. "I wish a report."

It came a few minutes later. "The attack was carried out successfully, honourable Admiral," said the strike leader, Commander Hirota. "I can report that five enemy battleships have been sunk and several smaller vessels. Surprise was complete. There was little anti-aircraft fire. A number of enemy planes got airborne, but most were shot down. Our losses were twenty-nine aircraft. I repeat, honourable Admiral, the raid was a complete success."

"A victory," Nagumo breathed. Clearly he had doubted its possibility. "A great victory." He turned to Asabe. "Signal the fleet to steam north-west with all speed. We must be out of here before the Americans can find us."

"May I speak, honourable Admiral?" Nicholas requested. Nagumo's shrug indicated that at this moment Nicholas could do anything he chose. Nicholas took the mike. "Commander Hirota," he said. "You say five battleships have been sunk. Is this certain?"

"Yes," Hirota replied. "I saw one explode, and the other four were settling when I left. One was capsizing."

"How many battleships were there?"

"There were eight battleships, honourable Commander. I do not think the other three were seriously damaged."

"What of the aircraft-carriers? How many of them were sunk?"

"There were no aircraft-carriers in Pearl Harbour, honourable Commander."

"Say again."

"I repeat, there were no aircraft-carriers in Pearl, honourable Commander."

Nicholas looked at Nagumo, who had paused in the doorway. Fighting a rising sense of panic, he kept his voice even. "Then report on the oil storage tanks. Have these been destroyed?"

"Regrettably, no, honourable Commander."

"Then how can you describe the attack as a success, honourable Commander?" Nicholas again looked at Nagumo. "We will have to refuel our aircraft and launch another strike, honourable Admiral."

"Have you gone mad?" Nagumo demanded.

"Honourable Admiral," Nicholas said urgently. "The aircraft-carriers and the fuel tanks were our prime objectives. That the carriers were not in harbour is a disaster, but we can at least destroy their fuel supplies."

"That is nonsense," Nagumo declared. "You . . . " he pointed, "cannot see the wood for trees. We have gained a great victory. Five enemy battleships sunk with no ship loss to ourselves. Now you would have me risk my entire fleet? The Americans will soon find us if we do not retire with all speed. As you say, their carriers not being in port could well be a disaster – if they find us. The fleet will retire with all possible despatch."

Nicholas stood to attention. "I wish to protest, honourable Admiral. Most strongly."

"Your protest will be entered in the log, Commander Barrett. But my orders stand." He returned to his day cabin.

"I know Admiral Yamamoto is like a father to you, Nicholas *san*," Awabe said. "But it can never do your career good to argue with an admiral, at least before other officers."

Nicholas would have liked to signal Yamamoto there and then, but it was still necessary to maintain radio silence. And before the fleet regained Japanese waters, Nagumo was again in the best of humours. "Gentlemen," he told his assembled officers when he visited the wardroom. "I have just received a signal from Admiral Yamamoto. In it he congratulates us upon our magnificent victory. But it is not we alone who have triumphed. Admiral Yamamoto signals that yesterday morning, 10 December, the battleship *Prince of Wales* and the battlecruiser *Repulse* were both sunk by our aircraft off the east coast of Malaya."

245

There was a moment of stunned silence, then a roar of "*Banzai!*" rose from a dozen throats.

Nicholas was more amazed than anyone. "Did the British not have an aircraft-carrier with them, honourable Admiral? Or at least air cover from Singapore?"

"There is no mention of any air cover. This is a great triumph. Do you understand, gentlemen, that within the space of one week we have sunk seven enemy capital ships? There has been no such victory since Tsushima, by any navy in the world. And there has *never* been such a victory over super-dreadnoughts. Gentlemen, we are invincible."

Nicholas could not help but admit he was right.

Yet he repeated his protest to Yamamoto when he regained the Admiralty. The admiral listened with his usual gravity, and nodded when Nicholas was finished. "The victory was certainly incomplete, Nicholas," he agreed. "However, it was a victory. It has set the world by the ears. The Americans are screaming treachery. Well, they would; owing to the utter incompetence of our embassy staff in Washington, it took them so long to decode the declaration of war that by the time it was presented to the State Department our planes were already over Pearl Harbour. The British are just screaming; it is a very long time since they have lost two battleships in one morning."

"I do not understand how this happened, honourable Admiral."

"Well, I must confess it was a mixture of good luck on our part and abysmal tactics on theirs," Yamamoto said. "*Indomitable* never reached Singapore. No one knows why, but we must assume that there was either some kind of accident or that she was considered more necessary somewhere else. If that is so, there was a serious misjudgement in the first instance. However, having reached Singapore, the two capital ships were under the protection of the fighter squadrons there. Yet when news was received of our landings further up the peninsular, they put to sea, escorted by only three destroyers, and proceeded beyond the range of their cover. One hates to criticise a fellow naval officer, and so far as I know Admiral Phillips has had a long and distinguished career, but what he did was madness. And yet, do you know, he almost got away with it? We knew very quickly he had entered the Gulf of Siam, and sent out both planes and submarines to find him, but they could not. As he couldn't find our landing parties either – the weather was atrocious – he had turned for home and was indeed within a few hours of Singapore when quite fortuitously he was found by an entire Air Flotilla on its way back *from* Singapore. A squadron of these planes was armed with torpedoes, in the hopes of finding the battleships in or close to the port. They attacked immediately, of course, supported by those still armed with bombs. Do you know, Nicholas, that we only lost four planes, while sinking two battleships?"

"They went down from bombs, honourable Admiral?"

"No, it was torpedoes which did the real damage, first by crippling their steering and then by hitting the ships themselves. It is a lesson in air power I hope all our admirals have learned very well. Poor Phillips won't have learned anything; he's dead."

Nicholas didn't know what to say. He had to be elated about such a victory, but over the Royal Navy? That hurt him much more than the partial success at Pearl Harbour. Grandfather had served in that navy. "I can tell you that our friends are impressed," Yamamoto said. "Hitler has declared war on the United States. Mussolini is expected to follow."

"And the American aircraft-carriers, honourable Admiral?"

"That they were not there is a nuisance. As is the fact that their fuel reserves remain intact. But one must be realistic, Nicholas. The Americans have three carriers presently available, we have six, with some more coming along. Now, we intend to proceed with our plan, to create the Greater East Asia Prosperity Sphere. We can only be stopped at sea. Thus the Americans are going to have to commit their carriers, very shortly. They have nothing else except those couple of old battleships which escaped destruction at Pearl Harbour. And they can expect nothing from the British, after that catastrophe off Malaya. While we . . . tomorrow morning, Nicholas, you are going to accompany me down to Kure."

247

"*Yamato* is ready?" Nicholas could not keep the excitement from his voice.

"She is in commission. Captain Hashiwara is taking delivery at this very moment. But as she is the flagship of the fleet, we also will take possession, tomorrow, eh? Now go home to your wife, and tell her the good news."

"It is no longer secret, honourable Admiral?"

Yamamoto slapped him on the shoulder. "We want the world to know, Nicholas, that we have the most powerful warship ever built. The ultimate warship. She makes *King George V* and the North Carolinas, even *Tirpitz*, into nothing more than heavy cruisers."

"Nicky!" Sumiko screamed, throwing both arms round his neck in a most unJapanese-like greeting. Behind her were her father and mother, Christina and Takeda, and Charlotte. "Oh, Nicky! I am so *proud*."

"Hail the victor," Yosunobe said, coming forward to shake his hand; he appeared to have forgiven Nicholas for their difference of opinion at the conference.

"We are all proud." Christina embraced him.

Only Charlotte was wistful. "There is no news from honourable Husband," she said.

"I am sure Major Mori is all right," Yosunobe said expansively. "The advance is going well. The British have evacuated Penang and are in full retreat."

"And our soldiers have landed on Hong Kong," Christina said, smiling at Nicholas; she knew where Linda Wells was. "They say the island is being laid flat in the fighting."

"Well?" Yamamoto said, standing on *Yamato*'s quarterdeck and looking around him. Nicholas could not help but be awed, for all his distraction. Here was indeed the mightiest ship that had ever put to sea. The Admiral had of course been piped aboard and then required to inspect a guard-of-honour. Then he and Nicholas had been taken on a tour of inspection by Captain Hashiwara, probably the proudest man in the Imperial Navy at that moment. They had descended to the engine room to look at the twelve boilers and the four-shaft geared turbines, which would enable her to steam at twenty-seven knots. They had looked at the fuel storage tanks, which contained six thousand three hundred tons of oil, and they had peered at the outer hull, where the belt armour was sixteen inches thick.

They had walked through the magnificent accommodation, for both officers and men, passed myriad sailors and marines standing strictly to attention; *Yamato* had a complement of two thousand five hundred. They had inspected the armaments, a lengthy business, for in addition to her nine mammoth eighteen-inch guns, mounted in three turrets – two forward and one aft – *Yamato* had twelve six-point-one-inch, in four turrets, twelve five-inch dual-purpose in six turrets, twenty-four twenty-five millimetre anti-aircraft guns, and four thirteen-point-two millimetre. She also carried seven reconaissance aircraft, fired from a catapult in her stern,

"This ship is unsinkable," Hashiwara asserted. "Her belt will cope with an eighteen-inch shell fired from as close as twenty-two thousand yards, and there is no other ship in the world with such a gun. While below the belt there is a seven-point-nine-inch anti-torpedo bulkhead, with a fourteen degree inclination. That means she can be hit by as many as twelve torpedoes without causing serious damage."

"Surely, honourable Captain, your principal danger will come from the air," Nicholas said.

"Agreed, Commander. But her decks carry nine-point-one inch armour. It is calculated that this will resist an aerial bomb weighing a ton and dropped from fifteen thousand feet. As for her attacking capabilities, those big guns will fire an armour-piercing shell weighing three thousand two hundred and twenty pounds a distance of forty-five thousand yards."

Now, having inspected the bridge and navigation machinery, they were on the quarterdeck; as the ship's beam was one hundred and twenty-one feet it was difficult to believe one was afloat at all. "She is a marvel, honourable Admiral," Nicholas said.

"Can you imagine a squadron of four of these, Nicholas?"

"I can imagine it, honourable Admiral. Will it really happen?"

"Oh, it will happen. *Mushashi* is already in the water, and *Shinano* is on the slip. The others may take a little longer, because of the steel problem. However, they will be built. And even two will be unbeatable. Why, this one alone is unbeatable."

"When do we take her into action, honourable Admiral?"

"Still anxious for glory, eh, Nicholas? She has still to make her shakedown cruise. As for action, our first business is to complete our occupation of Malaya, the Dutch East Indies, and the Philippines. It is all going according to plan. The Americans have already evacuated Manila and declared it an open city. Their resistance is virtually at an end. Singapore is the key. Once that falls, the Dutch East Indies are ours, then we can proceed with Phase Two, and move into New Guinea and the islands. For that we will need the fleet. Singapore! That is the secret."

"And Hong Kong, honourable Admiral?"

Yamamoto snorted. "Hong Kong can hardly be considered a fortress, Nicholas. I am surprised it has not surrendered already."

Hong Kong actually fell on Christmas Day. There were enormous celebrations in Tokyo, with firecrackers being set off and the ships in the harbour firing salutes. Nicholas and Yamamoto had by now returned to the capital, and Nicholas was forced to take part in the jollifications, for Christina and Sumiko and Charlotte and Alexander were as enthusiastic as anyone. He presumed Yamamoto would also be pleased, and was the more surprised to be summoned to the Admiral's office two days later, where he found his chief looking decidedly grim. "Sit down, Nicholas," Yamamoto said. Nicholas obeyed. "I have received a report on the taking of Hong Kong," Yamamoto said.

Nicholas waited, heart beginning to pound. "The British troops, actually they seem to have been mainly Indians and Canadians, fought desperately and well, and inflicted heavy casualties upon our forces. They did not surrender until advised to do so from London, when all hope of relief or succour was gone. Unfortunately, it appears that our men felt the resistance had been prolonged beyond reason, and

250

that a good number of their comrades had died unnecessarily. This is the official reason for what happened." He gave a little sigh. "Our troops appear to have run amok. There are reports of wounded prisoners being bayoneted in their beds, of civilians being shot in the streets, and of course, there seems to have been a great deal of rape. This, unfortunately, was universal, and extended even to the nurses in the hospital and other British women."

Nicholas swallowed. "You mean, it was Port Arthur in 1894 all over again. Only worse." No British women had been raped in Port Arthur.

"Probably for the same reasons. I do not think there can be any doubt that the sack was the result of orders. What happened in Hong Kong is being told around the world; there were neutral consuls present and they are taking care of that. This will bring great opprobrium upon our name, but at the same time it will cause the defenders of any other enemy positions we attack to think long and hard before fighting to the end. This may have a worthwhile effect. Particularly in Singapore."

"You condone what has happened, honourable Admiral?"

Yamamoto shook his head. "I do not. But war is a terrible business, and it is best fought brutally so as to end it the more quickly. And as it *has* happened, it must be used to the maximum advantage, as a psychological weapon."

"Is it possible to find out the names of the survivors, honourable Admiral?"

Yamamoto raised his eyebrows. "You mean the woman Wells? Did she not refuse your offer of marriage? And are you not now happily married?"

"Yes, honourable Admiral. I would still like to find out."

"I will see if I can discover what happened to the woman," Yamamoto agreed. "Nicholas, before this war began, you requested a sea posting. Do you still wish one?"

Nicholas looked up. "Yes, honourable Admiral."

Yamamoto nodded. "I think it might be a good idea, at least for a while. Before your wound, you were to command a destroyer. I know very nearly six years have passed, but there is a destroyer captaincy available now. I had hoped to promote you by this time, but it is felt that you have not seen sufficient active service. However, I have established that a year at sea will qualify you for your captaincy."

Nicholas stood up. "Thank you, honourable Admiral."

"Your ship is *Kasagi*, and she is lying at Sasebo. You will take command immediately."

"Yes, honourable Admiral."

Yamamoto pointed with his pencil. "There are to be no heroics, Nicholas. No acts of atonement for what happened in Hong Kong. I am sending you to sea to prove yourself as a fighting officer. Do that, and there are great possibilities ahead for you. Fail me, and in view of everything that has happened, I can hardly promise you a future at all."

Nicholas bowed.

I have been dismissed from the admiral's staff, Nicholas thought, as he went home, because he feels my sympathies will have been distorted by Hong Kong. He does not know that they were distorted long before that. Now I must either prove my worth, my loyalty, my devotion, or be cashiered. Without actually saying so, Yamamoto had made that very plain as well.

But he did want to fight, someone. Yamamoto had given him a copy of the Hong Kong report, and he had studied it in his office before leaving. It contained a purported eyewitness account by the Argentinian consul, who claimed to have seen British nurses, their wrists tied behind their backs, being gang-raped in the main streets of Victoria by Japanese soldiers. The same thing would have happened when the victors had invaded the government officers. In fact, decoding clerks were probably at more risk than nurses.

Linda, her hands tied behind her back, thrown to the ground and raped, again and again. The thought made him feel sick.

"I have been given a command at sea," he told Sumiko.

Her mouth made an O. "Just like that?"

"I applied for it some time ago. Now the posting has come through. I leave tomorrow."

Now her mouth puckered up. "You are leaving me?"

"Well, that is obvious. There is a war on, you know, Sumiko."

"Can you not even be here for the birth of our child?"

He took her in his arms, and smoothed her glossy hair. Did she even suspect that he was going to Sasebo in Kyushu she would insist on coming with him; she could always go on to the house on Shibushi *Wan*. But he did not want her to accompany him. He really did not want even to touch her, at this moment, because it was her father who had recommended the tactics used in Hong Kong. Of course, Yamashita was not in command of the force which had taken the island, but Yosunobe and the whole *Kempei-tai*, had no doubt aired their opinions to all the army commanders.

As for their child . . . did he really wish to bring another Japanese soldier into the world? Or even a sailor?

"I shall miss you, honourable Father," Alexander said.

Nicholas ruffled his hair. "As I shall miss you, Alex. But I shall soon be home. When the war is over."

"Honourable Mother says that the war will soon be over," the boy said, brightly. "Because we are winning every battle." He was, of course, referring to Christina, not Sumiko.

"And she is very probably right," Nicholas agreed.

"I do not wish the war to be over so soon," Alexander said. "I wish to fight in it."

"There will be other wars," Nicholas promised him. "And your first battle will be with Eta-Jima, eh? It is only a few years now."

It was actually a relief to be away from Tokyo, and plans and maps, not to mention relatives. Nicholas had felt at times like a spider, huge and ugly and bloated, sitting at the centre of his web and seeing which unsuspecting flies he could suck into his deadly embrace. Now he was going to be a fly himself. He felt almost clean again. And he was a fair-sized fly. *Kasagi* was one of a new breed of destroyers, laid down after Japan had definitely turned its back on naval treaties and the League of Nations; she had only been completed six months before. Displacing two thousand four hundred and fifty tons deep-loaded, she was three hundred and eighty-one feet long, and was designed to make thirty-five knots. Her main armament was six five-inch guns in three turrets, one forward and two aft. These were dual purpose, but were supported by a battery of anti-aircraft guns, and she also had eight twenty-four-inch torpedo tubes.

She had a complement of two hundred and forty officers and men, and they were lined up for Nicholas's inspection on the foredeck. The men's faces were gravely immobile, giving no indication of their feelings regarding this captain who was not even Japanese by blood, had a reputation for disobeying orders, and was reputed to be Admiral Yamamoto's *protégé*. To Nicholas's delight, however, his Executive Officer was Tono Kayasara, the midshipman who had stood beside him on the bridge of *Sawakaze* when the earthquake and *tsunami* had struck Tokyo *Wan*. Tono was the man who had actually commanded the destroyer on her sea trials, but he also seemed delighted to be reunited with his new commanding officer. "The ship is ready for sea, honourable Captain," he announced.

"Then we sail at dawn," Nicholas told him.

"Our destination, honourable Captain?"

"I will have to tell you when I open our orders, Lieutenant. Which will not be until after we are at sea."

"I am Tonoye, honourable Captain." The steward bowed. He was a little man, with the balding head common to so many Japanese, and wore steel-rimmed spectacles, again a not unusual feature with many Japanese.

"Welcome, Tonoye," Nicholas said, and looked around his cabin, small, but neat and as comfortable as the restricted space on a small warship would permit. Tonoye had unpacked for him, and the photographs of Sumiko, Alexander and his father were already in place on his desk.

"It was my privilege, honourable Captain, to serve with Captain Barrett," Tonoye said.

"Did you?" Nicholas was astonished. "You were not on *Kaga*?"

254

"No, honourable Captain. I was at Tsushima, with Captain Barrett."

"But that was nearly thirty-six years ago."

Tonoye bowed. "I was seventeen then, honourable Captain."

Nicholas realised he was going to have to maintain a very high standard, under the eyes of this overpersonalised veteran.

Kasagi sailed at dawn as instructed, leaving the Gotoretto Islands to starboard as she steamed south. The moment they were out of sight of land, Nicholas opened his orders. Lieutenant Tono stood in front of his desk as he read them. "We are to rendezvous with Vice-Admiral Ozawa's squadron in the Gulf of Siam," Nicholas said. "Radio silence will be maintained, but we will receive signals, and these will give us the coded reference numbers on the chart."

"Very good, honourable Captain. But who are we going to fight?"

"There is an Allied cruiser and destroyer squadron in the Dutch East Indies, based on Batavia. This needs to be dispersed or destroyed before we can put our people ashore on Java."

"You mean there is a possibility of seeing action?" Tono's eyes gleamed.

"I would say there is every possibility of seeing action, Lieutenant," Nicholas assured him.

By the time *Kasagi* joined the Southern Expeditionary Fleet at the end of the first week in January, Manila had fallen, together with the American naval base at Cavite in the Gulf of Manila, and the Filipino-American army was penned into the peninsular of Bataan; it was not expected that they would be able to hold out for very long. Singapore remained the principal enemy strongpoint in South East Asia, however, and it was expected that the resistance would be long and bitter, even if the Japanese were making steady progress down the Malayan Peninsular, and had even managed to land troops on the west coast.

"The Dutch Admiral Doorman has put together a squadron to defend the islands," Ozawa told his captains when he had assembled them in the wardroom of the heavy cruiser *Nachi*, his flagship. "However, he has only two heavy cruisers, *Houston* of the United States and *Exeter* of the Royal Navy. Some of you may remember that *Exeter* was one of the British cruisers which successfully engaged *Admiral Graf Spee* in December 1939. She was badly damaged in that battle but has since been entirely repaired. She is a dozen years old, displaces eleven thousand tons, can make thirty-two knots, and is armed with six eight-inch guns. *Houston* is eleven years old. She displaces just over eleven thousand tons, can make thirty-two knots, and has nine eight-inch guns, so she is an altogether more powerful vessel. In support are the Dutch light cruisers *De Ruyter* and *Java*, the Australian light cruiser *Perth*, the American light cruiser *Marblehead*, and we believe nine destroyers. *De Ruyter* is quite a new ship, seven and a half thousand tons, thirty-two knots and seven five-point-nine-inch guns. *Java* is an old vessel, just on seven thousand tons, but she can make thirty-one knots and has ten five-point-nine inch. *Marblehead* is nearly twenty years old, but she can still make thirty-four knots. She is nine and a half thousand tons and is armed with twelve six-inch guns; I am not sure that she should not be considered the enemy's most powerful vessel. *Perth* is another old vessel.

"Against this we have our two heavy cruisers, *Nachi* and *Haguro*, and our two light cruisers, *Jintsu* and *Naka*. *Jintsu* and *Naka* are old and small, it is true; they displace only seven thousand tons and are armed only with seven five-point-five-inch guns, but they are faster than any of the enemy ships: they can make thirty-five knots. *Nachi* and *Haguro* are in a class of their own, in this context. They displace more than thirteen thousand tons, have ten eight-inch guns, and can also steam at thirty-five knots. We also have sixteen destroyers available, and our light craft are all heavier than theirs.

"I can also inform you that we are merely the scouting squadron for Vice-Admiral Kondo's main striking force, which consists of the carriers *Akagi*, *Soryu*, *Shokaku* and *Zuikaku*, escorted by the battleships *Kongo*, *Hiei*, *Haruna* and *Kirishima*, three cruisers and destroyers. This force is operating south of Java, and will prevent any reinforcements reaching the Allied squadron, not that at this moment there appear to be any reinforcements available.

"So there is nothing for us to fear, and I know you are all looking forward to a fight. There will be one, never fear. For obvious reasons Admiral Kondo does not wish to take his big ships into the reefs and shoals of the Java Sea where they can be attacked by enemy aircraft unless it is absolutely necessary. The task of dealing with the Allied squadron has been left to us. But when we are ready. Our purpose is to engage and destroy or disperse the enemy while escorting our invading army to the Java beaches. However, the air force cannot at this time provide the necessary cover from their bases in Indo-China. They need landing fields further south, and that will have to wait until our campaign in Malaya is completed, or at least until Singapore is under siege. For the time being, therefore, we shall continue on patrol in these waters. Should the enemy seek to engage us, we shall of course respond, but it is not part of our plan to expose ourselves to attack by enemy aircraft or submarines until we can accomplish the most good. By the same token, our aircraft will soon be in a position to bomb the enemy ships. Until that moment, I must ask you to be patient. Thank you, gentlemen."

"So we wait," Tonoye grumbled in the privacy of Nicholas's cabin. "War is a matter of waiting, is it not, honourable Captain?"

"In this case we can afford the time, Tonoye," Nicholas pointed out. He felt that the size of the fleet commanded by Kondo was rather like taking a sledgehammer to crush a nut; technically it was stronger than that commanded by Nagumo in the attack on Pearl Harbour. Equally was he surprised by the extreme caution being shown by the Japanese commanders; it was almost as if they still could not believe they had got away with the attack on Pearl Harbour, and there could be no doubt that their success over the British battleships had made them extremely aware of the possibilities of an Allied air strike on their own ships – but there was little evidence that the enemy had any aircraft capable of carrying out such an attack. The clash between the lighter ships, when it came, would be more of a fight, but even so, the Japanese clearly held an enormous advantage. This was increased when Admiral Doorman led his little squadron in an attempt to attack a Japanese reinforcement invasion force, bound for Malaya, in the Straits of Macassar.

The squadron was immediately alerted and put to sea, but the Allies had ventured within range of Japanese shore-based aircraft and had been attacked and driven away in disarray long before the ships could get there. The planes reported several hits, especially on *Marblehead*, which they claimed was badly damaged.

"The gods are with us," Ozawa signalled the squadron.

It was galling to be leaving all of the work to the air force. "Do you realise," Nicholas commented to his First Lieutenant as they stood on the bridge gazing into the starry sky, "that so far as I know, none of our surface craft have as yet fired a shot in anger, except for the assault on Wake Island? She was sunk. But in exchange seven enemy capital ships have gone. It is an amazing way to fight a war."

However, only a few days after Doorman's abortive sortie, the waiting became worthwhile: Singapore surrendered.

The rapidity with which this seemingly impregnable fortress collapsed took everyone by surprise. The British and Commonwealth forces had actually retreated across the causeway connecting the island to the mainland on 30 January, but the causeway had then been blown up, and no one had had any doubt that a long and arduous siege had been about to begin. However, Yamashita had determined at least to try a *coup-de-main*, and had called for more troops. It had been these reinforcements Doorman had so gallantly but ineffectually attacked on 4 February. Three days later Japanese troops had crossed the Straits of Johore in small boats and obtained a lodgement on the north shore of the island.

From there on the campaign had been a shambles, from a British point of view. Nicholas, reading the report of the battle circulated around the Japanese fleet, could not believe that these were the descendants of the same men who for so long had made the defensive qualities of British infantry the wonder of the world. Yet at the same time he recognised that the attack had gone entirely as he and Yamamoto had planned it more than a year earlier. And as Yosunobe and Yamashita had planned it as well. The defenders' morale had been shattered by the ease with which the Japanese assault forces, on their bicycles, had got round their position on the mainland, and even more by the apparent confidence with which the Japanese penetrated the jungle – it was unfortunate for them that they had not spoken with people like Mori, Nicholas thought. In addition, they had been hampered by the enormous number of people crammed into Singapore itself, and by the tension and friction between Chinese, Malays, and British. They had also been obsessed by what had happened in Hong Kong, and deliberate Japanese acts of frightfulness on the way down the peninsular.

Even so, it was hard to believe that eighty thousand Commonwealth troops, if determined to make a fight of it, could not have held the north shore of the island, only some twenty miles in length, against attacks which by the very nature of the terrain could not, at least initially, be launched in any great force. But they had failed to do so, their morale apparently ruined by the successive defeats in Malaya proper and by another obsession, that the Japanese had spent all their lives fighting in and enjoying the jungle! The capture of the main reservoir had completed the debacle, and those eighty thousand men had surrendered to an army hardly greater. Ozawa was jubilant. "This is the greatest defeat ever inflicted upon the British Army," he told his officers. "Indeed, it is one of the greatest defeats ever inflicted upon *any* army in history. Even when Port Arthur surrendered in 1905 there were only fifty thousand men involved."

Certainly the capture of Singapore was the greatest victory ever gained by the Japanese Army. But it had to be set in the context of so many victories by the Navy by the middle of February: not only had the American fleet been virtually destroyed, two British battleships sunk, but the fortified island of Wake had been taken, the Philippines overrun, and already the extension of the empire to its designed extent had begun, as the island of New Britain, just north of New Guinea, had also been seized. In the port of Rabaul, New Britain had one of the finest natural harbours in the world, and engineers were already at work turning it into a huge and secure naval base. It really did seem as though the Plan was working, while the democracies seemed unable to cope with the catastrophe which had overtaken them.

But all depended upon securing that reliable source of oil from the Dutch East Indies, and by the end of the month, with Singapore now under complete control and the airfields at the south of the Peninsular functioning, the invasion force was ready to sail for Java.

Ozawa had already briefed his captains as to what he expected of them. They knew the Allied squadron was to the south and east, although Doorman had already been dislodged from Batavia by incessant air attacks and was now based on Surabaya, which was some distance away from Pelambang, the chosen landing place on Java. Yet it was felt that the Allied ships would surely make an attempt to get amongst the transports, and Ozawa's orders were that the squadron should take up a position on the eastern flank of the convoy, and act as a barrier. Expectation ran high as they proceeded south, the destroyers out in front of the cruisers. Binoculars swept the south and eastern horizons and great disappointment was expressed when they found nothing. It was not until noon that the signal was made: *Smoke bearing zero eight zero.*

Up came the glasses again, and the enemy force slowly came into sight. Nicholas counted fourteen ships, of which nine were definitely destroyers. That meant there were only five cruisers, instead of the expected six. "There is only one cruiser flying the Stars and Stripes, honourable Captain," Tono said. "And she is definitely *Houston*. *Marblehead* is the missing ship."

"So the pilots' claim to have badly damaged her was true," Nicholas muttered, and listened to the huge explosions as the Japanese heavy cruisers opened fire at maximum range. But the Allied ships advanced steadily, apparently undamaged,

260

and the signal came: *Destroyers will attack and use their torpedoes.*

"Full speed ahead, Lieutenant Mitsuru," Nicholas said into the engine room telephone. The response was immediate, and *Kasagi* raced through the calm sea, a huge white bone being thrown away from her bows; her seven immediate companions doing likewise.

"Torpedoes are ready, honourable Captain," Tono reported from the amidships telephone, where the tubes were situated.

"Stand by," Nicholas told him, gazing at the approaching ships.

By now the Japanese manoeuvre had been identified by the enemy, and destroyers were coming out to engage them. Nicholas gave the order for his bow guns to open fire, although with the ships on both sides rolling and twisting as they raced ahead there was little chance of hitting anything. Above their heads the heavier armament of the cruisers continued to roar, with *Exeter* and *Houston* doing most of the shooting on the Allied side.

Now the two flotillas were right up to each other, and the sea was peppered with plumes of white water, but even at this close range there were not any serious hits. The Allied ships loosed their torpedoes at the Japanese destroyers, but those far more deadly white wakes also went wide. Some of the Japanese replied, and a British destroyer was hit, but Nicholas was concentrating upon getting close enough to attack the enemy cruisers. "Range four thousand yards," said Midshipman Kiyota.

"Stand by, Number One," Nicholas said into his telephone.

Now *Exeter* was so close he could almost identify the men on the bridge. While continuing to fire at the distant cruisers with her eight-inch guns, she was using her secondary armament of four-inch quickfirers to deal with the impudent destroyer, and the sea to either side was turning into a maelstrom. But she was also presenting a target. The thought flashed through Nicholas's mind that had circumstances been only a little different he might have been on *Exeter*'s bridge instead of *Kasagi*'s, wearing the white tropical uniform of the Royal Navy instead of the dark blue of Japan. "Range three thousand yards," said Midshipman Kiyota.

"Hard a-port," Nicholas commanded. "Fire as you bear, Number One."

Kasagi came round in a tight circle, and as she did so the first four torpedoes entered the water with gigantic hisses. There was no time to follow their track, as Nicholas was commanding his ship to perform a complete circle in order to launch a second attack. "Reload those tubes," he ordered. "Ten degrees to port," he told his coxswain, but as he spoke *Kasagi* seemed to give a leap and he found himself on his hands and knees. For several seconds he could hear nothing above the immense ringing in his ears, then he smelt smoke. The ship was still charging ahead, but was making yet another circle, and he saw why; the coxswain had been hit by a flying shell fragment and lay dead across the wheel, which was jammed in its full port position. Nicholas scrambled to his feet, aware that he had lost his cap. He saw Kiyota also getting up; the boy was bleeding from a head wound and was shouting something, but Nicholas could not hear what he was saying. He reached for the coxswain, grasping his jacket to pull him away from the wheel and throw him to the deck. He then seized the spokes himself, and looked down on the shambles that was his foredeck. The shell had shattered the forward turret and torn a great hole in the deck, out of which smoke was pouring. But already the hoses were playing upon the tortured metal, while other sailors pulled the dead and injured away from the flames.

"Get down there and bring me a damage report," Nicholas told Kiyota, then reached for the telephone, which remained undamaged by the flying splinters which had killed the coxswain. "What is your situation?" he asked Tono.

"There is no damage aft, honourable Captain. But we have lost the range."

Nicholas looked up and for a moment saw nothing but smoke. Then he realised it was *Exeter* herself, very close, but also burning from a shell hit amidships. For the moment she was paying little attention to the destroyer, and Nicholas wrenched the helm to starboard to bring his ship round again. A rating emerged from the radio room.

"Message from *Nachi*, honourable Captain: *What is your damage?*"

Nicholas looked down at the foredeck, and Midshipman Hirota, climbing the ladder. The smoke was lessening. "Report!"

"The fire is under control, honourable Captain. But the forward turret is inoperable, and the damage extends down two decks. We have lost eight dead and seventeen wounded or suffering from burns."

"Are we making water?"

"No, honourable Captain."

"Make to flagship," Nicholas told the rating. "Forward turret out of action, some casualties, but am still able to fight the ship."

The rating bowed, and returned to the radio. Nicholas grasped the helm and attempted to discover what was happening. He realised that for the moment he was in a very vulnerable position. Presumably all the Japanese destroyers had fired their torpedoes, but only the one Allied ship was sinking. The Japanese flotilla had therefore retired to the shelter of the cruisers, as had the Allied destroyers. But *Kasagi*, having dropped out of the original line, was now some two miles away to the west, fairly close to the transports, and virtually isolated, while as smoke was still issuing from her foredeck it was obvious that she was damaged; if any of the enemy ships should decide to attack . . .

But even as he watched, Nicholas saw the Allied squadron turning away. "They are fleeing," Tono shouted exultantly through the telephone.

"Message from *Nachi*, honourable Captain."

Nicholas took the sheet of paper. *Withdraw and return to Singapore to have damage assessed.*

Tono emerged on to the bridge, as he no longer had a target for his torpedoes, and Nicholas gave him the paper. The Lieutenant read it, and then looked down at the foredeck, and gulped; he had not realised how severe the damage was. "Make to flagship," Nicholas said. "Repeat, am still able to fight my ship. Both after turrets and all torpedo tubes are functioning, and there is no damage to engines or navigating gear."

263

This last was stretching a point as the bridge was a shambles, but Ozawa would not know that.

Tono was summoning a replacement coxswain. "Course, honourable Captain?"

"We will rejoin the flotilla."

But as he gave the order the radio rating returned. *Repeat, take your ship to Singapore. Ozawa.*

"We have at least fired a shot, honourable Captain," Tono said.

Singapore no longer burned, but it presented a picture of utter desolation. The approach through the Dragon's Teeth was bad enough, but the harbour was a shambles, with wrecked and half-submerged vessels in every direction; it was impossible to say whether they had been scuttled or sunk by Japanese bombing.

The waterfront was also a mess of shattered buildings, but a dock had been cleared for *Kasagi* to berth alongside, and Captain Toyotomo, commanding the port area, came on board as soon as she was secure. "What news of the battle, honourable Captain?" Nicholas asked eagerly. "We heard firing again after nightfall."

"Yes. I understand that Doorman attempted to get round behind Vice-Admiral Ozawa's squadron when it grew dark, but our people were waiting for them, and had laid a minefield, in which a second British destroyer sank. Both *de Ruyter* and *Java* are also reported sunk, and *Exeter* is badly damaged. The remnants of the squadron are withdrawing to the east, with Admiral Ozawa in hot pursuit."

"And we are here, instead of there," Nicholas grumbled.

"Show me your damage," Toyotomo said. "It looked considerable from the dock."

He crawled in and out of the shell hole, went down to the lower decks, while Nicholas waited. "It is a very good thing that you are here instead of there," the captain said at last. "Do you realise that if you had run into any bad weather your ship would have been in danger. Now you must see if you can get her home."

"Home, honourable Captain?" Nicholas was aghast.

"I do not have the facilities here for such a major repair

as your ship requires, Commander Barrett. The docks are all smashed up, and will take weeks to put right. No, no, you must try to get her home. But if there is any sign of bad weather you must put into port. Fortunately . . ." he gave a grim smile, "all the ports between here and Japan – Saigon, Hanoi, Canton, Hong Kong, Wu-Chou, Ningpoo, Shanghai, Tientsin and Port Arthur, are in our hands. Is that not convenient? Do not look so downcast. You have the honour of being one of the first Japanese ships to be damaged in this war. Now, I recommend you give your men some shore leave and have some yourself, and sail at dusk tomorrow."

"I will do as you recommend, honourable Captain. But I have no wish for leave myself."

"But you must, Commander. Your father-in-law is here in Singapore. Did you not know this? He is anxious to see you."

Yosunobe came to the ship that evening, driven in a motor car which still had Singapore number plates. "Nicholas *san*." He embraced his son-in-law. "It is such a relief to see that you are unharmed. But this ship is badly damaged."

"A single shell, honourable Father-in-law. We lost some men. But I believe the battle was won."

"Oh, indeed. It was another victory. Now come and have dinner with me."

Nicholas looked out at the shattered city. "It is possible to have dinner, in Singapore?"

"Of course. We have put things to right."

Some things, and others in the manner of conquerors. Yosunobe drove Nicholas past Changi Prison, where it seemed all the European or politically incorrect Malays and Chinese were incarcerated, then up High Street, to look at the huge department stores, their plate glass windows shattered and the shops themselves gutted. "This was mostly done by the natives," Yosunobe explained, "before we arrived. There was a total breakdown of law and order."

Nicholas did not suppose there was much chance of a break down of law and order now; if the streets teemed with people and bicycles, there was not a white face to be seen, while every street was patrolled by armed Japanese soldiers and policemen. "The city is under martial law, of course," Yosunobe explained. "And there is a curfew. In another half-an-hour these streets will be empty; our men have orders to shoot on sight, anyone found out after dark."

"Is there much hardship?" Nicholas asked.

"There is much hardship," Yosunobe agreed. "These are a conquered people. But basically they hate the British, so we will soon have the city on its feet again. We are going to rename it Shonan, Light of the South. Does that not sound attractive?"

"Very attractive," Nicholas said. "And you are stationed here now, honourable Father-in-law?"

"Yes, until we have things fully under control. I know the place, and the people. I am useful for finding things out, because I can tell when people are lying, eh? I will show you, after dinner. We have arrived."

Nicholas was not at all sure he wanted anything to do with Yosunobe at work, but now they were at Raffles Hotel. He could only guess at the pleasure with which his father-in-law entered these hallowed portals, from which he had been turned away ten years before simply because of the colour of his skin. Now there were only yellow and brown faces, and the Malay waiters in their white jackets with brass buttons hurried forward and bowed obsequiously to the naval officer and the man from the *Kempei-ai*.

Nor was there any shortage of good whisky, apparently, or good wine with the meal, while the food was exquisite. "When you think that for a hundred years the British have been eating and drinking like this all over the world, while their slaves hurried to and fro doing their every bidding . . ." Yosunobe smiled. "Do you not think it is about time such decadence came to a halt?"

"So that our decadence may replace it, honourable Father-in-law?"

"Why not? Have a cigar." A waiter hurried forward with a box of Havanas, clipped the end of Nicholas's choice, and held the match for him. Yosunobe had also lit up. "Now," he said. "I am going to do some work. Come with me."

"At this hour?"

Yosunobe grinned. "I enjoy my work. This came up this afternoon, and I told my people to keep it until this evening. So I could show you the sort of thing I have to do."

"I am very tired, honourable Father-in-law, and we sail tomorrow . . ."

"This will amuse you," Yosunobe promised.

Nicholas allowed himself to be persuaded in preference to again giving offence, and drove with his father-in-law to the building appropriated by the *Kempei-tai* as their headquarters. Here guards presented arms, and they were admitted to what looked very like a police station. Well, Nicholas reflected, it was a police station – a *secret* police station.

There were several men in the charge room, and these came to attention as the officers entered. "The prisoners are in here, honourable Colonel," a sergeant said, and hurried in front of them.

Nicholas was surprised. "I did not know you held a military rank, honourable Father-in-law."

"Because I do not wear a uniform? There are many things you do not know about me, Nicholas."

The sergeant opened a door, and they entered a somewhat small room. There was no window and a single naked bulb hung from the ceiling. There were two straight chairs and a table. Again, it was like every interrogation cell Nicholas had ever seen in a movie; he had never actually been in one before. But there were differences. The chairs were bolted to the floor, and had no seats. So that the man who sat on one, stripped naked and blindfolded, his wrists and ankles tied to the chair back and legs, drooped through the centre. He was Chinese, and Nicholas could smell his terror, as his head turned from left to right when the door opened. Facing him, standing against the wall, was a guard. "What is his crime?" Nicholas asked.

"He attempted to pass a message to one of the British prisoners in Changi," Yosunobe explained.

"Is that so serious?"

"It is against the law. Our law. What is more, he managed to swallow the message before my people caught him. Is that not a suspicious act? Now he will not tell us what the message was. But he will have to." He spoke Chinese, rapidly, and the man's head jerked. But his lips clamped together. "You see?" Yosunobe asked. "He is obdurate. But he will speak in the end." He turned to the sergeant. "Did you find the woman?"

"Yes, honourable Colonel."

"Bring her in."

Nicholas retreated against the far wall, beside the guard. He wished there were some way he could leave without having his father-in-law laugh at him, but at the same time he was held by a horrible curiosity: this was an aspect of war of which he had only ever read – but which Linda could have experienced.

The door opened and the sergeant thrust a woman in. She was very young, hardly more than a girl, and was clearly from a good home; she wore a green *cheong sam*, somewhat crushed and disarranged, and expensive shoes. Her hair had once been neatly dressed but was now an untidy black mess. She was as terrified as the man, and trembled, while her eyes flickered from one to the other of the Japanese, resting for a moment on the tall, red-headed man. "This is the wife?" Yosunobe was astonished, in view of the obvious age difference.

"No, honourable Colonel. We could not find the wife. This is the mistress."

"Ah," Yosunobe said, and spoke to the girl in Chinese.

She listened carefully, her face slowly tightening. She had to moisten her lips before she could reply in a low voice. Yosunobe snorted, and his voice raised as he shouted at her. The girl looked Nicholas. "Can you let them do this?" she asked, in English, deducing his probable nationality.

Nicholas gulped. "Ah, so you speak English," Yosunobe said. "Then you can scream in English. Put her in that chair," he told his men.

The girl made no effort to resist them as her clothes were torn from her body and she was thrust into the chair, her arms carried behind her to be secured while her ankles were strapped to the front legs. She continued to stare at Nicholas. "You are a shit," she told him.

"Is she not a beauty?" Yosunobe asked, fondling her unusually well developed breasts. "You know, if you are a naughty girl," he said, "we are going to cut these off."

The girl hissed at him. The man had by this time realised what was happening, and began to speak in rapid Chinese. "Shut him up," Yosunobe said, and one of the guards hit the man across the face with his rubber truncheon. The man gasped and gave a little shriek.

"Now," Yosunobe said to the girl. "Tell me what business your lover had with Mr Brian."

"I know nothing of Mr Brian," the girl said.

Yosunobe pointed. "You love that man? Or is he just a convenience?"

The girl licked her lips. "I love him. We are to be married."

"You think so? He will not do you any good." He snapped his fingers, and one of the guards again swung his rubber truncheon, but this time from underneath the chair, slamming upwards into the man's testicles. He gave an unearthly scream, and almost burst his bonds. The girl seemed to coagulate. "You see?" Yosunobe asked. "Four more blows like that and his testicles will be smashed. He will never even erect again. Tell me about Mr Brian."

"I do not know about Mr Brian," the girl said, her voice slowly rising. "I do not *know*!"

"Do you not think she is telling the truth?" Nicholas asked. He was beginning to feel sick.

"I doubt it. These people are habitual liars." Yosunobe spoke to the man, who was still shaking and panting. When there was no immediate response, he signalled his guard, who delivered another savage blow to the man's genitals. This time the scream was almost animal, and tears rolled out from beneath the blindfold.

"You are killing him!" the girl shouted.

"Well, let me see if I can kill you instead," Yosunobe said, and snapped his fingers again.

The guards hurried forward with a length of thin wire. This was passed between the girl's legs and then up behind her back. Now it was her turn to gasp with apprehension as a guard took each end of the wire and lifted it so that it settled

269

into the flesh of her genitals. "It is the most simple thing in the world," Yosunobe explained. "But very effective. We simply raise the wire as high as it will go, and then saw it back and forth. I believe, if we had sufficient time, we could saw her in half. But of course they always tell us what we want to know after a few minutes."

"You shit!" the girl screamed.

"Take off the blindfold," Yosunobe said, and spoke to the man in Chinese.

The man blinked in the sudden light; his eyes were still filled with tears. Then he distinguished his mistress, and began screaming in Chinese. "You see?" Yosunobe said. "Now he wishes to tell us everything. He cannot bear the thought of this charming girl being destroyed."

"Thank God for that," Nicholas said. "It is time I was getting back to my ship."

"But we will still tickle her a little, eh?" Yosunobe said. "My men are entitled to their sport. And so am I."

"As the young lady says," Nicholas said, as evenly as possible. "You are a shit, honourable Father-in-law."

CHAPTER 11

The Working of Fate

A band played and streamers flew as *Kasagi* nosed her way into Sasebo. As far as Nicholas had been aware, the fact of her being damaged and returned to Japan had been a secret. Captain Toyotomo had commanded him to keep strict radio silence on his way home, unless he needed to make port because of stress of weather. But in fact the March weather had remained unseasonably good, and with heavy tarred canvas stretched across the gaping hole in her foredeck and her pumps on constant standby, the destroyer had been able to maintain a normal cuising speed.

It seemed that all Japan was there to greet her, including even the commander-in-chief. "You know of course that both *Exeter* and *Houston* were sunk in the pursuit?" Yamamoto asked, having inspected the damage.

"I heard it on the radio, honourable Admiral. So it seems that I have been the only failure."

"On the contrary, you are a national hero. All the squadron saw your gallant attack on *Exeter*."

"You flatter me, honourable Admiral."

"I am proud of you, Nicholas. And the war goes well. You also know, no doubt, that Rangoon has fallen, and that the Allied forces in the Dutch East Indies have surrendered?"

"I do, honourable Admiral."

"The only Allied position holding out in the whole southeast Asia complex is the island of Corregidor, and the surrender of that is merely a matter of time. Well, this frees us for the next important stage in our campaign: New Guinea and the Solomons. The Allies, of course, are in a state of panic and seem to think we are about to undertake full-scale invasions if India and Australia. They seem totally unaware of the logistical factor in warfare. Which may well explain their inability to wage war. In any event, we wish commanders of your capabilities in the front line. *Kasagi* is going to take some time to repair. *Yodo* will complete her refit in a few weeks time. You will take a month's leave, and then assume command. She lies in Yokosuka, so that should be simple enough."

Nicholas could not believe his ears. *Yodo* was one of the newest heavy cruisers in the Imperial Navy. Originally designed as a light cruiser to conform with the rules of the 1930 Treaty, she had been totally rebuilt following the withdrawal of Japan from the League and was now a fifteen thousand ton heavy cruiser, armed with eight eight-inch guns and capable of thirty-five knots. "But . . ."

"She can only be commanded by a full captain?" Yamamoto grinned. "As of this moment you are promoted captain. It should have happened long ago. It *would* have happened long ago, but for that lamentable incident with the *Sun Lily*. Anyway, it is better late than never. I will wish you good fortune."

"Where will I take *Yodo*, honourable Admiral?"

Yamamoto tapped his nose. "You will discover that when you have assumed command. Now go somewhere and enjoy yourself. Your wife is waiting for you at your home; she felt it would be improper for her to appear in public. But at least you will be here for the birth, eh?"

"Yes, honourable Admiral. But may I ask about the other matter?"

Yamamoto sighed. "Do you not think it would be most sensible to forget the girl? She is an enemy."

"I cannot forget the girl, honourable Admiral."

"Another reason why you westerners cannot wage proper war," Yamamoto remarked, "is that you are so infernally romantic. Well, at your request, I followed up the business." From his inside breast pocket he took an envelope. "It is all in there, Nicholas. I give it to you. But for your own peace of mind, I would strongly recommend that you burn that report, unopened. I wish you good fortune with your new command, Captain Barrett."

Lieutenant Tono was waiting to congratulate him. "I would take it as a great honour, honourable Captain, if I was allowed to continue serving under you."

"Well, I have already recommended you also for promotion, Number One. If you wish, I shall also put in a desire for you to be transferred to *Yodo*." Tono bowed, and withdrew.

Nicholas sat at his desk and regarded the envelope. Perhaps it would be simplest and best to take Yamamoto's advice, and burn the report unread. But it would not bring him peace of mind: after what he had seen in Singapore, he simply had to know.

He slit the envelope, and took out the sheet of paper inside.

From Lieutenant-Colonel Hessayu to Admiral Yamamoto Isoroku, Commander-in-Chief, Imperial Japanese Navy. Honourable Admiral, as requested I have conducted an inquiry into the situation of a woman named Linda Jeannette Wells. This Wells is a Caucasian British subject, aged thirty-four, employed as a decoding clerk in the office of the Governor of Hong Kong. She was resident in Hong Kong when the colony surrendered to the Imperial Army. She was arrested while in the act of destroying code books in her office. She was interrogated, and then placed with various other prisoners-of-war in a camp. She remains there pending further arrangements. Regarding her health, some injuries were sustained when she attempted to resist arrest. However, these were of a superficial nature. Her general health is good, although in common with most of the prisoners, she has lost weight. This is due to the fact that Caucasian women appear unused to a diet of rice. I await your further instructions, honourable Admiral.

Nicholas leaned back in his chair, his brain seeming about to burst out of his head. *She was interrogated.* Linda, tied naked to a chair while laughing men sawed a piece of wire to and fro between her legs? *Injuries were sustained when she attempted to resist arrest.* When she had attempted to resist rape? *She has lost weight . . . unused to a diet of rice.* She is being systematically starved to death? Slowly he folded the report and placed it in his

273

pocket, then got up. It was time to say goodbye to his crew.

"Honourable Husband." Sumiko could not bow as low as etiquette demanded. "The gods are with us."

"Let us hope they are," Nicholas agreed, kissing her forehead. Did she have any idea of what her father did? Could she? Even more did he not wish to touch her. But the real disaster was that her father was not alone in his bestiality: he had not been in Hong Kong. "When are you due?" he asked.

"It is another five weeks, they say."

"Then I may just make the birth. Because I have to go away next week."

"Go away? They told me you had six weeks' leave."

"It will be six weeks before I take command of my new ship," Nicholas agreed. "But before then I am required to undertake a mission. Do not ask me what it is, because it is secret and I cannot tell you."

She pouted, briefly, and then smiled. "I am remiss; I have not congratulated you upon your promotion. Is it true that a captain in the Navy is equivalent in rank to a colonel in the Army?"

"It is true."

"I am glad of that. Mori is home on leave too, you know."

"I didn't know. Is he all right?"

"Well, he was wounded. Not seriously, although Charlotte all but had hysterics when she heard about it. He has come back in a very odd frame of mind, however. The important thing is that he too has been promoted, to colonel. I would not like you to be inferior in rank to Mori."

"I would like to see him, see them both."

"You will. They are coming to dinner on Friday. I have invited my mother and Christina as well."

"With Takeda, I suppose?"

"Of course. Takeda is one of those fortunate men who never has to leave Tokyo. Unlike poor Father."

"Yes. Did you know I met Honourable Father-in-law, in Singapore?"

274

"Did you?" She squealed with delight. "I did not know you had been to Singapore."

"We stopped there to unload our dead and wounded following the Battle of the Java Sea. Honourable Father-in-law invited me out to dinner, at Raffles."

"Oh, that must have been splendid. I wish I had been there. I was never allowed to dine in Raffles. Is he well?"

"Very well," Nicholas said. "He seems to enjoy his work."

Yosunobe Aiwa was equally delighted to learn that Nicholas had encountered her husband, while Christina and Takeda were full of boisterous confidence: only that day it had been reported that General MacArthur, commanding the American-Filipino remnants still holding out on the island of Corregidor, had fled to Australia, officially recalled by President Roosevelt. "The rats are deserting the sinking ship," Takeda declared gleefully.

The news had also been received that Japanese forces had landed in the Solomons. Against all of this, an American air raid against Japanese shipping at Lae and Salamaua in New Guinea hardly seemed relevant. But as Sumiko had indicated, Mori and Charlotte did not seem to share in the general jollification. "Is it his wound?" Nicholas asked his sister, who sat beside him at dinner.

"It is more than that," she murmured, poking at her rice bowl with her foodsticks.

"Can you not tell me?"

"I think he would like to tell you himself. Will you come to see us?"

Nicholas nodded. "I will come tomorrow."

But he had more important things on his mind, and managed to have a word with Takeda in private. "You understand this is entirely confidential," he told his stepfather. "I do not wish Sumiko to know of it."

Takeda grinned. "I entirely understand, Nicholas *san*."

"Thank you. Is it possible?"

"To obtain the release of a prisoner-of-war? No, that is not possible, except as an exchange, and such things take a long

275

time to arrange. Anyway, the Allies hold none of our people. However, it might be possible to have a prisoner-of-war transferred for employment. I mean, we are employing all male prisoners in useful work, building roads and bridges and that sort of thing. We have not yet found anything suitable to do with the women, simply because we have discovered that Caucasian women, if required to perform any manual labour, die like flies. The men also die far too rapidly. They are simply unused to physical labour."

Nicholas kept his voice quiet with an effort; he needed this man's help. "Perhaps if they had adequate food, and were not worked quite so hard . . ."

"My dear fellow, they *are* prisoners-of-war, men who would not fight to the death. In any event, they have a long history of working other people, Chinese and Indian coolies and the like, just as hard. No, no, they must learn to take the rough with the smooth. But as I have said, it is possible to have a man transferred from one task to another, so long as he remains a prisoner, of course. Thus there is no legal reason why a female should not be transferred from one task to another, even if she is not at this moment performing any task at all."

"Tell me, honourable Stepfather," Nicholas said. "Do you not fear that one day you may have to answer for your . . ." he changed his mind about using the word crimes, "treatment of these people?"

Takeda looked at him somewhat blankly. "They are prisoners-of-war," he said again. Clearly, in his book that answered all charges. "Would you like me to have this woman removed from her camp, to perform domestic duties?"

"I wish you to give me permission to see her, first," Nicholas said.

He walked with Mori in the garden of the Colonel's house. "I am told the campaign was an enormous success," he remarked. "Well, that is obvious from the results. So the jungle must have proved less terrifying than you supposed."

Mori gave a little shudder. "It *was* terrifying."

"Did you encounter a lot of snakes?"

"A few. But they were nothing. One can shoot a snake.

276

The leeches . . . by the gods, they are the most unpleasant things I have ever encountered. Have you ever had a leech clinging to your asshole?"

"No," Nicholas said. "It is not something that happens in the Navy, I am happy to say. But was it not worth all the discomfort to win such a victory?"

Mori glanced at him, then looked away again. "I am a *samurai*, Nicholas. So are you."

"Yes," Nicholas agreed, uneasily.

"Thus we are honourable men. Oh, we subscribe to the principles of *bushido*, but the entire concept of *bushido* is one of honour, is it not?"

Nicholas could only wait; he knew what was coming next.

"But honour is a personal matter," Mori continued. "One cannot, and should not, inflict one's own concept of honour on an opponent. There can be no doubt that the Allied forces defending Malaya behaved in a dishonourable manner, by the standards of *bushido*. They were taken by surprise, they were afraid of us, and they were even more afraid of the jungle. They did not really wish to fight. And so they either ran away or they surrendered. When they surrendered, they were not, in their own opinion, behaving dishonourably. I have learned about this point of view from Charlotte. An English soldier, confronted with overwhelming force, considers it his duty to surrender and hopefully live to fight another day. Our soldiers cannot understand that."

"You mean your people sometimes refused to take prisoners?" Nicholas suggested.

"Oh, they took prisoners. Well, what can you do, when a man throws down his rifle and comes to you with his hands up?"

"They murdered them?"

"They did some things I shall remember to my dying day." Mori shuddered. "One group which surrendered were shut in a barn which was then doused with petrol and set on fire."

"Your men did this?"

"They were part of my regiment, yes."

"What did you do?"

"That is the most distressing thing of all, Nicholas. I have

277

fought in China. I know that soldiers sometimes behave like beasts in the heat of war, because war itself is bestial. But when they do so behave, they are punished. In this case, the men had been encouraged by their subaltern. I placed them all under arrest and forwarded a report to my colonel. Do you know what I received in reply? A letter of commendation to be read to the men, for their having shown the proper spirit of *bushido* towards the enemy!"

Nicholas nodded, grimly. "So then you tried to get yourself killed."

"What else was left to me to do, save *seppuku*? Perhaps that is what I should have done."

"I am glad you did not. It could well have sent Charlotte back into a mental state. But quite apart from that, this war is going to be over, some time, and then we are going to need men like yourself, untainted men, to make the peace work."

Mori stopped his perambulation, and gazed at the trees at the bottom of the garden. "You are speaking of when we have won the war, are you not?"

"Well, of course."

Mori turned to him. "And if we lose?"

"Lose?"

"It is a possibility. More, it is a probability."

"Mori, you are suffering from battle fatigue. I know what you saw was horrible, and I agree with you that the attitude of some of our senior people is repulsive. I put the blame at the feet of the government, having an ex-*Kempei-tai* officer as its head. But lose? We have accomplished everything we set out to do, and are well on the way to establishing our outer perimeter. In fact, there is no force on earth can now stop us doing so. The Germans are supreme in Europe . . ."

"You know they have not yet taken Moscow? In fact, that they are in retreat?"

"That is the weather. Next summer they will resume their advance. In any event, even if they do not take Moscow, Russia is shattered. Britain is being brought to her knees by the U-boat campaign. Within another six months America will have to face the fact of continuing the struggle, against virtually the rest of the world, by herself, or making the best peace she can. Anyway, has Japan ever lost a war?"

"You are whistling in the dark, Nicholas," Mori said. "All of these things that appear to be happening, none of them has actually happened yet."

"Not happened? What of our victories at sea? What of Singapore and the Philippines, the Dutch East Indies?"

"We have had the advantage of complete surprise. Can you argue that our course is wrong? No, you cannot."

"Whether it is wrong or not, Mori, it is the course dictated by our superiors, and as we are both serving officers in the Imperial Forces, we have no choice but to carry out our orders to the best of our ability."

"The orders ultimately come from the *Mikado*, do they not?"

"Well, of course. That is why they must be obeyed."

"And he issues them on the advice of his ministers, his generals and his admirals. At the present time, his orders are issued principally on the advice of Tojo Hideki, his prime minister. A man you have just described as a mistaken appointment."

"Yes," Nicholas said, more uneasily yet. "But as he *has* been appointed . . ."

"Nicholas, you are a student of history. Now, is it not a fact that has recurred time and again in our history, that when it is felt that the Son of Heaven is being wrongly advised, it is the duty of all right-thinking men to rise up and remove those wrong-headed advisers?"

"And our history is littered with the executions or the *seppuku* of such men who failed."

"It also contains one or two instances of men who succeeded, and are amongst the most revered of our ancestors. But even failure, in such a cause, would be a glorious death."

Nicholas stared at him. "By God," he said. "You're serious, aren't you? A conspiracy? This country is riddled with conspiracies. We had Yoshiye's conspiracy to start a war, now yours to end it. You will never have any support, Mori. Not as things are at present. Therefore I must beg you most earnestly to forget this absurd idea, and never

279

to mention it to anyone else. I will never betray you. But I certainly would not trust anyone else. And I am afraid that includes my own sister."

"Who happens to be my wife."

"Who also happens to be close friends with both Christina and Sumiko. The one married to an officer in the *Kempei-tai* and the other the daughter of one. You know how women cannot resist sharing secrets with their best friends."

"And you will not support me."

"No."

"Not even when it becomes apparent that Japan is losing this war, and that there will have to be a day of reckoning for the crimes we have committed?"

"Talk to me again when that looks like happening," Nicholas said, anxious to end so dangerous a conversation. He grinned. "I suspect we will be both quite old by then."

"He utterly rejects the idea," Mori said to Charlotte, as she lay in his arms that night, in the darkness and privacy of their own bedroom. "I am very disappointed."

"Why did he reject it?" Charlotte asked.

Mori sighed. "He says it is because there is no possibility of Japan losing this war. He is filled with Yamamoto's false confidence. But I believe he is afraid."

"My brother is not afraid of anything," Charlotte protested.

Mori hugged her. "Do not be so fierce. I am afraid too. But I am more afraid of what may happen if we just let events run their course."

"What are you going to do?"

"There is nothing I can do, at this moment. As Nicholas says, I will get no support while we are winning everywhere. But when that process comes to an end . . . I must wait, and watch. And perhaps talk to other people. Nicholas says I should not do this, but I do not have any choice."

"Can I help?"

It was his turn to speak fiercely. "No! Under no circumstances must you be involved. Or mention this to anyone. Anyone at all, Charlotte. You must understand this."

She kissed him.

*　　*　　*

"Honourable Captain!" Captain Yatsura bowed. As a captain in the Army he was Nicholas's inferior in rank. "What brings you to Hong Kong?"

"I wished to see for myself, the evidence of our victory," Nicholas said. "I have been to Singapore. But Singapore surrendered. Hong Kong went down fighting, as we would say at sea."

"That is true," Yatsura agreed. "They fought well. Unfortunately, the casualties were severe. But I was told you wish to visit the women's camp."

"That is why I am here," Nicholas said.

They stood on a dock, some distance from Victoria, where a motorboat bobbed on the sparkling blue water, waiting to take them to one of the outlying islands. Nicholas was glad to be away from Victoria, where even three months after the fall of the colony the evidences of battle and conquest had still been too evident in the shell-shattered buildings, the pot-holed streets, and above all, the crushed demeanour of the people. The Japanese had worked hard, and the docks were again usable, while there was an electricity and water supply of sorts, but as in Singapore they were ruling with an iron hand, and this showed. Equally, as in Singapore, there was not a white face to be seen. Nicholas did not know where the male prisoners had been shipped, or how many had survived and what their present condition was, but he was about to find out about the women. Yatsura sat beside him as they were ferried across to the island. "You have a personal interest in these women, honourable Captain?"

"In one of them."

"Ah, so." The captain refrained from any further comment, and a few minutes later they were tied up alongside another small dock and walking up the sloping path to the commandant's office. It was an attractive island, a place of little beaches and low hills, and trees; the walk was well-shaded. But beyond the administrative buildings was the barbed wire fence and the huts for the inmates, although these were not immediately to be seen.

"How many women do you have here?" Nicholas asked.

"Just over a hundred."

An orderly opened the door for them, and the young lieutenant seated behind the desk stood to attention, and bowed.

"Lieutenant Masaiye is the resident commandant, honourable Captain," Yatsura explained. "He knows all the women here."

"I wish to interview Miss Linda Wells," Nicholas said.

"Ah, so, honourable Captain," Masaiye said. "You will bring the woman Wells," he told the orderly, who hurried off. "Please will you sit down, honourable Captains." Nicholas and Yatsura seated themselves. "You wish to interrogate this woman, honourable Captain?" Masaiye asked.

"I wish to interview her, Lieutenant."

Masaiye considered this, obviously trying to determine the exact difference between the two words. "I understand she was interrogated, regarding the codes used by the British, when we took the colony. She was very difficult. She remains very difficult."

Nicholas frowned at him. "In what way?"

"Non-co-operative," Masaiye said darkly. "Food strikes, that kind of thing. Refusal properly to bow to her superiors. It has been necessary to punish her."

Before Nicholas could speak he heard the footsteps outside. Instinctively he rose, and both Japanese officers, who remained seated, looked at him in surprise. The door opened, and Linda was pushed in. She looked neither to left nor right, but stared straight at Masaiye, and gave a perfunctory bow.

"That is not deep enough, woman," barked the guard and raised his rubber truncheon, but Masaiye, who was watching Nicholas's expression, gave a quick shake of his head.

Nicholas gazed at Linda. She wore slacks and a shirt, and sandals. The clothes were crushed, but did not look particularly dirty. Her hair was neat. She was thinner than he remembered, but he had expected that. It was her face that had changed: her lips were clamped in a hard line, an expression which was also revealed in her jaw. He could not see her eyes. But he knew that she had come here anticipating punishment, and was bracing herself for it. "Honourable Captain Barrett wishes to speak with you, Wells," Masaiye said.

Linda stared at him for a moment, unable to believe her

ears. Then her head turned, sharply. As she saw Nicholas, her knees gave way and she slumped to the floor. "Up, woman!" shouted the orderly, again raising his truncheon.

Masaiye opened his mouth to give a command, but Nicholas acted before the orderly could hit the fallen woman. He took two strides forward, grasped the raised wrist, and twisted the man's body at the same time as he swung his toes into the back of the orderly's right knee in a classic judo manoeuvre. The man squealed with pain and himself hit the floor, heavily; his truncheon flew into a corner. The two Army officers looked utterly scandalised at such an attack by a superior. "I wish to speak with this woman, alone," Nicholas told them.

Masaiye and Yatsura exchanged glances. "This is very irregular, honourable Captain," Yatsura protested.

"I have given you an order," Nicholas pointed out. "Leave the room. And take that . . ." he pointed at the orderly who was just getting to his knees. "With you."

The two officers stood up, and Masaiye backoned the orderly to rise. Then all three of the Japanese bowed before leaving the room. Linda had also risen to her knees, and was gazing at the scene in consternation. Nicholas helped her to her feet, and sat her in a chair. "I must bow," she muttered, attempting to rise.

Gently he restrained her. "Not to me, Linda."

Her eyes were enormous, and filled with tears. "Has it been very bad?" he asked, sitting beside her.

She looked away. "You mean you do not know?"

"I have heard enough to suspect. But I would like to know, from you."

She glanced at him. "It has been worse than any nightmare. The battle was bad enough, because we were all in the middle of it, civilians as well as soldiers. But afterwards . . ."

He bit his lip. There was so much he wanted to ask, and dared not. "Yet you look quite well," he suggested. "And clean."

"Today was bath day. All of us. Hair-washing day. We do it under guard. Have you any idea what it is like to have to bathe and wash your hair in front of a lot of men? Alien men?"

He had no answer to that. "Why did you come here?" she asked.

"To see you."

"To be amused?" Her tone was bitter.

"To help you, if I can."

"How can you help me, now?"

"I can take you out of all this. I can take you somewhere you will not be beaten, or punished in any way, and where you will be given proper food to eat, and allowed to live a reasonable life."

She frowned. "Are you that powerful?"

"I am not powerful at all. But I *can* help you. Listen to me, Linda. It is permitted for a Japanese officer to obtain women prisoners for his household." Her head jerked. "As a maid," he added hastily.

"You must think I'm a fool."

"Well, what does it matter what you come out as? You would be away from all this. You would live in Tokyo."

"I would rather die."

"That is an easy thing to say. But if you remain here, and continue to defy the guards, you may well die, and it will not be pleasant."

"You are speaking of *your* people."

"I am speaking of young men who have suddenly been given unlimited power over a race which has always treated them as inferior. And in this instance, as you have said, over the women of that race."

"And you think that excuses them?" she suddenly blazed at him. "Do you know what they *did*?"

"Would you like to tell me?"

He was thinking of what had happened to her when she had been interrogated. But she preferred not to talk about that. "There is not a woman in this camp who has not been raped. There is not a woman who has not been beaten. There is not a woman who has not been humiliated. Do you know that we are required to bow to these . . . these animals? To bow to an exact position? One inch too high, or too low, and we are beaten."

"I know this is hard to accept. But . . . my wife bows to me whenever I enter my home. It is the Japanese custom."

"And if she does not do so to your exact requirement, you beat her with a stick, is that it?"

"No, I do not do that, Linda. But some Japanese men do."

"You are animals. All of you."

"We have a different culture, that is all. Do not pretend that British soldiers have not also behaved badly, from time to time. That they have not yet done so in this war is merely because they have not yet gained any victories. But I would suggest that were you being held in a British prison camp, there would be no bath days at all, whether or not you were watched by guards."

She glared at him, then her shoulders slumped. "I cannot leave my . . . my comrades. We have suffered together. We must live or die, together."

"You will have to leave them, some of them, when this camp is broken up, as will happen fairly soon. Then you will be sent to camps on the mainland. But not all of you will go to the same camp. I am merely going to make arrangements for you to be transferred sooner than later."

She gazed at him, willing herself to defy him. But the temptation to get out of these dreadful surroundings was too great, and she could solace herself with the thought that if he really intended to have her moved there was nothing she could do about it, anyway. "If any man ever touches me again, so long as I live," she said in a low voice, "I swear I will kill him if I die for it."

"I shall not touch you, Linda." But he could not forebear to add, "until and unless you wish me to." He went to the door where the two officers were standing together, looking out at the sea; no doubt they had exchanged opinions on what was happening. "Lieutenant Masaiye," Nicholas said. The lieutenant bowed. "This woman may be returned to the camp," Nicholas said. "However, the *Kempei-tai* are making arrangements for her to be transferred to another camp, in the near future. Until then, I do not wish her ill-treated in any way. Is this understood?"

Masaiye's eyes drifted towards Linda; he knew she spoke fluent Japanese. Then he gave another bow. "The order for her transfer should be here in about a month," Nicholas

285

told him. "Captain Yatsura, I am ready to return to the mainland."

He did not look at Linda again.

Nicholas returned to the news of the Japanese air strike on Colombo, and the subsequent victories in the Bay of Bengal. He wondered what Mori thought of that, but his brother-in-law had taken Charlotte on holiday down to Hakone. Instead he enjoyed a peaceful week with Sumiko and Alexander. Sumiko was due at the end of the month, so there could be no question of any sex between them, and this made their relationship easier. But he would have felt easier in his mind anyway. If he knew that he personally could never atone for some of the crimes that were being committed in the name of the Japanese people, he felt that he had accomplished something, as Takeda willingly signed the necessary forms for the transfer of Linda from imprisonment to domestic service. "She must be a rare beauty for you to have gone to so much trouble," he remarked.

"I would say it is more that we shared a rare beauty, once," Nicholas said.

"And at bottom, you remain a Western romantic," Takeda said. "However, it is not good to allow your romanticism to run away with you. Have you told Sumiko about this woman?"

"Not as yet."

"Then I would not do so at all. Because Christina has told *me* about her."

Nicholas did a double-take, as he wondered what else Christina had told her second husband. But Takeda did not look either aggressive or resentful. "There can be no doubt that Sumiko will be jealous," he went on. "And with you away so much of the time, well . . . I love my wife dearly, but she can be uncommonly vicious, and I suspect you would be exposing this mistress of yours to a great deal of contumely at the very least. If she is in your house as a servant, Sumiko would be within her rights to beat her whenever she chose." He grinned. "She might be better off in a prison camp."

"But she is being released as a domestic servant," Nicholas pointed out.

286

Takeda continued to smile. "That is what is on the paper. But once you get the woman to Tokyo, who is to say how she is employed? If I were you, I would set her up in an apartment somewhere, where she can come to no harm, and where you can visit her as and when you choose."

"You wish me to set up an alien Englishwoman on her own, in Tokyo? You would permit this?"

"I agree, to set her up on her own would not be sensible. But it is still the best idea to keep her out of your house. What you need is someone to share the apartment with her. Your current mistress. That is the ideal solution. Then you would have them both under one roof, and thus under one hand as well, so to speak. I am told this can be very amusing."

Nicholas sighed. "Takeda *san*, I do not have a current mistress, as you put it. I do not have a mistress at all."

Takeda raised his eyebrows. "You are a strange fellow, Barrett *san*. How can a grown man not have a mistress? Or have you been pining for this woman since 1936?"

"Well . . ." Perhaps he had. "I have just never had the time."

"And you have been stationed in Tokyo most of that time? Leave it with me. She can move in with *my* mistress for the time being, until we can sort something out."

"Takeda," Nicholas said. "No one is to lay a finger on Miss Wells, sexually. That includes you. I wish you to understand this very clearly."

Again Takeda raised his eyebrows. "Do you suppose I had that in mind?"

"Very probably, yes."

Takeda did not take offence. "As long as she is you mistress, Nicholas, I shall not touch her. You will not, I hope, mind if I look, occasionally."

Nicholas sighed again. But he knew he would do no better. "How soon will all this happen?"

"Not long. She will be here in a month."

"Damnation," Nicholas muttered. "I will be gone, in a month."

Takeda smiled. "But you will be coming back. Until you do, leave everything with me."

*   *   *

287

Three days later Nicholas was summoned to the Admiralty. "You will be pleased to know, Nicholas, that work on *Yodo* has been speeded up," Yamamoto said. "She will be ready to sail on the twenty-fifth. I therefore wish you to take up your position on board now, with a view to getting to sea with the greatest possible haste."

Nicholas bit his lip. "I understand, honourable Admiral. But . . . the twenty-fifth?"

"When is Sumiko due?"

"The thirtieth is the date given us by the doctor, honourable Admiral."

"That is bad luck. However, the baby will be here when next you return."

"Am I now permitted to ask where I am going, honourable Admiral?"

"I can tell you, yes, Nicholas, in the strictest confidence. You are going to join Admiral Takagi's Task Force at Rabaul. This is for the invasion of Papua and to secure the occupation of the Solomon Islands. Once they are in our hands we will virtually have completed our south-western perimeter, and can look to the north-west. As I have said, that is confidential, until you are at sea. And Nicholas, I would be greatly obliged if you would stay out of trouble, or even controversy."

"Honourable Admiral?"

"I have received a report from Hong Kong. Report! It is more in the style of an accusation. I assume you know that it is a court-martial offence for an officer to strike an enlisted man? Even if he is in a different service."

"He was ill-treating a prisoner, honourable Admiral."

"I also happen to know the name of the prisoner, Nicholas. Nothing will be done about this report, partly because you are my *protégé*, and partly because you are the son-in-law of a senior *Kempei-tai* officer, and the stepson of another, at least by marriage. But you should not count on this fortunate state of affairs lasting forever. Dismissed."

"Oh, I am so *angry*!" Sumiko declared, her small, swollen frame bristling. "For the sake of one week they cannot let you be here for my delivery? It is so unfair."

"Well, I think I am perhaps getting fairer treatment than most," Nicholas suggested; of course he could not tell her how, for the second time in his career, an adverse report was being quashed – without also telling her about Linda, and he knew that Takeda was right there. Takeda was, in fact, turning out to be a very decent and understanding fellow, even if he was a member of the secret police and had no doubt done some pretty awful things in his time.

"Where are you being sent, anyway, that is so important?" Sumiko demanded.

"That is confidential, my dear, as you know it must be," Nicholas said. "I promise you, I'll be up to say goodbye before I go." He would also need to say goodbye to Mori and Charlotte, who had just returned from their holiday. But he did not see them before going down to Yokosuka to join his ship. There he was greeted by Tono, to his great pleasure.

"Honourable Captain! My transfer has come through. I am again to be your Number One."

"And I am delighted," Nicholas said. "We sail on Monday morning." Tono bowed. He knew better than to inquire as to their destination.

Nicholas went down to his cabin, a far grander affair than on *Hatsuharu*, where Tonoye was already unpacking his gear. "Now we will really go to war, eh, honourable Captain?" he asked.

Nicholas agreed with him: *Yodo* was a delight, and became more so as he explored her, accompanied by Tono, Chief Engineer Commander Hasawa, and several other officers. Six hundred and sixty-one feet overall length, she had a beam of sixty feet and a draught of twenty-one. Her eight boilers drove four-shaft geared turbines which would produce one hundred and fifty-two thousand shaft horsepower and give a speed of thirty-five knots; all exhausts were exited through a single raked funnel immediately aft of the bridge.

Her main armament was of eight eight-inch guns in four turrets – unusual in that all were forward of the superstructure, with only one turret superimposed, which somewhat limited their field of fire except in broadside. In addition she also had eight five-inch dual-purpose guns, again

289

in four turrets, twelve twenty-five millimetre anti-aircraft guns, and twelve twenty-four inch torpedo tubes, arranged in four batteries. She also had equipment for six reconnaissance aircraft, although only five had actually been delivered. Nicholas had been disappointed never to have actually served on board *Yamato*, but he felt that this was much more of a ship, and less of a floating fortress. He could hardly wait to get her to sea and put her through her paces. And before him lay a three thousand mile voyage to Rabaul; across the open sea he would have to make it at a cruising speed of not much more than ten knots, which meant something like three weeks, with presumably not an enemy in sight. It would be a voyage to remember. Certainly one to enjoy.

Not an enemy in sight. As he was sailing on the Monday morning, 20 April, Nicholas had arranged to go up to Tokyo on the Saturday afternoon. This would enable him to spend the night and most of Sunday with Sumiko and Mori and Charlotte, before rejoining the ship on Sunday evening.

He was thus up early on the Saturday morning, checking the day log, which was kept even when the vessel was in port, and going over the various reports and requisition sheets presented by Tono, when Lieutenant Tosaburo, the gunnery officer, entered his day cabin after a brief knock. "Tokyo is under attack, honourable Captain," the lieutenant said.

Both Nicholas and Tono stared at him uncomprehendingly. "It is on the radio," Tosaburo said. "Besides, you can see it."

Nicholas and Tono ran out of the cabin and climbed the ladder to the quarterdeck. Here they found half the crew gathered – the other half was forward. All were staring to the north, at the distant flames, and now they could see planes too, low over the city, sliding in and out of the bursts of anti-aircraft fire. "There!" Tono pointed, and heads turned, to watch two aircraft coming in low over the southern end of Tokyo *Wan* and making straight for them.

"Action stations!" Nicholas bellowed. "Anti-aircraft batteries close up." Men raced for their gun positions. Tonoye arrived with Nicholas's binoculars. He levelled them, while his brain refused to accept what he was seeing. "B-Twenty-Fives," he muttered. "But that is not possible."

The Boeing Twenty-Five, the largest aircraft in service with the United States Army Air Force, was essentially a land-based bomber. But there was no US air base operational closer to Japan than Hawaii . . . and that was four thousand miles.

The planes passed right over the cruiser, while the machine guns and DP guns opened fired. The bombs were dropped, but on the yard rather than the ships, and then the enemy had gone, continuing to fly west. Either they had made arrangements to try to reach north Chinese airfields beyond the extent of Japanese penetration, or it had been a suicide mission. But Americans did not go in for suicide missions. Surely. "Sound cease fire," he told Tono, and the bugle rang out. The noise ceased, but his officers were looking at him. "Telephone fleet headquarters and ask if there are any orders," he told Tono.

That had to be his first priority. The second had to be to get to Tokyo: however much they had drifted apart since the war had started, Sumiko was his wife, and she was carrying his child.

Tono returned. "Headquarters asked if we had suffered any damage, and I replied negative, honourable Captain. They then said to carry on as normal."

"Very good. I shall go up to Tokyo immediately, Commander. Find out which of the men have families in the city, and give them twenty-four hours liberty. Every man to be back at his post by noon tomorrow." Tono bowed.

Nicholas went ashore. A bomb had actually landed in the yard, but the damage seemed slight, and far more to morale than any physical object: two men had been hurt by flying splinters. But the workmen gathered round the naval officer as he came ashore, shouting questions, principally, how could this happen? He could not tell them, even as he gained some slight inkling as to how the Americans in Hawaii must have felt on 7 December last.

He got into his car and drove up to the city. Predictably, the military had over-reacted and roadblocks had been erected as if they were expecting an invasion. However no one was going to prevent a captain in the Imperial Navy passing through. His first reaction on entering the city was surprise at how little evidence of damage there was, although the streets remained crowded with excited people, even hours after the raid. He drove straight to his home, which was also quite untouched, but there were only Alexander and the servants to greet him. "Honourable stepmother was taken ill when the noise began, honourable Father," Alexander said. "The ambulance came and took her to hospital."

"But you are all right?"

"No bombs landed near here. But how did the Americans come, honourable Father?"

"I imagine we will find out in due course." Nicholas hurried to the hospital, made himself known, and found that Charlotte and Christina were already there.

"The bombardment brought on the birth," Christina explained. "Is it not outrageous?"

Nicholas did not waste the time asking her what aspect of the situation she found especially outrageous, as he was already being escorted to the ward. "There is nothing to worry about, Captain Barrett," said the doctor. "Your wife became excited, and this induced labour, but the birth was very quick and easy and the boy is only a few days premature."

"Did you say, the boy?"

"You have a son, Captain. Would you like to see him?"

Nicholas was taken into the private ward, where Sumiko was sitting up in bed, the baby in her arms. "Oh, Nicky!" She turned up her face for a kiss, then held up the child for him to kiss as well. "Isn't he lovely? But Nicky . . . what *happened*?"

"Everyone is asking that," Nicholas said.

"Are we going to be invaded?"

"I don't really think that is possible," Nicholas said. "Except as part of some kind of suicide raid. There is nothing for you to worry about."

"But you must still go away?"

"Of course. We have the war to win."

*   *   *

292

He spent the rest of the day with her. Christina and Charlotte also came in, as that evening Takeda and Mori arrived. Takeda was full of self-importance, as usual. "They bombed Nagoya, Osaka and Kobe, as well as Tokyo and Yokohama. But the damage was very slight."

"How many planes were there?" Nicholas asked.

"We believe sixteen. There were reports of more, but only that number have been confirmed. The planes were all lost, of course. One came down right outside Tokyo. But even those which flew on to China will be lost. It was a senseless mission."

"Do you have any idea where they came from?"

"No doubt the captured airmen will be able to tell us." Takeda grinned. "They have been given to us for interrogation."

"They are prisoners-of-war," Nicholas protested.

"They were attempting to murder innocent women and children," Takeda argued. "At least here in Tokyo. As to where they came from, they emerged out of the ocean, so they must have come from aircraft-carriers. Can you imagine, sending aircraft-carriers to sea, and to within a thousand miles of our coast, merely to make a gesture?"

"It was hardly a gesture of a defeated enemy," Mori said quietly, and looked at Nicholas.

CHAPTER 12

The Limit of Success

Three weeks at sea, with a great deal on which to reflect, Nicholas thought as *Yodo* steamed south-by-east across the huge, limitless Pacific; their course to New Britain, of which Rabaul was the chief port, took them past the islands of Ogasawarashoto, which had long been Japanese, then the volcanic peaks of Kazan-retto, then the Northern Mariana Archipeligo, at the southern end of which was the American fortress island of Guam, only recently occupied, and then through the Caroline Islands. Acting on his orders, Nicholas did not touch at any of these places, and indeed, kept out of sight of them. But he used his reconnaissance aircraft to sweep as wide as possible, to either side. No doubt to locate and engage the American carrier which had launched the bombing raid on Tokyo would be to commit suicide – *Yodo* had not been designed to stand up to a concentrated air attack – but he still dreamed of doing so, and going out in one vast battle.

They found nothing, and although Nicholas also maintained radio silence, as ordered, he could listen, and a great deal of news there was to absorb, beginning with the Honkeiko Colliery disaster in Manchuria only the week after they had left Yokosuka. Some fifteen hundred people had been killed, and one's thoughts turned immediately to sabotage. Yet the war went from success to success, as Mandalay and then Corregidor fell. Not that the enemy seemed the least subdued. Apart from the raid on Tokyo, all Japanese ships were now being warned to look out for American submarines, which were showing greatly increasing activity: a Japanese liner was actually sunk off the coast of Hong Kong.

Nicholas doubled his watches, and *Yodo* arrived safely in Rabaul on 10 May, to discover it crammed with shipping, amongst them the two big new aircraft-carriers, *Zuikaku* and *Shokaku*. But clearly there was something wrong, as Nicholas quickly established through his binoculars: *Shokaku* was crawling with men repairing what looked like considerable damage. In addition to the warship, the harbour was crowded with transports, and with men, soldiers rather than sailors, in boats coming and going, and on the waterfront, staring at the new arrival.

The moment *Yodo* was moored up, Nicholas reported to Vice-Admiral Takagi on board *Zuikaku*. The admiral looked a tired and sombre man. "Welcome aboard, Captain Barrett," he said. "Your arrival is most timely."

"May I ask what has happened, honourable Admiral?"

"A temporary setback," Takagi said. "Three days ago we fought an engagement with an American task force. My squadron was covering Rear-Admiral Goto's invasion fleet bound for Port Moresby. But they were spotted by enemy aircraft, and attacked. It appears that the Americans had two aircraft-carriers in the area, as well as some battleships. So naturally we engaged them in return. It was a most unusual battle, because we never sighted a single enemy ship, from our own ships. Nor did they sight us. The battle was fought entirely with aircraft. That is unique, I fancy."

"Yes, sir," Nicholas agreed. "Have we captured Port Moresby?"

"That is what I meant when I said we had suffered a setback. The invasion fleet was escorted by the light carrier *Shoho*. She was attacked by American planes and sunk. Well, that was not a major disaster. *Shoho*, as I am sure you know, Captain Barrett, displaced only fourteen thousand tons and carried only thirty planes. But she was the only immediate escort to the troop convoy, as I was under orders not to hazard my big carriers in those narrow waters. And so it was decided to abort the invasion."

"You mean we have lost the battle, honourable Admiral?" Nicholas was aghast. Japan had not so far lost even the slightest skirmish in this war. But to have lost what sounded like a major battle, coming immediately on top of the raid on the mainland . . .

"No, no, Captain Barrett," Takagi said, somewhat irritably. "The invasion has been postponed, that is all."

"But with *Shoho* sunk, and *Shokaku* damaged . . ."

"That damage is being put right now. Tactically, we have won a great victory. We may have lost *Shoho*, but we have sunk both the American carriers, *Yorktown* and *Lexington*. I need hardly remind you, Captain, that those two were far superior in size and aircraft-carrying capability to *Shoho*."

Again Nicholas could hardly believe what he was being told, because *this* was simply too good to be true. "Honourable Admiral, you have completed what was left undone at Pearl Harbour. The Americans are down to one carrier. There is no doubt about these reported sinkings?"

"Reported? Our pilots actually saw *Lexington* explode."

"But not *Yorktown*?"

"When last seen, she was on fire and listing. She was then lost in a rain squall, and was not found again. Therefore it is obvious that she sank. But as a matter of fact I believe the Americans still have two carriers in the Pacific; they seem to have transferred a new ship, possibly *Hornet*, from the Atlantic theatre. That is as reported from our submarines operating off Hawaii. Is your ship ready for action?"

"As soon as she is refuelled. Is it your intention to complete the capture of Port Moresby, honourable Admiral?"

Takagi made an impatient movement of his fingers. "I am awaiting orders concerning that. I am also awaiting reinforcements. But I am told that these will not be available for some weeks yet."

Nicholas opened his mouth and then closed it again. It was not his business to tell an admiral his job, but if the Americans were reduced even to two carriers, neither of which was apparently in this area at all, then it seemed obvious to attack again just as rapidly as possible. Takagi had observed his expression. "I am sure your men will enjoy some liberty after their long voyage, Captain. See that they have it.

And take some yourself. When we resume our advance you will be very busy."

Tono and Nicholas stood on the bridge and watched the liberty boats ferrying their men ashore. "I doubt there will be enough comfort girls to go round," Tono said. "It will be a matter of standing in line waiting one's turn. But I have been speaking with Commander Nagachi from *Zuikaku*, and he tells me that senior officers may entertain on their ships."

"Providing there are girls available," Nicholas pointed out.

"I will find at least one," Tono promised. "I have been told that these Melanese women are the best in the world. Do you object to sharing, honourable Captain?"

"I will wish you good fortune," Nicholas said. "But concentrate on yourself." He had no interest in comfort girls at that moment; there was too much to be thought about. Perhaps it was because he had been in on the planning side of this war from the beginning, and therefore knew more than most about what Japan's true aims were. It was occurring to him that, as Mori had said, while nothing had yet gone disastrously wrong, nothing had yet gone absolutely right. Of course the over-running of south-east Asia was a triumph, and the quick surrender of Singapore an unexpected bonus, but all of that had been allowed for and expected as part of the nature of the surprise onslaught launched by Japan. It was in the achievement of the hinges upon which all of these tactical victories hung together that the plan was breaking down, and most disturbingly, it was doing so entirely because of the overcaution and uncertainty of the commanding officers.

Pearl Harbour, however dramatic a coup, and however impressive the sinking of five battleships in a single morning might read in a newspaper, had been only half a success – because Nagumo had been unwilling to take any risks. Now the assault on Port Moresby, which would have secured the southern perimeter so important to the future, had been abandoned because of the loss of one not very important carrier. It was as if Takagi and Goto had been children stretching out their hands towards a lighted bulb, and recoiling in dismay when they discovered it to be hot to the touch. And now, to sit around Rabaul doing nothing, while undoubtedly the Americans and the Australians were doing a great deal to the south of them, seemed the height of dangerous absurdity. Nicholas worked off his frustration by exploring the harbour and its environs, and most interesting, the volcanoes with which it was surrounded, and which, indeed, had created the harbour in some prehistoric cataclysm. The volcanoes went by attractively sinister names, The Mother, the North and South Daughters, Vulcan Crater and Matupi Crater. These last two had erupted only five years before, and caused the Australian administration to remove itself to nearby Lae; they continued to smoke and rumble.

He could also brood on the situation at home. Linda would have arrived by now, and been installed in the apartment of Takeda's mistress. He wondered if Christina knew Takeda had a mistress? She probably did, but she would not know who or where, so Linda was probably as safe as she could be – provided Takeda himself could keep his hands off her. While he was stuck in this smoking harbour, waiting, no man knew for what.

However, less than a month after his arrival, the fleet was startled by an announcement from the Admiral: "There has been fought the greatest battle of the war, off the island of Midway in the north-central Pacific. I am happy to tell you that the Imperial Navy, commanded by Admiral Yamamoto in person, has gained a great victory. The United States Navy has been defeated, and two of their remaining carriers have been sunk. As a result of this battle, the Aleutian Islands have been occupied. The gods are on our side."

"Is that not brilliant news, honourable Captain?" Tono asked. "The war is won."

Nicholas stroked his chin as he studied the signal. He had long learned that one could obtain more information by what was *not* said in a report, rather than from a plain statement of what might, or might not, be fact. He knew, because he had helped form the plan, that the northern wing of the perimeter had been intended to rest on the Aleutians and then Midway. So the Aleutians appeared to have been secured. But there was no mention of Midway having been occupied – a strange oversight if the island had been taken. But why had the island

298

not been seized, if the Americans had been routed? Then there was the statement about the carriers. The US Navy had lost *at least two* of its carriers. But according to every report previously received, the US Navy had only *had* two carriers available. Again, a strange phraseology.

He kept his thoughts to himself. Everyone else was in a state of euphoria. "Now we know why we have been kept waiting," Takagi told his captains. "Soon we will receive reinforcements from our victorious fleet, and then we shall resume our advance."

Nicholas hoped he was right. And a fortnight later Admiral Yamamoto came to Rabaul.

Yamamoto arrived entirely unannounced. This was obviously for security reasons, because he came by plane rather than on board *Yamato*, and with the victorious carrier fleet. He spent some time closeted with Takagi before his visit was properly announced, then there were guards-of-honour to be inspected and supper parties to be attended. At no time did the commander-in-chief give the impression of a man who has just won the greatest victory of his career. Neither was Takagi looking as happy as he should.

It was on the third day of his visit that Yamamoto inspected *Yodo*. "You have a fine ship," he told Nicholas and Tono. "Has she seen action yet?"

"Not yet, honourable Admiral."

"Well, I think she soon will. It has been a pleasure to meet you, Commander Tono."

Tono understood that he had been dismissed, bowed, and left the day cabin. Tonoye bustled in with green tea, and was then also dismissed.

Nicholas poured. "Am I permitted to ask what has gone wrong, honourable Admiral?"

Yamamoto frowned at him. "What makes you suppose something has gone wrong, Nicholas?"

Nicholas told him what he had found odd with the signal. "And then, I would have expected you to move all of your heavy ships south, if there is no longer any threat in the North Pacific, honourable Admiral."

"Sometimes," Yamamoto remarked, "it is a relief to know

that there are not many officers in the Imperial Navy with a brain as acute as yours. Then again, sometimes it is possible to wish there were more. Yes, Nicholas, there is something wrong. We have lost four carriers."

Nicholas sat very straight. "*Four* carriers?"

"*Akagi, Soryu, Kaga* and *Hiryu*, are all at the bottom of the ocean. Not to mention *Mikuma*, but in the context of such a catastrophe, one heavy cruiser is hardly worth mentioning."

Nicholas had the sensation that his ship was rolling in a heavy sea, although she was moored in a secure harbour. "But how did that happen, honourable Admiral?" It took an effort to keep his voice calm and even.

Yamamoto sighed. "Faulty intelligence, faulty tactics, faulty strategy on the day. Everything that could possibly go wrong, did. But most of all, it was faulty leadership. I should have been there. I can admit this to you, Nicholas, if to no one else. Instead, I was on *Yamato*, three hundred miles behind the carrier strike force. Our job was to clean up the American ships once their two carriers had been disposed of. Two carriers. There was error number one. They had three, but we were unaware of this, because Takagi reported that both *Yorktown* and *Lexington* had gone down in the Battle of the Coral Sea."

"He told me his pilots saw *Lexington* explode."

"Yes. That is undoubtedly so. But they lost *Yorktown* in a rain squall, and as she was on fire, when the squall ended and they could not find her again, they assumed she had gone down as well, and reported it so. And Takagi forwarded the report. One should never assume."

"You mean *Yorktown* did not sink, honourable Admiral?"

"I mean *Yorktown* was at Midway, Nicholas. In full fighting trim and with all her ninety aircraft operational. And we did not know this until it was too late. Mistake number two was Nagumo's decision to launch a second strike on Midway. I am told this was necessary because the first strike did not do sufficient damage. If that is true, then it was inefficiently carried out. The point is that to launch a second strike meant re-arming his planes. He was found by the Americans with his decks loaded with aircraft, refuelling and re-arming."

"He had no fighter cover?"

"Indeed. But he sent up his fighter cover to deal with the first wave of attack, torpedo planes. They were annihilated. But that meant his fighters were out of position when the second wave, dive bombers, reached him. Even then, he thought he was only faced with attack from two carriers."

Nicholas bit his lip, as he remembered warning the Commander-in-Chief, before Pearl Harbour, that Nagumo was not a carrier admiral. "Is the admiral . . . ?"

"Oh, he survived. When *Akagi* was definitely found to be sinking, he transferred his flag to a cruiser. Well, that was the correct thing to do, and at that time he still had one carrier left. But when she went as well, I had no option but to abort the attack. One of the American carriers sank, I am informed. But I could not risk my battleships against the remaining two without adequate air cover. I am quite sure *Yamato* can take anything the Americans can throw at her, but the others would have been sitting ducks. There is also another aspect of the situation which is most disturbing: the Americans knew we were coming. It could have been inspired guesswork, or just bad luck on our part. But if there has been treachery . . ."

The two men sat in silence for several minutes, then Yamamoto said, "We lost three and a half thousand men. Do you realise this is the first time the Imperial Navy has ever been defeated? I contemplated *seppuku*, Nicholas."

"I am glad you did not commit it, honourable Admiral."

"Why?"

"For three reasons, honourable Admiral. One is that you are my friend, more than my friend. The second is that although you were in ovarall command of the fleet, you were not on the field, as it were. You had no influence on the tactical way the battle was fought, and thus you cannot possibly be blamed for the way it was lost. And thirdly, we need you too much, to lead us."

Yamamoto gave one of his grim smiles. "It was the last that made the difference in my mind. Am I not exceedingly arrogant?"

"You are exceedingly realistic, honourable Admiral. But . . . what happens now?"

"My first reflection was that we had lost the war. Well,

we may well have done so: those four carriers cannot be replaced with a snap of the fingers – we already have a steel shortage. What is more important even than that, however, is that the two hundred and fifty pilots who died were our very best, men who had trained for years to be the best. Again, I cannot replace them with a snap of the fingers, yet I must have pilots. That means our new men will be poorly trained, and thus less efficient. However, when I considered the matter in more detail, I realised things are by no means as bad as I had first feared. The Americans are down to two carriers. But we also have two fleet carriers left, the two out there. Now, the enemy have the capacity to build ships far faster and in greater quantities than ourselves. But they will still need a year at least to produce any. Thus we still have that year to obtain the position we wish. That is why I am here. The Solomons must be fortified and held, and Port Moresby must be taken to make New Guinea and Papua secure."

"It should have been taken by now," Nicholas said bitterly.

Yamamoto nodded. "Once again, poor leadership. However, that can be rectified, and I am assured it will be. There must be no more mistakes. Now, it is fairly certain that the Americans will counter-attack in the Solomons. They have to. This time they must be defeated. We will have those two carriers yet."

"Yes, sir," Nicholas said enthusiastically. He wanted to fight, someone, anyone. "And in the north?"

"We shall have to do without Midway, that is all. But we will still have our perimeter, even if with a small dent in it." He stood up. "I have given you my thoughts because I have used so many of yours in my time. Nicholas, I count you one of my finest officers. Were I in complete control I would promote you admiral tomorrow, and make the defence of the Solomons your business. I cannot do this; there are too many political pressures at home against it. But I wish you to know that this is what is necessary. And remember, too, that if it should come to pass, I will back your actions to the hilt, even if they smack of insubordination, just so long as the insubordination is directed towards fighting the enemy."

"I am honoured by your confidence, honourable Admiral.

302

May I ask how the news of what has happened was received at home?"

This time Yamamoto's grin was savage. "At home Midway is being represented as a victory."

"But . . . when the ships do not return . . . and what of the families of all those men?"

"The ships have officially been reassigned, with their crews. That is all anyone at home can know for the time being. We are fighting a war. Oh, I know it cannot be kept secret for very long. It is our duty to make sure that by the time it is no longer a secret we will have gained sufficient victories for the fact of Midway not to matter." Nicholas bowed.

Nicholas sat in his cabin, alone, for some time after the Admiral had left. Having made the decision to live, and fight, Yamamoto was putting the best possible face on the situation. But as he had confessed, the war was lost. Or at least, it could no longer be won. Even if they succeeded in reaching the projected perimeter, it would be a case of standing siege rather than dictating peace from a position of strength. While if the Allies ever broke through and found out some of the things that had been happening . . . but the Allies already knew. It had been part of government policy that they should know, and be afraid.

It suddenly occurred to him that he was afraid himself. Not of death, but of condemnation by forces beyond his control. It had been possible to hope that a victorious Japan would be able to put its own house in order, deal with people like Yosunobe, and even Takeda; it would be an entirely different matter did their fate lie at the hands of victorious enemies who had only vengeance in mind. But there was more: the moral effect a defeat would have on a proud people who had never experienced it, as a nation. There was a terrifying thought.

Tonoye knocked before entering with a pot of tea. "Commander Tono would like a word, honourable Captain."

Nicholas nodded, and Tono bowed as he came in. "I trust the Commander-in-Chief had no bad news for you, honourable Captain?"

Nicholas squared his shoulders; for Yamamoto to lie to the entire nation was less difficult than for him to lie to his officers and men. "There was no bad news, Commander. The Commander-in-Chief merely reminded me that no matter how many victories we may gain, there are yet victories we need to gain."

"We are ready, honourable Captain, And our forces are growing. We have just been joined by a destroyer flotilla. The flotilla commander is Captain Takijo. He has signalled us asking if you and he could meet."

"Takijo! Indeed. Invite him on board, Commander."

"Hasueke!"

"Nicholas!"

It was several months since they had seen each other, now they embraced before stepping back to bow, formally: Nicholas was the senior, by a few months. "Now we are ready to fight the enemy," Nicholas said. "You weren't at Midway, by any chance?"

"No, sadly. Were you?"

"No."

"I was in the Dutch East Indies, on convoy duty," Takijo said. "We seem to have missed quite a show."

"Yes," Nicholas agreed. His friend obviously did not know the truth about the battle. "Have you seen action?"

"In a manner of speaking. I am bound to confess, Nicholas, that the American submarines are very bold. They sail within a few miles of our coasts and torpedo anything that moves. We have had a busy time."

"Any kills?"

"None that I can positively claim. I have seen oil slicks on two occasions after depth charging, but that is not in itself sufficient evidence. But are there submarines here also?"

"Not too many," Nicholas told him. "We're here to fight surface craft, I think."

For the next month the cruisers and destroyers patrolled the sea around the Solomons, seeking any American forces, but none were to be seen, although the Japanese were pouring more and more men into the islands and forti-fying Guadalcanal as rapidly as possible. Takagi having been relieved, as Yamamoto had suggested might happen, the naval squadron in Rabaul was now commanded by

Vice-Admiral Mikawa. For the moment he had little to do, and once again the Japanese were surging ahead, with an invasion force landed at Buna, north of Port Moresby, to complete the occupation of Papua by land. On Guadalcanal work commenced on building an airstrip. "Soon we shall have another aircraft-carrier operating in the South Pacific," Mikawa told his captains. "Only this one will be unsinkable."

But the Americans at last realised this, and also the potential of an operating airstrip on Guadalcanal, close enough to New Britain to make Rabaul untenable for the Japanese fleet. On the evening of 7 August, a Friday, the captains were summoned to the heavy cruiser *Chokai*, Mikawa's flagship. "The enemy are attempting to land on Guadalcanal and Tulagi Islands," the Admiral said. "They cannot be allowed to do so. Their invasion force is supported by a squadron of cruisers and destroyers. It is my intention to attack and destroy or disperse that squadron, immediately. We will sail at dawn."

Nicholas and Tokijo skook hands as they parted. "Now for the first time we are going to fight in harness, Nicholas," Tokijo said. "We must not fail."

Nicholas was aware of a growing sense of excitement. He was thirty-eight years old, and save for one unforgettable day off Java, six months ago now, had never been under fire. Equally had he never commanded a ship as large as *Yodo* into action. He wondered what he should tell his men. In the end, he merely announced over the tannoy, "*Yodo* will sail at dawn tomorrow to seek and destroy an enemy squadron operating in the Solomon Islands. I expect every man to do his duty."

His own orders were merely to follow the flagship, which seemed simple enough; as the largest of the seven cruisers in the squadron – even *Chokai*, the flagship, was under thirteen thousand tons compared with her fifteen – *Yodo* was second in the line. Disconcertingly, only one of Tokijo's ships was ready for sea, but he was not going to be denied and took command of her himself.

The eight ships got underway at four o'clock on the morning of Saturday 8 August, passed through St George's

305

Channel between New Britain and New Ireland, and steamed south-by-west along the south-western coast of Bougainville, the largest and most northerly island of the Solomon Group. The sun rose soon after they had passed through the channel, and it gave every promise of a most brilliant day, with hardly a cloud in the sky. Nicholas doubled his watches, both for aircraft and submarines, but for the moment they were untroubled, as the volcanoes of New Britain dropped astern and they looked at the peaks of the Emperor Range on Bougainville, nearly three thousand metres high.

Japanese troops had been landed on Bougainville some time earlier, but no one knew for sure how much of the relatively large island – it was some hundred and fifty miles long – was fully controlled, or if there were any sizeable enemy forces remaining. However, here again all was peaceful, as, steaming well within itself at thirty knots the squadron swung between Shortland Island and Treasure Island to enter New Georgia Sound, the thirty mile wide stretch of water known as The Slot. Takijo's destroyer was out in front of the flagship, an impressive sight with their battle flags streaming in the breeze and their white wakes carving through the bright blue of the sea.

They entered The Slot just after two o'clock in the afternoon. By now it was intensely warm, the sun seeming to hang immediately above the ships, causing the metalwork to be hot to the touch, while in the calm sea the only breeze was that whipped up by the ships themselves. But in the enclosed waters it was even more necessary to maintain a sharp lookout, and it was not possible to stand anyone down. Nicholas lunched seated in his chair on the bridge, a bowl of rice and a cup of green tea being served by the attentive Tonoye, while the islands of Choiseul and Santa Isabel raced by to the north-east, and the New Georgia Islands to the south-west. Like all of the Solomons these were volcanic, and rose from sandy beaches through lush green vegetation to stark, high, cone-shaped peaks.

By four o'clock the mountains of Guadalcanal itself were in sight, and now flags began to flutter on *Chokai*'s signal halliard. The admiral had been listening to the radio signals from Guadalcanal, although he was himself maintaining radio silence, and now he was sending: *Understand enemy force five heavy cruisers with destroyers in two groups intend passing south Savo Island to engage southern group squadron will then swing up north-east and round Savo Island to engage north group acknowledge.*

"Acknowledge, Commander," Nicholas told Tono, while he studied the transcript. There was no mention of attacking the landing force. But no doubt Mikawa was correct in seeking to destroy the covering force first, as opposed to what Doorman had attempted to do in the Java Sea. Although with the two forces so evenly matched, he would have supposed it might be a sensible idea to fight a holding action against the Allied ships while detaching two of his own to get amongst the transports and create havoc. But his business was to support the admiral. The sun was now fast drooping to the west, and at six o'clock it disappeared with tropical suddenness, plunging the islands into darkness, and the sea into stygian gloom. Now the only relief from the black was provided by the phosphorescent gleams of the wakes and waves streaking away from the bows, and the glimmer of the stern light on each ship. To the right Nicholas, his binoculars held to his eyes, could make out occasional sparks of red to suggest humanity amidst the trees; those watchers from the shore would have seen the battle squadron. What was really remarkable was that they had seen no sign of any enemy throughout the day. And now they were nearly upon them.

There came the drone of aircraft from overhead, at the same time as a radio message was received; the planes were reconnaissance machines from the Japanese fleet carriers which were hovering well north of the rocks and shallows of the islands. *Southern Group consists of Canberra and Chicago and two destroyers.*

Midshipman Funai was waiting at Nicholas's elbow with his book, reading by the glimmer from the binnacle lamp. "*Canberra* is a Kent Class heavy cruiser serving with the Royal Australian Navy, honourable Captain. Fourteen thousand tons deep load, eight eight-inch guns, thirty-one knots."

That made her, except in terms of speed, more powerful than any of the Japanese ships save his own, Nicholas realised.

307

"But she is an old ship, honourable Commander," Funai added. "Commissioned 1928. *Chicago* is a United States Northampton Class cruiser, eleven thousand tons, nine eight-inch guns, thirty-two knots. She also is more than ten years old."

And she also was more heavily armed than any of the Japanese ships, even his own. But the Japanese would have the advantage of surprise, even if the Allies would surely have been alerted to some impending danger by the reconnaissance machines earlier. Lights were flashing from *Chokai*. "Signal reads: *Yubari, Tenryu and Kako will turn to port when south of Savo, to engage North Force. Main body will deal with South Force and then join*," Tono read. "Further: *Yodo will engage Canberra*. We are honoured, honourable Captain.

Nicholas checked the chronometer: it was just on nine o'clock. "Pipe dinner. But all hands will eat at their posts, Mr Tono," he said.

The ships streaked onwards. Now their eyes were accustomed to the darkness they could pick out the black hump of Savo Island, which blocked the south-eastern end of The Slot. The passage between the islet and Cape Esperance on the north of Guadalcanal was just over five nautical miles wide, ample for manoeuvre as there were no reefs. And now, too, he could see lights beyond the passage, with more further off. The Allies were still disembarking and needing to see what they were doing, unaware that they were revealing themselves to their enemy.

"Eleven o'clock, honourable Captain," Tono reported. "All hands have eaten."

"Load," Nicholas said.

The hoists whirred and the eight-inch shells, each weighing some three hundred pounds, were sent up. Nicholas became aware of the tension in the men standing around him on the bridge, a tension which would be pervading the entire ship's company: only Tono and himself had previously seen action. "Midnight," Tono said.

Surely the enemy would know they were here now, Nicholas thought: they were abeam of Savo, and still hurtling south, speed now increased to a full thirty-five knots. The entire western horizon was blocked by Guadalcanal, and now

308

too they could see the red flashes of explosions where the Japanese were resisting the American landings. But perhaps the ships supposedly guarding the passage were also more interested in the fighting ashore than in their jobs: there had been no indication that the approaching squadron had been sighted. "Signal from flagship, honourable Captain," Midshipman Funai said. "*Alter course to port and open fire.*"

"Range?" Nicholas asked.

"Ten thousand and closing, honourable Captain."

"Port your helm. Lieutenant Tosaburo, fire when you are ready."

"I am ready now, honourable Captain. Shoot!"

The eight guns, all mounted forward of the bridge, exploded at the same time as those on *Chokai*. Tosaburo's gunlaying had been amazingly accurate in the darkness, and huge plumes of water rose to either side of the Australian cruiser. She was obviously taken completely by surprise, and although she promptly returned fire, her shooting was wild. The next salvo from the Japanese cruisers struck home. Vivid red flashes lit up the darkness and Nicholas almost thought he could hear the screech of tortured metal being torn apart.

"Radio signal from flagship, honourable Captain." Funai was back, and Mikawa had abandoned silence. "Reads: *Am shifting to Chicago. Keep firing into Canberra.*"

"Acknowledge," Nicholas said. "Keep firing, Mr Tosaburo."

Now Tosaburo had a clear target at which to aim, for *Canberra* was on fire in several places, lighting up the night sky, and by the glare they could also see *Chicago* being hit by a succession of salvoes from the other Japanese ships. But *Canberra* was going to be the first victim. Now she was ablaze from stem to stern, and her guns had ceased firing; *Yodo* had received not a hit in return. "Signal flagship," Nicholas said. "*Canberra* out of action. Request permission to turn to North Force."

Permission was received immediately, and *Yodo* left her blazing victim and steamed to the north-east, where the remaining Japanese ships were engaging the three cruisers and four destroyers of the North Force. These ships had been identified as all belonging to the New Orleans class, which

309

meant that they were bigger and slightly faster versions of *Chicago*. But they had obviously also been taken entirely by surprise. And although more heavily gunned that the ships attacking them, were already on fire in several places. The arrival of *Yodo* signalled their destruction. All three ships were in flames in minutes, and the Japanese continued to pump shells into them at a rapidly closing range, with hardly a shot being returned.

Message from flagship: *Congratulations on a job well done. The enemy force has been liquidated. This is a decisive victory. Squadron will adopt cruising formation and return to base.* Nicholas looked up from the signal to the burning enemy warships, then to the Japanese squadron, virtually undamaged, and back to the transports still unloading several miles to their south. If he could not hear, he could see the pandemonium down there, the flashing lights moving to and fro. The Americans anticipated total destruction, as had to happen, were the seven Japanese cruisers to steam towards them: they had absolutely no defence.

But the Japanese squadron was obediently forming line ahead, obeying its admiral's orders. "Shall I give the course, honourable Captain?" Tono asked.

Nicholas bit his lip. Yamamoto had said that he would support him in any insubordinate act, so long as it was towards the enemy. He was certain that Mikawa, as with almost every other Japanese fleet commander in this war, was erring in strictly obeying his orders – to destroy or disperse the escorting enemy squadron – in preference to acting in the *spirit* of the orders, which was surely to prevent the Americans landing on Guadalcanal, if he could. But to go steaming off by himself, towards no enemy warships . . . and suppose Mikawa knew something he did not? Not even Yamamoto could save him from a court martial, if he hazarded his ship, one of the best in the Imperial Navy, to no purpose, in direct contravention of his own orders from the admiral. "Lay a course to take our place in the cruising formation," he said.

When dawn broke the Japanese squadron was well up The Slot, steaming again in perfect nose to tail formation. The

310

weather remained calm, and visibility was excellent, and there was not an enemy in sight. The crews were jubilant, and although Mikawa had again enjoined radio silence, he did not interfere with the signals which were constantly being run up the mastheads as each captain congratulated his comrades on the enormous success. Which was even greater than they had supposed, as they listened on their radios to the frantic Allied interchanges from behind them. All three cruisers of the Northern force had sunk, and *Canberra* had also gone down, torpedoed by one of her own destroyers when it was realised that she could not be saved. Only *Chicago* seemed to have survived, but it was clear that she was badly damaged.

"Virtually a clean sweep, honourable Captain," Tono said. "Should you not be smiling?" He had known Nicholas long enough by now to be able to make that kind of remark.

Just as Nicholas had known him long enough to be able to reply, "The Americans are still putting men and material ashore on Guadalcanal, Mr Tono."

Tono gave him an old-fashioned look, and turned back to his executive duties, listing the number of shells fired and the various elevations and ranges, trying to correlate them to the observed hits. There was no damage report to be made, as *Yodo* had taken not a single hit. It had, Nicholas knew, been a most tremendous victory, quite on a par, regarding the number and size of ships involved, with Tsushima, the equalling of which was the dream of every Japanese admiral. But Togo, having destroyed three-quarters of the Russian fleet, had kept to sea in fog, rising wind and seas until the next day, to seek and destroy the remainder of the enemy – he had not immediately steamed back to Shimonoseki to claim his victory.

Nor was Mikawa to regain Rabaul unscathed. By midday, with half the journey covered, and not an enemy plane in sight, the Japanese lookouts were beginning to relax. It was Fujiko's destroyer which signalled frantically when it saw the tell-tale wisp of foam from the submarine's periscope, and dashed towards the enemy. But the submarine had clearly been watching the squadron for some time, and now with great deliberation fired her torpedoes before disappearing. Fukijo raced up and down dropping his depths charges, but without success, and meanwhile a huge explosion and tall column of smoke rose from the medium cruiser *Kako*, eight thousand tons and six eight-inch guns; she sank within minutes, taking most of her six hundred and twenty-five men with her.

The Japanese still claimed a great victory, as tactically the Battle off Savo Island was. For a while, indeed, it began to look like a strategical victory as well, as stunned by their losses, the Allies withdrew all transports and protecting warships from the Solomons, leaving the considerable force they had managed to land on Guadalcanal isolated. But these continued to fight to gain possession of the airfield, and within another ten days the Americans were again attempting to reinforce them, now supported by a proper naval squadron, including carriers.

This brought Vice-Admiral Nagumo Chuichi to Rabaul. Nagumo was still regarded by the Japanese people, as well as by the fleet at large, as a hero, for what he had accomplished at Pearl Harbour; few people as yet knew anything about the debacle at Midway. And certainly he seemed to have recovered his confidence. "Well, gentlemen," he told his assembled captains in the wardroom of *Zuikaku*, "Now we are going to see some real action, eh?"

Nicholas could not help but wonder if any of the other officers present were giving a thought to the absence of the other four heavy carriers from what promised to be another very important battle. But he had to respond when Nagumo singled him out to say, "Well, Captain Barrett, I understand that you have again been covering yourself with glory."

Nicholas bowed. "Now you will have a fresh opportunity, eh?" Nagumo said. "This will be the decisive battle of the war."

It occurred to Nicholas that he heard that before.

From the point of view of a cruiser captain, however, the opportunities for glory were slim. There was no lack of action: the Japanese were as determined to hold on to Guadalcanal as the Americans were to seize it, and before the end of the month a four-day battle, known as the Battle of the

312

Solomons, was fought in an effort to clear the area of enemy ships and allow sufficient men and material to be landed to secure the island.

This was a major action, in which each side had two fleet carriers supported by battleships, but as at Midway or the Coral Sea the surface craft never saw each other, the Japanese fleet remaining north of the islands and the American task force to the south. So it was a matter of watching one's own planes taking off and awaiting their return, and of watching for enemy planes coming in to attack. This did not mean there could be the slightest relaxation in vigilance, because apart from the enemy aircraft there were also US submarines in the vicinity. In fact, it was a far more exhausting form of warfare than the ship-to-ship action Nicholas had experienced in the Java Sea, for while the crews had to be on twenty-four hour standby, the only enemies they had to shoot at were fast-flying wasps or streaks of foam in the water; for men who so recently had watched their shells bursting on *Canberra* with devastating effect, this was most irritating. Worst of all the battle ended in a defeat. Very few Japanese troops got ashore, and when the light carrier *Ryujo* was sunk by American bombers, Nagumo, predictably, called off the attack. To be fair, his heavy carriers had also received hits, *Shokaku* being virtually out of action, but the Japanese pilots claimed to have damaged the American carriers as well. Nonetheless, the fleet and the surviving transports returned to Rabaul.

Yodo had once again escaped undamaged and without casualties; one or two bombs had entered the sea close by and there had been several seams strained, but these were easily repairable. Tokijo had also survived, Nicholas was glad to note, although not all of his destroyers, with their thin skins, had been able to cope with near misses as successfully as the heavy cruiser. The two friends met ashore to get drunk together and share a comfort girl. These were in great demand by the brooding, unhappy sailors. "Have you ever considered the future, Hasueke?" Nicholas asked, when they lay together, sated, to drink brandy, the girl between them, also drinking brandy.

"I do not think that is a good thing, for a naval officer," Tokijo said. "A consideration of one's next orders is far enough ahead to look. It is different when one is an admiral."

"Then you never think of the possibility of defeat." Nicholas remembered his conversation with Mori. So much had changed in so short a time.

"I think that is even more unwise. Besides, your men would be sure to guess it, and it would be bad for morale."

"I am not speaking of personal defeat," Nicholas said. "I am thinking of the possibility of Japan being defeated."

Tokijo raised himself on his elbow in consternation, and looked down at the girl. But she merely smiled happily. She spoke only a few words of Japanese, although she had a very good line in Australian swear words – and besides, she had taken advantage of the freely offered brandy bottle to become very drunk. "Japan has never been defeated," Tokijo said.

"And thus you think it is impossible."

Tokijo lay down again, and started playing with the girl's breasts; she giggled even louder. "It is certainly impossible to consider. You have become a very dour fellow, Nicky." Then he laughed. "But you were always a dour fellow, even at college. It is in the lap of the gods, Nicholas, whether we live or die, whether we win or are defeated. I know this is not a Christian philosophy, but there are times when one must accept the best philosophy available, and in time of war, that is the only one."

CHAPTER 13

The Narrow Waters

Nicholas could only hope that his friend was right. Because soon it became apparent that the gods were no longer with them. Following the repulse at the end of August the Americans secured their hold on Guadalcanal, and although the Japanese retained forces in the north of the island, the vital airstrip, named by the Americans Henderson Field, was made operational by the US Air Force. Now Rabaul was subjected to daily bombing raids, and it became obvious that there would have to be either a withdrawal or the airfield would have to be rendered inoperable.

It was chafing as much as exhausting to have to keep the crews on stand-by even in harbour, never knowing when the planes were going to strike, and it was a relief to be sent out in successive small squadrons to charge down The Slot and bombard Henderson Field, withdrawing again before they could be found by the American bombers. At the end of October, the Japanese Army commander on Guadalcanal reported that he and his men were within a few hours of recapturing the airfield, and Nagumo again took his ships to see, both to lend support and to make sure that the American Navy did not interfere. In the event, they did, and there was another long-range battle, which again turned out badly. *Shokaku* was so badly damaged she was out of action for several months, and although in reply the Japanese sank *Hornet*, which had by now been identified as the vessel responsible for the Tokyo air raid, this tactical success was more than negated by the loss of a hundred aircraft to only seventy American. Worst of all was the realisation that the

315

commander on the ground had been over-optimistic, and his men were nowhere near recapturing the airfield.

Vice Admiral Nagumo was withdrawn, with his carriers, both for repairs and to rest and recuperate. His successor, Vice Admiral Abe, summoned his captains to a meeting on board the battleship *Hiei* on the morning of Monday, 8 November. "I must inform you that the world situation is developing certain characteristics which may not be favourable to Japan," he informed them.

The officers waited. They were well aware that the land campaign on New Guinea was not going well, and that in fact the Japanese were fighting a succession of desperate rearguard actions as they retreated to the north. They had to do no more than look out of the window at the fires still burning on shore from the last American air attack to know things were not going well here either.

Abe cleared his throat. "There now seems no doubt that the Germans have received a severe defeat in North Africa, at a place called . . ." he peered at his notes, "Alamein. Additionally, we are receiving reports that a large Anglo-American force has been put ashore at the other end of North Africa. This does not immediately affect our situation here, of course, but it has become all the more imperative for us either to regain control of Guadalcanal or at least to destroy Henderson Field. It is my intention, therefore, to take my squadron down The Slot and bombard the airfield with every gun we have, until it is rendered unusable. This operation, which will completely occupy the Americans, will also serve to cover the landing of a troop convoy on the north of the island. Gentlemen, I must impress upon you that this time we *must* succeed in our mission. There can be no turning back. It is possible that we may sustain heavy casualties, but I know that every man will do his duty."

"And beside," Takijo smiled as he and Nicholas were ferried back to their respective ships. "Now that the carriers have been withdrawn, we are all expendable, eh?"

Abe was in fact attempting to repeat Mikawa's tactics, and hopefully, success of a few months previously, Nicholas realised. Only this time Abe intended to do what Mikawa

316

had failed to attempt, and get close enough to the American land positions and landing areas to blast them out of existence. But the situation had changed considerably since Mikawa's raid. Not only did the Americans have a task force concentrated south of the islands, and almost complete air superiority, but the Japanese ships available had also changed beyond recognition. True there were the two battleships, *Hiei* and *Kirishima*, but only one cruiser, Nicholas's own, was operable, due to bomb damage and various engine-room failures. On the other hand, Takijo now led a force of fourteen destroyers, and the battleships could certainly deliver a heavy punch when it came to bombarding an airfield.

As before, the plan was to attack at night, but this time the weather was not on their side. The squadron went down The Slot in pouring rain lashed with searing sheets of lightning, scarce able to see the stern lights worn on the ship ahead, knowing only that Fukijo's destroyers were out in front in three groups. *Yodo* was behind them, and the two battleships were astern of her. The entire crew was at their stations, the guns were loaded and the ammunition hoists whirred gently.

Nicholas and Tono stood together on the bridge, as they had so often in the past, not speaking, their minds concentrated on what they might encounter south of Savo, until Nicholas began to become worried. Having made this run before, he reckoned they had been far too long without seeing anything. The same thought had obviously occurred to the admiral's navigating officer, because through the darkness there came a flashing light: *We are south of the island. Put about.*

"Shit!" Nicholas commented. They were lost. But as he gave the order to come about and reverse their course, Midshipman Funai ran from the radio room, waving a piece of paper. "Signal from Captain Fukijo to the Admiral, honourable Captain."

"By radio?" Nicholas was astounded, as they were maintaining radio silence.

"In clear, honourable Captain. Message reads: *Have encountered enemy destroyers. Am altering course. Request instructions.*"

317

Nicholas peered into the darkness. The squadron was now steaming north, therefore they had not only passed Savo in the storm but also the American warships guarding the Sound. But even as the concept registered the night sky in front of him was brilliantly illuminated by gunfire, bursting into flame in every direction.

"Those are not only destroyers," Tono said, listening to the deeper reports of eight-inch guns.

Funai was back. "Message from flagship, honourable Captain: *Squadron will engage.*"

Also in clear. Well, it was all or nothing now. But even as he rang down for increased speed Nicholas wondered just who he was to engage, as he saw nothing ahead of him save flashing lights, and at least some of those lights were coming from Japanese ships.

But as they approached they could make out the vessels, illuminated by the brilliant lightning, and identify the larger gun-flashes as coming from American cruisers. Nicholas opened up with everything he possessed, shooting at anything larger than a destroyer, and for the next two hours it was an amazingly confused melee, with the smaller ships firing at each other and loosing off torpedoes in every direction, and with the battleships booming away with their eleven-inch guns. But Abe was intelligently letting his small craft do the naval fighting while he concentrated on bombarding his prime target, Henderson Field.

Nicholas was able to get some idea of what was happening on the American side by listening to their shouted communications, also in clear, from which he gathered that one of their admirals, Callaghan, had been killed, and that one of their cruisers was sinking as well. Dawn brought the evidence of at least a severe battle, as the surviving American ships had fled to the south, while the surface was littered with wreckage and boats and liferafts, and men. From prisoners he picked up Nicholas learned that the eight thousand ton cruiser *Atlanta*, the name ship of her class, a brand-new design armed with sixteen five-inch guns as opposed to the more normal eight eight-inch, had gone down, as well as four destroyers, and with them two admirals, Callaghan and Scott. Additionally it was admitted that a sister to *Atlanta*, *Juneau*, as well as the older and bigger – twelve thousand tons – cruiser *Portland*, had been severely damaged.

But any idea of claiming at least a tactical victory was negated by the sight of *Hiei*, the veteran forty thousand ton battleship, drifting helplessly, burning in several places and with her propellers damaged beyond repair.

Abe had been wounded, and the command was assumed by Vice-Admiral Kondo on board *Hiei*'s sister, *Kirishima*, and now signal flags were fluttering at the new flagship's masthead: *Squadron will withdraw*.

Nicholas and Tono looked as each other as they steamed north, past the stricken giant, abandoned to her fate, her decks crowded with men working the houses to keep the fires under control. "There was nothing else he could have done," Tono muttered, and now it was broad daylight they could expect a visit from the US Air Force.

And in fact the American planes, both carrier-launched and from Henderson Field, arrived soon afterwards. But Abe had calculated correctly, and instead of chasing his depleted squadron – in addition to *Hiei*, two destroyers had been sunk – the aircraft devoted their attention to completing the destruction of the battleship. *Hiei* continued to signal in clear for over an hour, before her last aerial was shot away, and soon after a reconnaissance aircraft reported that she had disappeared beneath an immense oil slick. The American planes had gone home to refuel, and in mid-afternoon the Japanese received some welcome news, the crippled cruiser *Juneau* had been torpedoed and sunk by the submarine I26.

"A cruiser for a battleship," Nicholas growled. "That is a bad rate of exchange, Mr Tono."

But only an hour later, with the day fading, ships were sighted to the north: they were the repaired cruisers from Rabaul, once again bringing the Japanese squadron up to strength. Immediately lights began winking from *Kirishima*: *Squadron will return to the attack*.

Nicholas could not believe his eyes as he read the command, but the battleship and the destroyers were already wheeling. Then he slapped Tono on the shoulder. "Now we have a commander!" he said jubilantly.

*   *   *

319

Kondo's brilliant stroke was a complete success. The American force had withdrawn to lick its wounds, and had not been replaced. The fourteen Japanese ships steamed past Savo without hindrance, and began pounding the airfield, a dramatic sight as the battleship's huge fourteen-inch shells slammed into the darkness and exploded with enormous gushes of red flame, well supported by the eight-inch of the four cruisers in support.

There was virtually no return of fire, and it was nearly dawn before Kondo signalled withdrawal. Then it was a matter of getting up The Slot as quickly as possible. Nicholas had an early breakfast, while remaining on the bridge, although, in common with all his men, he had had no sleep for forty-eight hours. He had, in fact, just told Tono to make up a roster and retire the crew in three watches below for a few hours rest when the enemy aircraft were sighted. "Cancel that order, Commander," he said. "We must see this lot off first."

In the narrow waters of The Slot there was not that much room to manoeuvre. Every ship opened up with its maximum anti-aircraft fire, but the enemy, both dive-bombers and torpedo-bombers, kept coming; without the protection that would have been afforded by a fighter screen there was insufficient fire power to deter them. Huge plumes of white water spouted to either side of *Yodo*, while she trembled to the chatter of her guns. One of the misses was near enough to send water clouding over the bridge screens, and almost immediately a report came up from the engine-room that they were making water.

"Keep the pumps going!" Nicholas snapped, hard put to make himself heard above the unending racket. But five minutes later the ship seemed to leap out of the water, and he realised that she had been struck by a torpedo, aft. "Damage report!" he shouted, as *Yodo* fell out of line, slowly turning to port. But he knew instinctively what had happened, and gazed in important rage as the next cruiser in line steamed past, her crew watching with anguished sympathy the plight of their big sister.

"Our steering has been hit, honourable Captain," Tono reported.

"Keep firing," Nicholas told him, while *Yodo* continued on her way in a slow circle.

"Message from flagship, honourable Commander." Midshipman Funai was breathless. "*How bad is your damage?*"

Nicholas hesitated only a moment. "Reply: Ship unmanoeuverable but will fight to the end." The boy gulped, and hurried off.

Now the planes, sensing a kill, had clustered in greater numbers about the stricken ship; the air was a mass of flying foam and screaming noise, and even as Nicholas watched, a torpedo-bomber swooped low out of the sky, making straight for amidships. The gun-crews had seen it too and were bringing everything they could to bear. Nicholas watched in fascinated horror as the huge silver fish splashed into the sea, not three hundred yards away, seconds before the plane itself disintegrated before the hail of bullets. Then he was lying on the deck, hurled there by the violent explosion beneath him.

Most of the men on the bridge had been knocked down, and several had been struck by flying splinters. Nicholas, on his knees, reached the engine-room telephone. "Damage report?"

There was no reply. He stared at the clinometer, and saw that the needle was already past the ten degree mark, while *Yodo* had now entirely lost way as thousands of gallons of water rushed into the huge gash in her hull. "Make to flagship," Nicholas said, staring after the squadron, which was now almost out of sight. "Am abandoning ship."

"There is no power to signal, honourable Captain."

The loss of power had also crippled the machine-gun batteries, which could no longer move but only fire aimlessly from their last position. It also meant there would be no tannoy. Nicholas seized a loudhailer and stepped on to the upper bridge wing, having to brace himself against the doorway because of the acute angle of heel. "This is the captain!" he bawled at the foredeck. "Abandon ship. May the gods go with you." He repeated the orders to the after deck, where the men fighting the fires stared up at him in dismay before hastily inflating their lifejackets.

"I must see to the men below," Tono said.

"I will see to them," Nicholas said. "You go now, Commander. Midshipman Funai, you go too. I thank you both for your gallant service."

"Look there, honourable Captain!" Funai cried.

Their heads turned, to see the destroyer racing towards them. Then they looked up, but the American planes were gone; they knew the cruiser was sinking. "May the gods be praised," Tono gasped.

"Then go!" Nicholas snapped.

"But you, honourable Captain . . ."

"I will be right behind you," Nicholas promised.

He slid down the ladders, still carrying his loud hailer. He was on the upper side of the ship, while most of the crew had already moved to the lower, where they could virtually step into the sea. He wrenched open the bulkhead door, stepped inside, and listened to the dreadful gurgling of the sea filling the hull. "Anybody down there!" he bawled into his loud hailer. "This is the captain speaking. Come up and abandon ship, now!"

After a moment men began appearing, scrambling up the ladders, giving hasty bows to their commanding officer as they sought the comparative safety of the deck. Nicholas went lower, until he reached a companionway where water gurgled over his ankles. "Is anybody there!" he shouted.

"Honourable Captain!" Tonoye stumbled towards him, then fell. His uniform was a mass of blood.

"Let me help you." Nicholas stooped beside him.

"Save yourself, honourable Captain," the steward gasped.

"And leave you behind? Who will make my morning cup of tea?" Nicholas dragged the wounded man to his feet and thrust him at the ladder. Tonoye fell again, and Nicholas picked him up again and hefted him over his shoulder. As he did so, he heard banging and shouts from below him. He looked down the next ladder, about which water was swirling waist deep. He laid Tonoye down, took a deep breath, and slid down the ladder. The bulkhead door was in front of him, bolted in two places. Who could have been so crazy?

He hurled himself at the door, pulled the bolts one after the other, and the half-dozen American sailors he had picked up earlier fell out. "Jesus Christ!" one gasped. "Thought we were gonners."

"Easy, sailor," said a petty officer. "This is the Jap captain."

The sailor goggled at Nicholas, who grinned. "I speak English. But we'd better get the hell out of here."

"You betcha." The men swarmed up the ladder, and reached Tonoye. Without a word the petty officer, a big man, threw the unconscious steward across his shoulders and went on climbing. It seemed to take an eternity, and all the while Nicholas was conscious of the increasing list; he knew the ship had only seconds to survive.

They reached the deck level, turned instinctively to their left, the downwards slope, and saw water lapping at the bulkhead door. "Up!" Nicholas shouted.

The petty officer took the unconscious Tonoye from his shoulder, laid him on the deck, and crawled upwards, pushing the inert body in front of him, helped by his panting comrades. They reached the open air, and Nicholas found himself kneeling on the bulkhead, with the rail above him. But there were lifejackets close at hand. He grabbed several of these and handed them out, inserted Tonoye's shoulders into one and tied it, then jerked on the inflating cord. As he did so, he felt the ship lurch beneath him, and then there was an explosion, followed immediately by another as the boilers burst. Pieces of wood and metal cascaded around him, and one struck him a painful blow on the arm. Desperately he thrust his other arm through the remaining life jacket and jerked the cord. Then he was under water, being sucked down with the sinking ship. The first Barrett ever to be killed in action, he thought, as his brain whirled and stars danced before his eyes and he heard the hissing of his life jacket inflating. He clung to it with all his strength, but his lungs were bursting and he had taken his first gasp of salt water before he was spewed into the air again by yet another explosion beneath him.

The sea around him was turbulent, and smothered in oil. This at least prevented any of the suction waves from breaking, but he was still tossed up and down like a cork, vomiting water and oil and breakfast, nearly choking because

323

his nostrils were filled with the muck, sneezing and coughing and spitting until he could see. Now the water was again calm, although the oil was everywhere. Slowly he began to hear again, men shouting, and the hum of engines. He clung to his lifejacket and saw the destroyer, some distance off, her engines virtually stopped as she picked up survivors. The gallant fool, he thought; she is a sitting duck for a submarine.

But the destroyer proceeded methodically about her task, and eventually approached close enough for even Nicholas to feel it was worth his while waving at it. He was spotted almost immediately, and one of the launches came towards him. Fifteen minutes later he was on the bridge, wrapped in a blanket and drinking hot green tea. "I knew we'd find you," Fukijo said.

"I knew you'd come looking," Nicholas said. "But you are taking a great risk."

"I just wish an enemy would show up," Fukijo said. "I would take great pleasure in blowing him out of the water. But we are nearly finished. I am afraid there have only been three hundred and eight survivors."

More than half the crew lost, Nicholas thought bitterly. "My steward . . ."

"Tonoye. Oh, yes, we have him. He is badly wounded, but not so badly that he cannot shout your praises. He says you saved his life."

"Only partly. Some American prisoners did most of the work. Did you pick them up?"

"We picked up six Americans."

"Thank God for that."

"You know, Nicholas, there is a school of thought that says we should throw them right back. But you do not subscribe to it."

"No," Nicholas said. "I do not. But I don't want those men taken back to a prison camp, either. I would like you to put them down in a rubber dinghy, give them a chance to make the shore or be picked up."

"May I ask why?"

"I think they may have saved my life. Tonoye's certainly."

Fukijo gave a brief bow; Nicholas was his senior officer, if only by a matter of weeks. "But you are wounded yourself."

"A scratch."

"Nonetheless, you must be seen to." He grinned. "I am in commnd now. You must go to the doctor."

Nicholas had no objections. He needed time to think, to evaluate what had happened. He went to the ladder and checked. "My Executive Officer, Commander Tono?"

Fukijo looked at *his* Executive Officer, Commander Uharu. The Commander checked his list, then shook his head. "Commander Tono is not amongst those rescued, honourable Captain."

"It seems that I am always congratulating you," Yamamoto said. He was first on board the hospital ship in which Nicholas, along with all the other wounded from the actions off Guadalcanal, had returned to Tokyo, and went straight to the cabin which his *protégé*, as the senior wounded officer, had to himself. "Home the hero. How serious is that wound?"

"I am afraid the doctors think it is more serious than I supposed, honourable Admiral," Nicholas confessed. "A piece of metal got itself embedded in my shoulder just before *Yodo* sank, and became infected."

"While you were saving your servant's life."

"While my ship was sinking, honourable Admiral."

Yamamoto nodded. "You were not the only casualty, you know. You have no doubt heard that *Kirishima* went the following day? Would you believe that she was crippled by shells from the *USS Washington* in a battleship to battleship gun duel? I suppose it is reassuring that such events are not entirely things of the past." He sighed. "At least Kondo and Abe were prepared to fight. But I am afraid it is necessary to face facts: Rabaul is now too exposed. I am withdrawing the fleet to Truk."

Nicholas was aghast. "Then . . ."

"Do not say it, Nicholas. Our outer perimeter has been breached. In fact . . ." he gave one of his grim smiles, "we never actually achieved it. But we still command a vast area of ocean, dotted with fortified islands. The Americans are going to have a hard time breaching *that*, and all the while we are growing stronger. You know *Mushashi* is now in commission?"

"I did not know that, honourable Admiral. But that is splendid news. And the others?"

Yamamoto's face was sombre again. "I'm afraid there will be no others."

"But . . . ?"

"We have insufficient steel to complete the programme. Also, we have other priorities. We have the two greatest warships in the world, but if they cannot get within range of the enemy – which seems impossible save for freak encounters like that between *Kirishima* and *Washington*, then they are useless as aggressive weapons. And we need to strike at the Americans; we cannot just sit back passively and wait for them to hit us. The third of our big ships, *Shinano*, is already close to completion, at least on the slip. I have ordered that she be converted into a carrier. Think of it, Nicholas. A seventy thousand ton carrier. She will be twice the size of any American ship."

"Are the Americans not building new ships, honourable Admiral?"

"Yes. I have no doubt they are, But they do not know about *Shinano*. She may well be the answer to our problem. However, it will be a year at least before she can possibly be ready, and in that time we must fight with what we have." He stood up. "You are to be transferred to the naval hospital. I know your wife and son and stepmother and sister are anxious to see you. Hurry up and get well, Nicholas. We have need of all the heroes we can find."

"I was not the only hero, honourable Admiral."

Yamamoto had gone to the door. "I know that. Every man was a hero. But some are more obvious than others. I am sorry about Tono. He was a good man."

"The very best. Do you know that we served together for nearly twenty years, honourable Admiral? We were on the bridge of *Sawokaze* when the earthquake struck."

"Then we will find you another such man, Nicholas."

"Nicholas! Oh, Nicholas!" Sumiko embraced him and then recalled herself, stood by the bedside, and bowed. "Honourable Husband, I have grieved for you."

326

Nicholas smiled at her. It was, after all, good to be home. "I shall soon be well," he promised her.

"Is he not a beauty?" She held up the baby boy for him to admire.

"He looks like you."

"I have named him Nicholas," she said. "Would you like to hold him?"

"When my arm is better," Nicholas said. His feelings towards his son remained too ambivalent. "I trust your father is well. Is he still in Singapore?"

"Oh, yes. He tells me he is very busy."

"I can imagine."

"You have brought great honour upon our house," Christina told him.

"I thank you, honourable Stepmother." Nicholas looked past her at Takeda, trim and smart in his uniform. Perhaps because his eyesight was fading, or perhaps because he wished to ape his revered chief, the *Kempei-tai* officer was wearing a pair of steel-rimmed spectacles. Beyond the glass it was impossible to see his eyes. But what message could he convey with his eyes? It was simply necessary to be patient.

"Honourable Father!" Alexander was erect and smart in his school uniform. "I am proud to be your son. My only fear is that we may win the war before I am old enough to fight for the Emperor."

"It is a possibility," Nicholas agreed. He had no idea how much these people really knew about what was going on. Certainly he did not think they knew enough.

"Nicky!" Charlotte kissed him.

It was difficult to grasp that his baby sister was now thirty years old. Because it many ways she remained a baby. Her complexion was clear, her facial structure young. Even her body, for all its large breasts and wide thighs, was that of a girl. At least to him. He thought she must make Mori very happy. But then, only Mori knew what really went on inside her mind, how much she had truly recovered from her breakdown. "Is Mori well?" he asked.

A shadow crossed her face. "Honourable Husband is in New Guinea," she said.

"Ah." He had heard only vague reports about what was

327

happening in New Guinea, but he did know it was about the roughest, most vicious fighting the world had ever seen. "Then perhaps we shall now begin to win there."

There was no answering smile.

"I must remain for a few minutes," Takeda told the nurse who came to usher them out. "This is official business."

The woman bowed, and left with the ladies; there was no nurse in all Japan who was going to argue with an officer in the *Kempei-tai*.

"Well?" Nicholas demanded, when the door had closed.

Takeda grinned. "Well what, honourable Stepson?"

"You know what I mean, Takeda *san*. Did the woman get here?"

"Of course she did, Nicholas. Was I not arranging it?"

"And she is well?"

"Physically, she is in the best of health. She has quite recovered from her interrogation in Hong Kong."

"By your filthy people," Nicholas growled.

"By officers who were doing their duty," Takeda pointed out. "However, what they did to her has undoubtedly left its mark. We have had much trouble with her."

"We?"

"My Suiko and I."

"If she has been ill-treated in any way, Konoye . . ."

Takeda smiled. "Did I not give you my word as a *samurai*? She has not been ill-treated. However, she has been difficult. She does not smile, and she does not go out of the apartment. Sometimes it is difficult to make her eat. We do this by telling her you are coming back to her."

"And this pleases her?"

"It is difficult to say," Takeda said, slyly.

"I wish to see her."

"Well, you cannot, until you can leave this place. And the doctors tell me that may not be for some time."

"Then bring her to see me."

"That would be the height of absurdity, Nicholas. Quite apart from the fact that an Englishwoman who is also a prisoner-of-war would never be allowed into a naval hospital, the fact of her presence in Tokyo would almost certainly become known. This could have serious consequences."

"Then I shall just have to get well as quickly as possible. Will you tell her I am in Tokyo?"

"No," Takeda said. "It might make her do something foolish. Your return will be reported in the newspapers in due course, but we will keep these from her. Never fear, she will be waiting for you." He got up. "This whole business has caused me a great deal of discomfort."

"In what way?"

"Well, questions were asked when I had the woman transferred. I naturally had to state that she was for my own use. This was accepted, but it has so been entered in my record. If Christina were ever to find out . . ."

"Doesn't she know about Suiko?"

"I do not think so."

"I am sure she knows you have a mistress, Konoye. All Japanese men have mistresses."

"That may be so. But if she discovered that my mistress is this Wells woman, who she in any event hates . . ."

"If she finds out, you will have to tell her the truth. Then she can hate me as well."

"You think it is that simple? There is also the matter of your behaviour in Hong Kong. This was made the subject of a report by the officer there."

"I know that. Yamamoto suppressed it."

"No, no. I suppressed it."

In his position, Nicholas could not afford to offend his stepfather by arguing about it. "Then I thank you."

Takeda glanced at him. "That still does not mean it has been easy for me. Rather has it been more difficult."

"So you would like a reward?"

"Do you not think I am entitled to one?"

"I am sure of it. And I will give you anything you wish, save for the one thing you wish most."

"She is just a woman," Takeda grumbled.

"Who is in my care. I did not bring her out of a prison camp to be raped again."

"Do you not intend to fuck her, when you are able?"

"I would like to do so, Konoye. But I shall only if she invites me to."

"And if she invites *me*?"

Nicholas gave a savage grin. "Do you suppose the sky will soon fall, Konoye *san*?"

But he was worried, especially when the doctors told him that it would be another month before he would even be allowed home for convalescence leave. And Takeda, pleading pressure of work, visited him less often. He needed help, and there was only one way for him to turn.

Charlotte usually only came to see him accompanied by either Sumiko or Christina, but he found a way to convey to her that he would like to see her alone, and she came at an odd hour the next day. "You have heard from honourable Husband?" she asked, the moment she had seated herself beside his bed.

"No. And you have not?"

"I get letters from time to time. He is very depressed. He is . . ." she bit her lip. "He says I should not speak of it, even to you. But you know of it. He told me so."

"You mean he has discussed it with you?" Nicholas was aghast.

She gave a quick, anxious smile. "I haven't told anyone."

"Obviously, or you wouldn't be sitting here."

She glanced at the door, which was closed. "He said you wouldn't join with him, because you did not think Japan could lose the war. But Japan is losing the war, isn't it, Nicky?"

"What makes you say that? There has been nothing like that in the newspapers, has there?"

"No, no. Of course not. But . . . one listens to little things. And every week the rationing gets more severe. They are even rationing rice. So, isn't it true?"

"I'm afraid it is."

"Then don't you see that Mori is right? We must make a negotiated peace while there is yet time. While the Navy and the Army are intact."

Nicholas sighed. "The Americans are demanding unconditional surrender, and that is simply not possible." He glanced at her. "You do see that?"

"No, I don't see that," she said. "Why not surrender. If we can't win? It's better than being destroyed."

"Charlotte, they'd take away our ships and our guns.

They'd take away our independence. They'd take away our history. My God, they'd take away the Emperor!"

"Would that be such a catastrophe?" she asked.

It was his turn to glance anxiously at the closed door. "Do you ever share any of these views with Sumiko or Christina?"

"I would not dream of it. They would not understand."

It was what he wanted to hear, although he doubted her reasons for not taking either her sister-in-law or her stepmother into her confidence were realistic. "Then there is something I wish you to do for me," he said. "What I have to tell you is as confidential as anything Mori has ever said. Will you promise never to repeat it to anyone?"

"Not even Mori?"

"You can tell Mori. But not by letter. You can tell him when he comes home. I will probably tell him myself, then."

"If he comes home," she said, gloomily.

"Of course he's coming home. Now listen."

She did so, her face gradually changing expression from bewilderment to disapproval.

"Takeda organised this?"

"Yes. He's not as bad as one might think."

"And you do not think he has told Christina?"

"I am quite sure he has not told Christina, for the very good reason that it would mean telling her about Suiko."

"Men! Mistresses! Do you think Mori has a mistress?"

"Ah . . . I really wouldn't know. It is the way of the world, Charlotte. And anyway, Linda is not actually my mistress. We had an affair, once. Briefly. But I couldn't let her try to survive in the hell of a prison camp. Will you go to see her?"

"It will mean going to the house of a *geisha*."

"I don't really think you could classify Suiko as a *geisha*, Charlotte. Will you do it?"

"If you will promise to help Mori, when the time comes."

"I promise. I will help Mori when the time comes." Because if such a time ever does come, he thought, we shall all be going to die, anyway.

Charlotte walked down the narrow street, pretending not

to be watching the numbers. Not that anyone paid much attention to her, as she wore a *kimono* and had her hair tied up in a bandanna. In the middle of the afternoon downtown Tokyo was a seething mass of people, hurrying, chatting, riding bicycles and ringing their bells. There were few cars to be seen; petrol rationing was the most serious aspect of the war from the point of view of the average non-military Japanese, and that had been going on for so long it was difficult to remember when fuel had been freely available. She found the number she wanted, and having already made up her mind, stepped through the street doorway without hesitation. She felt pleasantly excited; her life was normally extremely humdrum. Even sharing Mori's secret hopes and ambitions was not very exciting, because he kept insisting that she could never, must never, be involved.

Mori, like everyone else, treated her like a child. They understood so little of the truth, about life, and death. She had learned the truth on 1 September 1923. She had been standing on the lawn in front of the original Barrett house in Tokyo, waiting for her mother and sister. They had just started to come out of the house, Elizabeth in front and Mother behind, talking to her, when they had disappeared. She had blinked, and they had gone, together with the house. That meant, according to conventional thinking, that they were dead. They weren't, of course. They had simply gone to another place – although she had been educated as a Christian, Charlotte preferred not to think of it necessarily as Heaven. Heaven had always come across as rather boring, and she had no real wish to go there and be bored for eternity. But she did wish to join Mother and Liz, as soon as she could, wherever they might be.

That, of course, was not something over which one had any influence. That was in the lap of the gods, as opposed to God. Mori did not believe in God: he believed in the gods. And she believed that he was probably right; she never went to church any more, because it was too difficult to reconcile the religion she had been taught as a child with the religion of the society in which she now lived. She suspected Mother and Liz had also encountered that difficulty, since disappearing so suddenly. Which was why she did not feel that they could

332

be in the Christian Heaven. But wherever they were, they were undoubtedly waiting for her. Her mistake had been in saying so. No one had understood; everyone had thought she was mad. Even Mori, the kindest and most gentle of men, thought she was mad. But he was the only man, or woman, she had ever met, at least till now, who had made any serious effort to communicate with her, raise her to his level. She adored Mori.

Sumiko and Christina tolerated her because she was Nicholas's sister. Even Nicholas, she had always felt, did nothing more than tolerate her. But now he had turned to her for help. Her initial reaction had been disappointed shock that her brother, who she considered the finest of men, should turn out to be just like any other man, like Takeda, whom she despised. But that emotion had rapidly been replaced by an excited pride, that in all Japan she was the one he had turned to for help. She would have agreed even had he not promised to help Mori in turn. It was so exciting to share, with Nicholas, and with Mori. And now, perhaps, with this woman.

The hallway was dark and narrow, and a narrow flight of stairs led upwards; she reminded herself that Takeda was only a colonel in the *Kempei-tai* and would not be able to afford to keep his mistress in any enormous luxury. She climbed the stairs to the third floor, and knocked on the door. There was no immediate response, but she could hear someone moving about. Then a voice asked, in Japanese, "Who is there?"

But it was not a Japanese voice. "I am Barrett Nicholas's sister," Charlotte said.

Now there was complete silence for several seconds, before the lock turned. Charlotte stepped inside, closing the door behind her, and gazed at the woman waiting for her. Like herself, Linda Wells wore the *kimono*, but unlike hers, Linda's hair was loose. Her face was closed and watchful, but relaxed slightly as she took in Charlotte's colouring, and as Charlotte took off the bandanna and shook out her hair. "You look like Nicholas," she remarked.

"Where is the woman Suiko?" Charlotte asked.

"She is out. She is often out. How did you know I was here?"

333

"Nicholas told me. He asked me to make sure you were all right."

Linda's face closed again. "I am perfectly healthy. But I have been told that he has been wounded. Again."

"This is not as serious as the last time," Charlotte said, moving around the little apartment as she inspected the vases of flowers.

Linda knelt beside the low table and the teapot. "That is a great relief. Would you like a cup of tea?"

"Thank you." Charlotte knelt as well. "Do you love my brother?"

Linda raised her head. "I . . ." her cheeks were pink.

"I know that you had an affair," Charlotte said.

"He asked me to marry him, and I declined. Now I owe him a great deal. Perhaps my life."

"He wishes us to be friends. He thinks it would be easier for you to be friends with me, than with an ethnic Japanese."

"I am sure he is right," Linda agreed.

Charlotte raised her head as the door opened, expecting it to be Suiko. But it was Takeda.

Nicholas was released from hospital to spend Christmas at home, but he was still convalescent and confined for another fortnight. When he did go out it was with Sumiko at his side. Being at home made it more difficult for him to see Charlotte privately, but she managed to convey that she was visiting Linda regularly, and that the Englishwoman was all right. At the same time, however, he was aware of a certain tension in Charlotte, the reason for which she would not confide. He worried that she and Linda were not hitting it off, and began counting the hours until he would be able to visit her himself.

But there were other, more important things to worry about. In mid-January Admiral Yamamoto called, a tremendous compliment to be paid by the Commander-in-Chief to one of his captains, no matter how good friends they were. "When will you be ready for duty?" Yamamoto asked, when Sumiko had left them alone together.

"Another week, honourable Admiral."

Yamamoto nodded. "Good. You will return to work

in the strategic planning department. In fact, you will head it."

"Sir?" Nicholas was at once startled and disappointed; he had hoped for a battleship.

"You wish to go back to fighting, eh? Well, we may all have to do that. But first we must have some kind of a plan. Did you know that we have lost Guadalcanal?"

"No, honourable Admiral."

"The decision was made to evacuate a week ago, but the Americans are advancing anyway. They are now bombing Rabaul nearly every day. B-17s. We have no defences against them, so as I told you would be necessary, I am evacuating there as well, save for a skeleton garrison who will fight to the last man. But there is worse. We have also lost Papua, which means, in the long run, that we have lost New Guinea."

Nicholas could not believe his ears.

"Buna has fallen, and the Americans and Australians are advancing in every direction. The fact is that since losing those carriers at Midway we simply do not have the counter-attacking capability to maintain our perimeter."

"May I ask, honourable Admiral . . . were there heavy casualities in New Guinea?"

"There are heavy casualties everywhere, Nicholas. Our men are fighting magnificently. Their problem, and ours, is that because of American air superiority they cannot be adequately supplied with either food or ammunition, nor can they be given any aerial support, whereas the Americans, having decided to take a position, merely smother it with bombs first. This situation has to be reversed. We have to devolve a plan to bring the American carrier force at least to battle, and destroy it. The entire fate of the empire depends upon this, Nicholas. This is why I want you back in the operations room."

"I am flattered, honourable Admiral."

But his mind was elsewhere, as Yamamoto could tell. "You are concerned about Colonel Mori."

"I would be afraid for my sister's sanity, were he to be killed, honourable Admiral."

Yamamoto nodded, and stood up. "I will make inquiries. But Nicholas, you do understand that having our friends and loved ones killed, indeed, being killed ourselves, is something we may have to grow very used to, over the next year or so."

"I understand this, honourable Admiral."

This was difficult to accept in the peaceful winter sunshine of Tokyo. Apart from the raid last April, no bombs had ever been dropped on the city, and Doolittle's raid had been more of a propaganda exercise than an effective piece of aggressive warfare. At a distance of three thousand miles and more, New Guinea and the Solomons seemed an eternity away, as did what was happening there. And he was staying in Tokyo, for the immediate future, Nicholas reflected. He was torn two ways about this. One half of him wanted to be commanding his ship into battle, time and again, until he was killed – that was his conscience talking, a conscience which kept reminding him that he was on the wrong side of this war, and that it was a side whose honour had been too deeply stained for forgiveness. The other half was merely grateful that he should be allowed to survive, that much longer, to be with Linda.

But had that been a terrible mistake? He stood outside the little apartment block for several minutes before summoning the courage to go in. Charlotte would have told her he was well again, and would be coming. But would she want to receive him? He went up the stairs, and knocked.

"Who is there?"

Definitely Japanese. "Captain Barrett."

"Ah, so." The key turned, and he looked at a small pretty woman, wearing a *kimono*, and with her hair loose. She appeared somewhat agitated to see him, but he supposed that was reasonable.

"You'll be Suiko."

She bowed. "You wish to see Linda?" The name was almost a song, as it came from her lips.

"Please."

"You will come in?" She stepped aside, and when he took off his shoes and entered, she closed the door behind him. Nicholas looked around him. Charlotte had described the apartment, and he knew that it contained two rooms. The inner door was open. "She is in there," Suiko said. "I go out now, soon."

"That would be very kind of you," Nicholas said.

She knelt before her mirror and began putting up her hair. Nicholas hesitated a moment, then crossed the floor and without looking into the inner room, tapped on the door. "I am here," Linda said.

Nicholas drew a long breath and stepped inside. When last he had seen this woman she had been a prisoner, on the island off Hong Kong, having been beaten at best, beaten and raped at worst: he still did not know the truth of that. But the evidence of mistreatment had been abundant. Now . . . she looked almost as he remembered her, in the house on Shibushi *Wan*, how many years ago?

She wore a *kimono*, but her hair was loose, and she pushed it from her eyes and forehead in an embarrassed gesture, then she rose to her feet and gave a hasty, and incongruous bow.

"You do not have to bow to me," he protested.

"All Japanese women bow to their superiors," she pointed out. "I learned that, in the prison camp. And besides, Colonel Takeda insists upon it."

"Takeda," he said.

"He is my saviour, is he not? He has told me this, often enough. I do not object to bowing to him, honourable sir; Suiko and your sister also do so."

There was a lot to be done, here, he realised. "You knew I was coming?"

"Your honourable sister told me so, honourable sir. I am pleased to learn that you have recovered from your wounds."

He went closer, took her hands. "Linda, I am Nicholas, remember? I am not your master, or your superior. I wish to be your friend. Your . . ." he bit his lip.

She raised her head. "My lover? I understand this, honourable sir."

"If you say that again, to me, I shall . . ." he did not know what he would do.

Linda bowed. "You will beat me. I understand this, honourable sir."

He still held her hands, and now he exerted sufficient

337

pressure to force her to her knees, joining her on the *tatami* mats. "Linda," he said. "I am Nicholas. I love you. I think I have loved you from the moment of our first meeting. I will always love you. I was shattered when you refused to marry me. Thus I married someone else. That does not affect my love for you. Nor can I blame you for your decision, in view of everything that has happened. I brought you here to save your life. Whether or not you wish to know me when peace is made . . ."

"Peace?" she asked. "Can there ever be peace with you, or what you stand for?"

Again he bit his lip, while Linda freed her hands. Then she untied her sash and shrugged the *kimono* from her shoulders. "You have come here to fuck me," she said. "And you are my master."

"What is your assessment of the situation?" Yamamoto asked his Director of Operations.

"That it is not as bad as it might be, honourable Admiral," Nicholas said. He picked up his wand and went to the wall chart. "We hold the Aleutians. That is a sally port, if you like, on the extreme wing of any American advance in the North Pacific. We did not manage to take Midway, but we hold Wake, and this controls the gap between the Aleutians and the Marshall and Gilbert Islands. We hold these, and in support we have the base at Truk, with our main fleet, able to attack any American fleet which attempts to come through the Central Pacific, while they will of course also be subject to attack by our land-based bombers from Eniwetok and Kwajalein in the Marshalls. We have been forced to evacuate Guadalcanal, and as you say, honourable Admiral, that puts Rabaul within easy reach of American land-based bombers. But we still hold the northern Solomons, and more especially Bougainville, just as we still hold the Bismarck Archipelago. We may not be able to maintain a fleet in those waters, but the Americans still have to drive us out. We have evacuated Papua, but the northern half of New Guinea proper is still in our hands, and they are going to have to drive us out of there as well. Farther west we are in complete control of Indo-China right up to the borders of India. What we still hold is not so very much less than our original planned perimeter."

338

"So you think we should sit back and congratulate our-selves," Yamamoto remarked. "And forget about those lost carriers, those lost battleships, the fact that we have been defeated on more than one occasion."

"I think it is very necessary that, as we say in English, honourable Admiral, we should not lose sight of the wood because of the trees. In every war there are some lost battles, and in every war there are some heavy casualties to be borne. But I believe that if we follow an intensely defensive attitude for the next few months, until our new aircraft-carriers are ready, it will be to our best advantage. We have failed to capture one island, and lost possession of two or three more. That is not a catastrophe. And we must not forget that the Americans are also fighting a life and death war in Europe."

"I find your optimism most encouraging, Nicholas," Yamamoto said. "And as you say, our carrier fleet is being restored. *Shokaku* is now fully repaired, and she and *Zuikaku* are of course the nucleus. And our two new twenty-eight thousand tonners, *Junyo* and *Hiyo*, have now both joined the fleet. I have also recommissioned *Ryuho*. But there is still a gap. *Taiho* will be launched this month. She is even bigger and better than the Shokakus; thirty-seven thousand tons, and I am promised she will make thirty-three knots. I am also converting the two seaplane carriers, *Chitose* and *Chiyoda*. They will be ready next year. They are small, less than fifteen thousand tons each, and not as fast as I would like, but beggars cannot be choosers."

"But that is splendid, honourable Admiral. Now we have a carrier fleet in being again."

"Yes," Yamamoto said, drily. "We have a fleet of six carriers, two of which are under fifteen thousand tons. The Americans also have six at the moment, including their two new Essex Class ships, thirty thousand plus tons and carrying ninety-one aircraft each."

"But the odds are surely even at this time, honourable Admiral."

"At this time. Do you know how many ships of this Essex class are currently building in the States? Fourteen!"

Nicholas gulped.

"And I am informed that there are another eleven on the drawing board, just awaiting slip space. Each of thirty-four thousand tons! Each capable of carrying ninety-one aircraft. That will be a carrier fleet of twenty-six ships, with an air flotilla of two thousand, three hundred and sixty-six planes, probably operational by the end of 1944. We will have *Taiho* by then, and the two Chitose ships."

"And nothing else?" Nicholas was aghast.

"I have been given the money, and more important, the steel, for some new ships. I have gone for speed and hitting power. There will be six. The prototype is *Unryu*, and this will be the name of the class. They will be only about twenty thousand tons full load, but they will carry about sixty aircraft each, and most important, they will make thirty-four knots to the Essex's thirty-two. But we need to be realistic about this: we will still be pitting six ships against twenty-five, and in those circumstances, I do not think an extra two knots is going to make very much difference."

"But when we have *Shinano* . . ."

"Oh, quite, Nicholas. She will be the greatest aircraft carrier the world has ever seen. It is just possible that she may make the difference. But I am told that she also cannot be ready much before the end of 1944. So, we have eighteen months to hold on. And we must hold on. I agree with your assessment of the situation. It must be our business to make sure all our commanders in the field understand it too, and realise that it is a matter of buying time. For this purpose I intend to undertake a series of visits to all our advanced positions. The personal touch, eh?"

"Yes, honourable Admiral. Am I to accompany you?"

Yamamoto shook his head. "You will remain here, Nicholas, and plan for the coming battles. You will work on the assumption that we manage to hold for the rest of this year, and that 1944 will be the decisive year of the war. The Americans may have the bigger force by then, so we must work on concentrating *our* forces in small, hard punches, which will whittle down the American strength. That is your responsibility."

"Yes, honourable Admiral." Nicholas stood up, and bowed.

"I would like to have your preliminary plan on my desk when I return from my visit to the Solomons," Yamamoto said.

"It will be ready, honourable Admiral."

"Of course. Nicholas, before you go, I would like to ask you a question."

Nicholas waited. "I am concerned that you seem to have a great deal on your mind," Yamamoto said. "I trust there is no domestic problem distracting you from your duty?"

"There is none, honourable Admiral," Nicholas lied.

Yamamoto nodded. "That is good. Our situation is such that total concentration is necessary, upon the matter in hand."

"I understand, honourable Admiral."

Nicholas realised Yamamoto would be very angry, were he ever to find out the truth. And it was almost certain that he would, eventually. But there was no way he could now stop himself, move his feet from the path on which he had embarked that day in Hong Kong. He was, in fact, living not a double, but a triple life. On the surface he was the dedicated officer in the Imperial Japanese Navy, a favourite of the Commander-in-Chief, happily married to a beautiful and adoring wife, the adopted father of a fine boy and the actual father of another, devoting all his time and energy to the preservation of Japanese power. But beneath that surface he had sworn to bring that power down the moment the cracks that were appearing everywhere became evident. And beneath both he possessed and loved an alien mistress, even if she was of his own race.

There was the distraction which Yamamoto had perceived and considered dangerous. The first two were interlocked. He did wish to preserve the power of Japan, if that were possible, but only in order to reinstate the totally honourable society in which his grandfather had found fame and fortune. He knew that should the Empire start to crumble, then the state would even more be taken over by the *Kempei-tai*, and when that happened, they, and even the state they represented, would have to be brought down to

341

prevent Japan being regarded in history as the most evil of countries.

But Linda . . . it was a peculiar sensation, in the middle of the Twentieth Century, absolutely to possess a woman. Linda had no rights, not even the right to life, outside of his determination. And she was aware of this. Thus there could be no love between them, at least until equality was restored. He endeavoured to be as kind and gentle to her as possible. He took her presents, and tried to make her smile. But, possessing her, he could not stop himself from wanting to make love to her: he was a man, not a monk. This too she realised, and offered herself to him without the slightest hesitation. Without love.

There were times he felt the most wretched man alive. As Charlotte undoubtedly understood. Where he would have supposed the event, taken together with his promise, might have brought his sister and himself closer together, it had somehow distanced them even more than in the past. Charlotte seldom looked him in the eye any more, and seemed almost ashamed to be in his presence.

And there was nothing he could do, driven on the one hand by his desires, and on the other by his duty. Thank the gods for his duty. He worked on his plan, which was actually to withdraw from the Bismarck Archipelago and even the remainder of the Solomons, slowly and deliberately, in the hope of drawing the Americans into that apparent gap, and then striking them from Truk with everything Japan possessed, and thus gaining that decisive victory which was so necessary before the huge bulk of the Essex Class carriers arrived. He was not sure how Yamamoto would react to such a drastic step, with its inevitable political repercussions at home before such a victory could be gained, or even worse, if the Americans failed to take the bait, but it was the plan with the most chance of success, he was sure.

He was at his desk in the Admiralty putting the finishing touches to his concept, on the morning of 19 April, a Monday, when his door was opened without a knock, and the lieutenant who was his secretary entered, almost forgetting to bow in his agitation. "Whatever has happened, man?" Nicholas demanded.

"Honourable Captain," the young man stammered. "It has just come in on the secret code machine. Admiral Yamamoto is dead."

CHAPTER 14

Bloody Sunset

"Sit down, Captain Barrett." Koga Minseiko was a dapper little man, with somewhat anxious features. This was not the least surprising, in view of the shoes he had been commanded to fill, but Nicholas recalled that the admiral had always had an anxious approach to his profession. He was in fact an amazing choice as Yamamoto's successor, even if he was the next most senior admiral in the Imperial Navy. Although he had taken over from Yamamoto as commander of the China Seas Fleet in 1939, since the outbreak of war he had been in charge of the Yokosuka Naval Base, and had never been engaged in combat. But presumably it was felt that men like Nagumo and Kondo, who had actually led Japanese fleets into battle, had suffered too many defeats to be given overall control of the war at sea. "This is a trying time for us all," Koga remarked, when his Director of Operations was seated.

"Indeed, honourable Admiral. May I ask how it happened?"

"Admiral Yamamoto's plane was attacked by American Lightning fighters just north of Bougainville. It is almost as if they knew he was going to be there, but of course that is impossible; his itinerary was known only to a few people, and transmitted to his landing fields in our most secret code. Thus it was sheer bad luck."

Nicholas remembered what Yamamoto had said about treachery, following the Battle of Midway. But this sounded more as if the Americans had somehow succeeded in breaking the secret naval code. Although even that, a disaster

344

in itself, could not be as great as the loss of the Admiral. "You mean, he went down in the sea, honourable Admiral? Then . . ."

"Sadly, Captain Barrett, his plane crash-landed on the island. His body has been recovered, so that there can be no question of the fact that he is dead. I am sending *Mushashi* to bring him back to Japan for a state funeral. We can do no less. I know he was a close friend of your family, and I offer you my condolences. However, he is now the past. It is my task to look to the future. That future does not look bright. I wish you to bring me up to date on Admiral Yamamoto's plans."

"I have a summary of what we were working on here, honourable Admiral."

Nicholas held out the folder, and Koga opened it and began perusing the pages. Nicholas remained seated before the desk, as he had not yet been dismissed. Koga read for several minutes; he clearly had great powers of concentration and absorbtion. At last he raised his head. "The future looks even less bright than before, according to your notes, Captain."

"If we could bring about that decisive battle, honourable Admiral . . ."

"That is a dream, Captain. You wish to fight this battle north of the Solomons? That would probably suit the Americans very well, as they would have the support of their land-based bombers from Guadalcanal. The decisive battle, when it is fought, requires us to have the support of *our* land-based bombers."

"With respect, honourable Admiral, but the nearest such support would be Truk or Saipan. That would be to bring the Americans into the very heart of our island empire."

"Or *lure* them, Captain. This is something I shall have to consider very deeply. But it need not concern you."

"Honourable Admiral?"

"You have done an admirable job as Director of Operations for Admiral Yamamoto, Captain Barrett. I congratulate you. However I know how anxious you must be to get back to sea, with a command. I am giving you *Haruna*. She is refitting in Kure. You will join her immediately. I hope this pleases you, Captain Barrett."

Nicholas swallowed. "This pleases me very much, honourable Admiral," he said uncertainly.

Haruna was a sister ship of *Hiei* and *Kirishima*, and thus, in moving up from a fifteen thousand ton heavy cruiser to a thirty-five thousand ton battleship he was receiving a considerable promotion. But the fact was that the ship was thirty years old, and had been designed as a battlecruiser before being rebuilt. He knew how vulnerable battlecruisers were in modern warfare, even after they had been converted to battleships. Koga could tell that Nicholas was not being entirely truthful. "You will find her a good ship," he said. "She has been completely rebuilt and refurbished. You will command her to success, Captain. Your orders await you at Kure."

Nicholas stood up and bowed.

"I'm afraid I have been fired," he told Sumiko. "For the second time in my life."

"You, honourable Husband? From the Navy? That is impossible."

"No, no. From my desk job at the Admiralty. I suppose you could say I have been kicked upstairs. To command a battleship."

"Nicky!" she screamed with delight. "Oh, what an honour. A battleship!"

"A very old battleship, I'm afraid. Just about the oldest there is."

"But . . . then you will have to go to sea."

"Of course."

"Back to the war? You could be sunk again."

I very probably shall, he thought. But instead he took her in his arms and kissed her. "Most men are only sunk once in their lives," he assured her. "I've had mine."

"When will you come back?" Linda asked.

"I don't know. But I will, come back."

She shuddered, and hugged herself. "Without you . . . I would go mad."

It was the first time she had ever acknowledged that he

meant anything to her at all. He kissed her. "Stay sane. I will come back. Promise me you will never do anything stupid."

"That allows a personal interpretation of the word, stupid," she said. "What is going to happen, Nicky?"

He shrugged. "Japan is going to lose the war."

Her mouth made an O as she stared at him. "*You* can say that?"

"I can face facts, if that is what you mean. The important question is, how we lose it. If we could end it tomorrow, in a negotiated peace, we would have nothing to worry about, even if it meant giving back some of our conquests. But that is impossible. The Allies have called for unconditional surrender and the return of *all* our conquests. This would be unacceptable, quite apart from the implied threat to the Emperor in an unconditional surrender. So we must fight on. Our second option, or hope, is to win an important, perhaps decisive battle. This has not now happened for a year. If we could do this, we might be able to force the Allies to that negotiated peace we seek."

"And if you cannot win such a battle?" she asked.

"Then we will have to fight to the last man."

"And at the end of it, you would still have lost all of your conquests, lost everything in fact."

"Except our honour."

"Do you really believe that?" She gave a little shiver. "You lost your honour in Hong Kong, and Singapore, and Nanking even before that. But you know there is another alternative, Nicky. If there was enough resolution amongst sufficient men, and women, to overthrow the government and dissociate themselves from the acts of the government, the Allies might well be willing to negotiate. After all, Nicky, revolution was not unknown in the days of the *shoguns*, when it was felt that they were taking a wrong line."

"Charlotte has been talking to you," he said. "The fool. Have you discussed this with anyone? Suiko?"

"Of course not."

"Takeda? He comes here quite often, does he not?"

Her face seemed to close. "Yes. But I do not discuss such things with him. I do not discuss anything with him."

347

"Thank God for that." He held her hands. "Listen to me. Charlotte's ideas are utter dreams, and dangerous dreams. The Japanese people may have revolted against the *shoguns*, but very seldom successfully. And they would never revolt against the *Mikado*."

"It would be against his government," she insisted. "Against Tojo. And have you not agreed to help? Charlotte has said so."

"I agreed to help, yes. If it ever became a practical possibility. I will try to get back to you as soon as possible. Until then . . . stay away from any plots. If there should be a betrayal, and you are arrested by the *Kempei-tai*, I would not be able to help you."

He visited Charlotte before leaving Tokyo, and to his amazement was welcomed by Mori. But was this shattered creature really his brother-in-law? Mori's left arm was in a sling, he walked with a limp, and his face was a mass of scars, some of them jagged. "An American bomb," Mori explained. "But I am one of the lucky ones. I was evacuated, not left to die."

"From New Guinea?"

Mori shrugged. "Does it matter where? Yes, it was New Guinea."

Nicholas embraced his sister. "How bad is he?"

"His leg is permanently shortened, and he has lost two fingers from his left hand." Her face twisted. "He suffered this for the emperor." Her voice was loaded with contempt.

"And now you are going back to sea," Mori said. "Sumiko telephoned us the news."

"If you go to sea you will be killed," Charlotte said.

"Perhaps."

"But you are going, because you want to be killed."

"I am going because I have been ordered to do so, Charlie."

"You should stay, and help us. You promised to do that."

"If I stay, I will be disobeying orders. Thus I will be cashiered and probably sent to prison. That will not do much to help you."

348

"He is right," Mori said.

"Men!" Charlotte commented. "All you do is talk. When it comes to the moment, you can do nothing."

"This has not yet come to the moment." Nicholas embraced her, then shook Mori's good hand. "I will come back, when the time is right. Until then, take care of Linda."

Even more than Tokyo, the Inland Sea made all thought of war a remote nightmare. And yet, even in these peaceful surroundings, there were nightmares enough. Virtually opposite the island of Eta-Jima, where he had spent four happy years, was the secluded beach where he had first bathed with Christina, and begun the path to hell. He could not prevent himself from stopping there for a moment. There were people swimming. But these were boys, healthy and happy animals. And then, Kure. Nicholas knew the city well; the ferry from Eta-Jima had used it. From its location, secluded from the sea and yet possessing a relatively deep-water harbour, it had been chosen as a shipbuilding port as long ago as 1886. Since then it had become one of the major shipbuilding centres in Japan: *Yamato* had been built here. And here, waiting for him, her refit completed, was *Haruna*.

Even at nearly thirty years old, she remained a beautiful ship, although her shape was antiquated by modern standards, with her relatively straight bow, her stern gallery, and her three curiously staggered funnels. There had been four ships in the Kongo Class – Kongo herself was still in service, although both *Hiei* and *Kirishima* were at the bottom of the sea – and they were unique in that they were the last ships built to a non-Japanese design, by Sir George Thurston of Vickers. *Kongo* had actually been built at Vickers in England, but the other three had been built in Japan, *Haruna* at the Kawasake Yard in Kobe. Designed for twenty-seven and a half thousand tons, the ships had come out at just over thirty-two thousand, full load. Capable of making twenty-seven knots and armed with eight fourteen-inch guns, they had been, when new at the start of the Great War, very formidable ships, and unsurpassed as battlecruisers until the British had built *Hood*

349

towards the end of that conflict.

However that had all been a long time ago, and the ships had been rebuilt as part of the fleet modernisation programme put in hand by Yamamoto in the 1930's, emerging in fact, as fast battleships, capable of thirty knots. *Haruna* now displaced over thirty-six thousand tons, full load, although she was of course dwarfed by ships like *Yamato* and *Mushashi*, and was much smaller than the new British and American ships, not to mention *Tirpitz*. But she was still a formidable fighting vessel. "All present and correct, and ready for sea, honourable Captain," reported Commander Yakobe, the Executive Officer.

"Then let us open our orders," Nicholas said.

These were, in the first instance, to proceed south to the new naval base being constructed in the Lingayyen Islands, not far from Singapore. *Haruna* arrived there in the summer of 1943, to find most of the major units in the Imperial Navy, including *Yamato*, moored in the calm tropical waters. This concentration was in itself an admission of defeat, as it meant that the Imperial Navy was now forced to base itself close to its source of oil, Brunei and the Dutch East Indies, rather than having its oil brought to it wherever it might be most useful – too many tankers were being sunk by the American submarines. Soon the fleet was joined by *Mushashi* as well, the great ship having carried out her duty of returning Admiral Yamamoto to Tokyo for a state funeral. Best of all, Nicholas found himself again serving under his first squadron commander, Vice-Admiral Ozawa Jisiburo, who had led him into battle in the Java Sea. Such a concentration, and such a commander, promised great things, but the fleet remained in the Lingayyen Archipelago for very nearly a year, save for the odd patrol into the Indian Ocean or in the waters around the Philippines. This was galling, as there was a great deal of fighting going on to their west. It was particularly galling to Nicholas, as he could guess the reason why: Koga had not come up with any viable plan for bringing the Americans to battle, and as the new commander-in-chief was quite lacking in Yamamoto's offensive spirit, he did not see him ever doing so.

350

Meanwhile, his business was to keep up his men's morale. This was difficult, as during the second half of 1943 the Americans really moved into high gear. Throughout the summer they continued their advance in the Solomons, and then began to surround Rabaul by knocking off the various fortified islands close to the great base, without ever actually assaulting the immensely strong position. The Imperial Fleet continued to oppose the enemy wherever possible, but Koga seemed determined not to risk his battleships or carriers where the Americans held air superiority, and the actions were mostly fought at night between cruisers and destroyers. Nicholas longed to be with them, with Tokijo, but at the end of July he received word that Tokijo was dead, drowned when his ship was torpedoed. Tokijo was his oldest friend. Indeed, now that Yamamoto was also dead, with the exception of Mori he had been his *only* friend, and he had saved him from death by risking his destroyer after the battle off Guadalcanal. Now he too was gone, while I sit in safety three thousand miles away, Nicholas thought, brooding in his cabin.

Nor was the news from Europe any better. The Allies had landed in Sicily and forced the resignation of Mussolini, while the Germans were still reeling from their overwhelminmg defeat at Stalingrad. "It is a serious situation, honourable Captain," Yakobe remarked.

Nicholas agreed with him: he had never felt more helpless, while the psychological duality of his situation was growing almost unbearable. He did not know what was happening back in Tokyo; the news of successive defeats had to be filtering through, and if Mori were to act rashly disaster could be overtaking everyone he loved. He should be there. At the same time he wanted to be here, to take part in the last climactic battle, whenever it was fought. Whenever. Koga seemed to have no plan for stopping the American advance, and the so-called strongpoints which would hold out until the new fleet was ready proved false hopes. In November the Americans assaulted the Gilberts, in January the Marshalls, and having secured these two vital archipelagoes, in February a huge sea and air bombardment was hurled at Truk, ending its existence as a naval base. The

Americans had torn a great hole in the perimeter, and now there was no question that there had to be a fight.

The fleet's morale was not improved when in March *Mushashi* was torpedoed by an American submarine. In a sense the event was reassuring, as the battleship appeared to confirm her reputation for being unsinkable, by absorbing the damage and continuing on her way, but she had to be very hastily repaired, as what was intended to be the decisive battle was looming. This was because, only a few days after the damage to *Mushashi*, the fleet was astounded to learn that for the second time in a twelvemonth they had lost their commander-in-chief. Koga took off from the island base at Panau to fly to Mindanao in the Philippines, and was never seen or heard of again. In his case there was not even any wreckage. But that he had gone down in the sea, whether by engine failure or enemy action, no one could doubt.

For several days the Imperial Navy was left an inert monster, then the name of the new C-in-C was announced, and a great sigh of relief went through the fleet. The new man was Admiral Toyoda Suemo, who, like Nicholas – although vastly senior – had been a *protégé* of Yamamoto: everyone felt that at last they again had a fighting sailor at their head. From Nicholas's point of view, the news was even more of a relief, as he knew that Toyoda and Tojo hated each other. But presumably there had been no other man senior enough and with sufficient grasp of the situation to take the command. That Toyoda was determined to take the fight to the enemy was made manifest only a few months later, when the fleet was ordered to sea, to fight what was, predictably, described as the decisive battle of the war. In the fact the battle, named after the Philippine Sea, was another disaster. The surface ships never caught a glimpse of each other. The Americans were now attacking the Marianas and Guam, and Toyoda's plan was that their fleet should be lured east of the islands, by the appearance of the Imperial Navy in the Philippine Sea, whereupon they would be attacked by all the planes the Japanese carriers could muster. It was well understood that the Americans had a two-to-one superiority in aircraft, but Toyada's scheme was to negate this by using the air bases he still held in Saipan and Guam: his bombers

352

would attack the US Task Force, do what damage they could, fly on to Saipan and Guam to refuel and re-arm, and then attack again, on their way back to their carriers, thus delivering a double blow inside the space of only a few hours. The dream was to catch the Americans with their fighter protection dispersed, as had happened to the Imperial Navy at Midway.

But there was one catastrophic flaw in the plan: the initial attack, meant to catch the Americans by surprise, had to be a success. Instead it was a disastrous failure. Warned by their radar of the approach of the Japanese planes, the Americans were able to get their defences up and more than half of the attackers were shot down. The attenuated force returning from Saipan a few hours later was similarly roughly handled, with the result that less than a hundred of the original five hundred odd planes returned to the carrier fleet – and by then that fleet had itself been torn apart.

The Imperial squadron was a strong one: five fleet carriers, including the brand new and immensely powerful *Taiho*, appropriated by Ozawa as a flagship, four light carriers, and five battleships, including the two superships, *Mushashi*'s repairs having been completed. The crews were at action stations from the moment the assault aircraft took off, and then it was simply a matter of waiting for them to come back. In Nicholas's case, hoping that some enemy ships might break through and come after them, and give them a chance to do some shooting themselves. However, the planes had hardly disappeared when there was a warning that submarines had been sighted. Speed was increased and the fleet assumed battle formation while destroyers scurried to and fro. Then without warning there was a huge explosion from *Taiho* and the flagship burst into flames. Nicholas and Yakobe and their crew could only stare in horror at Japan's newest carrier in dire trouble.

The submarines seemed to have disappeared, having struck their decisive blow, and again the fleet could only wait, listening to the orders going out from the burning flagship that she would be unable to recover any aircraft. The morning dragged on, and Nicholas had just told Yakobe to have the men served their midday meal at their stations

353

when there was another alarm, with an equally devastating outcome. Before the destroyers could react there were three huge explosions from *Shokaku*, and she too began to burn and list. It was very obvious now that they were in the presence of a major disaster, compounded by the fact that they had to remain roughly in position to recover the attack planes. But when these started to return soon after two, the disaster was even greater than feared. As there were so few planes left Nicholas felt that had he been in command of the fleet, it might be better to abandon them and take his ships to safety, but this ruthless consideration did not apparently enter Admiral Ozawa's mind, and the planes were still landing on the remaining effective carriers when, just after three, the disaster was completed.

For six hours a skeleton crew had been fighting the flames on *Taiho*, watched anxiously by the rest of the fleet. Ozawa had of course transferred his flag, but if the great carrier could be saved something would have been rescued from the debacle. Now, without warning, there was an explosion which shattered some of the screens on *Haruna*, over half a mile away; an enormous pillar of smoke reared skywards, while pieces of debris, metal, wood and men, scattered about the rest of the squadron. Nicholas was momentarily blinded by the unforgettable flash; when he could see again, *Taiho* had disappeared. And now, as if that had been a signal, *Shokaku*, whose crew had also been fighting desperately for survival, keeled over and plunged beneath the waves. In the space of a few minutes Japan's two largest carriers had been lost.

It seemed that even Ozawa was overwhelmed by what had happened, and for some time there were no orders. He had just commanded the fleet to finish retrieving their aircraft when more planes were sighted, and these were Americans. At least there was at last an enemy to be fired at, but Nicholas knew that his old battleship was now just as vulnerable as *Yodo* had been, for the fighter cover put up by the remaining carriers was frighteningly thin. Thus it was the old business of weaving to and fro while *Haruna*'s anti-aircraft batteries seared the sky with

354

tracer bullets and the afternoon became a kaleidoscope of flaming planes and exploding bombs. And once again, too, he knew the sickening impact of a bomb striking home, aft of the bridge, sending smoke and flame billowing into the clear blue sky.

But on this occasion the attack was not pressed home: not only was the tropical dusk closing in, but the Americans were operating at extreme range, and had only a few minutes over their targets. It was later learned that a good number of them ran out of fuel and had to ditch before regaining their carriers. The raid had again been a victory, however. The twenty-eight thousand ton carrier *Hiyo*, hardly older than *Taiho*, was sunk, and in addition to *Haruna*, *Shokaku*'s sister *Zuikaku*, and the newest of all the carriers, the fifteen thousand ton *Chiyoda*, were badly damaged. When Ozawa withdrew the remnants of his squadron under darkness it was in the knowledge that his carrier fleet, together with their planes, had been virtually liquidated.

For Nicholas and his men, it was a matter of fighting the flames for the next twenty-four hours, never knowing when they would be attacked by an enemy submarine. The men hardly looked at one another. There was no disguising the magnitude of this defeat. At Midway, they had at least claimed an American carrier. In the Philippine Sea there had been nothing to claim at all. The battered fleet regained the Lingayyen Islands, where repairs were immediately put in hand. Damaged as she was, *Haruna* would normally have been returned to Japan, and Nicholas was desperate to be so ordered, for by now reports were coming in of heavy American bombing raids on the Japanese homeland itself. Some of these were from bases on the Chinese mainland, but when, following their tremendous victory in the Philippine Sea, the Americans conquered Saipan they were within bombing range of Japan from that base as well. Admiral Nagumo, the veteran of so many unsuccessful battles, was in command and committed *seppuku*. But no ships were allowed home. Repairs had to be effected on the spot, and by working round the clock *Haruna* was again ready for action by the end of July.

*   *   *

355

By then a new sensation had rocked the nation: General Tojo had been forced to resign. He was replaced at co-premiers by General Koiso and Admiral Yonai, while General Umezu took over as chief of staff. The "Razor's" departure sent a sense of excitement spreading through the fleet, a combination of anger, despair, and defiance. It was now impossible to conceal from anyone that things were going very badly. The crews were caught up in a growing mood of frustration, that they, who had ruled the Pacific for the first six months of 1942, should now, two years later, be at the mercy of an enemy they never even saw, except as fleeting, deadly darts in the sky. The will was to seek out the enemy and fight him ship to ship, even if it meant their own destruction.

It was a mood which was apparently reaching up to the command level as well. At the beginning of October, their new fleet commander, Kurita Takeo, summoned his captains to the wardroom of his flagship. It was the twelve thousand ton, ten eight-inch gun heavy cruiser *Atago*, which he preferred to use as a headquarters instead of *Yamato* or *Mushashi*, because of her great speed – she could make thirty-five knots – and manoeuverability. "Gentlemen," he said, "the decisive moment is at hand."

The officers, as etiquette demanded, sat with backs straight and faces rigid, but they could not prevent their eyes rolling; they had heard all this before. "The Americans are now poised to assault the Philippines," Kurita told them. "We have long known this is the way they would continue their advance, in preference to the northern isles. Not only do they regard the Philippines as a much easier target than mainland Japan, but there is also the matter of MacArthur's bombastic promise to the people of the Philippines: I shall return. Well, I can tell you that this return has already begun: American transports are at this moment unloading their men and material in Leyte Gulf."

This time not even etiquette could prevent a rustle going round the wardroom: had they been caught with their pants down again? But did it matter whether their pants were down or up, Nicholas wondered, in view of the American superiority in ships and men – and planes? "Now," Kurita

356

went on, "as I have said, we have long anticipated this moment, and have laid our plans for it. This is an immense American operation, involving two task forces, virtually their entire Pacific Fleet, and untold numbers of men. If they can be given a decisive check now, any further advances will be put back at least a year. But there is more. In another fortnight there is an election in the United States. Roosevelt is standing for an unprecedented fourth term. There are many people who question the wisdom of this, who question the entire way in which Roosevelt has handled this war. If, immediately before the election, he were to be dealt a severe defeat, then the whole tide may turn in our favour. It has thus been decided to risk all, to gain all. The plan has been code-named the Sho Plan, the Victory Plan." He nodded to his secretary, and a huge wall chart was unfolded against the bulkhead.

Kurita picked up his wand. "The Americans are working to a plan which supposes that we are unable to oppose them. As I have said, they have two task forces available. One is the landing group, which is poorly protected by a few escort carriers. That is now in Leyte Gulf." He touched the map. "The overall commander of this task force, which is called the Seventh Fleet, is Admiral Kinkaid. Under his command, but operating as a separate unit, is a so-called Support Force, commanded by Admiral Oldendorf. This consists of six old battleships, *Maryland*, *Mississippi*, *West Virginia*, *Tennessee*, *California* and *Pennsylvania*. All of these ships are well over twenty years old. They displace around forty thousand tons and are armed with twelve fourteen-inch guns; obviously they are no match for *Mushashi* and *Yamato*, quite apart from the remainder of the squadron. However, the Americans also have their second Task Force, called the Third Fleet, and commanded by Admiral Halsey. This is a very powerful combination, including eight fleet carriers and four modern battleships. It would be very difficult to defeat this force, because of its air superiority. Therefore we are not going to try."

He looked from face to face with the air of a conjuror who has just pulled a very large rabbit out of his hat. "This Seventh Fleet is situated just north of the Philippine

357

Archipelago. The Americans obviously consider that should the invasion force be attacked, Halsey would be able to send his pilots to its aid. This would be correct did we not have a plan of our own. Our plan is that Admiral Ozawa, with our remaining carriers, that is to say, *Zuikaku* and the three light carriers, supported by the battleships *Hyuga* and *Ise*, will attack Halsey's Third Fleet."

There was a collective gasp of dismay. Kurita smiled. "A suicide mission, I will agree. But is not all war suicide? The point is, Admiral Ozawa will make contact with Halsey, then turn and run. Halsey will most certainly pursue. He is not called "Bull" for nothing, and besides, he will perceive this as his opportunity to destroy the last of our carriers. From our point of view, the important factor is that he will be lured out of range for supporting the Seventh Fleet.

"That leaves us with the eighteen escort carriers commanded by Kinkaid, and Oldendorf's old battleships. But Oldendorf is himself going to be lured out of position by our Southern Force. The command of this will be shared by Admirals Shima and Nishimura. It is even more of a decoy force than the Northern Force, as it will contain only two battleships, *Fuso* and *Yamashiro*, supported by some cruisers and destroyers. As I say, its business will be to draw Oldendorf from his position covering the landings. While this is happening, our main force, the Central Force, *this* force, will steam through the centre of the Philippines, use the San Bernadino Straits, and emerge immediately north of Leyte Gulf. Then we will have the invasion fleet at our mercy. Can you imagine what half an hour of *Mushashi* and *Yamato* would do in the midst of a fleet of transports guarded only by a few escort carriers? Gentlemen, we have it in our hands to turn the tide of this war by the destruction of an entire American army. We sail at dawn."

The excitement permeated the fleet as the orders were given by each captain to his crew. "Can we do it, honourable Captain?" Yakobe asked. His eyes were alight with the determination to do or die; he was young, inexperienced, and fanatical; there were too many like him in the Imperial Navy, now, Nicholas thought. But perhaps inexperienced fanaticism was what was needed, over the new few days, at least. It was an impossibly complicated plan, but for that very reason . . .

"I see no reason why not, Commander," he said. "Provided we all do our duty." And that our admiral does not lose his nerve, he thought.

The Central Fleet duly departed the Lingayyen Islands, putting in first to Brunei to top up their fuel, and then standing out for the Philippines, their course east by north. Kurita intended to pass north of the long island of Palawan, the most westerly of the group, before turning east for Mindoro and the tortuous passage between the islands for the Strait of San Bernadino. This would bring it out north of the island of Samar, at the southern end of which was Leyte Gulf. The day was fine and the squadron, which in addition to the six battleships included twelve heavy cruisers, two light cruisers and fifteen destroyers, and in terms of any warfare before the coming of aircraft was a most powerful force, was making virtually full speed, huge white bones thrusting away from the bows while the smoke from their funnels belched into the clear blue sky. Obviously they must be visible for miles, Nicholas thought, seated in his chair on the bridge of *Haruna*, but there was no sign of any enemy aircraft. Perhaps the gods were at last on their side.

Palawan was sighted at dawn the following morning, 23 October, and then slowly unfolded several miles to starboard as the sun rose from a clear sky to indicate another brilliant day. Yakobe stood beside Nicholas to admire the squadron; the battleships at the moment were steaming two abreast, with the cruisers outside them and the destroyers ahead and astern. "Are we not the finest navy in the world, honourable Captain?" he asked.

Nicholas was considering his reply when the signal lieutenant ran on to the bridge. "Submarines, honourable Captain. Fleet will disperse and regroup."

Nicholas swung his head left and right. He could see nothing untoward, but already sirens were screaming and the ships were peeling off according to their previously agreed plan. "Helm hard to port," he commanded the coxswain.

Even as the big ship started its turn there was a shout and a tremendous bang. All heads looked in the direction of the noise, to see *Atago* listing while smoke plumed into the air. Nicholas gulped. Not only had the Americans found them, but they had known exactly which ship to attack: the flagship. "Zigzag pattern!"

Haruna twisted to and fro, and now Nicholas saw another deadly streak of foam, passing close by to starboard. That had been avoided, but now there came another of those heart-stopping explosions, and the heavy cruiser *Maya*, a sister to *Atago*, began to go down. *Atago* herself was sinking, her crew being taken off by her destroyers. Nicholas wondered what would happen if Kurita elected to stay with his ship? But that would be dereliction of duty with the battle still to be fought.

Meanwhile, a third heavy cruiser of the Atago Class, *Takao*, had also been hit, although not as badly as her sisters. But she was ordered to drop out of the squadron, and, Kurita having resumed command from *Yamato*, they continued on their way; the destroyers appeared to have driven off the submarines with their depth charges, although there was no indication that they had managed to sink one. The sudden attack, and its devastating consequences, quite took the elation out of the crew. Yakobe had a very long face, and Nicholas had to remind him that the only important factor was that the battleships should get through to destroy the transport fleet. The Commander did not look reassured.

There were no further attacks during the 23rd, and by dawn next morning the squadron was rounding the southern end of Mindoro Island and turning up for the passage into the Sibuyan Sea, right in the heart of the archipelago. No one on board *Haruna* had had more than a few minutes sleep snatched at his post and Nicholas did not suppose it had been very different in the rest of the fleet. Now it was a case of all hands standing to, for this was the vital day. If they could get through the Sibuyan Sea and reach the San Bernadino Straits without detection, their mission could be achieved. But their mission *had* to be achieved, even if they were attacked. It was another glorious morning, and the scene was

360

again dramatic in the extreme. The sea was shallower here than out in the ocean, with vivid blues interspersed by no less attractive greens. Overhead the sky was decorated with scattered white clouds. And to either side could be obtained distant glimpses of lush green vegetation punctuated with mountain tops. It was to a degree reminiscent of The Slot, but here there was even less room to manoeuvre.

And even less chance of escaping detection, Nicholas thought, as, soon after breakfast, he heard the first sighting. "Aircraft approaching bearing zero six zero."

From the north-east, exactly where Halsey's task force was situated. That figured, but where was Ozawa's decoy group which was meant to lure the American fleet carriers away? "Fire as they bear, Mr Hamashita," Nicholas told his gunnery lieutenant. There was no hope of avoiding the enemy attack by zig-zagging here, without risking collision either with another ship or with the rocks that littered both sides of the passage.

Every ship opened up as the Americans zoomed in. Planes exploded as streams of tracer bullets carved through the air. But enough got through to launch their bombs and torpedoes. Nicholas kept waiting for that unforgettable tremble which would mean that *Haruna* had again been hit, but to his amazement when, after a frantic fifteen minutes, the Americans disappeared, there was no damage report. Then he realised why: the enemy had concentrated their efforts upon the two super-battleships, and especially upon the new flagship; *Mushashi* was indeed on fire in several places and had a slight list, to indicate that she had been struck both by bombs and at least one torpedo. Of course, she was unsinkable, and there did not appear to be any diminution in her speed, but it was still a disagreeable thought that she could at least be wounded.

The respite was a short one. The squadron proceeded into the Sibuyan Sea, and turned east for the straits, still a hundred and seventy nautical miles distant, a matter of something like six hours at thirty knots, allowing for the various alterations in course that would be necessary to pass by the several islands in the way. But their arrival

361

at dusk seemed on schedule, until the appearance of a second wave of American planes just on noon. The pattern was the same, as ignoring the hail of shot put up by the smaller battleships and the cruisers and destroyers, not to mention the superships themselves, the aircraft went straight for *Mushashi*, clearly their intended victim.

There was something quite terrifying in the way they ignored every other target in their determination to destroy the giant. Nicholas watched with a sense of detached horror as more and more bombs exploded on *Mushashi*'s decks and superstructure, and as the great ship trembled to the blows from two more torpedoes. Was any ship unsinkable? But if *Mushashi* were to go . . . She was clearly seriously damaged. Her immense fordeck sloped downwards towards the surface of the sea, instead of tilting slightly upwards like a launching platform. And now too there came a signal to reduce speed to twenty knots; this was clearly because the flagship could no longer maintain her designed speed. Nicholas gave the command to the engine room himself, while his officers muttered at each other, and he could see his men also clustering together as they began to consider the unthinkable.

But the speed reduction meant a serious interference with their schedule.

The third American wave came in the middle of the afternoon, and the tactics were repeated. Nicholas and Yakobe watched helplessly as explosion after explosion wracked the flagship, and by the time the planes withdrew her bows were nearly awash, she was on fire in several places, and it could be seen that her decks were a shambles. Nicholas saw a destroyer go alongside to take off the admiral and his staff and transfer them to *Yamato*, but he was taken totally by surprise by the orders which were now signalled: *This attack is aborted. Ships will return to base*. He stared at Yakobe in consternation. "Abort the attack? It will soon be dark, and we still have *Yamato* and four other battleships."

"Orders must be obeyed, honourable Captain," Yakobe pointed out.

"Dammit, we knew there had to be casualties, that this had

362

to be a suicide mission, if necessary, so long as the invasion force is destroyed," Nicholas grumbled, and remembered Yamamoto's promise, that he would forgive any disobedience of orders, so long as it was directed towards engaging the enemy. But Yamamoto was dead. On the other hand, Toyoda was his disciple.

"Shall I give the command, honourable Captain?" Yakobe asked. "The squadron is turning."

Nicholas's shoulders slumped. "Give the command."

Haruna began her turn, and as she did so, the Americans came again. This was the heaviest and most concerted attack yet; they could see they had the Japanese squadron on the run, just as they could tell that *Mushashi*, even *Mushashi*, was mortally wounded.

The anti-aircraft batteries chattered and the sea was filled with foaming explosisons. Nicholas saw the heavy cruiser *Myoko* take a direct hit from a bomb, men, metal and smoke hurled skywards. But she remained afloat. *Yamato* was also hit. But the main attack was, as before, reserved for *Mushashi*, and at last the great ship fell out of the line, turning away to the north, her foredeck beneath the waves, which lapped at her forward turrets, while her propellers were starting to show. Nicholas did not care to estimate how many thousands of gallons of water had to be in her hull to create such a situation. She was definitely sinking, her only hope to be beached on the island of Boac before going down.

By now the sun was setting fast, and within a few minutes *Mushashi* had disappeared into the gloom. The squadron closed up, their position, and course – back to the west – clearly delineated by the burning *Myoko*. But the crews were exhausted, and it was unlikely the American bombers would return during darkness. Tomorrow the squadron would have to face the submarines waiting west of the archipelago. "Stand down the watch below, Mr Yakobe," Nicholas said.

"Will you rest, honourable Captain?"

"I'll grab a sleep in my chair. But you take an hour, Commander."

"I too will remain on the bridge, honourable Captain."

363

"Yakobe, I am going to need you fresh tomorrow. Get some rest. What is it, Lieutenant?"

The signals officer was wildly excited, "Message from flagship, honourable Captain: *Squadron will resume attack.*"

"Let me see that." Nicholas virtually snatched the piece of paper. However welcome the order, it was still quite inexplicable.

He handed it to Yakobe, who glanced at it, and grinned. "We can but obey orders, honourable Captain."

"Indeed. Give the command, Mr Yakobe." Nicholas went on to the bridge wing to look out at the dark shapes of the other ships, all reversing the courses save for *Myoko*; she continued on her way to the west, now again fulfilling a valuable role, for if she would be useless in any fight, she would continue to indicate to any watchers that the Japanese were retiring.

But what had brought about Kurita's change of mind, and heart? Nicholas would have liked to feel this had been the Admiral's plan from the beginning, to convince the Americans that he was retreating, and just wait for darkness to advance again. But somehow he felt that was unlikely. He wished he could have been a fly on the bulkhead of the admiral's cabin on board *Yamato* to listen to the discussion, surely animated, which had led to a re-assertion of the aggressive spirit.

But the important thing was that they were returning over the water which had already cost them so dear. They regained the position where they had last seen *Mushashi* soon after eight, and here were joined by the destroyer which had accompanied the stricken ship in its search for the shallows. The news was flashed through the fleet that she had not done so; when within sight of Boac, at seven-thirty, *Mushashi* had turned turtle and gone to the bottom. It had taken a dozen torpedoes and a dozen bomb hits to sink her, but the important point was that there was no such thing as an unsinkable ship any longer.

"All we can do now is avenge her," Nicholas told his crew over the tannoy, and Kurita certainly seemed intent upon doing that. Speed was increased as the battle squadron streaked past the southern end of Burias and into the

364

Burias Passage and the southern extremnity of Luzon. Soon they sighted the small islands of Capul and Dalupin which marked the north entrance to the Samar Sea. Now they altered course hard to port, and passed through the Straits of San Bernadino into the Philippine Sea. The time was midnight.

The squadron now stood due east for Cape Espiritu Santo on the north-eastern extremity of Samar. There they would turn south for the last hundred and fifty miles of their journey, taking them into Leyte Gulf. But it was off Espiritu Santo that Halsey's Third Fleet had been last reported, and all the binoculars were out, scouring the night sky. "Nothing in sight, honourable Captain," Yakobe reported.

The ships raced south through the darkness. By now they knew that their surprise had been complete: they could hear the exchanges between the various American radio operators. They had been seen by shore spotters emerging from the strait, and Kinkaid, learning that Oldendorf's old battleships were momentarily expecting an engagement with Shima's and Nishimura's Southern Force – seen on their radar screens – and was therefore unavailable for protecting duties further north, was under the assumption that his northern flank was still in the care of Halsey. Now he was discovering that Halsey was many miles away to the north, chasing Ozawa's virtually unarmed carrier force. Nicholas could imagine the panic that was going on in Leyte Gulf, as the Americans realised that dawn was going to bring a squadron of Japanese battleships into their midst, with only the small escort carriers to defend them.

And there was the dawn, the eastern horizon bright with the promise of the coming day. Now the land to starboard was clearly visible, and in front of them, just over twenty miles away, the headland of Calicoan, beyond which was Leyte Gulf. *Squadron will first destroy or disperse the escort carriers*, came the orders from the flagship.

Binoculars swept the southern sky as visibility improved. "There!" Yakobe said.

"There!" said Lieutenant Hamashita.

365

The escorts were scattering to present less of a target. But they were also flying off their aircraft to attack. "Bandits bearing one-two-five," said the lookout above them.

The crew were already at action stations, and the machine guns started belching tracer streams. Nicholas ignored them. His business was a carrier, if he could get one. He would never have a better opportunity. "Range twenty thousand yards, bearing one-four-zero," Lieutenant Hamashita said.

"Fire as you bear, Mr Hamashita," Nicholas replied.

The fourteen-inch guns belched flame and smoke and steel, and *Haruna* trembled and rolled away from the enormous force she had just released. All the squadron was firing now, the deeper booms of *Yamato*'s eighteen-inch dwarfing the explosions of the other guns. The sea to the south became dotted with white, and then with black and red as one of the carriers caught fire. It was impossible to determine whose guns had scored the hit, but there were a multitude of other targets, and the headland was racing at them . . . "Message from flagship, honourable Captain," said Lieutenant Kano, the signals officer. The young man's face was quite distressed.

Nicholas took the sheet of paper, frowned at the words: *Attack is aborted. Squadron will return to San Bernadino Strait with all possible despatch.* He raised his head, looked at the scattered fleet of escort carriers, listened to the whine and boom of the planes attacking them; the Americans had not yet scored a hit and at least two of their ships were on fire. The invasion fleet was within ten miles, a helpless target. "There must be a mistake," he said. "Ask for a repeat of the message, Mr Kano."

The lieutenant bowed and ran back to the radio cabin. Nicholas handed the message to Yakobe, who read it, and then shrugged. "We must presume the Admiral knows something we do not, honourable Captain."

"We are on the verge of succeeding in our mission, Mr Yakobe," Nicholas reminded him. "Nothing was to distract us from that, or should now."

Kano was back. "Message confirmed, honourable Captain. It appears that Admirals Shima and Nishimura have been defeated and destroyed, and that Oldendorf's battleships are steaming towards us. Additionally, Admiral Kurita expects to be attacked by planes from Halsey's fleet."

"In the name of the gods!" Nicholas shouted. "Halsey's fleet is chasing Admiral Ozawa, is it not? As for Oldendorf . . . Six old battleships, against *Yamato*? Hasn't that been the Navy's dream since she was commissioned? Anyway, they cannot get here for at least six hours."

The lieutenant remained standing to attention, but Yakobe was pointing. "The squadron is turning, honourable Caaptain."

Nicholas looked at the other battleships in impotent fury. But he had come here to do or die. In fact, by the terms of their orders, as he understood them, he had come here *to* do and die. I will forgive anything, Yamamoto had said, so long as disobedience is directed towards the enemy. Toyoda could hardly lack that spirit, as he had created this plan in the first place. "Course will remain unchanged, Mr Yakobe," he said. "We will engage the invasion fleet."

Yakobe opened his mouth, then closed it again. He looked at the signal lieutenant. "What reply am I to make to the flagship, honourable Captain?" Kano asked.

"You will make no reply, Lieutenant. We will simply ignore the signal."

The young man gulped, and looked at Yakobe. "With respect, honourable Captain," the commander said. "But you cannot disobey an order given in battle."

"I can and I will, when that order itself disobeys an order given by a higher authority," Nicholas told him. "You have my orders, Lieutenant Kano. Carry them out. And you, Commander, tell the gun crews to stand by."

He left the two officers staring at each other, and stepped out on to the bridge wing. The headland was momentarily coming closer, and as *Haruna* was the only ship continuing to steam south, the aircraft were now clustering about her. But as yet she had not been hit, and her huge guns continued to belch smoke and flame at the distant escort carriers. Another few minutes would bring the transports in sight, and then . . .

"Honourable Captain," Yakobe said behind him.

Nicholas turned, expecting yet another order from Kurita, which he intended to disobey, and looked into the barrel of a

367

revolver. "Regrettably, honourable Captain," Yakobe said. "It is my duty to place you under arrest."

Nicholas stood up as the door to his day cabin opened. Except for half-an-hour's exercise a day on the quarter-deck, he had been confined in here all the way back to the Lingayyen Islands, and indeed for the four days since they had been again safely moored. He had had no com-munication with the Admiral, save for a signal, addressed to Commander Yakobe rather than himself, confirming and congratulating the Commander in his action. Yakobe had shown his captain the signal, his face expressionless. But there could be no doubt he was pleased with himself. "I wish an interview with the admiral," Nicholas had said.

Yakobe had bowed. "I am sure the admiral will summon you as soon as is practical, honourable Captain."

That had been several days ago, and the Commander had remained scrupulously correct, even if there could be no doubt that he felt his captain was deserving of a court martial. Well, Nicholas thought, that could not happen too soon. He would have a great deal to say at a court martial. As far as he was concerned it was Kurita who had disobeyed orders, twice. And his evidence was going to be supported by facts. The squadron had regained their base without suffering another casualty, for all Kurita's fear of attack, from either Oldendorf or Halsey. And because of the admiral's loss of nerve the entire Sho plan had turned into a disaster. Ozawa's carrier fleet, such as it was, had been blown out of the water. So had Shima and Nishimura's Southern Force. So had *Mushashi*. In all the Japanese had lost four aircraft-carriers, three battleships, six heavy cruisers, four light cruisers, and eleven destroyers, a total of some three hundred thousand tons of ships, together with not less than ten thousand men. The Americans had lost three small carriers and three destroyers, totalling thirty-five thousand tons. Their invasion fleet had not been disrupted in any way, and men and material were being poured ashore at Leyte. What had been going to be the great reversal of fortune by the Imperial Navy had turned out to be its final and most crushing defeat. For what use was a squadron of five battleships, without air cover? Far better had they all gone down, if they could have taken most of the American transports with them.

But now at last . . . the door opened, and he gazed at his father-in-law. "Well, Nicholas *san*," Yosunube remarked. "This time you have really overstepped the mark."

"I wish a court-martial, honourable Father-in-law."

"That is for others to decide. For the time being, I am to take you back to Tokyo."

"Well, that is something. I am grateful, honourable Father-in-law."

Yosunube's smile was cold. "I think you should know, Nicholas *san*, that I am taking charge of you, not as your father-in-law, but as an officer in the *Kempei-tai*."

CHAPTER 15

Darkness

Nicholas's head came up. "I have committed no treason."

Yosunobe went to the door and opened it to show Nicholas the four armed men standing there. "Some would say that disobedience of orders under fire constitutes treason. Your escort awaits you."

"What you really mean is that I am to be spirited off my ship and away from the fleet in secrecy," Nicholas said.

Yosunobe smiled. "Why, yes. That is exactly right. Will you go quietly, or will you be dragged? Oh, there is one thing I almost forgot." He produced a pair of handcuffs. "Hands behind the back, please, Nicholas *san*."

Nicholas hesitated, knowing an enormous temptation to cut loose and take them all on in one glorious last five minutes. But it would not be a last five minutes; there were too many of them for them to need to kill him. Then he would be dragged away, a bleeding mess, to their torture cells. Well, perhaps he was going there anyway, but as long as he was alive, and fit and strong, he had a chance – he could not accept that Toyoda would allow one of his senior officers to be tortured to death. He put his hands behind his back, and listened to the click of the lock as the steel settled around his wrists. "I have long wanted to have the opportunity to do this to you," Yosonube remarked. "Ever since the day you caused me to lose face before Admiral Yamamoto and General Yamashita. Is it not true that everything comes to he who waits?"

They were taken ashore by the waiting launch, and boarded

the aircraft, also waiting for them on the runway. An hour later they were landing in Singapore. Yosunobe kept up a stream of conversation throughout the flight, a mixture of banter and insults and threats. Nicholas endeavoured not to listen. He was bracing himself for what might lie ahead, telling himself again and again that survival was all that mattered, until he could reach Tokyo.

A car drove them from the airport to the *Kempei-tai* headquarters. "No Raffles this time, eh?" Yosunobe said jocularly.

"When do we leave for Tokyo?" Nicholas asked.

"Tomorrow morning. But we have the night in front of us, eh? There will be nothing to do tomorrow, save sleep. It is a long flight." He gestured with his stick, and Nicholas entered one of the interrogation rooms, followed by two men.

"There is really no need for this," Nicholas pointed out. "You only have to ask, and I shall tell anything you wish to know. I have nothing to hide."

Yosunobe grinned. "I know this. But it would be such a shame to have you in my power and not at least enjoy myself. Will you undress yourself, or would you like my people to assist you?"

Survive, Nicholas told himself. He had survived so much, beginning with Christina, that he could surely take this in his stride. "I will undress myself," he said. "If you will free my hands."

Yosunobe nodded to one of the guards, and the handcuffs were removed. "You will, I hope, be sensible," he said, "and not attempt violence. Or you will be beaten very badly."

"I will not attempt violence," Nicholas assured him.

He stripped, and sat in the waiting seatless chair. His arms were taken behind him and secured, as were his legs. Never before had he felt so *exposed*. "Now," Yosunobe said. "All you have to do is scream, Nicholas *san*."

Nicholas clamped his teeth together, and tried to control his mind as Yosunobe took one of the guard's rubber truncheons, and walked round him, occasionally flicking him. Each flick induced a remarkable sensation, as all feeling ceased in the area struck at the moment of the blow, and then came rushing back with an intensity which

371

made crying out a necessity. Nicholas bore it stoically while he was hit on the arms and legs, on the neck, lightly . . . "I could kill you with that blow," Yosunobe told him. He was hit on the chest and in the stomach, before his tormentor turned his attention to his genitals, kneeling to obtain a better position and flicking them time and again, while Nicholas clamped his jaws so tightly he could almost feel his teeth cracking, and tears ran down his cheeks. But no sound escaped his lips. "You will never fuck my daughter again," Yosunobe jeered at him.

Nicholas reckoned he was entirely right, even without any physical disability: were he ever to find himself alone with Sumiko again he would very probably strangle her. And her father, of course. And the child? In his present mood, perhaps him, too.

Eventually even Yosunobe grew tired of tormenting him, and went to bed. Nicholas was left sitting in the chair, every inch of his body from his neck to his ankles a mass of pain. Yet that slowly wore off during the long flight the next day, and he was even able to snatch some exhausted sleep, despite the fact that his wrists remained manacled throughout the journey. But at last, Tokyo. "I wish to see see Admiral Toyoda," he told Yosunobe.

Yosunobe grinned. "The admiral will see you, as and when he chooses."

"It is my right to put my case to my commanding officer," Nicholas said.

Another grin. "You have no rights, Nicholas *san*, unless we choose to give them to you."

A curtained van was waiting on the runway, and Nicholas was taken directly to the *Kempei-tai* headquarters outside the city. It was a building he knew well, although he had never been inside it before. There he was handed over to guards who again stripped him naked and beat him before he was thrown into a cell. The sense of outrage grew, but with it now a sense of panic. He was clearly not going to be court-martialled. That would be to allow him to criticise the Navy, the way it had fought this war, and especially the way Kurita had fought the Battle of Leyte Gulf. He could understand the reasoning behind this, but now he realised he was not even going to be allowed to see Toyoda. Presumably this was because Toyoda did not wish to see him. He had become an embarrassment to everyone. And there was no Yamamoto to step in and save him from the consequences of his insubordination.

Then what of his family? Did they know anything of the affair, or where he was? Takeda had to. But Takeda never came near him, either. Had he told Christina? How Christina would laugh, especially if she knew what had been done to him. Sumiko? He was not sure what Sumiko's reaction would be. However hateful the very thought of her had become to him, he felt she was genuinely fond of him. But she was certainly more fond of her father.

Charlotte? And Linda? They would be going mad with anxiety. And in the case of Charlotte . . . Mori? But Mori was a dreamer, hardly less light-headed than his wife.

He tried to adopt a reasoned approach. This was made easier because after the first day he was no longer beaten or assaulted – just ignored. He was fed a subsistence ration of rice, and exercised, by himself, for half-an-hour every day. The guards occasionally poked him with their sticks, and jibed at him, but made no serious attempt to hurt him. Now his principal misery was a combination of boredom, apprehension for his family – in which he included Linda – and lack of knowledge about what was happening in the world, and in the war. But that the situation was deteriorating quite rapidly soon became apparent; he had returned to Tokyo on 8 November, and had indeed glimpsed a newspaper headline announcing that Roosevelt had again been elected president. Then nothing. But on 24 November the air raid sirens screamed as over a hundred massive B-29's scoured the sky above the city, raining down bombs.

Nicholas's guards were terrified, and were even prepared to talk about what was happening; the target had been the Musashi works which manufactured aero-engines. Apparently damage had been severe. And only three days later the Americans were back. To compound matters and make it appear as if the very universe was now fighting the Japanese, on 7 December, the third anniversary of the attack on Pearl Harbour, Tokyo was rocked by a severe earthquake. Nicholas felt the prison tremble and watched cracks appearing in the walls. He remembered how his mother and sister had been sucked into the rubble of their collapsing house, and wondered if that too was to be his fate. Then his thoughts turned to escaping, as the cracks became wide enough to climb through. But his guards had realised this as well and were waiting to take him to another, undamaged cell. He begged them for some information as to what had happened in the rest of the city, but they didn't appear to know much more than he did.

But even the earthquake was nothing compared with the events of 16 and 17 February, when on consecutive nights Tokyo and Yokahama were attacked by over a thousand bombers. The B-29's of the previous year had clearly come from bases in China, having been flown there from India: there was no way they could have used the flight deck of an aircraft-carrier. But these planes were equally clearly carrier borne, which indicated that the American fleet was now operating within range of the Japanese mainland. "You realise that the war is lost?" Nicholas asked his guards. "Why does the Emperor not make peace?"

They merely swore at him and beat him with their truncheons.

The culmination of the growing number of raids came on 9 March. Nicholas was exercising in the yard when the sirens went. His guards immediately hurried him back to his cell, but before they got there he saw the planes, super-fortresses, swooping low over the city. Clearly these were not looking for military targets, and equally clearly they were not using high explosive bombs. His guards stood with him, staring open-mouthed as the planes passed in procession, almost untouched by the scant anti-aircraft fire. Then they saw the smoke and the flames, everywhere. "Incendiaries," someone gasped.

The window of Nicholas's cell looked out at the inner courtyard of the prison, and he could not see the city itself. But he could see the smoke, an immense pall which entirely blotted out the sky; unlike London, which had survived

374

incendiary attacks in the Blitz, the houses in Tokyo were built of paper rather than brick. Now he was really frightened, as the fires burned, it seemed out of control, for several days; it was difficult to believe that anyone could have survived such a holocaust. But still no one would tell him what was happening outside the prison, until, a fortnight after the incendiary raid, the door of his cell opened, and he gazed at Takeda Konoye.

Takeda wore the uniform of a full colonel, and looked as fit and well as ever Nicholas had seen him. And as imperturbable. "Well, Nicholas *san*," he said.

Nicholas did not bother to bow. Nor was he any longer interested in pleasantries. "You have taken a long time, Takeda."

Takeda looked around the cell. "You have not been comfortable here?"

"What makes you suppose that?" Nicholas asked sarcastically.

"I know it has been hard," Takeda said. "But had there been a court martial you could well have been shot by now. And all of this time your friends have been working for you."

"Tell me how," Nicholas suggested.

Takeda glanced at him, while he strolled around the cell. "You will discover, how. Would you like to leave this place?"

Nicholas could not believe his ears. He dared not. "It is possible," Takeda said. "For you to walk out of here within the hour."

"There has been a revolution?"

Takeda smiled. "Of course not. But there is work to be done. Would you like your rank back? No, no, would you like a promotion?"

"You mean I am going to be reinstated? Just like that? You must think I am a fool."

"No one has ever mistaken you for a fool, Nicholas. I am here to offer you reinstatement, yes. With the rank of Rear-Admiral. In return for an important service, a service vital to the future of Japan."

375

Nicholas sat down. "You mean I am to lead some kind of suicide mission."

"You have always thought in apocalyptic terms," Takeda said, and sat beside him. "I will agree that it has become necessary, in recent months, to employ suicidal tactics in an attempt to stop the American advance. This has had its successes, but, sadly, has not achieved the results for which we had hoped. It seems that within a matter of days they will have succeeded in taking Iwo Jima. They have already gained the upper hand in the Philippines. And the British have just recaptured Mandalay. This suggests that they will soon regain Burma. And once Iwo Jima falls the Americans will no doubt attack Okinawa. Should Okinawa fall, they will be within round-the-clock bombing range of Japan. Briefly, it can be said that the war is developing in a direction which is not in our best interests."

Nicholas could only wait; his stepfather was perfectly serious. "Thus it were best ended," Takeda said, gazing at Nicholas in an ingenuous fashion. "However, as is well known, the Americans have adopted a most intransigent attitude towards us. In this they are of course supported by their European allies, and especially the British and the French, desperate to regain their former colonies."

"And perhaps to avenge their dead," Nicholas suggested.

"Have we not got dead to avenge? More than they. Do you know what they did to Tokyo a fortnight ago? Twenty-six square miles of the city have been devastated, eighty-four thousand people killed, more than a hundred thousand injured, more than a million made homeless. They have achieved almost as much damage as the Great Earthquake."

Nicholas's head jerked. He had not realised it had been so bad. "My family . . ."

"*Our* family has survived, Nicholas. That includes your woman, although I have had to move her and Suiko to a fresh apartment. But they may not survive another such raid. None of us may. Thus, as I say, it must be ended." He gazed at his stepson.

"I am supposed to assist in this process?"

"You are of their blood. You will be able to speak their

376

language. You will have the rank of Rear-Admiral, and the authority to speak on behalf of the Emperor."

"Does the Emperor really expect me to do this? Does he not know that I have been beaten and humiliated by his people?"

"He is sorry for this. But you did disobey orders when under fire. He also knows that you have a wife, and two sons, and a sister, whom you love deeply. He does not know that you have a mistress you possibly love even more, but I know that."

"I see. I do as you wish, or they die, is that it?"

Takeda made a deprecatory gesture with his hands. "They may well do so, as I have said, from the American bombing. However, I must inform you, Nicholas, that I have information that Colonel Mori and his wife, your sister, are the centre of a subversive group which had as its aim the overthrow of the government of General Tojo."

Nicholas caught his breath. "You were obviously not aware of this, of course," Takeda went on without blinking. "Or you would not have permitted it. Yet it is so. The matter was reported to me by your own dear wife, Sumiko, who learned of it from Charlotte. I was shocked, and could not believe it. But I soon had one of our agents infiltrate one of their meetings, and now I have proof. I have so far kept that proof to myself. And as it appears certain that this irrational behaviour has been induced by a fear of Japan losing the war, were the war to end, I would see that it remained suppressed. In any event, it was directed, as I say, against Tojo, and he no longer matters. However, if the war were to drag on, and our situation continue to deteriorate, it would be necessary to place all possible subversives under restraint. I am sure you would not like Charlotte to find herself in here. You might have to listen to her screams as she is interrogated."

Sumiko, Nicholas thought. One day . . . but again, survival until that day. And he would include this man in his vengeance. "You do not leave me with much option, honourable Stepfather," he remarked. "However, I hope you do not expect me to perform a miracle. Have not the Americans declared that they will accept nothing less than unconditional surrender?"

377

Takeda waved his hand. "That is a negotiating position."

"I would not be too sure of that."

"It is a negotiating position," Takeda repeated, "because they do not understand what is involved. They do not understand the forces with which they are dealing. It is up to you to tell them this and convince them that what they propose is impossible. Our soldiers, our seamen, but more important, our people, are prepared to die for the Emperor and the Empire. The Americans must decide whether they wish to die in pursuit of some abstract idea of vengeance. We had twenty thousand, nine hundred and nineteen men on Iwo Jima, commanded to fight to the end. Now that it has fallen, we have been informed that twenty thousand, seven hundred and three of those men are dead. Only two hundred and sixteen have been taken prisoner. To achieve this result, the Americans landed two full divisions, after weeks of air and sea bombardment. They have suffered more than nineteen thousand casualties, including well over four thousand dead. There are a hundred million people in Japan prepared to fight to the end. How good are you at arithmetic?"

"You are saying that the Americans will require a thousand divisions and will suffer two million casualties before they can conquer Japan."

"Those are certainly the figures they need to look at," Takeda agreed. "And all of this while they are still waging a war in Europe."

"And should I be able to convince them, what are our terms for peace?"

"Your business is to convince them that a negotiated peace is better than this absurd demand for an unconditional surrender. Once they have conceded that point, a cease fire can be arranged while we discuss terms. Are we agreed?"

Nicholas had already made up his mind. This was the best hope for peace, a peace which would save all of their lives. Personal feelings would have to be left until later. "I would need to see my family, first."

"That is not possible, Nicholas. This negotiation must be carried out in absolute secrecy. I have given you my word as a *samurai* that they are all well, including Linda. And when

378

you return from your mission, why, then you will be reunited with them."

"Whether I succeed or not?"

"Whether you succeed or not. Providing that you do your best." He gave a quick smile. "You will, of course, have an aide. Well, two aides, who both speak good English."

"I understand," Nicholas said. "When do I commence this mission?"

"We are negotiating now. It should be with the next month."

"Where?"

"Our concept is that it should take place in the Portuguese colony of Macao."

Nicholas nodded. "And until then?"

"For security purposes, you must remain within this prison. However, you will be given a suite rather than a cell, and be treated as an honoured guest. Ask, and you shall receive."

"You are too kind," Nicholas remarked.

Takeda stood up and bowed. "Well, then, honourable Stepson, I congratulate you upon your promotion. I will leave you now to inform my superiors of your agreement."

"There is just one more thing," Nicholas said. "Whose idea was it that I should be your representative at these negotiations?"

Takeda bowed. "I had the honour to put forward your name, Nicholas. And the Emperor was pleased to accept it."

"Then tell me this: does my father-in-law know of it?"

"He does."

"And he approves?"

"Ah . . . no. He does not approve. He argued against it. But that is of no importance. Yosunobe's star has set; he was Tojo's man."

"May I ask why you were in favour?"

Takeda bowed again. "Are you not my stepson?"

Certainly he was as good as his word. No sooner had he left than Nicholas was taken from his cell and installed in a comfortable three-room suite, within the prison, given silk *kimonos* to wear and female servants to attend to his every wish. He was also measured for his new uniform. He was invited to request the company of a *geisha*, and this he accepted, as he was anxious to discover how much manhood he had left, after his sexual beatings. In the event, he was reassured.

Then it was a matter of waiting. As Takeda had prophesied, only a few days later, on 1 April, the Americans landed on Okinawa, and another intense struggle commenced. There were well over a hundred thousand Japanese troops on Okinawa, as well as a large civilian population, and Nicholas gathered that they had all been instructed to fight to the bitter end. In fact, every weapon Japan possessed was to be thrown into the struggle, and on 5 April even *Yamato* put to sea. She was the only Japanese battleship remaining operational, and she was still the greatest battleship ever built. Now indeed she was on a suicide mission, to do a Leyte Gulf all on her own, sail into the midst of the American task force off Okinawa, and hopefully right through it, guns blazing to left and right, and keep on going until she beached herself, where she would be fought to the last. She never got there. Two days later she was attacked by planes from Task Force Fifty-Eight, and after being hit by thirteen torpedoes and six bombs, capsized and sank, taking all but fifty of her complement of two thousand five hundred men with her.

She had been the ship, Nicholas recalled, that Yamamoto and himself had been going to sail to victory, time and again. Now, her going meant that the era of the battleship, which had truly begun with the Battle of Tsushima in 1905, was finally over, after just forty years. Nicholas also realised that with every day his bargaining chips were being whittled away. But the forces on Okinawa continued to fight with utter determination, and on 12 April all Japan cheered when it was announced that President Roosevelt had died of a brain haemorrhage.

Nicholas doubted that tragedy was going to make much difference to the conduct of the war. Indeed the very next night following the announcement, Tokyo was ravaged by B-29's, bombing at will as the city's anti-aircraft defences had been reduced to rubble. From the *Kempei-tai* headquarters he looked out at the raging fires and found it difficult to believe there was anything left to destroy. He could only hope that Takeda had indeed managed to remove the family out of the city.

Two days later he was visited by Captain Yamaguchi from the Navy, and Major-General Kawasabe of the Army, who informed him that the embassay was ready.

All travel was dangerous, because of the activity of the American Air Force. The envoys took off at night for the flight down to Hong Kong. This meant that they had to pass over almost the entire length of Japan south of Tokyo, and Nicholas was astounded at the number of fires he saw blazing throughout the country. His companions, who had to know where he had spent the past six months, as they had actually joined him at the headquarters, made no comment, and he asked no questions. But matters were obviously more serious than he had been able to gather from his cell window.

They landed at Hong Kong without mishap, and this was like entering another world. Most of the damage caused during the assault in 1941 had been repaired, and Hong Kong had not been bombed by the Allies. Here a fast motorboat was waiting for them, to rush them the few miles further south to Macao. An hour later Nicholas, flanked by his two aides, was seated across a table from two American officers, an admiral and a general, who were also flanked by an aide each. "Yours is a fairly well-known name, Admiral Barrett," the General said. "You have a kind of in and out track record. Of British descent, but fighting for the Japanese against the British . . ."

Nicholas glanced at the information sheet he had been given. "Are you not of German descent, General? Or, for that matter, is not General Eisenhower equally of German descent?"

The General flushed, and frowned. "Then there is the matter of the *Sun Lily*, against which we have the testimony of Petty Officer Browning that you not only rescued him and his companions from drowning, but set them ashore."

Nicholas shrugged. "In the one instance, I was obeying orders, in the other, lacking orders, I was obeying my instincts as a seaman. But really, gentlemen, I did not come here to discuss a personal matter."

"You might find it useful," the Admiral said. "We're compiling a list of war criminals who will have to answer for their crimes when this is over. It's a matter of debate whether your name should be on it. I reckon you should be interested in that."

"I am interested in the task I have been given, gentlemen. Which is to convince you that physically to conquer Japan, whether or not it is at all practical, will cost you more than it could possibly be worth, and that the only sane answer to the problem that confronts us both is a negotiated peace."

The eyes facing him across the table were hostile. "Why should we agree to that, Admiral Barrett?" asked the General.

Nicholas repeated the arguments given him by Takeda.

"Do you seriously expect us to believe that a whole nation would voluntarily commit suicide on behalf of some heathen idea represented by a pop-eyed pipsqueak with spectacles?"

Nicholas kept his temper. "Do you seriously expect me to believe that a nation with no ideals other than to make as much money as possible and live as expensively and wastefully as possible, is going to risk two million of their favourite sons to find out?"

They glared at him, and he smiled at them. "And suppose we threaten just to blast you out of existence with bombs?" the General inquired.

"I doubt there is enough high explosive in the world to destroy a whole country, General. You would have to land, eventually."

"Well, as to that," the General said, "let me tell you . . ."

"General," the Admiral interjected. "I guess we've talked enough. We'll report back to General MacArthur and he will no doubt inform President Truman of your stand, Admiral Barrett. You can tell your people they'll have our answer in due course." He stood up. "I'll bid you good-day." He did not offer to shake hands.

"What do you think?" Kawasabe asked, as they bounced over the waves on their way back to Hong Kong.

382

"I think that we should brace ourselves for a fight," Nicholas told him. "At least at this moment. Whether, when they've had time to reflect, they may be more reasonable, is another matter."

In Tokyo, Nicholas was taken to a meeting of the war cabinet, headed by the new prime minister. Mr Higashikuni listened to what he had to say with quiet anxiety. "You do not consider the response was positive?" Admiral Yonai observed.

"From those officers, no, honourable Admiral. But this may in itself be a negotiating position."

"We must assume that it is not," the Prime Minister said. "We thank you, Admiral Barrett, for your efforts on our behalf."

Outside, Nicholas was required to report to Admiral Toyoda. It was a very long time since he had last seen the Admiral, and he arrived at the temporary Admiralty, the original building having been too badly damaged for further use, in a state of some shock. He had had to drive through the streets of Tokyo, and see the destruction caused by the bombing, the misery of the people, many of whom were camping out in the ruins of what had been their homes. But he was also aware of the tremendous anger they felt at what had happened to them. Whether this anger was directed against the enemy or the politicians and generals who had led them to this disaster was difficult to determine. "Barrett *san*." Toyoda gave a brief bow. "Welcome back."

"Do you know where I have been, these past six months, honourable Admiral?"

Toyoda sighed, and gestured him to a chair. "You will understand that you placed me in a very difficult position. You *did* disobey orders. I could not, at that juncture, permit a court martial which could have been very damaging to the prestige of the Imperial Navy." He smiled. "However much I agreed with you."

"So you let the *Kempei-tai* have me."

"They were, and still remain, a powerful force. It was necessary for you to disappear for a while, yes. I am sorry if they ill-treated you. It is the nature of the beast. However,

383

I made it perfectly plain to them that you were not to be killed or permanently injured in any way. I knew we would have need of you, soon enough. And now you sit before me, looking as fit as ever."

"Thank you, honourable Admiral," Nicholas said, with as much sarcasm as he dare risk. "And now?"

"I have no doubt that you would like a command at sea." Toyoda spread his hands. "I cannot give you one."

"There is nothing at all?"

"Nothing. You know that *Shinano* has gone down?"

"*Shinano*? I did not even know she had been completed."

"Well, she never was completed. But she could float. So I was commanded to send her to sea, with as many planes as we could muster, to attack the Americans off Iwo Jima. It was another suicide mission. But this was more suicidal than most. She was sunk only a hundred miles south of Kyushu. The whole thing was a deadly secret, yet it seems that at least one submarine was waiting for her."

"There must have been several submarines. How many torpedoes did it take to sink her?"

"The survivors estimate she was hit twice."

"Twice, and sank? *Shinano*? She was a sister to *Yamato* and *Mushashi*. It took a dozen torpedoes each, plus bombs, to sink them."

"That is true, Barrett *san*. But they were finished ships. *Shinano* had not yet had her interior watertight bulkheads fitted."

"And you sent her to sea? To fight?" Nicholas could not believe his ears.

"I obeyed orders, Admiral Barrett. As you become more senior, you will discover that disobeying orders becomes more difficult. In any event, I have no sea command to offer you."

"You mean *Haruna* is gone too?"

"As a matter of fact, *Haruna* is still afloat. But she is very badly damaged, and is in port in Kure, undergoing repairs. She will not be ready for sea for another six months, and we fear that may be too late."

"You expect the Americans to attempt an invasion before then? Surely they have to take Okinawa first?"

384

"That is true. But we do not expect that to be long delayed. Have you heard the news from Europe?"

"What news?"

"Simply that Hitler has committed *seppuku*, at least after his own fashion. An unconditional German surrender is expected any day now. That means the war in Europe is over, and the Americans will be able to turn their entire resources upon us. I think the final battle will be fought quite soon. But we will fight it, Barrett *san*. You will take command of the dockyard at Kure. Apart from *Haruna*, which still has her guns, there is virtually a brigade of sailors and marines quartered there. Like you, they have run out of ships. Your orders are to put the port in the best possible state of defence, and then, when it becomes necessary, defend it to the last man. Is this understood?"

"Understood, honourable Admiral. Am I allowed to take my family with me?"

"If that is what you wish to do, certainly."

Nicholas went to see Takeda. "I gather your mission was not an immediate success," his stepfather remarked.

"I never expected it to be. With events in Europe going their way, the Americans are not going to negotiate now. I have received a shore appointment, to command the garrison at Kure. I would now like to visit my family."

"Of course. They are in Mito. Well, it is safer there."

"Who, exactly?"

"Well, Sumiko, and the boys, and Christina."

"Where are Charlotte and Mori?"

"Mori has been posted to Nagasaki."

"Nagasaki? Will that not be one of the first ports the Americans will invade?"

"Very possibly. But there is nothing I can do about it. I had nothing to do with the posting."

"What of this evidence you possess against them?"

"I told you, it is suppressed."

"But Sumiko knows of it. And Christina?"

"Of course. Sumiko told her. It was she told me."

"Then the whole world knows of it."

"I told them to keep it to themselves, because there was

insufficient evidence to arrest Mori. I told them that until I could accumulate such evidence, it must be kept secret. They believed me."

"Takeda," Nicholas said. "I would like to know why you are doing this?"

Takeda licked his lips. "You are my stepson."

"And you, honourable Stepfather, are a liar. And a poor one. However, I am grateful. Now tell me where I can find Linda."

"She is in Hakone. Charlotte is with her."

"What did you say? She is not with Mori?"

Another quick lick of the lips. "They . . . we . . . thought it best."

"I see," Nicholas said, not seeing at all. There was a great deal going on about which he knew absolutely nothing. Yet it all concerned him, or his. "Very well. It is my intention to go to Hakone, now, pick up both Linda and Charlotte, and take them with me to Kure. Have you any objections to this?"

"Ah . . . no. They are your women. But what of Sumiko? She is your wife."

"If I laid eyes on Sumiko, I would very probably strangle her."

"And your sons?"

"I will have to consider the matter. As you suggest, they are probably safer in Mito than in Kure, at least for the time being. I will say goodbye, Takeda. And again, thank you."

"I did what I thought best," Takeda said. "But Nicholas, remember that I still have that evidence."

Nicholas couldn't determine what Takeda meant by that last remark, save a reminder that for Charlotte or Mori to recommence their activities might force him to act. He entirely agreed with his stepfather, for once; his sister and her husband had been fantastically lucky, and even if he was sure Takeda was grinding some private axe, he was not at this moment prepared to quibble: he had himself been enormously lucky, knowing as he did the way the *Kempei-tai* worked, virtually as a state within a state. Whatever his stepfather was up to, he had to accept that but for Takeda he could well be dead, or still locked away in a cell. In any event, he was too happy to be seeing them again, to be able to take care of them himself, no matter what the future held. And the boys? They were a problem which remained to be solved. They were his own flesh and blood, the very fruits of his loins . . . but their mothers were the two women he hated more than any other women in the world. The women he could love came first.

The Hakone Range rose behind Yokohama. It was dominated by the greatest mountain in Japan, the sacred peak of Fujiyama. But beneath the hallowed, snow-covered slopes were many lesser peaks, interspersed with delightful valleys and deep, still, lakes. In the winter it was a playground for skiers; in the summer it was even more a paradise for fishing and walking, for observing nature at its best. This summer the crowds were absent; everyone was at work, preparing for the unthinkable, the possible invasion of Japan. But the heart of the country continued unchanged, and the village to which Nicholas had been directed by Takeda was as typical as any Japanese, with neatly terraced rice paddies rising up the hillsides, watered by carefully controlled sluices to admit the nearby lake as required.

Takeda had provided him with a car and sufficient petrol, both to make this stop and then reach Kure. What he did after that was up to him. But in Kure he would be in command. Now he pulled up before the one house of any size in the village, instantly surrounded by a group of small boys and girls, gaping at the automobile, while their mothers and grandfathers studied him from a more discreet distance – men of service age were almost entirely absent – for none of them had ever seen a man wearing the uniform of an admiral before.

The door was opened for him by Suiko herself, her eyes nearly popping out of her head as she recognised him. "Honourable Admiral," she gasped, bowing level with the floor.

"Admiral?" Charlotte stared at him from an inner doorway.

Nicholas handed his shoes to Suiko, and stepped past her. "Did you not know I had been promoted?"

387

She allowed him to take her into his arms. "We have been told nothing, save that you had been arrested."

"One of those things." He held her close, but her body remained stiff, and he was already looking past her, at Linda, waiting in the inner room, her face too the picture of amazement. And alarm, he realised. His sister and his mistress were more alarmed than pleased to see him! He kissed Charlotte on the forehead, released her, and went towards Linda.

"I did not expect ever to see you again," she whispered.

"I'm a very bad penny," he reminded her, and held her close. But her body too remained stiff. He realised that there was a great deal he had to learn, about what had happened in his absence, but that he would have to move slowly and carefully. And remember Takeda's words, that he could still arrest Charlotte, whenever he chose? "Pack your things," he told them.

"But . . . Colonel Takeda . . ."

"You can forget Colonel Takeda, as of now."

She gave a little shiver. "Are we going to Mori?" Charlotte asked.

"We are going to Kure. But I will make it possible for you to see Mori."

"Oh, I'd so like that. Come on, Linda. We must hurry." Linda looked as if she would have protested again, then changed her mind and followed Charlotte to pack her few belongings.

"What is to become of me, honourable Admiral?" Suiko asked.

"That is up to you. Have you not heard from Colonel Takeda recently?"

"Not for several weeks, really. He sends us money. But he has sent me no messages. I cannot stay here by myself."

"You are welcome to come with us if you choose."

"Only for the journey, honourable Admiral. I have a sister in Hiroshima. If you will take me to Kure, I can easily get to Hiroshima. It is only a few miles."

Kure was like another world. There had been some bombing, as it was known to be a naval base, but the Americans had

388

been concentrating their efforts on the larger industrial centres, and the Inland Sea was as beautiful as ever. Just across the water was Eta-Jima. Nicholas lost no time in visiting the Academy, where he was welcomed both as a hero and ex-student and with the deference due to his rank. "We await the arrival of Barrett Alexander," the Commandant told him. "He will carry on your illustrious name, honourable Admiral."

Hardly less rewarding was his welcome from the surviving crew of *Haruna*. Yakobe had been transferred, and it appeared that few of the seamen had agreed with his decision to place their captain under arrest in any event – at least in retrospect. While Tonoye immediately resumed his position as the Admiral's servant. "Those men love you," Linda remarked, in some surprise, when he escorted her to the dockyard to look at the battered old battleship.

"We have adventured together," he said. "But then, so have you and I, Linda." She shivered.

She remained an enigma to be unwrapped, but he knew he had to take his time. And suddenly he had a great deal of time. Suiko duly departed for Hiroshima, and he was able to arrange for Charlotte to go down to Nagasaki, and be with Mori. He sat with his sister the evening before her departure. "You understand that Takeda knows about your plot?" he asked.

She nodded. "We were betrayed, by Sumiko."

"You were crazy to trust her. I warned you about this."

"She is your wife."

"Was my wife. There can be nothing but hatred between us, now. And her father was an officer in the *Kempei-tai*. You owe Takeda your life."

"Yes," she admitted, her shoulders bowed.

"Now . . . you realise it is too late for anything, save the defence of Japan."

"Why do we have to defend something to which we have never truly belonged?"

He sighed. "You will have to ask that question of Fate. And Grandfather. Mori certainly has no choice. But Charlie,

389

listen to me: survival is the key. There is yet a lot of living to be done. Mori must remain at his post. But the moment the Americans begin their invasion, you must leave Nagasaki and return here."

"I will stay at the side of my husband," she declared.

"Very well," he agreed, having already resolved to write to Mori himself. "Tell me something: has Takeda discussed this business with you at all?"

Her face seemed to close. "Of course he has not." But he knew she was lying.

He could get nothing more out of Linda, even when they were alone. "He came to see Suiko regularly," she said. "And there were times he spoke with Charlie. I was not present all the time. I do not know what there was between them."

Nicholas felt that she too was lying. But again he was reluctant to probe. It was enough that he had her with him, that they could live together as man and wife. This she seemed prepared to do, without any reservations. Out of gratitude? He dared not suppose it was out of love. What frightened him was that her acceptance of him might have an entirely different cause, something of which he knew nothing. He had to find out, but as with Charlotte, he felt it was a case of hurrying slowly, because of his fear of losing what he had of her – even if it was nothing more than her passive acquiesence in his desire.

Meanwhile there was enough to be done, putting Kure into a state of defence. The news continued to be bad. He had only been in the seaport two days when Germany – as had been anticipated – surrendered unconditionally. Meanwhile in Okinawa the fighting was the bloodiest of the Pacific War, with the Army counter-attacking the US forces with desperate intensity, always to be hurled back in the end. The onset of heavy rains, however, slowed the American advance towards the end of May.

Not that this meant any real respite on the home front, which was continuously subjected to air attacks, the American planes roaming almost at will. Kure was still not seriously attacked, but they could see the aircraft zooming overhead on their way to fire bomb Osaka and Nagoya, Kobe and Yokohama, and of course, Tokyo, time and again.

At the end of May Toyoda resigned. His successor was Nicholas's old commander Ozawa Jisiburo, who promptly made a tour of inspection of all his remaining bases. "Well, Barrett *san*," he said, standing on *Haruna*'s bridge and looking out at the Inland Sea. "Will her guns fire?"

"They will, honourable Admiral."

"It will happen, soon," Ozawa said.

Apart from the Navy, Nicholas's task was to mobilise the entire seaport. He conscripted both men and women to fill sandbags and build defences, and when they were finished their manual labour he armed them with rifles and had his marine sergeants drill them and teach them how to use their weapons. They responded with a will, although he had no idea what the Americans, when they came ashore, would make of having to fight a regiment of old men and women wearing *kimonos*. "Shouldn't I help?" Linda asked.

"Do you wish to? This is for fighting the Allies. There'll be British soldiers amongst them."

"I feel so guilty, sitting here, doing nothing while everyone else is working so hard."

"You're still supposed to be my prisoner," he pointed out. "My private *geisha*. I think it is best you keep a low profile."

She hugged herself. "If, four years ago, anyone had told me the sort of life I would lead for those four years . . ."

"The sort of nightmare, you mean?"

Her mouth twisted. "In many ways, a nightmare, yes. But . . . what is going to happen, Nicky?"

"They are going to invade." He listened to the drone of the air raid siren. "When they reckon we have been softened up enough."

"And then?"

"To coin a phrase used by your Churchill, we are going to fight them on the beaches and in the towns, in the fields and in the hills. We have a lot of hills in Japan."

"Do you really think these people will do that?"

391

"Do you really think the British are the only people with the fortitude to die for their beliefs?"

"No. Of course not. It's just that . . . the Germans swore to fight to the end, and then surrendered."

"Correction, my dearest girl. The *Nazis* swore to fight to the end, and then surrendered. I don't think the German *people* had any ideas in that direction. And with due respect to Hitler, he was an upstart revolutionary, not the inheritor of a throne more than two thousand years old and always held in a direct line of succession. These people will fight for a way of life they believe they will lose forever if they submit."

"Do you believe that?"

"Yes, I do. Perhaps not quite as apocalyptically as the Japanese. But if they lose this war Japan will never be the same again."

"That might not be a bad thing. Because they will lose, no matter how hard they fight. You do understand this, Nicky?"

"I understand this."

"But you will fight with them to the end."

"I have sworn an oath to do so."

"But you won't . . ." she bit her lip. "You will accept defeat, when it comes."

"I have been ordered not to do so, Linda."

"You can't be serious!"

"Listen to me. There is nothing for you to fear. All of your papers are in my safe. You have but to present them to the Allied authorities, and you will be repatriated to England."

She stared at him. "Do you think I care about *that*?" she cried, and he saw that her eyes were filled with tears.

"My dearest girl," he said. "Do you seriously mean you care about what happens to me?"

"You stupid man," she snapped.

Nicholas took her in his arms.

The next three weeks were the happiest of his life, despite the continuing grim news, as by the end of June the Americans had completed the conquest of Okinawa, in the course of which over a hundred and thirty thousand Japanese soldiers and over forty thousand civilians had either been

killed or committed suicide, nearly eight thousand planes had
been shot down, and six major warships had been sunk. On
the American side, more than twelve thousand men had been
killed and well over seven hundred planes lost. There could
be no doubt that the staggering casuality figures probable in
an invasion of mainland Japan remained valid.

Then on 23 July, Sumiko arived at Kure.

Nicholas had been on board *Haruna*; it had been decided
not to repair the old battleship sufficiently to go to sea –
there was insufficient steel available – but she could still
fire her guns, and she had now been joined by all that
remained of the Imperial Navy, the old, World War I
battleships *Ise* and *Hyuga*, each close on forty thousand tons
and armed with twelve fourteen-inch guns, and the brand
new twenty-thousand ton aircraft-carrier *Amagi*. He found
it ironic that at the end he should be in overall command
of the ship named after the vessel his father should have
commanded twenty-two years before. Equally he found it
ironic that after all his dreams he should actually command
a battle squadron which could do nothing but wait to be
hit; even if he or his superiors had been tempted to mount
another suicide mission, there was simply insufficient fuel to
travel more than a few miles.

The big ships were moored off the port, and he travelled
to and fro by launch; soon, he reckoned, he would be
using a sailing dinghy. But for the moment Kure remained
an island of peace and almost tranquillity, as the Allied
bombers, passing overhead almost every hour of every day,
sought more important targets. His house was close to the
shipyard, and he walked back, to be greeted by Tonoye,
who wore a very long face. Before Nicholas could ask him
what the problem was, he heard the chatter of voices, and
felt at the same time as if he had been kicked in the
stomach.

Yet he could not help but respond to the greeting he
received from the boys, Alexander, grave and serious in
his school cadet's uniform, and Nicholas, a bouncing little three-year-old. He swept the boy from the floor and
into his arms, before responding to Alexander's bow. "We

have missed you, honourable Father," Alexander said, and Nicholas felt inexpressibly guilty.

Behind them was Sumiko, face hostile. "We waited for you to send for us, but you never did," she accused. "And now . . ." she glanced at Linda, who had also entered the room, and was waiting quietly against the wall. "You have been betraying me, all of these years!"

"Now, Sumiko," Takeda remonstrated. He had followed Linda into the room. "I told you . . ."

"Just what have you told her?" Nicholas demanded. He was the senior officer, and thus the senior person, present. "And what are they doing here?"

"Ha!" Sumiko commented. "Should a wife not be with her husband? Sons with their father?" She gave Linda another furious look.

"I had to bring them, Nicholas," Takeda explained. "Kure is about the only safe place left in Japan. Have you not heard that Allied warships are lying off the north coast of Honshu and bombarding the towns? Mito has been blown to bits. And as she was coming anyway, well, I had to explain the situation."

"You did, did you," Nicholas commented.

"You are a mean and despicable man," Sumiko told him.

"I am also your husband," Nicholas reminded her. "And commandant of this port. I am also aware that it was you betrayed my sister to the *Kempei-tai*."

"You hear him?" Sumiko demanded. "Arrest him, Konoye, and lock him up. He has just virtually confessed to treason."

Takeda coughed. "I have no authority to arrest an admiral in the Imperial Navy," he pointed out.

"And until he obtains such authority," Nicholas said. "You, and everyone here, are under my jurisdiction. Remember that. You will obey my orders."

"I think it is best that you do as he says, until things sort themselves out," Takeda advised. "And that goes for you too, my dear," he said to the inner doorway.

Nicholas looked past him with his mouth open. Christina stood there, an anxious smile on her face. And behind her was Yosunobe Asawa and his wife. "You brought *them* here?" he demanded.

"I explained . . ."

"There was nowhere else to go," Nicholas said. "That bastard? I am sworn to kill him. With my bare hands, if I have to."

Yosunobe gave a nervous grin. "I did what I had to do, Nicholas *san.*"

Nicholas started towards him. Sumiko gave a scream. The two boys, watching open-mouthed, backed against the wall, Little Nicholas clinging to his brother's hand. Christina and Yosunobe Aiwa were also clutching each other. But Takeda stepped between the two men. "Nicholas, I beg you, now is not the time for fighting amongst ourselves."

Nicholas's brief burst of temper had already faded; Yosunobe, in civilian clothes and entirely lacking his old arrogance, was actually a forlorn, contemptible figure, more to be pitied than hated. "He is not staying here," he said.

"No, no," Takeda assured him. "He is on his way to Hiroshima."

"My parents live in Hiroshima," Aiwa explained. "But we thought you might wish to see your sons."

"Thank you," Nicholas said. "Then you had better be on your way."

Aiwa looked at her daughter. "And me?" Sumiko demanded. "You are expelling me as well? You have no right to do this."

"I have every right," Nicholas growled. "After your betrayal of Charlotte."

Sumiko started to weep. "Nicky," Linda said.

All heads turned to look at her. "I think Sumiko should be allowed to stay," Linda said. "If she wishes to do so."

"You . . ." Sumiko screamed.

"If you wish to do so," Linda said again, quietly.

"With you?"

Linda looked at Nicholas. "Yes," he said. "With Miss Wells."

Sumiko looked from one to the other, then at the boys.

"We would like to stay with honourable Father, honourable Mother," Alexander said. Sumiko's shoulders slumped.

Takeda seized Nicholas's arm and led him aside. "Where is Suiko?" he whispered.

"She said she had relatives in Hiroshima," Nicholas said. "Have you told Christina?"

"No, no. Only about Linda. Linda . . ." he licked his lips, while peering at Nicholas. "She has . . . ?"

Nicholas frowned. "What?"

"Ah . . . no matter. I must get the Yosunobes out of here."

Before Nicholas could consider what he might mean, he had hurried across the room. Sumiko accompanied her parents to the door, while Christina continued to glare at Linda. "You are of course welcome to spend the night, dear Stepmother," Nicholas said. "I assume you will be accompanying Takeda when he leaves?"

"Ha!" Christina commented, and looked up as the sirens began to wail.

"They do that every day," Linda remarked.

"However, you will take shelter," Nicholas said. "Down . . ." he checked as there was a huge explosion near at hand: the entire house trembled. "Jesus Christ! They're after us, this time. Get down to the cellar." He ran for the door.

"Let me come with you, honourable Father," Alexander begged.

Nicholas hesitated. But it would be too dangerous. "No. You stay here. Look after your brother and the women."

He went outside, encountered the Yosunobes and Takeda coming back in. "They are bombing the harbour," Takeda gasped.

"You cannot send us out into that," Yosunobe Aiwa begged.

"Get into the cellar," Nicholas snapped.

"Nicky!" Linda had followed him. "Don't . . ." she bit her lip. "Be careful."

For her situation, should he be killed or even seriously wounded, did not bear consideration.

"I'll be back. Are you coming, Takeda?"

Takeda gulped. He was a desk soldier, and had never been under fire.

"I need every man," Nicholas told him.

The sky was filled with planes, and for the moment they

396

were concentrating their attack on the moored warships. The entire harbour and the sea beyond was a mass of pluming white explosions, often enough accompanied by sand and mud sucked up from the floor of the shallow bay. The battleships were responding as best they could, but stationary as they were they were being hit at will. "Take command of the shore batteries," Nicholas shouted, pointing to where they too were firing wildly and ineffectively into the sky; the brown cloudbursts of their exploding shells were well below the height at which the bombers were flying; Nicholas needed only a glance to realise that these were carrier-borne aircraft, not heavy bombers . . . and also that there were RAF roundels to be made out amidst the American stars. The victors were gathering for the kill.

He reached the dock, and found his launch still intact, although the crew were ashore taking shelter. "I will go to *Haruna*," he told them.

Somewhat reluctantly they boarded and cast off. Within seconds they were swamped by the waterspouts all round them, and it was almost impossible to see. Nearer at hand there came a huge explosion as *Ise* was struck; her anti-aircraft guns kept firing, but she was already beginning to list. Miraculously the launch survived, and they came into the side of *Haruna*, which continued to bear a charmed life as the bombs rained all around her.

At last the attack ceased as the planes soared away, and Nicholas and his officers could take stock of the situation. *Ise* was finished; she had sunk but the sea was so shallow her upper works remained above water, and indeed her anti-aircraft batteries could still be fired. *Amagi* was on fire, and would clearly never fight again. *Hyuga* had also been damaged. Only *Haruna* had so far survived. Nicholas was very tempted to send her to sea, but he had no orders to do so, and with her nearly empty fuel bunkers she would not get very far in any event. As she was doomed, it would be better for her to go down in the company of her fellows, he supposed.

He sent the launch ashore to find out if all was well there, although the bombers had paid little attention to the city itself. He himself had no time to return ashore as he went from ship to ship, inspecting the damage himself, encouraging and exhorting, before returning to *Haruna* for a hasty meal and then falling asleep in his old cabin. He was awakened by the screaming of the sirens. The bombers were back.

This time the Allies meant to finish the job. Nicholas stayed with his men on *Haruna*, sending their tracer streams screaming into the air, while all around them the day again became a gigantic waterspout, interspersed with clouds of black smoke and leaping red flame. The attack commenced early in the morning, but the day rapidly grew black as the bombs were this time also dropped on the city itself, until all Kure seemed to be on fire. Nicholas saw *Amagi* go up in a cloud of smoke, and *Hyuga* begin to capsize. Like *Ise*, she could not go right down because there was insufficient water, but she settled on her side. Then it was *Haruna*'s turn. A bomb struck the foredeck with a huge blast which blew out the bridge screens and scattered death and destruction in every direction. Hardly aware of the blood dribbling from half a dozen splinter wounds, Nicholas himself helped man a hose to direct at the flames, but then there came another shuddering explosion from aft, and the deck began to tilt.

"She is finished, honourable Admiral," gasped Commander Abe, the senior surviving officer after Nicholas himself.

Nicholas reflected that, like her sisters, she would not be going very far. But as a fighting machine she was certainly finished. "Tell your people to abandon ship," he said.

There were few liferafts left; most men merely jumped into the water to swim ashore. Nicholas looked for the launch, but that too had disappeared or disintegrated. Then he looked at the town, and the heavy pall of smoke which rose into the morning sky: it seemed thickest over the harbour area. He made sure all his men were off, and then dived into the calm sea himself. It all seemed so much more civilised than when *Yodo* had gone down in The Slot. He reached the shore without difficulty, increasingly aware of the burning sensations from cuts and slashes he had not even felt before. Commander Abe was waiting for him, actually standing to attention and bowing in his sodden uniform – he had lost his cap. "Have these men changed and fed and armed," Nicholas told him.

"Your orders, honourable Admiral?"

"Are unchanged; we hold the port."

Then he hurried home, to pause in horror. His house had been hit by a bomb. It still burned, and the garden was a shambles. His mind raced back to the September day in 1923, when he had come upon a sight just like this, in which his mother and sister had been buried alive. Now . . . "Father!" Alexander ran to him, Little Nicholas as ever behind him.

Nicholas embraced them and looked past them, at the others, smoke-stained and frightened, but alive. "The house collapsed on top of the cellar, honourable Master," Tonoye told him. "But I managed to force open the trap and get us out."

"He was magnificent," Linda said. "He saved our lives."

"We wish to leave this place," Yosunobe Asawa muttered.

"I will find transport," Takeda said. "For Hiroshima." He looked at Sumiko.

"I will come with you," Sumiko said. "This place is a shambles. And it is not safe."

"Very well," Nicholas agreed. "But the boys will stay here."

"You cannot do that," she shouted. "When the bombers come back, they will be killed!"

Nicholas looked out at the sunken ships, the devastated harbour, the burning town. "I don't think the Americans are going to bother about Kure again," he said. "In any event, the boys stay with me."

"Oh . . ." for a moment he thought she would also change her mind, but Alexander was not her flesh and blood, and she was too frightened to care about Little Nicholas.

"I will be in touch," Takeda said, as they left, intending to go to the railway station and see if any trains were running. In any event, it was only just over five miles from Kure to Hiroshima, so they could walk if they had to. He bowed to Nicholas, then half turned towards Linda, changed his mind, and followed the others.

Nicholas also looked at Linda, and caught both her little

399

shiver and her expression of absolute revulsion before she brought herself back under control. "Tell me," he said.

She glanced at him. "Tell you what?"

He bit his lip, and was interrupted by Alexander.

"What are we going to do, honourable Father?"

"See what we can salvage from this mess, and then find somewhere to sleep."

Tonoye rounded up some of the survivors from *Haruna* and they got to work. There wasn't much to be rescued from the burned out house, and as the whole town was a ruin Nicholas opted for a tent on the beach, where most of his men were encamped already. "Isn't this fun?" Linda asked the boys, as they ate their supper around a campfire on the sand.

"Are you our new mother?" Little Nicholas asked.

Linda looked at Nicholas. "Yes," Nicholas said.

After the boys had been put to bed in sleeping bags, guarded by the faithful Tonoye, Nicholas and Linda walked away from the camp, along the sand. "How is it that men can fight so gallantly one minute, and be absolutely bestial the next?" she asked.

"Because gallantry and bestiality are two sides of the same coin. They both require an excess of adrenalin at any given moment, and a certain psycopathic disregard for what most of us call civilised behaviour."

She glanced at him. "Are you like that?"

"I've never really had the opportunity to find out, for which I suppose I should thank God."

"I have been told that you have been cited for gallantry on several occasions."

"I could say I've been lucky."

"The adrenalin must have done a bit of flowing."

"Absolutely. But you see, at sea, one never actually looks upon the face of the man one is fighting, at least until the battle is over, and even then only occasionally. Obviously passions run high, but they are impersonally directed. We never kill anyone with our bare hands, or a sword or bayonet, or with a bullet fired at point-blank range. Most important of all, we are never in the position of having done one of those things, and while still in the grip of the killing syndrome finding ourselves facing a woman sheltering behind the man."

"In other words, you condone what happened in Hong Kong. And a thousand other places."

"No," he said. "I could never condone something like that. But I believe I can understand how and why it happened."

"A serving officer who is also a philosopher," she remarked, but without bitterness.

"Linda, if I hadn't been a philosopher, I would have killed myself long ago." They walked in silence for a little while, then he asked, "Would you like to talk about the future?"

"No."

He considered this. "A couple of weeks ago, I got the feeling that you had revised your feelings about me, just a little."

"If I may paraphrase what you just said, if I had not let myself fall in love with you, I would have killed myself."

"Well, then . . ."

"But you are about to be killed, and your country is about to be destroyed, and I . . ." her shoulders humped.

He caught her arm. "Tell me. Tell me about Takeda."

She sank to her knees on the sand, her flesh slithering through his fingers. "He found out about Charlie's group."

"He told me that. But suppressed it."

"At a price."

He knelt beside her. "You?"

"Yes. But also Charlie. It was Charlie he really wanted."

"By God," Nicholas muttered. "I thought he was my friend."

"He was just a man, with two women of an alien race at his mercy," she said. "Nicky . . ." she caught his arm in turn. "See? Even I can philosophise."

"Takeda," Nicholas said, and stood up.

"Nicky! He still has the evidence. And even if you are an admiral, he is still a colonel in the *Kempei-tai*." She shuddered. "He would tell us, what they would be doing to you."

"Wasn't that what they did to you?"

"It was . . . nothing personal, with me. Nicky, promise me you'll do nothing stupid."

"Will you marry me?"

She gazed at him. "You are married."

"That is something I mean to sort out."

"Will you leave Japan, when this is over?"

He sighed. "No."

"Nicky . . ."

"I may not look like a Japanese, but these are none the less my people. And there are going to be an awful lot of pieces to be picked up. I must play my part in that. So . . ."

"Just let's live these next few weeks, Nicky."

It was what he wanted to do too. And he could even have been happy, despite the burned-out town, the wrecked ships, the general air of defeatism which pervaded the men he was supposed to command in resisting the Allies, when they came; he had Linda, and the two boys, and however hard he worked salvaging what was possible from the ships, gathering whatever food they could find, however primitive the conditions under which they had to live, they were worth coming home to. But always the thought of Takeda twisted in his mind, and his gut.

And in the event, they did not have a few weeks. They had barely a few days, until the morning of 6 August. It was just after eight o'clock, and they were breakfasting on the beach, when Tonoye spotted the small group of planes approaching from the south-west. "Are they coming for us, honourable Father?" Alexander asked. Linda had already taken Little Nicholas into her arms.

"I don't think so," Nicholas said, frowning. The Allies had not bothered to bomb Kure again since the destruction of the fleet. He levelled his binoculars. "Only five planes. Looks more to me as if they're just inspecting the damage they've caused, deciding where to attack next. Yes, there they go." Four of the planes had peeled off and were flying away in differing directions. The fifth held its course, but to the south of Kure, to pass over Hiroshima. "Nothing for us today," he said.

There was a blinding flash of light, and such a trembling that he thought there was an earthquake. He found himself on his hands and knees, gazing at Linda, who had also been

402

knocked over. Fortunately both of them, and the boys, had been looking away. Tonoye, who had been serving the meal and had still been watching the plane, had his hands to his face and was moaning. "What *happened*?" Linda asked.

"I don't know." Nicholas got up, stared at the hills, beyond which lay the city. He was still aware of shock waves, although thanks to the high ground these were not particularly severe. Then he saw the cloud, rising out of the valley in which Hiroshima was situated, mounting higher and higher until he estimated it was more than thirty thousand feet, and slowly forming a gigantic mushroom. His men gathered round him, also to stare. "There has been a big explosion," someone said, ingenuously.

Caused by that single plane? Nicholas wondered. But he had a problem closer at hand, in both Tonoye and several other sailors who had been looking in the direction of Hiroshima when the blast had happened. They had been blinded by the flash. That was not uncommon, but they remained blinded. Nicholas and Linda and the other stewards bathed the afflicted men's eyes, and then Nicholas used his radio to call up the commander of the Hiroshima garrison and discover what had happened. He received no reply. "I must go down there," he said.

"Is it safe?!" Linda asked.

"I don't know. But I have to find out."

"Then send someone. You are the commander here. You cannot leave your post." He knew she was right. But at the same time, however much he now loathed them, his family had been in the city. Eventually he did the correct thing, and sent a patrol to see what had happened.

They returned with quite horrific news: Hiroshima had ceased to exist. When he first heard this, Nicholas thought they had been drinking. Then he realised they were telling the truth. "The entire city has been incinerated, honourable Admiral," Petty Officer Matsuo told him.

"By a single bomber?"

"There was only a single explosion, honourable Admiral!"

Nicholas scratched his head. But Matsuo's tale was born

403

out by the other members of the party, who told of tens of thousands of people apparently burned to death, lying in groups on the roadside, of entire blocks laid flat with only the odd wall or steel upright standing, and of tens of thousands more suffering from burns and shock. "What can it mean?" Linda asked.

"I wish to God I knew. A bomb must have struck a chemical plant, or something like that." But there was no huge chemical plant in Hiroshima. He remembered what the American general had said in Macao: suppose we just blast you out of existence? He must have known, even then, that his side possessed such a weapon.

He would have gone down himself, searching for Sumiko, at least, as his duty to his wife demanded, but Matsuo told him that the entire heart of the city was no more, and that all communications had broken down. As he had to assume that the use of this new and unthought of weapon must herald the invasion, he could not possibly leave his post to go searching amongst thousands of refugees. And in the event he was rather glad he had not gone, as the next day Matsuo and his companions came down with a severe attack of vomiting and diarrhoea. "Do you think the Americans can have used some kind of poisoned explosive?" Linda asked, aghast.

By then Nicholas had contacted Tokyo, but his superiors were as mystified and horrified by what had happened as anyone else. He was told he would be receiving orders shortly, but that in the meantime he was to continue his preparations for defending Kure. At least, he reflected, the problems of dealing with Yosunobe and Takeda had been solved, as, in the grimmest possible way, had the problem of his marriage.

Hiroshima had been destroyed on the Monday. No further orders had been received when on the Thursday morning Nicholas was amazed to see a car bouncing down the road towards the encampment. From it stepped Mori. "Mori!" The two men bowed to each other, then embraced. "But it is good to see you," Nicholas said. "You have never met Linda."

Mori bowed again, visibly embarrassed.

404

"Where is Charlotte?"

"I left her behind in Nagasaki. Well, I couldn't risk bringing her up here; there have been all manner of rumours of people falling mysteriously ill . . ."

"They are not all rumours," Nicholas said grimly. "But she is well?"

"Very well, apart from being worried about you. That is why I decided to come up here and find out for myself. I have tried to call you, both by telephone and radio, but I could not get a reply."

"All the lines are down between here and the south. As for radio . . ."

"What of your family?"

"If you mean my wife and in-laws and step-parents, they are all dead. My sons were here with me, thank God."

"What is going to happen, Nicholas?"

"If the Americans do have a bomb which can wipe out entire cities in a matter of seconds, and is poisoned into the bargain, well . . . they can destroy all Japan without putting a man ashore."

"But that is barbaric!"

"Yes," Nicholas agreed. "But it is we who sewed the wind. Now it is up to our superiors in Tokyo."

"Well, I must be getting back to my post in the south. I should not really have come away. But as you say, it does not look as if the Americans are going to need to land." He bowed to Linda. "I shall remember our meeting, Miss Wells. Nicholas . . ." he held out his hand, and was interrupted by Alexander, running from the radio tent.

"Honourable Father! Honourable Father!" Then he saw Mori, and stopped, and bowed. "I did not mean to interrupt, honourable Father. But . . ."

"What has happened now?"

"It is on the radio, honourable Father. There has been another city wiped out. By a single bomb!"

Nicholas and Mori stared at him in consternation. "Which city?" Nicholas snapped.

Alexander swallowed. "Nagasaki."

Mori gave a great shriek of despair, and fell to his knees.

Nicholas felt like doing the same thing. Instead he stared at Linda, and she came to him.

"Oh, Nicky! I am so terribly sorry."

"Mori . . ." The colonel had regained his feet. Now, without a word, he ran back to his car, got behind the wheel, and drove off.

"I should go too," Nicholas muttered.

"But you can't abandon your command."

He chewed his lip, but knew she was right. Besides, there was nothing he could do to help his sister. There seemed nothing he could do to help anyone. That afternoon news was received that the Russians had denounced their agreement with Japan and invaded Manchuria with an army of more than a million men. "The bastards," Tonoye growled. Even blind he insisted upon making tea.

The following day Radio Tokyo announced that Japan was willing to surrender, providing the future status of the Emperor was assured. This was promptly rejected by the Allies. Nicholas and Linda and the boys could only wait for the next bomb to be dropped; they could at least reflect that Kure was too small, and already too badly damaged, to be worth it. But on the following Tuesday the message came through to all commanders, that Japan had surrendered unconditionally, and that they were to remain at their posts and maintain order until further instructions were received. *Seppuku* was strictly forbidden.

"It's over," Linda said.

"I wonder," Nicholas said.

The following day Takeda arrived.

It was early in the morning when the car pulled up on the road behind the camp. Linda had been on the beach with the boys, while Nicholas was at the tent being used as his office, trying to contact Tokyo to discover whether or not he was to continue salvaging the big ships. He looked up in concern as Linda came in, face flushed. "Where now?" he asked. "I thought we had surrendered."

"Takeda," she said. "Nicky . . ."

"Stay here," he told her, and went outside. Takeda looked immaculate, as always. Nicholas could only stare

406

at him in amazement, tempered by anger. "We thought you were dead."

"I was not in Hiroshima when it was hit. But my wife and family are dead. As are *your* wife and family. Now . . . there are warrants out for my arrest. For the arrest of all senior *Kempei-tai* officers. Nicky, you must help me."

"Help *you*?"

Takeda's eyes flickered, and Nicholas knew his stepfather had looked past him, at Linda, standing in the tent doorway. "Your threats are no longer effective, Takeda," he said. "Now there are only your crimes to be answered for."

Takeda licked his lips. "But for me, that woman would have died long ago, in some stinking prison camp."

"And I am grateful," Nicholas said. "So I will not place you under arrest, as I should. But you will yet answer to me, for breaking your word, and for what you did to my woman."

Another quick flick of the lips. "Answer to you?"

"You are a *samurai*, are you not, *honourable* Stepfather? I would imagine you have your swords in that car."

Takeda's eyes narrowed. "You wish me to commit *seppuku*? Now? I refuse. The Emperor has forbidden it."

"I did not suppose you would. But I also have my *samurai* swords, Takeda *san*."

Takeda stared at him. "You wish to challenge me to a duel, with swords?"

"I have just done so," Nicholas told him.

"You?" Takeda's lip curled in contempt.

"Nicky!" Linda gasped.

By now a considerable body of the men had assembled. Nicholas turned to them. "This man," he said, "has dishonoured my woman and my sister. Have I not the right to seek satisfaction?"

The men murmured their agreement. As they all adored Nicholas and hated the *Kempei-tai*, they would have agreed with whatever Nicholas proposed.

"Oh, I will fight you," Takeda said. "But how do I know these people of yours will let me go when I have won?"

Nicholas beckoned Commander Abe. "Commander, I give you my last order as your commanding officer. Whatever the outcome of this duel, Colonel Takeda is to be allowed to leave, unharmed, if he wishes and is able to do so."

Abe bowed. "The order will be obeyed, honourable Admiral."

"Well, then," Takeda said. "Killing you will be a pleasure, Nicholas *san*." He returned to the car for his weapons.

Nicholas went to his tent to fetch his own swords. Alexander followed him. "Can you beat him, honourable Father?"

"I do not know. We were both trained as swordsmen in our youth. It all depends who has practised more since then."

"But you have not practiced at all, honourable Father."

Nicholas squeezed the boy's shoulder. "Perhaps he has not, either. But you must remember, no matter what happens, he is to be allowed to leave, afterwards."

"When I grow up, I will kill him."

"Hopefully, by the time you grow up, swords will be a thing of the past, in Japan," Nicholas told him.

Takeda was waiting, surrounded in a huge circle by the sailors and marines, and even by some of the townspeople, who had heard the rumour of what was about to happen. The *Kempei-tai* colonel had taken off his tunic, leggings, and boots, and was barefooted on the sand. He did not look the least apprehensive. Nicholas also undressed, left his clothes where Linda and Little Nicholas were standing. Linda's face was tight with apprehension, but she knew better than to attempt to interfere now, while to speak at all might upset Nicholas's concentration.

Nicholas drew his sword, slowly, listening to the slither of steel against steel. Takeda had already drawn his weapon, and was holding it, blade down, in front of him, both hands clasped on the hilt. Now he raised the weapon, holding it in front of him in both hands, while he moved slowly to the right. Nicholas followed his example, but moved to *his* right. For a few seconds they circled each other, gazing into each other's eyes, testing each other's will, then Takeda uttered a great shout and leapt through the air, covering the distance between them in three bounds. As he started the third bound he began his swing, bringing his sword over, round and then up again before delivering a tremendous blow. The whole

408

movement performed a figure-of-eight, which would have sliced almost in two any flesh and bone it encountered. But Nicholas had known what was coming, and jumped out of the way, before immediately launching himself into a similar manoeuvre. Equally, Takeda had expected the riposte, and had turned, maintaining a perfect balance despite his leaps. Now the two swords clashed and sent sparks into the air, the blades scraping along their lengths until the two men thudded into each other, their fists and brief hand guards smashing together.

Takeda grunted, and tried to throw Nicholas backwards, but he lacked the strength and so jumped backwards himself, bringing up his sword as he did so. Nicholas swung again and again sparks flew as the two blades met. But this time Nicholas did not propel himself forward, but instead leapt back. Takeda, braced to withstand a shoulder charge, stumbled. He brought up his blade as before, but was too late to intercept Nicholas's next swing. Nicholas's sword swept his aside and continued on its way, biting deep into Takeda's left arm. Takeda gasped and looked down; the arm had been all but severed. Then he looked up again, but Nicholas's sword, having swung one way, was returning, urged on by all of his strength. This time the red-stained blade struck the colonel at the base of the jaw, and all but wrenched his head from his body. He fell without a word. "*Banzai!*" shouted the sailors and marines. "*Banzai!*"

Nicholas dropped his sword; there was blood on his hands as well. He turned to face Linda.

"Is it over?" she asked.

"It can never be over," Nicholas said. "What men like Takeda, and Yosunobe, and their sort, did, will stain Japanese history for a thousand years." He sighed. "But as long as there are men like Mori, and Yamamoto, and old Togo, there is always hope."

"What are you going to do?" she asked.

He shrugged. "Wait for the Americans to arrive, and hand over my command."

"They may try you as a war criminal."

Nicholas grinned. "I think I have enough going for me."

"And after that? You can't mean to stay here?"

409

"I must. This is my home. These are my people."

"Despite all?"

"Linda, there is not a nation in history which has not gone through a trauma like this; Japan's has just been encapsulated by time, a matter of medieval thought and practice being thrust into the twentieth century, armed with modern weapons and fired with the ambition to prove themselves the equal of any people on earth. I agree with you, there are going to be some horrendous questions to be answered, but when they *have* been answered, there is then going to have to be an enormous job of reconstruction, of minds and people as well as places. I'm not going anywhere while I can play my part in that. But I'm going to see you get out of here just as quickly as possible."

She bit her lip, and looked from him to Alexander and Little Nicholas, and then to Tonoye, waiting with the inevitable pot of tea. "Forget it," she said. "I think I'd like to stay as well."